Love in another time, another place.

STELLAR REVIEWS FOR ANNE AVERY'S
ALL'S FAIR:

"Wonderfully imaginative and beautifully written...a superb futuristic romance."

—Phoebe Conn,
author of *Lady Rogue*

"Ms. Avery lets loose her wonderful imagination to spin a vivid and compelling love story into a top-notch reading experience!"

—*Romantic Times*

"*All's Fair* is an excellent futuristic romance... emotionally poignant!"

—*Affaire de Coeur*

AND FOR *A DISTANT STAR:*

"*A Distant Star* sweeps the reader into strange and wonderful worlds filled with high adventure and love. This is my kind of futuristic romance!"

—Kathleen Morgan,
author of *Firestar*

"*A Distant Star* is a must read for all futuristic romance fans...Anne Avery has a bright future in this genre!"

—*Affaire de Coeur*

⋆ Futuristic Romance

Love in another time, another place.

LOVE AND WAR

Rhys took a step forward, then another, and another, until he was once more only inches from Calista. He brushed the tip of one finger suggestively across her lips, then trailed it along her jaw. "You can't deny you want me, Calista, and as long as we're partners...."

The flush rising up her throat and across her cheeks had to be from anger, Calista told herself. He was deliberately provoking her. There was no way—absolutely no way in space—that she could be responding to the nearly imperceptible tracing of his finger against her skin.

She slapped his hand aside. "As long as we're partners, we'll keep our relationship on a professional level, Fairdane. And when we're not partners...." She stopped, unexpectedly shaken by the thought, then swallowed, took a deep breath, and continued. "When we're not partners, there won't be any relationship. Period."

Other *Love Spell* Books by Anne Avery:
A DISTANT STAR

ALL'S FAIR

ANNE AVERY

LOVE SPELL **NEW YORK CITY**

To Angel Smits, Claire Freeman, and Donna Robinson,
critique partners extraordinaire.
And especially to Kathleen Morgan,
whose generosity of spirit and honesty of vision
have meant so much to me and my writing.
Thank you all.

LOVE SPELL®

March 1994

Published by

Dorchester Publishing Co., Inc.
276 Fifth Avenue
New York, NY 10001

Printed in the United States of America.

ALL'S FAIR

Chapter One

Calista York dropped out of hyperdrive into a perfect orbit about the planet of Karta, inordinately pleased with herself and life in general. That pleasure was considerably diminished three minutes later when she spotted a second ship already in orbit and eliminated entirely when the computer identified the ship as the *Fair Trade*.

For an instant, she considered forgetting the whole affair, but the temptation of being named trade representative to the Dorinor of Karta was too great. A few years as rep and her fortune would be made. After so many years of struggle, she would be able to put the past behind her—forever.

She wasn't about to let the owner of the *Fair Trade* be named rep in place of her. Not without a fair fight.

Well, a fight, anyway.

If Rhys Fairdane really were after the position, she wouldn't put it past that sleazy slime bucket to use

7

every dirty trick known to get it, and then invent a few more just for the hell of it—and to irritate her.

The communications panel chimed, indicating an incoming message in normal space. It was the *Fair Trade*, no doubt, since the Kartanese were notorious for disliking anything technical, including space communications systems.

Briefly, Calista considered refusing to answer. But Fairdane knew she was here—he would have spotted the spatial distortions caused by her incoming ship long before she entered orbit—and he was perfectly capable of interpreting her refusal to answer as a sign his presence had upset her. The three moons of Tolkat would fall before she'd give him that satisfaction.

With a curse she'd learned on Darneb II and found particularly satisfying at times like this, Calista slapped the respond button, then cued the view screen. Might as well confront him right off. The man could smell fear a parsec away and there was no sense in . . .

The view screen was a mistake.

It was also a mistake to catch her breath in a distressingly audible gasp, or to let her eyes widen until they couldn't grow any wider. But she couldn't control either of those automatic reactions to the sight of him, naked from the waist up—which was, thankfully, all the screen revealed—with droplets of water glistening on his bare chest and a broad, lopsided grin on his face.

He hadn't changed. His hair was still long, black as the depths of space, and pulled back in a queue at the nape of his neck. Thick, straight brows shadowed dark eyes that gleamed like Risian soul stones. The flat planes of his cheeks were cut by the same strong lines running from beside his nose to the edge of a mouth that was far too full and sensual for such a masculine face. His jaw hadn't softened. It was as darkly shadowed as ever, even though he was clean-shaven.

His body was, well, perfect. He was broad-shouldered, slim-waisted, with smoothly rounded muscles that slid easily beneath his skin. Even now, five years later, she could remember how distractingly tempting it had been to run her fingers across his chest, through the dark, silky hair that followed the curve of his breast then came together in a tapering vee. . . .

Thank the stars the image shown on the view screen ended at his waist.

"Well-bred people don't come to the view screen unless they're properly dressed, Fairdane!" Calista snapped, irritated by her involuntary reaction to him.

"I have a towel," he protested. "See?"

With an air of injured innocence he held up a large towel for her inspection. As though an unexpected thought had just occurred to him, he glanced down at the half of his body hidden from view, then smiled apologetically.

"Does it count if I *was* wearing it?"

"No, it doesn't! And most people use dry booths rather than a damp, disgusting rag—"

"It's not damp when I start, and it's not a rag. I pay good money to have these specially made on Ardole," he protested, clearly hurt. "You ought to try it, Red. I don't know how many times I offered to dry you off—"

"And stop calling me Red! I'm not a redhead and never have been."

"I know." He grinned. "That golden hair is stunning no matter whether it's on your head or . . . elsewhere."

"Why, you—"

9

"But you've the temper of a true redhead, Red. It's not your fault," he added with the air of a man determined to be fair. "I realize you can't help it if your genes got mixed up and—"

Goaded, Calista reached for the weapons panel.

"Now, Red, you know better than that." He frowned and shook his head with the gloomy expression of a parent who is sadly disappointed in his offspring. "My shields are up. Knowing your temper, I put them up the minute I realized who was dropping in. Besides, I have as much firepower as you. There's no sense in wasting a good energy charge."

He was right. And knowing he was right made her even madder. She'd never won any of their verbal sparring matches and, much as she'd like to, she probably never would.

"Given that rusty junk heap you call a spaceship, I'm surprised you found your way to this part of the galaxy," Calista said at last in a sweetly conciliatory tone. "Did you get a new computer to help figure out the coordinates? I wouldn't have thought you could have managed, otherwise."

"Haven't changed much, have you?" He grinned. "You know, I was reading just the other day that the ancients used to preserve their food with salt and vinegar. Since those two ingredients seem to flow in your veins instead of blood, I'll bet you'll live to be two hundred and still look as gorgeous as you do today."

"Jealous, Fairdane? Maybe you should try changing that weak blood of yours." Calista did her best to assume an expression of motherly concern. "You're really not looking up to par, you know. Sort of wasting away, not quite the man you used to be."

He sighed. "You're right, of course. It's the women. They take a lot out of a man, but what can I do? I can't just turn the darlings away. That would be far too cruel."

Unreasonable jealousy stabbed at Calista. It wasn't hard to imagine him with a beautiful woman adoringly draped on each arm and a few more trailing lustfully in his wake.

"You have all my sympathies." Calista forced aside a vivid mental image of him lying with one of the beauties her imagination had conjured up. "So tell me, Fairdane. What brought you here? Knowing your fondness for the comforts of life, I find it hard to believe you came this far from galaxy center just to escape your more demanding admirers."

"Right again," he said, clearly struck by admiration for her insight. "It cost me a pang or two, I'll admit. Though if I'd known you were going to be here, I wouldn't have hesitated for a moment, Red. I want you to know that."

"No doubt." Calista angrily repressed a sudden, and totally absurd, desire to believe him. "So why are you here?"

"As direct as ever, aren't you? I might ask the same of you. What's enticed you away from that lucrative run between Sogral III and Magruder Station? I'd heard you were making credits so fast even you couldn't count them."

How, by all the devils of Dormat, had he found out about that deal? Had he been tracking her? Calista wasn't sure if she was more flattered—or disturbed.

It was tempting to believe he still thought as much about her as she did about him. Tempting, and irrational. There was no profit in clinging to the past and never had been. And profit was what life was all about, wasn't it?

That and independence. She wasn't about to give up either. Not for him, not for any man.

11

"Calista?"

He sounded wistful, but that had to be her overactive imagination.

"I'm here on business, Fairdane. What did you think? Surely even you wouldn't be so arrogant to think I'd come halfway across the galaxy just to see you."

"You're right. I wouldn't be that arrogant. Not after the way you walked out on me five years ago. And certainly not after your masterly trashing of my negotiations with the Celignians a year ago." The friendly, bantering note was gone from Fairdane's voice, replaced by a sharply bitter tone.

"You were treading on my turf and you know it. Did you think I'd let you take that deal away from me?" Calista was grateful for her rising anger. It provided far better protection from him than just exchanging insults.

"You—" Fairdane broke off abruptly, clearly struggling to regain control of his rising temper.

He took a deep breath, which swelled his chest to disconcertingly impressive proportions, then exhaled loudly. "I'm warning you, Calista. Don't think you can pull something like that with the Kartanese. You're not getting that trade rep position, no matter what dirty tricks you dream up to use against me."

"Oho! So you think the Dorinor's dumb enough to name you as rep, instead? Well let me tell you—"

Fairdane didn't give her a chance to tell him anything. The view screen went blank and although Calista pounded furiously on the send button for the communications panel, insistently demanding he reopen the channel, he refused to answer her signal.

With one last, frustrated thump on the comm panel, Calista sank back in the pilot's chair. She'd always known it—the fates didn't play fair. Certainly not with her. If they had, they would never have brought Fairdane into her life. Or they would at least have ensured that once free of him, she'd never again have had to deal with that obnoxious male.

Instead, he kept thrusting himself into her life. He'd crossed her path three times since she'd left him, and he'd won in two of those three encounters.

Well, not this time. Not if it took the last ounce of guile she possessed. She'd fight dirty if she had to. He certainly did, whether he had to or not.

Calista shut her eyes and leaned her head wearily against the chair. They'd spent five minutes talking— all right, fighting—and she felt as exhausted as if she'd just spent the day battling space pirates trying to steal her cargo.

Worse, her body still ached with the intense and disturbing physical need the sight of him always roused in her.

It wasn't fair, damn it. It just wasn't fair. You'd think after five years she could forget how good it had been to make love to him, and to have him make love to her.

Surely she ought to be grateful for the return of her privacy and her independence, things she'd treasured ever since her escape from the slave quarters on Andrus at the age of fourteen. Yet Calista still found herself—far too often for her peace of mind—wishing he were there on the ship with her. She didn't even want him by her side, necessarily. It would have been enough just to know he was there.

Without him, the ship sometimes seemed so— empty. And that was crazy.

From the time she'd won her first small scout ship off a drunken miner in a game of bakal when she was nineteen until she'd had the misfortune to get involved with Fairdane six years later, Calista had treasured the privacy that was hers and hers alone. But then she'd made the mistake of taking him on for that deal with the Andorians, who refused to deal with the female of any species. Four weeks later they'd each had more money than they knew what to do with and, in a riotous celebration, had somehow ended up in bed together.

She still couldn't face a glass of draknir without an unpleasant queasiness twisting her stomach.

Even after they'd both recovered from their massive hangovers, when her brain should have been working a little better, it had seemed like a good idea for Fairdane to remain on the ship.

With a grimace, Calista recalled her solemn, carefully reasoned, and totally insane efforts to justify his staying. There might be other chances for a deal with someone like the Andorians, she'd assured him. Two heads were certainly better than one, he'd agreed with equal solemnity. Combining their trading talents just made sense, they'd both said. After all, hadn't they each made more money on that last negotiation than either of them could have made working alone?

Calista sighed and forced her eyes open. Even now, when she could happily contemplate the possibility of blowing his ship out of the sky if given half a chance, she had to admit that their partnership had worked, at least for the first year or so.

But being good together in bed wasn't enough. Neither was making money, though she would have put up with a Toregan toad, warts and all, if the relationship could have been as profitable as hers and Fairdane's had been.

The problem was, the man had come to think he owned her. He'd tried to tell her what to do, how to do it, and when. He'd decided she needed protection, and had irritated her to her soul by his constant hovering when they were on a dangerous planet. He'd even had the gall to trick her so that she missed the chance to obtain a trade agreement with the people of the Utali star system. All because the Utalis collected women for their harems—or so *he'd* said.

The final straw had come when he'd humiliated her in front of other traders by telling her he wouldn't allow her to deal with the Zogret. Too dangerous, he'd said. They couldn't be trusted if you were nose to snout with them.

She'd dumped an entire pitcher of ale over his head, tipped his plate of fried gosaak in his lap, and left. She never had found out if he'd picked up all his possessions, which she'd summarily shoved out the airlock into orbit the minute she'd returned to the *Independence*.

No one had the right to tell her what to do. Not anymore.

Calista pushed herself up out of the chair. A shower—a nice, long, *cold* shower—would feel good right now. She glanced at the blank comm screen and the instruments that told her the *Fair Trade* was still there. Almost within transport range—if she'd been interested.

Which, of course, she wasn't.

Fairdane had been wrong in any case, Calista thought. She'd made a considerable profit with the Zogret, and the phaser burn she'd received as she left had been worth it. Most traders never made it off planet at all.

So he still wanted her.

Rhys glared at the hard, aching evidence of his desire and silently cursed the unreasonable fate that had tied him, against his will and better judgment, to a woman who seemed determined to drive him mad.

15

It had been five years. That should have been more than long enough to have forgotten her, forgotten the feel and taste and smell of her.

It wasn't.

Often, in the long, lonely hours of the night onboard ship, he'd lie awake thinking of her, wanting her, remembering all the times she'd shared the night with him, all the dark hours that had flared to brilliant light with the passion of their joining.

He could remember the sweat-slicked texture of her skin as they'd lain together afterwards. He could see the blue of her eyes glinting through the thick, dark lashes, taste her swollen lips, caress the tangled, golden mane spread across the pillows.

Rhys sighed, then shifted uncomfortably on the pilot's chair. Even the damp towel flung across his lap was insufficient to quench the heat of his skin or hide the physical evidence of his need.

Would he ever stop wanting her? Stop thinking of her?

It wasn't just the nights that returned to mock him. He still found himself glancing up from his work, expecting to hear her footsteps in the passages or her muttering to herself as she worked. In the months they'd been together, she had become a part of his life, a part of his being as no other woman he'd ever known had been.

Yet she was so damned serious, so intense. There was a vast capacity for laughter and joy hidden beneath the hard shell she'd built around her emotions, but she'd rarely ever allowed that side of her to show, even with him.

He'd never understood why she kept that part of herself so well hidden. For himself, he'd learned long ago that laughter and a flippant, easygoing manner were the best disguises for one's true feelings. If you never revealed that something mattered, then no one ever bothered trying to take that something away.

It was a lesson Calista should have learned.

Rhys's fingers tightened around the padded arms of the pilot's chair, digging deep into the pliant fabric.

His glance slid to one of the view screens. A brilliant blue and green and white orb seemed to float there, slowly spinning against the infinite dark of space. It was a planet of the Kartanese system—not the second planet he was orbiting now, but the third. A precious jewel of teeming oceans and rich, fertile lands that had never known the hand of man. Or that of any other intelligent creature, for that matter.

But just because it was uninhabited didn't mean it was unclaimed. By Imperial law, the third planet belonged to the Kartanese, the huge, dragonlike creatures who occupied the desert world below him.

With other species, he might have negotiated for the right to colonize the third planet. The Kartanese, however, were famous for their distaste for contact with other races. And as the Empire's only producers of the costly and coveted saitha silk, they were far too wealthy to be tempted by the relatively paltry sums he could offer.

But if he could use the position of trade rep to his advantage, then maybe, just maybe . . .

A muscle in Rhys's cheek jumped as he set his jaw.

He wouldn't let Calista have the position. He couldn't let her have it. All she wanted was the profits from the silk trade, but his goal was far more important than mere money.

He'd sought this world, or one like it, for so long that he'd come close to believing it would never be anything but a dream, a tempting, eternally elusive dream he would chase forever—alone.

Only once had he dared hope that he might, at last,

have found someone to share that dream.

Once had been more than enough. Never again would he allow himself to care that much, to need someone that badly. Never.

Rhys angrily flung the towel aside and stood.

No matter that the golden-haired witch had suddenly reappeared in his life, and at such an inopportune moment. No matter that just the sight of Calista was enough to heat his blood and make him ache with the wanting of her.

She wouldn't disrupt his life as she had five years before.

He would never give her the chance.

"Master." The worker prostrated itself on the floor, not an easy task for a heavy-bodied creature with thick, clumsy legs. Even though it was the chief of the thousands of workers so carefully tending the precious eggs, its words were scarcely distinguishable because its pale, round face was rubbing the paving stones.

"I have come as you bid me, O Great One. My life is the life of Karta, my soul your servant so long as breath is in my body and—"

"Yes, yes, I'm sure you're doing a superb job, but that's not why I called you here." The Dorinor, regally seated on his haunches with his wings folded and his tail wrapped around him, gestured impatiently with one clawed forefoot.

"As you say, Master," the worker said, scrambling to its feet. It tucked its own two hands into the heavy pouch that hung from a belt around its waist and bowed deeply. In the dim light of the chamber, its pale gray fur showed eerily white. "I serve you and yours to—"

Before the worker could get into full swing, the Dorinor interrupted again. "Over a full cycle of the

18

sun has passed since you installed the equipment. Is it working as we'd hoped? Will you be able to open the new caves this year?"

The worker flushed, a sure sign of nervous fear. "No, Master," it said, much more hesitantly than it had rattled through the traditional salutations. "The equipment seems . . . adequate, but that is all." The exterior of the pouch bulged as the worker wrung its hands. As if seeking assistance, it glanced at the Dorinor's silent companion, but no help was offered from that direction.

"If that's true, why didn't you let us know sooner? Why have you made me call you from your work when you could have—" The Dorinor's shrill, clicking tirade stopped abruptly when his companion intervened.

"It is only a worker, Master, and does not know any better," the companion said soothingly. "The fault is ours for not asking. You cannot blame a worker for being what it is."

With a chittering sigh, the Dorinor sank back onto his stone platform. "You're right, of course, Karnor. You usually are. If only—" His head wobbled with frustration on his long neck. "But times change and so must we."

He rolled one golden eye at the trembling worker but when he spoke, his voice had lost its shrillness. "I know you and the other workers are doing the best you can," he said slowly, "but in the future, I want your reports to include information on this new equipment and not just on the condition of the eggs. Do you understand?"

"Of course, Master," the worker said, clearly relieved at the mildness of the rebuke. It bowed low once more. "We will do just as you order, Master. You may be sure of that. Your merest wish is our command, your commands a sacred charge that—"

19

"Yes, yes," the Dorinor muttered impatiently. This time, both forefeet came up to indicate the worker was dismissed.

Once the worker had bowed its way out of the chamber, the Dorinor focused his glowing eyes on Karnor. "Have we made a mistake, old friend? Should we even have tried these off-world abominations the strangers call machinery? Are the gods expressing their displeasure at our choice?"

Karnor used one forefoot to scratch the thick, black hair on his abdomen while he considered the question. "Did we have a choice?" he asked at last, sadly. "The gods seemed none too pleased before or they would not have allowed the changes in the sacred caves. Perhaps we simply chose the wrong machinery."

"Or the wrong representative. What do you think? Will these two new strangers serve us better than the last one did?"

Karnor's mouth wrinkled in distress. "I certainly hope so," he said plaintively. "The last one failed us completely. And he tasted so bad. All that fat. I know my duty, but I really don't want to be forced to eat these two, as well. I'm not sure my stomach could handle it."

The Dorinor nodded and clicked his teeth in distaste. "I couldn't agree more, though you'll remember I *did* warn you to remove those artificial skins they wear, first."

Silence fell as the Dorinor, too, scratched his abdomen in perplexed thought. "They're most unpleasant creatures, but we need their services and they seem ready to do our bidding in exchange for the right to sell the fibers." His tail twitched. "Odd how the strangers crave the fibers. Larr swears it is because they like the color, but I find that difficult to believe.

Yet why else would they pay so much for something of so little value?"

A second hand joined the first in its scratching. "Even this concept of payment I find very difficult to understand. Larr says they have no workers and so must have other creatures make the things they need. It doesn't sound like a very sensible way to organize matters."

"The strangers don't seem very sensible, under any circumstances." Karnor drummed his claws on the edge of the Dorinor's platform. "And now, by selling the fibers and buying their machinery, we begin to adopt their ways, too."

"Perhaps these new strangers will find the solutions we seek." The Dorinor's words were optimistic. The tone of his voice was not.

"I hope Larr is right about these new strangers." Karnor grimaced. "I *really* don't think my digestion could handle two."

Chapter Two

The heat was appalling and the earth beneath Calista's feet was little more than ash, every trace of moisture long ago baked out by the relentless sun that dominated the steely sky of Karta.

Slowly Calista pivoted on her heel, studying the forbidding gray rock that loomed like prison walls on all sides. If she hadn't checked, then double-checked the coordinates Larr had given her, she'd be tempted to beam back to her ship. The place was hardly auspicious for her first face-to-face meeting with the Dorinor's personal representative, but the site was his choice, not hers, and she would have put up with a lot more discomfort for the chance to be named trade representative.

Calista squinted against the heat and light, trying to picture the Kartanese here in their native setting. The few info-tapes she'd found had been of poor quality, but she had no difficulty in imagining one of the great creatures shown on the tapes soaring above the barren rock, its huge wings outstretched to catch each updraft, it massive body and long neck and tail strangely graceful in the hot, gray vault of sky.

What she couldn't imagine, however, was how such a creature could ever have created saitha silk, the extraordinary fabric that was the sole export of Karta and one of the most coveted—and costly—commodities in the galaxy.

She'd had the chance, once, to touch a scrap of the silk. Even now Calista could remember the energy that had flowed through her fingers with that brief contact, the sense of well-being that had lingered for minutes afterwards. A few days of wearing a gown made of the silk was enough to temporarily restore lost youth to an aging matron, power and virility to a decrepit male. And constant use of the fabric added decades to the life of the wearer. It wasn't hard to believe that people had killed for the chance to possess enough of the fabric to make a complete garment.

Now that trading in the silk was strictly controlled by Imperial decree, there wasn't as much mayhem involved, but there was just as much profit. More, maybe. The Kartanese produced only a small quantity of silk every year, far less than the demand for it, and prices rose steadily.

Since the Kartanese themselves never went off planet, anyone lucky enough to be named trade rep could quickly—and very, very easily—make a fortune. Calista had calculated that a five percent commission would earn her more in a year than she had earned in the ten years she'd been working as a trader.

Larr had promised her ten percent.

It was enough money to buy her freedom, the *real* freedom that for so long had been just beyond her reach.

Calista's hands clenched into two fists. No one—and certainly not Fairdane—would take this chance from her.

No one.

As though summoned by her thoughts, Rhys suddenly materialized four feet away from her. At the sight of her, he broke into a raffish grin.

"Red! How nice to see you again!"

"Don't—"

"Call you Red. You've said that before." His grin, if possible, stretched even wider. "It's a habit I just can't seem to break, but don't get excited. Once the Dorinor names me rep—"

"There's not a spacer's chance in hell of that, Fairdane!" Calista resisted the urge to plant a fist in the middle of that smug smile, but it took an effort.

"Well, since this isn't hell, despite the heat, that won't matter much." Rhys slowly turned on one heel, calmly surveying the area around them. "Nice place. If you're a Kartanese. Myself, I prefer something a little greener."

"Your preferences probably don't interest the Dorinor much." The insult was sadly flat, but Calista found herself incapable of anything more biting—she was too distracted by the clinging fit of Rhys's protective black skin suit to concentrate.

It was downright impertinent of the man to wear a suit that highlighted every bone and powerful muscle in his body.

Impertinent, and damned irritating.

At the very least he could have worn an over-robe, as she had, which would have disguised the blatantly masculine lines of his body. But that would have been a demonstration of consideration, and being considerate wasn't one of Rhys's strong points—at any rate, not where she was concerned.

24

Rhys abruptly completed his inspection of the area around them and turned back to face her. To Calista's chagrin, he caught her just as she was glaring at his firmly rounded posterior.

She flushed, which irritated her even more. If the man wanted to fight dirty, it was his choice. She wasn't about to let him get the advantage right from the start.

"Hot, isn't it?" she said, her gaze innocently fixed on the rocks fifteen feet behind Rhys's shoulder. Calista lifted the collar of her over-robe and waved the fabric as though trying to fan herself. "I don't think my suit's working right. It's not compensating for the robe."

With a slight frown to show her annoyance with the improperly functioning suit, Calista slowly ran a finger down the front seam of the robe. The heavy blue fabric parted, revealing the glistening silver-blue fabric of the skin suit beneath.

"I told the computer a week ago to fix that clothing generator," Calista complained, "but it doesn't seem to have done any good. This skin suit was fresh this morning and it hasn't even lasted a full day."

She flapped the edges of the robe. Instead of stirring a cooling breeze, the motion simply served to drive more hot air up over her throat and face. It didn't matter. She wasn't about to stop yet. Her strategy was working too well.

Covertly, Calista watched Rhys. The trader's eyes were glued to the opening of her robe and to the brief, tantalizing glimpses she was providing of her own shapely body in its skintight suit.

With Rhys's darkly tanned skin it was hard to tell, but she could have sworn he was flushed. Calista pushed her advantage.

"Do you think Larr or one of the Kartanese will show up soon?" Calista dropped one edge of her robe, carefully letting it fall to the side so the curve of her breast was outlined against the dark fabric. She tugged at the round collar of her suit. "If we don't get out of this heat soon, I'm going to have to transport back to my ship and change."

"Why don't you do that? Then when our escorts arrive, I'll just tell them you've decided to drop out of the deal." Rhys's taunt would have had more effect if it hadn't been for the hoarse, slightly breathless catch in his voice.

"You'd like that, wouldn't you?" Calista glanced up but Rhys wasn't looking at her face. His gaze was firmly fixed on her fingers, tugging at her collar, and on the silver-blue sheen of her suit where it stretched over the full curves of her breasts.

"Yes, I'd like that." His words came out in an even hoarser, scarcely audible whisper.

Calista ran her finger a few inches down the invisible center seam of her suit. The fabric, released from the stress of conforming to her body, immediately pulled apart to reveal the soft white skin beneath.

"Well, I wouldn't." To hide her satisfaction at Rhys's completely involuntary intake of breath, Calista put a bite in her words. "I'd rather stand in this heat stark naked than—"

Stark naked!" Rhys's head snapped up.

For an instant—an all too brief but *very* satisfactory instant—his mouth gaped and his eyes glazed over with the sudden heat of his desire. Then his eyes flashed, hard and black, and his mouth snapped shut with an audible pop.

"Why, you—" Three swift strides brought him to within inches of her.

In spite of herself, Calista flinched at the almost palpable wave of anger that emanated from him. Her hand froze in the act of opening the seam farther.

"Go ahead, Calista. Open your suit. Let the air dry your skin. Maybe the Kartanese will give you a discount on some saitha silk, as long as you're here."

Calista closed her suit with an angry, upward jerk of her hand. "I won't need discounts, Fairdane, since I'll be the rep. And if you think—"

The sound of footsteps on stone interrupted her. As one, Calista and Rhys whirled about to confront the new arrival.

Arrivals, Calista amended silently. The boots of the tall man at the head of the approaching delegation crunched on the hard, rocky soil. The two creatures slightly behind and on either side of him made no sound at all.

The info-tapes hadn't prepared Calista for the Kartanese in person. They were huge, yet their four claw-footed legs carried them easily and totally silently over the rocks. Their bodies, with the exception of the long tails curled over their backs and the wings furled at their sides, were covered with what looked like thick, coarse black hair that reflected iridescent hues of blue, purple and green in the harsh sunlight.

But it was their eyes that held Calista fascinated. They were like multicolored gems, glittering in the light. The brilliant orbs gave the creatures a clear view on all sides and behind them. Right now, they were focused squarely on Calista and Rhys.

The Kartanese halted fifteen feet away from them, but the creatures were so tall that when they bent forward and stretched out their long, graceful necks, their heads were only inches from Calista.

Fascinated, Calista found herself staring, transfixed, at the beast on her right. After a moment of her intense scrutiny, the Kartanese blinked, then retreated, drawing its neck in and straightening so its head was at least six feet above hers. From that position of advantage it tucked in its chin and stared silently down at her, a thoroughly magnificent, intimidating creature.

"Welcome, traders."

Calista jumped. She'd forgotten the man leading the two Kartanese. He shouldn't have reminded her. She had a bone or three to pick with him.

"You've got your nerve, Larr," she began, glaring up at him. "What do you mean—"

"I trust you both had a safe journey." If Calista's heated greeting irritated him, Larr's bland smile gave no hint of it.

"The emphasis should be on the word 'both,' Larr." Rhys's words were far calmer than Calista's, but they carried the same message.

"Ah, yes." Again Larr smiled. "That will be explained in due time. Meanwhile, the Dorinor awaits us. If you'll follow me?"

Without waiting for their response, Larr turned and retraced his steps. The two Kartanese remained unmoving, their gaze fixed on Rhys and Calista.

For an instant, Calista hesitated, irritated by Larr's arrogant assumption that she would follow him rather than demand the explanation she wanted.

"Shall we?" Rhys was watching her, one eyebrow raised in inquiry. "I'd say ladies first, but I doubt you'd appreciate the gesture."

"Don't pretend to be the gentleman, Fairdane," Calista snapped.

One corner of Rhys's mouth twitched in irritation. "At least you'll never pretend to be a lady, Red."

"You got that right." Calista swept in front of Rhys, her long robe billowing about her legs, and headed after Larr. Behind her, she could hear Rhys's footsteps on the gravel.

She wasn't aware the Kartanese had moved until

the shadow of one's head and neck swung across the path. Calista glanced up, startled to find the creatures were now flanking them. She hadn't heard even the slightest roll of a pebble under their feet.

A few minutes walking brought them to a narrow defile between the cliffs. Larr led them around an outcrop of gray stone and through an enormous, arching entrance that must once have been a natural tunnel into the rock. At some time in the distant past it had been carefully reshaped into a semicircular passage. The entrance was more than large enough for the two Kartanese to enter, side by side. It dwarfed the three humans.

A hundred feet in, the tunnel came to an abrupt end. A dozen smaller tunnels, each just large enough to accommodate an individual Kartanese, showed black against the dark stone.

At the entrance to the fourth tunnel on the left, Larr halted and turned to face Calista and Rhys. His thin, sharp-featured face showed palely in the dim light.

"This passage will take us to the Dorinor's chamber. Before we enter, are either of you carrying weapons of any kind?" he asked.

"You told us to come unarmed, Larr." Calista's words were sharp, impatient. She wasn't about to tell him about the long, slender strip of plasteel that lay just beneath the seam of her left sleeve, or the superfine length of wire woven around the neck of her robe. Neither was detectable by any but the most sophisticated of modern equipment.

The plasteel, scarcely more than a millimeter thick, made a lethal weapon. Wielded by a trained fighter, it could slice through hide and muscle with ease. Calista had learned to use it when she was scarcely ten years old. The wire with its multitude of uses had more than once been handy in a tight spot.

She'd carried weapons like them for years—a trader never knew when that extra bit of protection might mean the difference between living and dying.

"No weapons at all?" Larr's left eyebrow raised in query. Neither Calista nor Rhys responded. "You surprise me."

Rhys shrugged. "And you told us—me, at least—to come unarmed, Larr. Let's get on with it."

"It's gratifying to find you both so . . . compliant."

Larr bent slightly to stare directly at Calista. The bland smile with which he'd greeted them was back in place.

"If you wanted to chat, Larr, we could have done that much more comfortably on the *Independence*." Calista peered past the Kartanese representative into the relatively cooler darkness of the tunnel beyond. "Do we have an appointment with the Dorinor or don't we?"

Larr's smile grew slightly wider but he said nothing. Instead, he turned and, picking up a glow-light from a shelf near the entrance, led the way into the tunnel.

The light didn't do much more than illuminate the side of Larr's robe. Ten steps into the tunnel and Calista found herself instinctively stretching out a hand in front of her to prevent a collision with any invisible obstacle. Another twenty steps or so and even the palest hint of sunlight from the tunnel's opening had disappeared.

Without intending it, Calista found herself moving closer to the vague, black form of Rhys beside her. His masculine, well-muscled bulk was some small comfort, at least.

The comfort didn't last for long.

With a roar that reverberated in the darkness, a Kartanese suddenly filled the passageway before them.

At least, Calista assumed it filled the passageway.

All she could see were two glittering eyes and what seemed like a hundred huge, white, and very sharp teeth—no more than a foot in front of her.

"Run, Calista!"

Part of Calista's view was blocked as Rhys threw himself between her and the Kartanese. Calista tugged the plasteel strip out of her sleeve and spun around.

Two more glittering eyes blocked the passage behind them. The second Kartanese gave a shrill hiss and opened its mouth to expose a set of teeth that were, if anything, even bigger than its companion's.

"We're trapped!" Calista took two steps back and bumped into Rhys. She raised the plasteel, ready to defend herself against an attack she knew they couldn't withstand.

"Enough!"

Larr's voice, cutting through the dark, startled Calista. She'd forgotten him entirely. And what had happened to the glowlight?

As if in answer to her question, Larr suddenly switched the light on. This time, its glow illuminated the passage completely.

But even that wasn't sufficient to make the Kartanese looming in front of her any less intimidating. It hissed again and opened its mouth wider, exposing a dozen more razor-sharp teeth.

In spite of herself, Calista shrank back, grateful for the bulk of Rhys behind her. From the strung tension that held his body rigid, she guessed he wasn't any happier about his view.

"Tsk, tsk, tsk." Larr stepped away from the wall of the tunnel, gravely shaking his head. He bent to study Calista's weapon. "And you said you were unarmed."

Calista's fingers tightened around the plasteel's narrow handle. All it needed was one quick flick of

31

her wrist to put an end to that smug smile.

"Did you arrange this for our entertainment, Larr?" Rhys's voice was only slightly less cutting than the plasteel he held.

"I didn't have to, trader. There are Kartanese guards like this one posted in every tunnel leading into the caves." Larr didn't even glance at the creature blocking the passageway before them.

"Not to mention the secure-detects you've mounted along here." Calista forced a note of disdain in her voice.

Larr grinned. "There is no equipment here, Trader. None."

"Then how did the Kartanese know we were still carrying weapons?" Rhys demanded.

"The guard sensed them." Larr gestured toward the Kartanese that had originally attacked them.

"That's ridiculous! Even the most delicate sensors have trouble detecting plasteel," Calista protested.

Larr shrugged. "Don't ask me how they do it. Perhaps they're psychic. But I assure you, the guard knew you were armed."

"You knew we were." Calista wasn't guessing.

"Let us say, I assumed you were. Most traders are."

"Nothing quite like being proved right, is there, Larr?" Rhys tossed the plasteel against the far wall of the tunnel.

Calista hesitated for an instant, then flung her weapon after Rhys's. "Satisfied, Larr?" She took two steps forward, only to be drawn up short when the guard hissed rather nastily and swung its head down, teeth bared, to within inches of her face.

This time Larr laughed outright. "I will be when you drop your other weapons, as well."

The man would have been struck dead on the

spot if Calista could have put some physical punch behind her glance. Briefly—*very* briefly—she considered refusing, but another menacing hiss convinced her otherwise.

Without taking her eyes off Larr, Calista tugged the wire free and tossed it after the plasteel.

"Satisfied now?" she demanded. Bereft of her weapons, she felt more exposed than she would have if she were totally naked.

Larr turned toward Rhys. "And you, trader?"

Clearly annoyed, Rhys slid a second plasteel from his sleeve, then bent and tugged a third from the inside seam on the leg of his skin suit.

Calista's eyebrows raised. What had he planned to do with *three* of the things, for star's sake?

"Let's get on with this, Larr," Rhys snarled, tossing his weapons on the small but growing pile at the side of the tunnel. "I'm not finding this very amusing."

Rhys stepped forward to glare at the Kartanese blocking their path. The guard hesitated. It stared at Rhys, hissing softly, then reluctantly backed into an enormous niche cut into the wall. Once settled in its guard post, the creature was nearly indistinguishable from the black rock of the tunnel itself. Only its eyes and the small, irritated hiss it made as they went past revealed its existence.

The going was easier now that Larr had turned the glow-light up. As they moved deeper into the hillside, they began passing numerous cross tunnels. Each had walls and floors worn as smooth as the tunnel they followed, as though countless generations of Kartanese had polished the rock in their passing.

Bereft of her weapons, Calista tried to stay alert to possible dangers but found her senses determined to play her false.

She strained her ears to catch any hint of Kartanese

33

approaching from the cross tunnels but all she heard was the firm scrunch of stone with each step Fairdane took. She strained her eyes to peer into the darkened passages, trying to see beyond Larr's glow-light, but it was Fairdane who filled her vision.

Why had he thrown himself between her and the Kartanese guard? He owed her nothing and she'd made it clear she wanted nothing from him. So why risk himself for her? What possible motive could he have had?

The answer was, of course, none. And that bothered her even more.

More than three feet separated them, yet Calista would have sworn his arm brushed against hers, would have sworn it was his breath and not just the faint movement of the air in the passage that slid down her cheek and jaw and throat.

And with each step she took, every foot they progressed deeper into the Kartanese caves, her anger at the man grew. She refused even to consider that anger was a far safer emotion than the others that tugged at the edges of her consciousness.

What right did he have to come back into her life? Especially now? What had he expected to gain by showing up in that damned skin suit? Did he think she was some simpleminded female incapable of controlling herself at the sight of a well-built male body?

And he shouldn't have jumped in like that, as if she weren't completely capable of defending herself. Just who did he think he was?

The man was an arrogant, swaggering . . . *man*, that's what he was. She'd spend the rest of her life cleaning garbage scows before she'd let him take this chance to be trade rep from her.

Rhys was finding that Calista's silence worried him a whole lot more than her verbal barbs. At least when she was snapping at him he knew what she was thinking about. This way . . .

Rhys's jaw set. It didn't matter what she was thinking. He was going to be trade rep and that's all there was to it. The fortune the position would bring him could make an enormous difference—to his mother, to Glynna. To all of them. Not the wildest, most convoluted machinations of which Calista was capable would succeed in winning her the position that was already his.

But why had Larr asked both of them in the first place? Rhys eyed the tall, slender form of the Dorinor's personal rep with misgivings. He'd worried that problem ever since the *Independence* had dropped into orbit beside him, and he was no closer to an answer now than he had been then. Larr must know that he and Calista hadn't worked together for years. *Had* to know it. So why were they both here?

Rhys wasn't any closer to an answer by the time their small party emerged from the tunnel onto a stone ramp. The ramp led to the floor of a fair-sized cave illuminated by sunlight streaming through openings in the ceiling high above them.

He blinked, startled by the sudden transition from dark to relative brightness. He would have sworn they'd been moving deeper into the caves, but it seemed he was mistaken. Judging by the placement of the openings, the cave was situated somewhere on the hillside above the original entrance.

Despite being close to the surface, however, the cavern was as cool as the tunnels they'd just come from. Rhys had to admit, however, that "cool" on this planet of baked rock was definitely a relative term.

Without stopping to give their eyes a chance to adjust to the increased light, Larr started down the ramp ahead of them. For an instant, Rhys hesitated, unwilling to move forward until he could see more clearly. A sharp, warning hiss from one of the Kartanese behind him convinced him of the wisdom of going on, anyway.

Before he could take one step, Calista swept in front of him, head high. Irritated, Rhys came very close to grabbing her and pulling her back beside him. He stopped himself at the last moment.

She was going to play that game, was she? She'd pulled the same sort of stunt before. Pushing in every chance she got, elbowing him aside, speaking before he'd had a chance to open his mouth. There were times that strategy had worked very well.

It wasn't going to work this time.

The thing was, he couldn't beat her by playing her game with her rules.

Ignoring the two impatient Kartanese following hard on his heels, Rhys moved down the ramp and across the expanse of worn stone floor in a slow, arrogant swagger. He could think of nothing better calculated to annoy Calista and incite her to lose her temper than to feign a nonchalance he was far from feeling.

As he crossed the cave, Rhys strained to see beyond the shafts of light into the shadows beyond, into the dark where the Dorinor must surely be. Yet each time he glanced to one side or the other, his gaze was drawn back to the sight of Calista passing through the golden light, her hair a luminous aureole about her.

She was . . . beautiful. Exquisite.

It made him mad as hell that, without trying, she was still capable of driving every thought out of his head but those of her.

With a growl of disgust, Rhys forced his attention back to the matter at hand. He couldn't afford to lose the position of trade rep. He couldn't stand to lose it to Calista.

Before them, Larr came to an abrupt halt at the edge of the shadows that engulfed the far edge of the chamber. Calista stopped two feet from Larr. Rhys pushed his way between them, blatantly ignoring Calista's angry glance.

For a moment, Rhys was blind, the shadows a vague wall of black after the pale sunlight that filled the rest of the cavern. Then the shadows took on form and Rhys blinked, startled. The Dorinor was larger than the Kartanese guards that had accompanied Larr. Even seated—or was the proper word reclining?—on a low platform, the creature towered over the three humans before it.

"Welcome, strangers."

The translator behind Rhys's left ear changed the Dorinor's rasping sibilants into an approximation of human speech. Odd that the device had made no effort to translate the guards' hisses. Threats obviously came across clearly no matter how they were presented.

"Greetings, Excellency." Calista was first to speak.

"Excellency." Rhys nodded politely in greeting. He'd barely stopped himself from glowering at Calista.

The Dorinor's head swung down so its—his? hers? Rhys couldn't decide and the info-tapes had given no clue to the Dorinor's sex—eyes were on a level with theirs. Without speaking, it studied first Calista, then Rhys, then Calista again.

"You are the male," it said at last, its gaze on Rhys.

"Yes, Excellency." Rhys couldn't help blinking in surprise. Whatever opening he'd expected, it certainly wasn't this.

"And you are the female," the Dorinor said, turning toward Calista.

37

"Of course!" The question clearly irritated Calista, but she added, more calmly this time, "You're quite right, Excellency."

"Ah." The Dorinor's head swung up and back. The creature straightened, then stared at the two of them while slowly scratching its belly. "Larr was right, Karnor," it said to the silent Kartanese sitting on a second, lower platform to the side. "They do send their females out."

He, then. The Dorinor had to be male. Out of the corner of his eye, Rhys studied Larr. The man remained unmoving, expressionless. After all these years, he was probably accustomed to being talked about as though he weren't present. But then, a man could put up with a lot if it meant earning the kind of profits being the Dorinor's personal representative must surely bring.

"Have you known each other long?" the Dorinor asked, swinging back to Calista and Rhys.

"Well, we—" Calista began

"I knew her in a very ancient sense of that word several years ago, but I don't think I ever figured her out." Rhys felt a twinge of satisfaction. His use of archaic references irritated the very devil out of Calista. She probably wasn't familiar with the expression, but that wouldn't stop her from suspecting him of the worst.

"We've worked together before," Calista admitted, keeping her gaze firmly fixed on the Dorinor. "However—"

"I prefer to work alone," Rhys interjected smoothly. It was *his* turn to reject her. He'd waited five years and he'd never have a better chance.

Calista's head snapped around. Rhys watched her struggle to bite back the angry retort hovering on her lips.

"We have very different styles of working," he added, turning back to the Dorinor.

"That's right." Calista's effort to restrain her temper showed in the quivering tension in her voice. "I think you will find that I'm able to deal with even the most difficult customers, Excellency. A successful trader has to be willing to take chances, and I've been *very* successful."

"On the other hand, long-term profits require a good working relationship between trader and client." A successful trader also didn't let the competition get the upper hand in negotiations, but Rhys wasn't going to mention *that* to the Dorinor. "I'm still working with my first customers, Excellency. There aren't many traders who can say the same."

"You have to grow, Excellency, if you're to stay profitable." From the cool, reasoned tone, Calista had her temper back under control. At least for now. "There are so many opportunities, so many—"

"Yes, yes. I understand what you are saying," the Dorinor broke in, seemingly irritated at the rapid-fire exchange. He paused, his gaze roaming over the three humans standing before him, then mumbled in what must have been the Kartanese version of an undertone, "At least, I think I do."

The translator could only reproduce words, not emotions, but Rhys could have sworn he detected a note of puzzlement in the Dorinor's voice.

"In any case," the creature continued before either Rhys or Calista could interrupt, "Larr has explained the differences in your methods of operation." The great head nodded slowly, thoughtfully. "It pleases me to know that, even as humans, you understand the gods assign a task to each individual, a role no other can fill. It is best so."

The Dorinor once more brought his head down to

Rhys and Calista's level. For what seemed an eternity he studied them, then nodded again, once, twice. "Larr was right."

"What do you mean, Excellency?"

Trust Calista not to be able to keep silent for very long, Rhys thought. He wasn't sure exactly what the Dorinor intended, but based on the creature's comments, he had his suspicions and he didn't like them. Not one little bit.

"What do I mean?" The Dorinor seemed surprised that Calista should ask. "I mean that you two will serve us well, working together as trade representative for Karta."

Chapter Three

"No! No way. Absolutely not. Never. Under no conditions. I will *not* work with you, Fairdane!"

Rhys settled deeper into his seat and glared across the table at the angry woman seated on the other side. In spite of himself, he couldn't prevent the small twitch of amusement tugging at the corner of his mouth. Calista always looked gorgeous when she was mad. It was, he supposed, the result of the fire it brought into her blue eyes.

"That's the trouble with you, Red," he said at last. "You're always so wishy-washy in your opinions."

Her lips gave an answering twitch, but there wasn't a speck of amusement in the expression. "Did you expect I'd leap on the deal with a cry of joy? I'm going to be the trade rep, Fairdane, and you are *not* going to be my partner."

"You're partially right, anyway. I'm *not* going to be your partner. But it seems to me we might discuss some alternatives in light of the Dorinor's little bombshell."

"I don't know what kind of sneaky deal you hatched with Larr—"

"Larr offered me the position," Rhys snapped, irritated. "He sure as hell didn't say a word about you being in on the deal, so I don't know what kind of underhanded tricks you—"

"Tricks! You talk about tricks?" Calista slapped her palm against the tabletop, then shoved her chair back and stood up abruptly. "If ever there was a master of trickery, it's you, Fairdane. But regardless of what you're up to, there's no way I'll let you get away with stealing this deal from me."

"I'm not stealing the deal from you. It was never yours to begin with. It's mine, and inviting me up to your ship to discuss the matter was a waste of time."

"Then why did you accept my invitation, Fairdane? Did you make the mistake of thinking I'd give in to your wiles? Don't think I don't know what you're up to when you put on that oh-so-charming smile and that smooth manner. It doesn't fool me and—"

The communications panel chimed, interrupting her. She glanced toward the panel in irritation, then back at him, clearly debating whether to continue her tirade or answer the incoming call. Since there wasn't anyone else in the sector who would be calling them except Larr, the decision was easy. Calista threw him one quick glance that carried a warning Rhys had every intention of ignoring, then stalked across the room to key the comm panel to respond.

In spite of his irritation at her arrogant assumption that he'd give in to her, Rhys couldn't help watching Calista. It would have been impossible not to. The silver-blue skin suit she wore displayed her slender, delectable body in thoroughly distracting detail.

The minute they'd beamed onboard her ship, she'd slipped the over-robe she'd worn off her shoulders, letting it fall in a puddle of color at her feet while she calmly stepped out of it and led the way to this meeting room. From the casual way she'd completed the maneuver, Rhys had no doubt she'd planned it carefully, and all for his benefit. It was her method, he supposed, of exacting revenge for his own blatant display with his black suit.

Rhys shifted uncomfortably on his chair. He could only hope his efforts at annoying her had been as effective as hers had been at distracting him. His suit was becoming uncomfortably strained—at least in spots. He casually leaned back and propped a foot on the chair next to him, grateful that the table was between him and Calista, hiding the proof that her tactics were as successful as she'd undoubtedly hoped.

Calista stepped back just as the comm screen cleared to reveal Larr's smooth, handsome features. From the tension Rhys could see in her shoulders, it was clear she wasn't any happier about the interruption than he was.

"How nice to hear from you, Larr," Calista said sweetly. She strolled back to the table, then propped herself on one corner in a graceful, subtle display that wasn't lost on Rhys, whatever Larr's reaction. It was all Rhys could do to keep from scowling.

With an effort, he forced his features to assume an expression of polite blandness. He couldn't use sex appeal in the negotiations like Calista, but that didn't mean he didn't have a few advantages on his side. She was too passionate and quick-tempered to keep her emotions in control for long, and Rhys was fully prepared to use that weakness against her if he could.

If he could. All his trader's instincts told Rhys the Dorinor's offer wasn't going to change. He'd work with Calista, or neither one of them would be rep. But that didn't mean he wouldn't try to turn the negotiations his way.

"Traders." Larr nodded in greeting, a polite and totally noncommunicative smile on his lips. "I trust you have had sufficient time to discuss the Dorinor's offer and come to a satisfactory agreement."

"We've had time to discuss it, Larr," Calista snapped, "but there's no way in space I'm going to work with this oaf." She gestured over her shoulder at Rhys but her gaze didn't waver from the screen in front of her. "You offered the position to me. Me, not both of us together. I'll be very happy to take on the job, but I work alone."

"Indeed." Her sharp words hadn't ruffled Larr's smooth smile one whit. He glanced over at Rhys. "And you, trader? Do you have an opinion?"

"You know I do, Larr." Rhys rose to stand at the edge of the table, only inches from Calista. The position gave him a slight advantage in height and freedom of movement. Even though he didn't take his gaze from Larr, he could feel the irritation radiating from her. "I'm quite pleased to accept your offer. But I do have some suggestions."

He glanced at Calista and smiled sweetly before turning back to the screen. "You and I, Larr, know the Dorinor's interests can best be served by someone with a cool head and an established reputation for success. I'd be pleased to discuss—"

"Not a chance, Fairdane." Calista slipped off the edge of the table, then moved forward two steps so that she partially blocked his view of the screen. She turned to Larr. "Your offer—"

"The only offer that matters is the Dorinor's. And

that means the two of you work together as rep." Larr's voice carried a flinty edge this time round. "Take it or leave it. I want to know your answer now."

Calista's chest swelled with indignation. "I—"

Before she could say more, Rhys stepped forward and wrapped his arm around her shoulders with an air of companionable bonhomie. A good trader knew when the other side wasn't going to budge. He'd settle for what he could get. "We accept."

Calista spluttered a protest but Rhys tightened his grip in warning. Even though her body stiffened at his presumption, one glance at her expression was enough to assure him she wasn't going to destroy the deal by refusing to work with him. She might have a temper and she might not like him, but she wasn't a fool, either.

"Excellent." Larr beamed. "I'll tell the Dorinor. I'm sure he'll be very pleased."

"There are just a couple of questions—" Rhys didn't have a chance to finish his sentence. The view screen was blank.

He didn't have a chance to say anything to Calista, either. Without warning, she twisted free from him and planted her fist squarely in the middle of his solar plexus. Hard.

Rhys grunted and doubled over, clutching his belly.

"That's for your patronizing, arrogant—"

"You wanted . . . to lose . . . the deal . . . entirely?" Rhys demanded. His breath came in short gasps, which robbed his objection of some of the strength it might otherwise have had.

"I didn't want you making my decisions for me, Fairdane." Calista backed off a foot or so. Hands on hips and feet aggressively planted wide apart, she stood watching while he slowly straightened.

"Furthermore," she added as he tenderly rubbed his

abused stomach muscles, "I want it understood that if we have to work together, we work *together*. Don't start thinking you're going to have everything your way, because you're not."

"How are you going to enforce that rule, may I ask? More physical violence?" Rhys leaned back against the edge of the table, wincing slightly. Calista must have spent some of the time since they'd split up in perfecting her techniques for barroom brawling.

"I'll do whatever I have to, to protect my interests. You tried to run everything your way last time. I'm not going to let you get away with those high-handed tactics this time around."

Resentment rose in Rhys. Resentment, and a biting little doubt. Was that why she'd walked out on him? Because she'd thought he was trying to have things his way?

He'd always figured she left him because she couldn't stand having to share the trade with him. That, and the fact that she liked having everything her way, all the time.

But now, with her standing only a couple of feet away, her whole body stiff with resentment and defiance, Rhys couldn't help wondering if maybe there had been another side to the whole affair that he'd never considered. Maybe he *had* been a little prone to demand they do things his way.

Yet if it hadn't been for his cooler, more rational approach, who knew what problems they might have run into?

"No comment, Fairdane? I'm amazed. I thought you always had a smart comeback for everything."

Rhys scowled. Calista's chin was up at the pugnacious angle that always made Rhys think about strangling her because it gave him such a clear shot at her long, graceful neck.

"There's no point wasting my breath on a senseless argument, York. You've never listened to reason before. Is there any reason I should expect you to now?"

Two quick steps brought Calista to within inches of him. She was tall and he was propped against the edge of the table. That put their eyes on the same level. Rhys met her glare directly, then immediately wished he hadn't.

This close, he could see the tiny flecks of silver in the intense blue of her eyes, and every one of the thick, dark lashes that edged her eyelids. Her skin was as fine and as delicately tinted as he remembered, and her lips . . .

Rhys took a ragged breath, then stood abruptly.

The move wasn't necessarily an improvement in the situation, since it brought them even closer together.

By all rights, Calista should have stepped back, given him more space. He couldn't back up, after all. But she didn't budge. She just tilted her chin higher and glared up at him.

Somehow, the glare didn't have quite the same effect it had had a few minutes before.

This time, instead of narrowing with anger, her eyes widened and the irises expanded until only a narrow rim of sapphire was left. Instead of tightening in anger, her lips parted, revealing just a hint of her tongue. Rhys could hear the soft escape of air as she expelled a quick breath.

The sound was enough to make the muscles of his lower abdomen tighten in a sudden spasm of heat and desire. Whatever he'd been about to say died on his lips and Rhys had to gulp to choke the words back down.

"You . . . I—" Calista bit her lower lip, then took a deep breath and tried again. "I'm going to be the

47

boss this time around, Fairdane," she said. Despite the strong words, her voice lacked the aggressive challenge that had been there a moment before.

"Is that right?" Even those short syllables were an effort to get out. Rhys was finding it hard to concentrate on anything except her quickened breathing and the way her lips moved as she talked, the way the tip of her tongue had peeked out, very briefly, after she'd stumbled over her words.

Calista nodded. Rhys could hear the slight sound her hair made as each silken strand swung forward and back with the motion. "That's right."

He had to bend his head to catch the words. Was it his imagination, or could he feel the heat of her breath against his face? They were so close, her lips were so near . . .

Calista abruptly thrust out both hands, hitting him squarely in the chest and shoving him back against the table.

"Whaa—?"

"I want you off my ship, Fairdane. Right now."

Rhys could have sworn he caught a note of panic behind Calista's harsh demand, but her attack had taken him by surprise. For the life of him, he couldn't think of an intelligent response.

"*Now*," she insisted, her eyes wide—almost wild.

Rhys straightened, caught between anger and confusion at her attack. He felt like shoving her back, which would have been childish. He also felt like taking her into his arms and kissing her until she begged for mercy.

Even now, with her eyes flashing blue fire, that particular mode of revenge held an undeniable appeal.

"Do I have to throw you off my ship, Fairdane?" Calista demanded.

Rhys almost snapped back at her, but the words died

on his tongue as an even better response occurred to him. He grinned. It would drive her crazy.

"All right. I'm going." Rhys keyed his comm link. Then, an instant before his transporter picked him up, he saluted her and added, "Partner."

Partner!

With a cry of frustrated rage, Calista lunged forward, but Rhys disappeared in the transport beam before she could reach him.

For what seemed like minutes, she stared at the empty space where he'd stood. Then she sank, trembling, into the chair beside her.

Having him here so close—so dangerously close—had shaken her far more than she'd ever have thought possible.

Damn him! What right did he have to disrupt her life like this? What right did he have to rouse all those old desires she had struggled for so long to suppress?

Partners! Calista leaned back in the chair, her eyes scrunched shut against the thought. Partners with a man who could rouse her to rage or physical passion with equal ease and who had no scruples at using both abilities to his own advantage.

All it had taken was to be near him again and she'd lost all control, forgotten every intention she'd ever formed about not caring anymore. How would she be able to endure working beside him in the months to come?

She wouldn't. It was as simple as that. She couldn't possibly work with Rhys Fairdane.

Yet if she didn't, the opportunity to be the Kartanese trade rep would be gone.

Calista's eyes flew open at that thought. Every argument against working with Rhys always brought her back to that unpalatable truth. If she threw away the chance to be rep, she'd lose the single best opportunity she'd ever have to buy her freedom, as well.

If there was one thing Calista was absolutely sure of, it was that freedom was going to be expensive. *Very* expensive. A runaway who wanted to buy free from her legal owner had to pay five times her normal market value. Given her success as a trader, her market value would be exorbitant. And that didn't even begin to count the cost of the intermediaries she'd have to hire to act for her, or the credits she'd need afterward to keep on trading.

Assuming, of course, that no one recognized her from her past life first.

Though it was unlikely anyone remembered the scrawny, hostile wench who'd escaped Andrus so long ago, Calista couldn't afford to take chances. If she were identified as a runaway slave and taken captive before she could gain her independence, everything she had would be forfeit to the owners she'd fled years before.

She couldn't—*wouldn't* go back. From the moment she'd understood what freedom meant, she'd worked for nothing else. Every time she'd been punished for being slow, or awkward, or simply a slave, she'd vowed to be free. Every time she'd gone to bed cold, tired, and hungry, she'd dreamed of it.

She would die before she'd ever return to that living hell she'd escaped but never completely left behind.

The sooner she had the money to buy free, the safer she'd be. Nothing she had achieved so far, not even her most profitable negotiations when she was still working with Rhys, had brought in the kind of money she could earn working for the Kartanese.

For a moment, Calista hesitated, mentally weighing the price of her freedom against the cost of working with a man capable of enraging and arousing her, all at the same time.

Involuntarily, her eyes turned to the end of the table, where they had stood only minutes before.

She wanted Rhys Fairdane.

No matter how much she might try to lie to herself, she couldn't deny it. She had wanted him from the moment he'd first appeared on her comm screen, and the closer she came to him, the more she wanted him.

With an angry expulsion of breath, Calista pushed out of the chair.

She was taking the job, Rhys Fairdane or no. Her goal was to gain her freedom and she would do whatever was necessary to ensure she succeeded.

If Fairdane thought he could use her weaknesses against her, he had another think coming. Calista York had never let a man get the best of her before, and she wasn't going to start now.

"We'll use my ship, of course."

"That scow bucket? Might as well park it in Pirates' Alley on Graustaak VII and invite the thieves in for lunch!" After more than seven hours negotiating the terms of the trade rep agreement with Larr and Rhys, Calista's patience was wearing thin. It didn't help that Rhys looked as cool and unruffled as he had when they'd started.

Almost. Calling his beloved *Fair Trade* a scow bucket had definitely put a dent in his emotional armor. She wasn't completely sure, but Calista thought she could detect the faint hint of an angry flush under his dark skin.

With exaggerated calm, he leaned back and casually hooked his elbow over the back of his chair. Even though the heavy wood and fabric chairs around

Larr's office table were well-constructed, the joints on his chair creaked ominously.

Rhys smiled across the table at her, but Calista didn't miss the angry gleam in his dark eyes.

"I wondered when you'd be reduced to insults," he said pleasantly. "You've held up so well until now, York, that I was beginning to worry about you."

"About me, Fairdane?" Calista returned the smile, but it wasn't easy. Being this close to him for so long had strained her admittedly limited powers of self-control, and the reason wasn't entirely due to the complexities of the negotiations. Try as she might, she couldn't ignore the involuntary heat that rose in her at the mere sight of his massive body lounging so casually across the table from her.

"That's right. I—"

Whatever Rhys had been about to say was cut short by Larr's sudden, "That's quite enough!"

Calista glanced at the Dorinor's rep in surprise.

Larr had taken the chair at the end of the table, a strategic choice that had both reinforced his position of control and allowed him to watch their expressions during their hours of dickering over the contract that Rhys and Calista would sign with the Kartanese. Until now, he had maintained a demeanor of bland politeness that had failed totally to disguise his knack for shrewd, hard bargaining. His patience, however, appeared at an end. His usually smooth features were drawn tight in annoyance with their petty exchange of insults and his lean body was tense with disapproval.

"It seems you have forgotten that both your ships are now contracted for the Dorinor's use. *I* will tell you which you will use and when."

Calista started to protest, but a warning glance from Rhys made her think better of it. Instead, she keyed a few quick commands into her hand comp, requesting it search through the lengthy document they'd been working on. When the screen displayed the paragraph in question, Calista couldn't help scowling. There it was, Section 23, Subsection 36, paragraph 11, line 5. She'd missed it entirely.

Which could only be blamed on the deleterious influence of one Rhys Fairdane.

Unfortunately, the glare she threw that reprobate fazed him not at all. He simply assumed a subtle but undeniably smug expression of superiority and turned back to Larr.

"I didn't see any problems with using the ships when we covered that section of the contract," he said, deliberately not glancing at her. "However, I would like to know what you have planned, Larr."

"That's easy enough. The *Independence* is the faster ship," he said. Before Calista could even begin to preen, he added, "But the *Fair Trade* is larger and more versatile. Each has its advantages and I intend to make use of them."

Calista glared at Rhys. He stared back without speaking.

"Very well, if neither of you has any more questions—" Larr glanced inquiringly at Rhys, then Calista. When neither spoke, he pushed back from the table and stood. "Then let's get on with business."

Without another word, he turned and left the room. Rhys was on his feet at the same instant as Calista, and both were headed toward the door before Larr was out of sight.

As she snapped her hand comp to her utility belt, Calista's mind raced. But instead of concentrating on what lay ahead, all she could do was wonder what else she had missed in the contract. Especially what she might have missed that Rhys hadn't.

It wasn't like her not to notice even the most obscure points in the fine print, and it didn't bode well for the future if Rhys's presence could befuddle her enough to make her miss it now.

Somehow she was going to have to learn how to ignore the big oaf. Fighting with him didn't work—he always seemed to have the last word. Sexually teasing him didn't serve, either. She didn't need to remind herself of the sparks that always flared between them.

That left strangling him.

The corner of Calista's mouth twisted in disgust. Unfortunately, she remembered quite clearly the sections in the contract that dealt with the death of either one of them, so strangling was out, too.

For right now, she tried to concentrate on where they were going and what they passed on their way. A trader never knew when familiarity with her surroundings would come in handy—or be essential for her survival.

Like the chamber they'd conducted the negotiations in, the halls and rooms they passed had all been hewed from the dark gray rock which seemed to form most of Karta. The difference between these passages and those they had passed through during the meeting with the Dorinor was that these were human-sized and had obviously been cut with the aid of equipment usually used in hard-rock mining operations.

The complex was lighted by self-contained white globes set in the ceilings and at regular intervals along the walls. Hidden fans kept the cool air circulating, creating a comfortable environment for humans that was especially welcome after the oppressive heat of the planet itself.

Three times they passed rooms occupied by one or two people working at desks and computer banks, but

Larr made no effort to introduce them to anyone, and none of the workers so much as glanced up to watch them pass.

He came to a halt at last before a sealed metal door set deep in the surrounding rock, then turned to face them. "Have either of you ever touched saitha silk?"

His question brought Calista's attention back to him with a snap. She'd been studying the palm lock and the seal around the edges of the door with professional interest, but whatever lay behind the door, it seemed, was going to be a far greater attraction.

Larr didn't wait for a reply. "We keep the finished silk in this room. My people are all carefully screened and extremely honest, but it never hurts to be cautious." He smiled, but the smile didn't reach his eyes. "I thought you might like to see the commodity that is going to make you both very, very wealthy."

He turned back to the door and pressed his left palm against the glowing lock. A second later, the light winked out and a slight hum signaled the door was opening.

Despite her eagerness to see what lay inside the room, Calista couldn't help studying the door mechanism as they passed through. Top quality and very well done. Which meant it wouldn't be easy to break in, even with the right tools and all the time in the world.

Was Larr the one responsible for this well-built labyrinth? she wondered. Or had it grown in stages over the years? For the first time, Calista found herself wondering what kind of administrative structure the thin blond man had built to support the valuable trade he managed. How long had he been at the game? She didn't even know how old he was.

Those questions, however, could wait. With a quick mental note to herself to follow up on them the first chance she got, Calista turned her attention to the small room on the far side of the security door.

The chamber, like every other one they'd seen, was cut from solid rock and lit by the ubiquitous white globes. The furnishings consisted of a massive table in the center of the room and deep shelves mounted along the walls. With the exception of six medium-sized leather chests, the shelves were empty.

Rhys came to a halt at one end of the table. Calista chose to stand at the opposite end. She spared one quick glance at him, but he seemed as puzzled and as disappointed by the nearly empty room as she was. Somehow, she had expected the vault containing the most costly commodity in the Empire to be more impressive.

Larr crossed to the shelves, pulled one of the chests down, then carried it back to the table. The chest was perhaps three feet wide by two feet tall and about the same deep. Despite its relative bulk, it didn't seem to be heavy for Larr easily swung it up onto the table.

Calista was finding it hard to repress her growing excitement at finally being able to touch the exquisite silk that people were prepared to spend fortunes to acquire. Larr, however, seemed to take pleasure in tormenting her. Instead of opening the chest, he rested his hands on the lid and let his gaze travel from Calista to Rhys and back again.

"The silk," he said, "is always stored in leather chests if it's not being worn. Even when it's being made into a garment, it's cut on a leather-covered table and sewn by hand. That's necessary to maintain its restorative powers."

Calista watched Larr's long, slender fingers rub across the surface of the chest, along the seams at the sides. She didn't need the lecture and she'd happily have ripped the lid off the chest in order to see the contents if she could have gotten away with it. Larr, however, seemed to be taking great delight in delaying the revelation.

"If the silk is left around metal or man-made materials for too long," he continued, "it . . . dies. That's the best way to put it. It becomes nothing more than a fragile, plain piece of rather crude fabric. But when handled properly—"

With frustrating care, he untied the leather lacings that held the chest shut, then slowly lifted the lid to reveal a mound of ivory-colored cloth that seemed to have been unceremoniously dumped inside. He fumbled with the jumbled mass of cloth for a moment, then pulled a length free.

Calista's first reaction was one of disappointment. In all her years as a trader, she'd only seen two people wearing garments cut from the valuable silk. In both cases, the simple garments had molded to their wearers' forms with surprisingly sensuous elegance. Their color, like the color of the fabric in the chest, had been a pale, off-white, but in each instance there had been subtle highlights that had drawn her eye as they shifted with each movement, every change of light.

This cloth, however, was far from impressive. She'd seen bolts of finely woven cotton cloth that were more interesting. Calista couldn't help letting her disappointment show on her face. She glanced up at Larr and was irritated to find him watching her, a slight smile of mingled amusement and condescension on his lips.

"You're disappointed, trader," he said softly. The smile widened. "Perhaps this will change your mind."

With a sudden flick of his hands, he tossed the end of

the fabric across Calista's head and over her shoulder, as if it had been a shawl.

"I don't—" The words were cut short by a gasp as Calista struggled for air against the sudden, icy fire consuming her flesh.

Chapter Four

From somewhere, Calista heard Larr's voice. The words made little sense. She tried to turn, tried to run, but all she could do was sink to her knees under the onslaught of nerve-racking sensation.

"No, don't touch her, Fairdane. Give her body a chance to adapt to the effect of the silk."

The silk? Dimly, Calista struggled to understand. How could crude fabric cause this much pain?

"Rhys!" The name was barely a whisper, choked out between the spasms racking her body. But weak as it was, he heard her plea.

"Calista. Calista! Do you hear me? Take the silk off. Take it off!"

He was there. She could hear him, but what was he saying? A dark face with glittering black eyes swam into her field of vision. Rhys would help her. Calista focused on that thought. Rhys would know what to do.

His eyes grew larger, darker. Calista concentrated, trying to anchor her whirling senses to those two dark orbs staring down at her, cutting through the cloud that held her captive.

Rhys.

The name was a benediction . . . and a promise. And with that promise came an easing of the pain.

Rhys.

Like honey on the tongue. A name to be savored. Calista tried to say it, tried to call to him, but her body refused to respond.

It didn't matter. He was there. She could see him, feel him bending over her.

The pain ebbed and in its place came a slow tingling, then a rush of sweet sensation, of energy and physical well-being unlike anything Calista had ever known. The effect was far more welcome, but just as disorienting as the pain.

That didn't matter, either. She had Rhys to cling to. *That* was what mattered. He was there and he wouldn't leave her so long as she needed him.

Calista smiled. She could feel it lifting the edges of her lips. "Rhys," she whispered, reaching toward him as she clumsily tried to free herself from the length of silk.

"Damn you, Larr! What have you done?" With a vicious oath, Rhys tore the silk from around her shoulders and dragged her into his arms. "Calista! Can you hear me?"

He was shaking her, but Calista didn't mind. At least she knew what he was doing—what she was feeling. Slowly the world righted itself and her mind cleared. Yet as her control returned, Calista's anger rose. Her head was still spinning slightly, but she pushed free of Rhys's protective embrace, then stood and turned to confront Larr.

"Just what in space happened, Larr?" she demanded. Her legs still felt wobbly and she was grateful for Rhys's bulk behind her, yet at the same time she felt a vague sense of loss that the silk was gone.

"It was the silk, trader." Larr, apparently, hadn't moved a micron. He stood calmly beside the open leather trunk, watching her with a cool expression of amusement on his handsome features. "It doesn't take long, but it *is* painful to adapt to the influence of so large a piece. Especially for one as young and healthy as you."

Calista's brown furrowed in thought. She touched the edge of the trunk. "It hurt so much . . . But then I felt as if I were floating, as if—" She shook her head, frustrated by her inability to describe exactly what she'd felt.

"If you hadn't taken it off so quickly, you would have discovered just how energizing the silk can be." Larr gathered up the length of silk he'd flung over Calista and carefully placed it back in the trunk. He closed the lid and retied it before turning back to face them.

"I wanted you to know how potent the silk is. You know of its powers of rejuvenation, but most people don't talk about how painful it can be to adapt to using it." He shrugged. "Perhaps they don't care. If you're old and rich and just spent half your fortune on a garment that can restore years to your life and appearance, I don't suppose the temporary pain matters."

"And everyone goes through whatever the hell you just put Calista through?" There was a note of harsh accusation behind Rhys's query.

Larr nodded, unimpressed by the accusatory tone. "To a greater or lesser degree." His gaze roamed over Calista. There was a speculative glint in his eye that was impossible to miss.

"Actually, trader," he said, "you recovered extremely

quickly. Usually someone in your excellent physical condition finds it much harder to adapt. It has something to do with the way the silk takes the body's energies and feeds them back—amplifying them, so to speak."

"And none of your customers complain?" Calista found that hard to imagine, despite the energizing effects of the cloth.

"Of course not." Larr picked up the trunk and restored it to its position on the shelf. "The ancients searched for a Fountain of Youth, I'm told. We've found it in the silk. Why would anyone complain?"

"But can't you change it? Do something so it isn't so uncomfortable to adapt to?" Calista's rising irritation with Larr's smug self-satisfaction made her take a step forward. She instantly regretted the move, for it made her head start spinning again and brought into question her ability to make her legs do what she wanted them to.

Instantly, Rhys was at her side, his big hand warm and comfortingly strong at her waist. At any other time, Calista knew she would have deeply resented his support. For right now, she could only be grateful he was there to keep her from collapsing in an ungainly heap on the floor.

"You should have left the silk on longer," Larr chided. "If you had, you wouldn't feel so weak now."

"Surely the scientists could find out what causes the reaction and find some way to prevent it." Rhys spoke sharply. His attention was fixed on Larr, but Calista had a sudden suspicion his question was intended more to draw attention away from her momentary weakness than it was to express any real interest in the conversation.

The ploy didn't seem to work. Larr glanced first at Rhys, as though intending to answer his question, then at Calista. The corner of his mouth quirked upward slightly. He turned back to face Rhys.

"You forget," he said, "that the silk doesn't tolerate contact with anything metal. Even those who make it into garments use bone needles and knives to work the fabric. Every effort to study the fabric with an eye to replicating it or its effects has failed."

Larr paused, then smiled. A real smile this time, comfortably complacent and self-satisfied. "That's why you are both going to be very wealthy. There is nothing on the market anywhere that can begin to compete with the silk. And there is nothing like the prospect of regaining their lost youth to tempt old and wealthy people to part with some of their riches."

He moved around the table and headed toward the door. When both Calista and Rhys hesitated, he paused at the threshold and said over his shoulder, "Come along. It's time we celebrated our agreement."

Although her moment of weakness had passed, Calista kept her eyes fixed straight ahead during the short walk, unwilling to reveal her intense awareness of Rhys striding silently beside her. She should have been embarrassed. At least, that would have been her usual reaction—embarrassment and anger that someone should have seen her in anything less than perfect control of the situation. Yet she felt none of those emotions.

Instead, somewhere deep in the core of her was a little warm knot of—what? Appreciation? Certainly she was glad he'd been there. His presence, the knowledge that he would let no harm come to her, had helped her fight against the overwhelming pain and confusion the silk had generated.

It wasn't so simple, however. And that lack of simplicity, her inability to fully understand the emotions his support had engendered, bothered Calista.

Calista didn't have time to mull over this new and disturbing perspective on her relations with Rhys. Larr led them into a large, comfortably furnished room whose far wall was formed of filtered, protective glass.

The view from the window was stark, yet breathtakingly beautiful—a sweeping vista of the gray-white stone peaks and dry uplands of Karta that made the breath catch in Calista's throat. She hadn't realized just how high in the mountain Larr's facilities were set.

As though drawn, Calista and Rhys crossed the room to stand before the window, drinking in the harsh, majestic scene. At that moment, one of the Kartanese sailed past, its wings outstretched, floating on an updraft in a graceful, lazy motion that was strangely at odds with the creature's latent power and ferocity. Sunlight glinted on its dark skin, drawing brilliant flashes of iridescent blue, purple and green.

Awed, Calista could only stand silently watching as the Kartanese turned once, then, with a powerful downbeat of wings, rose even higher and was gone.

"He's beautiful," she whispered. She hadn't intended the comment to be heard, but Rhys's hearing was too acute for him to miss it.

"Incredible, isn't it?" he said, clearly as impressed by the sight as she had been.

"No matter how often I've seen them flying past this window, I still marvel at their grace." Larr's voice, coming suddenly from right behind her, startled Calista.

She turned to find the Dorinor's rep standing only inches away holding three delicate-stemmed glasses filled with a sparkling lavender liquid. He extended one glass to her, gave the second one to Rhys, then raised his own in a toast.

"To your new venture," Larr said, saluting first Calista, then Rhys. "May it prove far more profitable than you ever dreamed—for all of us."

Calista had no trouble drinking to that.

Five days later, Calista stared down at the command console of the *Independence* and reminded herself, for the four thousand and seventy-fifth time, of Larr's toast.

Profit. That's why she was in orbit above the planet, Sindrakis. That's why she had pushed her ship to high speed in order to get here as quickly as possible. And that's why she would manage, somehow, to tolerate a few more days of Rhys's presence on board her ship.

Maybe.

She gritted her teeth. The trouble was, there wasn't anything she could point to that he had done to irritate her. He was polite, tidy, and kept to himself, spending most of his time, it seemed, in the communications center. He hadn't started any fights and had gone out of his way to avoid her when she was in the mood to pick one herself—no mean feat with a ship as small as the *Independence*. Not once had he tried to tell her what to do or how to do it.

He was driving her absolutely crazy.

She'd tried to convince herself it was just because she wasn't used to having anyone else on board. The explanation might have worked if it weren't for the fact that she found herself listening for his footsteps in the passageways, even when she knew he was working in another part of the ship. Or that she had, once or twice—well, all right, three times—deliberately sought him out when she hadn't seem him for several hours at a stretch. She'd even invited him to share her meals, against her better judgment and despite a warning voice in the back of her head that insisted she was asking for trouble.

Worse, she hadn't had a good night's sleep since he'd come on board. Even though she'd deliberately assigned Rhys to quarters on the opposite side of the ship from her personal rooms, she'd found herself waking in the middle of the night, straining to catch any sound that might indicate he was moving about, wondering if he were asleep and, if so, if he were dreaming of her.

Calista began to wish she'd thrown *him* out the airlock when she pitched his possessions all those years ago. It would have made things a lot simpler right now.

"We're in orbit?"

The query brought Calista bolt upright in her chair. She spun around to find Rhys standing in the doorway, watching her. He was dressed in thigh-hugging breeches and a loose top that did nothing to disguise the breadth of his chest or the heavy muscles of his shoulders and arms. As always, his hair was drawn back in a queue at the back of his head. The severe style only served to highlight the strong lines of his face and the dark glitter of his eyes.

Calista drew in a deep, steadying breath and tried to ignore the heavy heat that was rising from somewhere in her lower belly.

"That's right," she said, clipping her words short so he wouldn't suspect how his presence affected her. "I've already signaled our contact that we've arrived."

"Good." He crossed to stand next to her, his attention fixed on the view screen that showed the planet below them. "Not too prepossessing a planet from here, is it?"

"What is? After you've seen a few, they don't seem so

impressive anymore." Calista fixed her gaze firmly on the screen, but even that didn't blot out her awareness of him.

"A few do."

Calista glanced up at him, her attention caught by the odd tightness in his voice. From this angle, seated beside him, she could easily see the sudden tensing of the muscles at the side of his jaw.

Before she could comment, he added, "But that's not important now. When are we supposed to meet this Rudgo Beyloraff?"

"I haven't received a response yet, but judging from Larr's urgency, I wouldn't think we'd have to wait long."

Rhys nodded, once, then stepped away from the screen. "I've already checked the trunk with Beyloraff's shipment and attached the transport ID. We can bring it down whenever we're ready."

Calista couldn't miss the excitement tingeing Rhys's voice. The same eagerness was rising in her at the thought of the deal ahead. Whatever their differences, she realized suddenly, watching Rhys pace the narrow confines of the bridge, they had that much in common—they were both traders to their core.

The unexpected thought eased some of the tension within her. "I've already confirmed that Galaxy Reserve Services is standing by, ready to transfer the funds from Beyloraff's account to ours once the deal is firm."

Calista couldn't prevent a little quiver of eagerness at the thought of the size of the pending transaction. "Do you realize, Fairdane, that this will be one of the largest deals we've ever handled? And we haven't had to do anything but show up!"

Rhys stopped in his pacing and turned to face her. "I've thought about it, York," he said, an unexpected grin spreading across his face. "And there's a whole lot more like it, just waiting for us to come along."

"I almost feel guilty about taking all his money and leaving him with nothing but a leather box and a bunch of silk," Calista admitted, flashing Rhys an answering grin. "But I want you to know I'm not going to let a trivial little thing like guilt get in my way."

She leaned back in her chair and propped a leg over one arm. "He wants that silk and we're the only ones who have it. On the other hand, he has all those nice, shiny credits that *we* want. I'd say both sides have an advantage."

"Let's just make sure we don't lose ours." Rhys leaned against one edge of the command console, openly studying her in a way that was both disconcerting and irritating.

"What exactly do you mean by that, Fairdane?" Calista frowned. She'd heard that tone of voice from Rhys before and she didn't like it any better now than she had the first time they'd worked together.

"We don't know Beyloraff and we don't know how he operates. As the new Kartanese trade reps, we're fair game, so don't rush in and muck things up before I've had a chance to—"

"Before *you've* had a chance!" Calista brought both feet down on the floor with an angry thump.

It had been precisely this sort of overbearing, know-it-all behavior that had made her pitch his possessions out the airlock five years earlier. She'd taken orders as a slave on Andrus and she still took orders—if someone paid her enough.

She wasn't taking orders from Rhys, but she was damned if she'd let him draw her into a fight right now. Too much depended on their working together effectively, regardless of their personal feelings.

Calista came to her feet in a jump that left her pilot's

chair rocking. "I'll meet you in the transport chamber when we're ready to beam down," she said curtly.

Head high and eyes straight ahead, she strode past Rhys and out the door.

Watching her go, Rhys thought sourly that it shouldn't be possible for a man to hold two mutually exclusive thoughts at one and the same time.

He'd like to strangle Calista. It would be satisfying, at least once, to keep her from snapping at him or assuming that she always knew best.

On the other hand, he couldn't look at her without wanting to make love to her. He badly wanted to get his hands around her throat—as well as a few other portions of her luscious anatomy. That possibility had been driving him mad ever since he'd boarded her ship five days before.

Five days and already she'd thoroughly disrupted his life. He couldn't eat, couldn't sleep, and was going quietly and rapidly crazy with wanting her.

Which wasn't going to do him a damn bit of good, since she persisted in keeping him at a safe and icy distance, both emotionally and physically. She was, Rhys thought sourly, like a Gorwalii prickle bear, all sharp points and bad temper. At least where he was concerned.

He'd tried to convince himself it didn't matter, that they could work together without reestablishing the sexual relationship they'd had before. That idea was nothing short of delusional. He wanted Calista and he knew she wanted him. How could any two people who wanted each other so badly work together on a strictly platonic, professional basis?

If he thought about it too long, he'd go mad. And madmen didn't make good traders. He couldn't afford to risk the trade rep position because of a little raging lust. There was too much riding on the profits he could earn and the influence he hoped to gain with the Kartanese.

Rhys grabbed the back of the still-rocking pilot's chair, irritated by the reminder of Calista's angry departure. The chair stopped abruptly.

The negotiations ahead were only the first of what he intended to be a very long string of *very* profitable trade deals. He wasn't going to let Calista muck it up, and he wasn't going to let her drive him crazy.

The trouble was, he couldn't see how he was ever going to manage that particular feat.

Sindrakis, according to the computer records, was a successful agricultural world whose feudal society tied the bulk of the workers to the land and concentrated its wealth in the hands of a very few.

It seemed to be an awful lot of wealth, however. Discreetly, Calista assessed the reception area where they'd been told to wait. Walls, floors, furnishings, and ornaments were all of the finest quality credits could buy. And the credits had bought an impressive array of items from a dozen worlds spread halfway across the galaxy.

She was still trying to decide if the choice of waiting area had been a clever ploy or a strategic mistake on Rudgo Beyloraff's part. On the one hand, he'd more than proved that, if he didn't own the credits themselves, he had access to more than enough to pay for whatever amount of silk they'd be willing to sell. On the other, now she knew they could push the negotiations to squeeze the maximum financial advantage possible from the deal.

Calista glanced over at Rhys. He was discreetly running the fingers of his right hand along the carved arm of his chair. His expression, his graceful, slouching posture, even the seemingly idle play of his fingers along the carving would have convinced any observer he was bored and, perhaps, somewhat sleepy. His pose, Calista knew, was totally spurious.

Rhys caught her watching him. Without changing expression, he shifted slightly in his chair, then briefly extended his right hand so the palm rested on the chair arm and the fingers were stiff and straight, pressed tightly together. To an observer, it would have appeared he was growing restless with waiting.

To Calista, he'd just conveyed the message that he expected negotiations to be fairly easy and that they should push for the greatest advantage possible.

It had been over five years since she'd last used any of the complex, unspoken communications they'd worked out between them, but she still remembered. The knowledge gave her an odd sense of excitement. She'd forgotten how much . . . fun it could be to work with him, to share the thrill of trying to outguess the other side and shape the negotiations their way.

Casually, she scratched the second finger of her right hand against the edge of her jaw in acknowledgment of his message. If there was an unseen observer, she gave no hint that she was even aware of Rhys's presence. No one was in the room with them, but that didn't mean there weren't hidden spy eyes or voice traps. In fact, their being left alone guaranteed they were being observed.

A sharp stab of disappointment hit Calista. Negotiating a deal was more satisfying if the opposite side was just as good as you. Tougher, maybe, but more satisfying. Leaving a trading team alone in the hope they'd reveal something was one of the oldest tricks in the book, and one of the most useless. A good trader never revealed anything, and Calista knew she was very good indeed. So was Fairdane, she mentally added. However much he might annoy her.

For the first time, she found herself looking forward to working with Rhys. Maybe they could recapture something of what they'd once shared. Maybe . . .

"Honored traders."

"Honored host." Rhys was on his feet and nodding politely to the elegantly garbed individual who stood in the doorway. Calista couldn't tell if it was male or female.

"His Excellency will see you now and most humbly begs your pardon for having kept you waiting," the attendant added, bowing slightly. "He was detained by the press of business and was not informed you had arrived. The individual responsible for the oversight has been severely chastised."

I'll just bet, Calista thought to herself as she stood. More likely, the "individual" in question had just reported that the two traders hadn't said anything for the past hour or more, so "His Excellency" might as well get on with the negotiations.

"We are honored that His Excellency could see us so quickly," Calista lied. She put on her most charming smile and gestured to the room around her. "Waiting in such surroundings as these could scarcely be considered a penance."

And that was another lie. Calista tightened the muscles of her buttocks, trying to relieve the discomfort of having sat still for so long. She'd never figured it out, but waiting rooms the galaxy over always seemed to be furnished with the hardest, most uncomfortable chairs available.

"If you would follow me—" The attendant bowed again, then led the way out of the room and down a short corridor to massive double doors set in a wall of sculpted stone. Calista didn't have a chance to more than glance at the carvings, but they seemed about what you could expect in any official building—boring, uninspired, and chauvinistic. Probably cost a fortune, too.

The attendant tapped discreetly on the right-hand door. After a moment's pause, both doors swung open, revealing an even more sumptuously furnished chamber on the other side. This room, however, was bustling with activity. A number of people, every one dressed exactly like the attendant who had escorted them, were bent over papers piled on a huge table at one end of the room, conversing in hushed but urgent tones. Others, their arms loaded with more papers and several less easily distinguishable items, streamed in and out of a door at the opposite end of the room.

Either Rudgo Beyloraff thrived on chaos, or he'd staged this busy scene for their benefit. Calista rather thought the latter explanation was the more accurate, though what he'd hoped to accomplish with so inept a performance she couldn't imagine. Perhaps he'd just wanted to inflate his importance and hint that he was a power to be reckoned with, that neither she nor Rhys should expect to push him around.

Not that pushing Rudgo Beyloraff around would be an easy task, Calista conceded wryly as the official behind the enormous desk in the middle of the room rose to his feet. The man had to weigh at least three hundred and fifty pounds. Probably more.

As Beyloraff stood, the commotion in the room stilled instantly and all eyes turned nervously toward him. He didn't seem to notice. Instead, he beamed at Rhys and Calista and came around the end of his desk, his arms outstretched in welcome.

"Honored traders!" he boomed. "Welcome to Sindrakis. We have been awaiting you."

As he waddled toward them, Calista discreetly studied the expressions of the people within her range of vision. Though most had managed to assume masks of polite interest, she thought she detected hints of nervousness, resentment or anger on a few faces.

Beyloraff, she decided, weighing up the evidence so far, was demanding, unreasonable, and probably cruel. And he had all the power. That would make him difficult to deal with since he would be used to having his way and would expect to get it in the negotiations for the silk, too.

Well, she wasn't going to let him have it. Calista turned her attention back to him. She made sure her face bore an expression of polite respect, but it wasn't easy repressing her rising distaste for the man. She didn't like tyrants and bullies and Beyloraff looked to be both.

She didn't even glance at Rhys. They'd worked together too often for her to wonder about his assessment of the situation. It would be very similar to hers.

"Welcome!" Beyloraff stopped about four feet in front of them. At least, that's how far away his feet were. His belly was a good two feet closer. He beamed at Calista, then Rhys. "Larr told me there would be two new representatives arriving with our shipment, but he failed to tell me your names."

"I'm Calista York, Excellency," Calista said, bowing slightly. She wasn't going to give the man the satisfaction of receiving anything more than a polite inclination of her upper body. Anything deeper would have verged on the subservient.

"And I'm Rhys Fairdane." Rhys's bow was a little lower, but then a man of his size and obvious physical strength didn't run much risk of being thought weak.

"We're delighted to have the opportunity to do business with you," Rhys added smoothly. "Larr explained that you, as purchasing agent for the government of Sindrakis, are a regular customer. We always like doing business with regular customers. It's so much more . . . pleasant."

Calista couldn't help glancing up at that. The smile on Rhys's lips was one of perfect goodwill and amiability. His whole body radiated the message that he couldn't possibly be more pleased at the chance to deal with such a distinguished man of the universe as Rudgo Beyloraff.

It was Rhys's slight pause just before the word "pleasant" that gave her the real message, however. He'd just told Calista how he thought they should conduct the meeting. She wasn't going to argue. The tactics he proposed suited her perfectly.

Rhys would take the lead as a smooth but eager-to-please trader. That would induce Beyloraff to relax and become overconfident. He'd start thinking that if Rhys, an obviously powerful male, was going to be so easy to deal with, then he could effectively forget about Calista.

That would be his biggest mistake, because he wouldn't be ready when she eventually jumped into the negotiations with hard demands and even harder objections to any offer he'd make. Confused by having to deal with a physically powerful but clearly weak male on the one hand, and a slender but hard-nosed and aggressive female on the other, he'd lose track of where the negotiations stood. And that would be all the opening they'd need.

Calista had a hard time repressing her satisfaction. She was going to enjoy this, and she knew Rhys would, as well.

With a great display of officious activity, Beyloraff

ordered chairs, drinks, and food to be brought. It took three people to move the massive chair that had obviously been specially made to accommodate his corpulent body. Once settled, and with the requisite polite toasts and trivial chitchat out of the way, they got down to business.

Chapter Five

Less than two hours later, Beyloraff had drunk more than he should have and was waxing overconfident under Rhys's soothing patter. The man's insufferable arrogance and rudeness to those who served him had given Calista a thorough distaste for him and an eagerness to get on with the final stages of their negotiations.

From an occasional glint in Rhys's eyes, she could see he felt the same, but only someone who knew him as well as she did would have guessed that fact. To an observer, he seemed to have imbibed just as much of the heady wine as his host. Right now he was engaged in a rambling and totally unconvincing explanation of exactly why they couldn't quite offer the quantity of silk that Beyloraff wanted at the price he'd proposed.

Calista could feel the eagerness rising in Beyloraff. He sensed a weak adversary and was already gloating at the outrageous profits he anticipated.

Profits he would never see. Neither she nor Rhys had any desire to cheat Beyloraff. Only fools let themselves be tricked by greed at the expense of long-term profits. But they wouldn't let him get the best of the deal, either.

"I'm a reasonable man, trader," Beyloraff said. He tucked in his three chins and considered that pronouncement. His eyes crossed at the effort, ever so slightly. "Eminently reasonable. I can see your side of the matter and I don't want to take advantage of you."

He swallowed a hiccup, then leered at Rhys. "I'm willing to come to an . . . mmm . . . an accommodation."

Rhys beamed. At least he tried. The attempted smile was somewhat out of focus. "That's excellent, Excellency." He giggled. "Excellent Excellency. I like that."

Beyloraff smiled condescendingly. "For instance, there would be a little matter of the invoices."

"Invoices?"

So that was the way Beyloraff played the game. Calista forced herself not to reveal her disgust. It wasn't easy, even though both she and Rhys had expected something of this sort after their review of their predecessor's records.

Adjusting the invoices was a time-honored way of cheating both sides and leaving the pockets of the negotiators a little fatter than they would be otherwise.

There were a number of ways to work that game. The most likely approach would be for them to write Beyloraff an invoice for a smaller amount of silk than they actually delivered, in which case Beyloraff would retain the additional fabric for his own use or illegal resale. There would be a second invoice, which they would use, that showed the full amount of silk delivered but listed a lower sales price. The difference between the money they received from Beyloraff and the money shown on the invoice Larr would see, would go straight to their pockets.

From Beyloraff's overconfidence, Calista decided her predecessor must have been . . . "accommodating" in the past. Well, that entertaining little sideline would end right now.

"Our invoice will comply with all Imperial and Sindrakis laws, Excellency," she said firmly. Her unexpected entrance into the conversation made the purchasing agent jump. No mean feat, considering all the fat that had to be moved in order for Beyloraff merely to flinch.

"I wasn't—" Beyloraff's words were sharp with irritation, but Calista cut him off.

"We register the invoice immediately via subspace, so there's no possibility of anyone questioning the transaction. The silk is already packaged, ready for you." Beyloraff tried to interrupt, but Calista didn't miss a beat. "It's the same amount you've always ordered from Karta."

She smiled. Charmingly. Even in his befuddled state, Beyloraff saw her warning and remained silent. "I have an invoice already made out showing the price Trader Fairdane quoted you, Excellency. It's higher than your previous payment," *and probably less than you—or rather, your superiors—really paid last time, you jerk,* she thought, "but he's explained the reasons for that increase."

"But, but . . . that's absurd!" Beyloraff's indignation might have been more intimidating if he hadn't slopped wine down his front when he waved his goblet around in agitation.

79

"Not at all, Excellency. That's business. I'm sure a man of your experience realizes that."

"This is intolerable, trader!" Beyloraff turned his anger on Rhys. "I won't put up with this kind of intimidation. I don't have to buy the silk if you feel my overly generous offer isn't acceptable."

"That's quite all right, Excellency," Rhys commiserated. The corners of his mouth drooped in an inane expression of masculine sympathy for Beyloraff's situation. "We understand. There are a couple of other clients who would be happy to—"

"No, that's not . . . I mean, I'm sure we . . . Well, after all—!" Beyloraff was practically slobbering in his efforts to regain the advantage.

Rhys leaned toward Beyloraff with an air of man-to-man confidentiality. "Women." His head wobbled slightly as he indicated Calista. "You know how they are. And when Trader York makes up her mind—" He shrugged in recognition of any male's inability to comprehend or rationally deal with the opposite sex.

"Here's the invoice, Excellency. You'll see that everything's in order. As soon as you've signed and we have confirmation that your bank has transferred the credits to the Kartanese account with Galaxy Reserves, we'll beam down the silk." Calista coolly extended her hand comp.

"Absolutely not! I won't deal under these terms." Beyloraff was on the edge of his chair by now, but getting to his feet so he could stomp off in outraged indignation wasn't possible. The servants who would have helped him out of the chair had already been dismissed.

"No problem, Excellent uh, Excellency." Rhys rose to his feet and, weaving slightly, beamed down at the Sindrakis agent. "We understand. No hard feelings and all that, but we have other appointments an—"

"All you have to do is thumbprint your approval, Excellency." Calista continued to offer the hand comp to Beyloraff. "A quick review of the invoice will show you that everything is in order and exactly as we discussed."

"No, no, York. Can't bother his Excellency." Rhys frowned disapprovingly at Calista's unseemly pushiness. "Very busy man, his Excellency. We'll jus—"

"All right! I'll sign!" Beyloraff wrenched the comp from Calista's hands and, muttering darkly, reviewed the invoice's contents. For an instant he wavered, but a quick glance at Rhys, tugging at Calista's sleeve as though to drag her off, and then at Calista, who sat waiting with an expression of dispassionate determination on her face, seemed to convince him of the futility of further protest. With a sudden release of pent-up breath that sounded incredibly like a snake's hiss, he jammed his right thumb in the thumb plate to confirm his acceptance of the contract.

Calista smoothly took her hand comp out of his grasp before he could fling it at her. A quick check of the document confirmed that everything was in order and that Beyloraff's authorization had already set the necessary transfers of credits in motion.

Ignoring both Calista and Rhys, Beyloraff pulled his own hand comp out from under his voluminous robes and angrily keyed in a series of commands. Whatever his screen showed him seemed at least somewhat reassuring, because the skin around his eyes relaxed slightly. He glared up at his now unwelcome guests.

"The credits have been moved to your account. Now where's my silk?" he demanded, his voice grating with repressed fury.

Fat men shouldn't let themselves get in such a rage, Calista decided, eyeing Beyloraff. The agent was panting with the exertion of his temper tantrum.

She checked her comp to confirm that the transfer of credits was complete, then nodded to Rhys.

Rhys beamed at Beyloraff. "I'm delighted with our agreement, Excellency. It's such a pleasure—"

"Where's my silk?"

Rhys frowned, clearly hurt by his good friend's rudeness. "I'll bring it down immediately, but—"

"The silk, trader." Beyloraff spoke between gritted teeth. His patience was clearly at an end.

"Of course." Rhys pulled out his own hand comp and gave the command for the transporter to beam down the already prepared merchandise. When the leather trunk containing the silk materialized at his feet, he stooped and released the ties, then threw back the lid so Beyloraff could have a clear view of the trunk's contents. "It's all here, Excellency."

"It better be." Beyloraff's voice was still harsh, but his attention was fixed on the silk that gleamed dully in the light. "Deshant! Trel!"

At the shouted command, two attendants immediately appeared at the far door and scurried across the room to Beyloraff's side. They bowed quickly, then, at Beyloraff's command, brought a small table and placed it near the agent's chair. A minute later, the trunk was on the table and the silk in Beyloraff's hands.

Calista couldn't repress a shudder at the memory of how the silk had rocked her senses. Rhys evidently caught her reaction, brief though it was. He wrapped his hand around her arm in a comforting clasp that instantly dispelled the unpleasant queasiness rising within her.

She threw him a quick glance of gratitude and took a deep breath, forcing her mind back to the present. "Are you satisfied with the quality of the merchandise, Excellency?"

At her question, Beyloraff's head jerked up. He'd been so engrossed in the physical sensations generated by the silk, he'd almost forgotten their presence. He didn't appreciate the reminder. His head sank into the folds of fat around his neck as he hunched his shoulders angrily. His eyes glittered with resentment.

"I won't forget this, traders."

Calista met his hostile gaze directly. "I'm sure everyone will be pleased with the quantity . . . er, quality of the silk, Excellency."

It was all the hint she'd give him. Even if he couldn't fill his pockets through an underhanded arrangement as he had in the past, Beyloraff could still garner favor by appearing to have acquired more silk for the same amount of credits. Calista had no doubt he would milk the changed circumstances for every possible drop of advantage to make up for his lost revenues.

Their leave-taking was far shorter and far less cordial than their arrival. Rhys maintained his pose of slightly inebriated but very happy trader until they were safely onboard the *Independence*. The instant they had fully materialized on the transport platform, however, he straightened with a whoop and swept Calista into his arms to swing her around in a dizzying circle.

"You're brilliant, York! Brilliant! Our beloved Rudgo would have throttled you if he could have gotten out of his chair!"

Calista wrapped her arms around his neck. Laughter bubbled out of her. Her grin was so wide it threatened to break past her ears.

"Excellent Excellency, huh, Fairdane? You must have swallowed more of that wine than I thought!"

"Not on your life. Horrible stuff, that was." He stopped swinging her, but he didn't let her down. Instead, he drew her even more tightly against his chest, holding her feet off the ground and the length of her body pressed close against his.

Head tilted back, Calista gazed up into his dark, lean face. Was it his smile that made her heart suddenly somersault beneath her ribs, or the way his eyes softened as he looked at her?

There was so much about him she remembered. The vague shadow of beard beneath his smooth-shaven skin. The small, white scar that cut through the edge of his lower lip. The slight crease that formed in one corner of his mouth when he smiled.

This close, Calista could see lines of dark gold in the deep brown-black of his irises. His pupils had expanded until the black merged with the brown in a dark pool that seemed to draw her in, deeper and deeper, then deeper still.

His lashes were as thick and dark as ever, long enough to cast even darker shadows across his eyes. In a sudden surge of heat, Calista remembered those lashes brushing against her skin as he'd explored her body in that tormenting, glorious lovemaking they'd once shared.

A small moan—half desire, half regret—escaped her.

The moan was faint, so faint it was scarcely audible. But it—and Rhys's odd, choked gasp of response— were enough to break the mind-drugging spell that threatened to descend on them.

With a shaky laugh, Calista unwrapped her arms from around Rhys's neck, then, placing her hands on his shoulders for leverage, arched back and away from him.

The move wasn't such a great idea—it gave her a little more distance from his tempting mouth and his eyes with their dark, unspoken promises, but it also forced her hips to press far more suggestively against his.

Even through the heavy, formal garments they'd worn to their meeting with Rudgo Beyloraff, Calista couldn't avoid noticing just how quickly his body had responded to hers. The hard evidence of his desire, pressed so close against her own aching heat, caused an involuntary shudder to course through her body.

"We need to celebrate, Fairdane," she said, forcing an unconvincing grin. She pushed harder against his shoulders, trying to get free, but his grip around her waist only tightened.

"What do you suggest?" His voice was rough, slightly hoarse and breathless. He gulped, then his mouth twisted in mocking amusement. "Draknir, maybe?"

At the mention of the strong, sweet drink that had been her undoing after their first negotiations, five years earlier, Calista flinched. The reminder of how easy it would be to lose control, to let herself become involved again, was all the impetus she needed. With a small exclamation of disgust, she wriggled free of Rhys's arms.

Once her feet were firmly back on the floor, she backed up three steps, then planted her fists on her hips and glared at him. "I was thinking of tea, or possibly some Earth-grown coffee. But coffee's too expensive and tea, I suppose, isn't quite your style, is it, Fairdane?"

Calista was aware of an odd feeling of gratitude behind her irritation. If Rhys hadn't goaded her, she might easily have given in to the hungry promptings of her body.

"Not quite." Rhys had his voice under control and that old, infuriating smile on his lips. He took a step forward, then another, and another, until he was once more only inches from her.

Calista stood her ground, but she resented the need

to tilt her head back in order to look up at him.

"I was thinking of something a little more . . . mmm . . . physical, shall we say?" He brushed the tip of one finger suggestively across her lips, then trailed it along her jaw. "You can't deny you want me, Calista, and as long as we're partners—"

The flush rising up her throat and across her cheeks had to be from anger, Calista told herself. He was deliberately provoking her. There was no way—absolutely no way in space—that she could be responding to the nearly imperceptible tracing of his finger against her skin.

She slapped his hand aside. "As long as we're partners, we'll keep our relationship on a professional level, Fairdane. And when we're not partners—" She stopped, unexpectedly shaken at the thought, then swallowed, took a deep breath, and continued. "When we're not partners, there won't be any relationship. Period."

She paused for a moment, wondering if he would refute her, hoping . . . No, darn it, she wasn't hoping anything of the kind. She'd be crazy to want him to protest that there ought to be—had to be—more to their relationship than mere business.

When he didn't say anything, Calista snapped, "I'm going to set the coordinates for Lyra. Our appointment with the buyers there is next on the schedule." Without another word, she spun about and stalked out of the room.

Rhys let out the breath he'd been holding with a great whoosh of mingled relief and chagrin when the door slid silently shut behind Calista. He brushed his sleeve across his forehead, then took a couple of wobbly steps forward and slumped down on the edge of the transport platform.

Thank all the gods of any planet he'd ever visited that just enough of his trader's instincts had been functioning to get him out of the mess his exuberance had almost dumped him into.

What had he been thinking of, to sweep Calista up in his arms like that? He ought to have known better. He couldn't even be close to her, let alone touch her without having his pulse race and his limbs go weak. Holding her pressed tight against him had been the act of a madman. It had opened every soft curve and firm angle of her for his heated exploration—if he'd had the courage to risk it.

Worse, she had wanted him at least as much as he had wanted her. That knowledge had nearly destroyed the last, small spark of rationality in him. If she hadn't pushed away from him—and he hadn't remembered that the best way to defend himself was to provoke her to anger—they might even now be lying on the floor, their clothes half torn off and their bodies wild with the sensations coursing through them.

Rhys groaned, but couldn't help glancing at the spot where they'd stood. The surface of the transport platform was opaque plaston—hard, cold, durable, and extremely uncomfortable for any lovemaking. They wouldn't even have noticed. He was sure of it.

What he wasn't sure of was whether or not he wanted to resume their relationship as lovers. Oh, there was no doubt that she set his blood burning as fiercely and achingly as she ever had. And he had no doubt that she wanted him as badly as he wanted her.

But unchecked fires—of any kind—were capable of consuming everything in their path. He didn't think he could endure having Calista back in his life and his bed—not if they were to be torn apart by the same misunderstandings that had separated them before.

Somehow, they had to make their new relationship work. He wasn't sure how they were going to manage that feat when they hadn't managed five years earlier, but they would. They had to. He was too close to the goal that had been driving him for so long to lose it now.

A vision of a rich, green planet with blue oceans and fat white clouds and land that stretched as far as the eye could see rose in Rhys's mind. A planet whose jungles and vast prairies were teeming with living creatures—and not one sentient being. The third planet of the Kartanese system.

He'd been searching for the planet, or one like it, for longer than he cared to remember. If he worked this new relationship with the Kartanese just right, that planet could be his. His and his people's.

No use thinking about it, Rhys chided himself. For right now, it was enough to concentrate on whatever the next deal brought. He couldn't afford to make a mistake, and that included not letting Calista's presence interfere with the work at hand.

Though they hadn't done badly so far, Rhys conceded as he left the transport chamber and headed toward the quarters Calista had assigned him. He'd been surprised at how quickly everything had come back to him—their system of signals and cues, the way they'd read each other's body language and understood each other's thoughts. He'd never even come close to establishing that same rapport and easy, effortless communication with anyone else.

The door to his quarters slid silently open in front of Rhys, startling him. He paused in the doorway, studying the room before him as if for the first time. Though it had been set up as quarters for paying passengers the room was, in many ways, like Calista herself—an eminently practical space, totally lacking in frills or adornments. Hard and apparently unwelcoming.

At least at first glance.

Closer inspection revealed unexpected touches of softness and sensuality.

The walls, furniture, and fittings were in shades of gray and brown, colors seldom associated with any of the softer, more feminine traits. Yet it didn't take long to realize that the browns came from finely finished woods set in the walls as decorative trim or used to make the few simple tables and extraordinarily comfortable chairs. The seemingly stark gray walls were covered in a subdued fabric that was smooth and cool to the touch. The gray carpet was thick and springy beneath his feet.

The bed appeared a hard, uninviting box, yet it was the most comfortable bed he'd ever slept in. Rhys couldn't help but grimace at the thought. With thoughts of Calista disturbing his rest, he hadn't been doing much sleeping lately.

The reminder was about as welcome as having a bucket of cold water dumped over his head. With a rough exclamation of disgust, Rhys swung about and headed on down the corridor. The exercise rooms weren't far away. A couple of hours hitting things suddenly seemed like a very good idea.

Over the next two and a half weeks, whenever she and Rhys weren't engaged in negotiations with customers, Calista kept her nose glued to a tutor comp. When she wasn't studying or checking the operations of the *Independence*, she was in the exercise rooms, pushing her body until she collapsed, exhausted.

It required a bit of planning and a preternatural alertness, but except for when they met to discuss the next deal, she managed to avoid Rhys almost completely. Her success, however, was probably as much due to his efforts to avoid her as hers to avoid him.

He seemed to spend an inordinate amount of time in the communications center talking to stars knew who. Calista suspected he was operating some kind of profitable little business on the side, but she didn't care so long as it kept him away from her.

Her behavior, skulking down back corridors and rising at odd hours, was cowardly. Calista had to admit it. But right now, she was so confused she needed all the distance she could get.

On the one hand, her unwelcome and uncontrollable physical awareness of Rhys, her constant craving for his touch, were beginning to affect her ability to concentrate. On the other, she reveled in the excitement and satisfaction that came from working with him. If it weren't for her intense dislike of the culture on their next customers' world, she'd be looking forward to the negotiations.

Tarkis II was a planet noted for its extraordinary mineral wealth and its rigidly structured social system that elevated males and kept females in positions of subservience. A review of Larr's records had shown the Tarkisian rulers, a Committee of Four composed of old men who had held the reins of power for over sixty years, were some of their most profitable customers.

Calista's upper lip curled in distaste. The thought of selling any more of the silk to those four irritated Calista. No, irritated wasn't the right word. It made her downright mad. Rudgo Beyloraff and Tarkis II were excellent examples of how she *didn't* want to manage the silk trade.

As soon as she could, Calista was going to change a few things. Starting with a more careful scrutiny of the people and societies with whom they did business. The silk was so limited in quantity and so widely coveted, they shouldn't have any trouble adjusting their customer list.

The present list contained far too many customers whose wealth and power came from the sweat of those who had no say in the matter. The previous trade reps seemed to have selected their customers based who had the greatest political power and would return the greatest profit for the least effort. Easy enough, when you controlled the whole game. But not very . . . ethical.

Right now, however, there wasn't a whole heck of a lot she could do.

With a muttered imprecation against all arrogant, money-grubbing, power-hungry males, Calista tightened the belt of the dress she would wear on Tarkis. The garment itself was an insult. With its filmy fabric, short skirt that rose halfway up her thigh, and open neckline that plunged to her navel, it didn't even qualify for the epithet skimpy. She might just as well have gone naked, but she didn't have any choice in that, either. All females were required to wear the . . . whatever you called it. Period.

If Rhys hadn't needed a female escort to prove his status, she would have stayed on the ship and let him handle the negotiations rather than suffer the humiliation of appearing in public clothed in little more than a scrap of cloth. But no Tarkisian male of any standing ever went out without a female dutifully following behind to open doors, carry his possessions, and generally wait on him hand and foot. That meant she was going, whether she liked it or not.

Rhys had better be sure they made a *big* profit on this deal, Calista decided. If they didn't . . .

She grabbed the small bag of personal items she'd

need for their required two-day stay and stalked out the door.

If they didn't make a substantial profit, she'd figure out a way to make Rhys pay for her having to appear a subservient idiot. Even if it *was* only in front of people who were so mealy-headed they thought that kind of behavior was normal.

Rhys was waiting for her by the transport platform. He was dressed in the elaborate costume considered proper for an upper-class Tarkisian male. His expression revealed the embarrassment common to all males suffering from the usually justified suspicion that they looked like fools.

Calista's gaze started at the shining lavender ribbon that pulled Rhys's long, black hair into a queue at the nape of his neck. Though he usually used a simple bit of cord, the ribbon wasn't too outrageous. But from there down, matters degenerated rapidly.

Under a sweeping, lavender-colored cape, Rhys wore a full-sleeved silk shirt with lace ruffles, an ornately beaded and feathered . . . jacket, she supposed you'd call it, thigh-hugging leather breeches, and painted boots. A large leather bag lay on the floor by his feet. Its sides bulged with whatever was stuffed inside.

The only thing that saved him from looking absolutely ridiculous was his impressive size and chiseled, masculine features. Despite the absurd clothes, there was no way anyone could miss the hard, powerful lines of his muscular body. Which didn't keep Calista from bursting into laughter at the most outrageous ornament in her partner's outrageous costume.

"What is *that* thing?" Calista choked, pointing to the bejeweled cup that arrogantly jutted out from the tight leather at Rhys's crotch.

"That," Rhys said, staring down at the offending ornament, "is a codpiece."

"A codpiece?"

"That's not what the Tarkisians call it," he admitted. "Their word for it is a little more graphic. I had the computer search for another word that might be a bit more . . . uhm . . . socially acceptable."

"It's disgusting! What kind of arrogant—"

"Exactly." Rhys grinned. "I believe the Tarkisians added it to their wardrobe using the time-honored principle of 'if you've got it, flaunt it'."

"Who would dream up an outrageous costume like that?" Calista had to force herself to keep from staring at the blatant adornment.

"The same person who thinks your whatever-it-is scrap of cloth is a reasonable choice for everyday wear." Rhys leered suggestively at Calista's skimpy costume. "Though I have to admit, on a body like yours, my dear, the idea has merits."

"It's damned drafty, is what it is," Calista snapped, tugging at the edges of her top in a futile effort to pull them closer together.

The computer had been unable to provide any information about what kind of undergarments she was supposed to wear, so she'd chosen a pair of tight briefs to cover her bare bottom. Unfortunately, she hadn't managed to think of anything practical that would confine her full breasts without making her look even more ridiculous than she already did. That left her with the necessity of having to concentrate on keeping her back straight and chest out in an effort not to let the fabric sag and thus expose her to the view of all and sundry.

It was going to be a *very* long two days.

With a grumble of disgust, Calista shifted the strap of her small bag higher on her shoulder, then stepped up on the transport platform.

When Rhys didn't move to follow her, Calista couldn't help snapping, "Well? Aren't you anxious to show off your stylish little ensemble?"

His smile carried just a hint of condescension. He shifted position slightly, letting the lavender cape fall back to expose the full glory of his costume.

Calista couldn't help but notice the way the light glinted off the fake jewels set in that—what did he call it? Cogpiece? No, that didn't sound right.

The thought of what lay behind the ostentatious piece of bad taste brought a flush to her face. She glared at Rhys while he languidly took his place on the platform, then announced, "You forgot your bag."

The revolting smile on his face became even more condescending. "No, I didn't. You did. Remember, *you're* the servant here."

"If you think—"

"Now, now. What would the Tarkisians think if I showed up carrying my own bag? We don't want to give them the impression they might be able to put one over on the Dorinor's new trade rep, would we?"

For a moment, Calista wavered. He was right, of course. But that didn't make the matter any more palatable.

It wasn't as though she'd never had to make concessions in terms of dress or behavior before. After all, she'd be the first to admit that the "perfume" she'd worn when negotiating with the Grulls had been enough to choke a Zantha rock snake, and *they* didn't have noses! But carrying Rhys's bag was pushing things just a tad too far. She should leave it right where it sat and . . .

"York?"

At the softly voiced query, Calista glanced up to find Rhys watching her. From the slight arch of his right eyebrow, it was clear he knew precisely what direction her thoughts were taking.

"Business before satisfaction, York," he added. "Silk or no silk, the Tarkisians will boot us off the planet as fast as we arrive if we don't play the game by their rules."

Calista set her jaw, just to let him know what she thought of the whole arrangement, but without another word she stepped off the platform, picked up the bag and slung it over her left shoulder, then took her station on the platform a respectful three steps behind Rhys.

Chapter Six

When they arrived, the area around the transport platform seemed filled with dozens of brightly plumed and strutting creatures. These strange beings eventually sorted themselves out into six Tarkisian males whose costumes made Rhys look sadly drab and dowdy in comparison.

Each male was closely followed by at least one female, if not more. The women were as scantily clad as Calista, but, unlike her, they seemed to find nothing to laugh at in the spectacle of so many males parading around like a flock of hens that had run through a costume wardrobe.

One of the gaudiest specimens of Tarkisian manhood pranced forward to welcome them, plumes waving and spangles flashing. "Sul Sullinian, Master Merchant," he gushed, extending his hand to Rhys. "Welcome, Trader Fairdane. We have been looking forward to your visit."

96

Sullinian was immediately followed by his five flamboyant colleagues. As the five clustered around Rhys, Sullinian stepped back, as though content to be pushed aside. Watching him, Calista knew that wasn't the case. The man's sharp gaze was fixed on Rhys, studying him carefully. The Tarkisian was no fool, no matter how poor his taste in clothing. He was using the confusion of Rhys's arrival to study the new trade representative. It was a tactic Calista might have used herself.

After the florid welcomes were out of the way, one of the extra females, eyes politely downcast, took the bags Calista carried, leaving her free to follow after Rhys.

At a respectful but attentive distance, of course, Calista thought sourly.

Sullinian's overdone welcome was just a prelude to an elaborate and exhausting tour of the notable public buildings, gardens, and monuments of the planet's capital, Trais. And as if five hours of playing tourist weren't enough, Sullinian had planned an elaborate meal with an array of government officials and their accompanying entourages.

Calista, teeth gritted, was forced to stand behind Rhys's chair throughout the entire meal, even though another woman had been assigned to attend to the honored representative of the Dorinor of Karta.

It didn't help that the climate was hot, humid, and thoroughly uncomfortable. At least her absurdly abbreviated costume was designed to accommodate the weather. The garments Rhys wore had to be swelteringly oppressive.

Calista smiled. Poor Rhys.

After so many hours of keeping a politely vacuous expression on her face, the muscles in her cheeks were beginning to ache. Her back didn't feel so great, either.

97

She'd never stood up straight for so long in her entire life. If she had anything to say about it, she never would again.

As soon as she had buyers to replace the Tarkisian rulers, Calista vowed silently, she'd cut off the supply of silk to Tarkis II. She couldn't change the society itself, but she'd rather be fed to Fallite sand worms, piece by piece, than do anything to help keep these pampered males in power.

When the dinner began to break up at last, one of the guests who had imbibed more liquid refreshment than was good for him suggested a tour of a section of town whose name Calista didn't recognize. The area's function wasn't hard to guess, however, based on the answering titters and lewd remarks from the other guests.

Rhys pleaded exhaustion and politely declined.

Not a very clever excuse, Calista decided as she rushed solicitously to his side when he gestured her over. Rhys Fairdane had the endurance of an ox. He didn't look exhausted. Bored, maybe. Uncomfortable, certainly. But not exhausted.

Definitely not exhausted, she thought waspishly a moment later as she caught him appreciatively eyeing the gaping neck of her gown as she bent over him. Calista straightened abruptly, almost knocking a tray loaded with sweets from the hands of a serving girl who was attending the dignitary seated beside Rhys.

"If I could be shown to my quarters?" Rhys asked, smiling ingratiatingly at his host.

"Of course!" Sullinian leered at Calista, then winked at Rhys. "A man must recuperate, after all!"

Hearty guffaws greeted the sally. It took a moment for Calista to realize they were all staring at her. Worse, more than one had a hungry light in his eye. She'd become so used to being treated like one of the decorative fixtures, she found herself blushing at the vulgar attention. The blush only increased her fury and chagrin.

That did it! She wouldn't need alternative buyers to cut these louts off from their supply of silk. If Larr hadn't already agreed to provide the silk requested, she'd have happily broken off negotiations right now. After all, there wouldn't be a whole lot Rhys could do about it if she beamed back up now and left him to explain the change in plans.

In the general confusion as the guests milled about talking, Calista found herself momentarily separated from Rhys, trapped between the serving women who were clearing the table and the cluster of female attendants who were trying to gather any of their masters' possessions that might have been left behind.

Calista was attempting to catch a glimpse of Rhys in the crowd when one of the attendants, her attention apparently fixed on the items she was clutching in her hands, bumped into her. A small metal case tumbled from the woman's hands to spill coins across the floor and under the feet of the bustling servants.

With an exclamation of disgust, the dark-haired woman quickly knelt to retrieve the coins. Calista, without thinking, bent to help her. Gathering up the coins nearest her, she extended them to the attendant. "Here you go."

"Thank you." The woman leaned closer to take the coins and said, so softly that Calista could scarcely hear her, "Meet us tonight, an hour after turning. In the gardens near the Jaynat Palace." Before Calista had a chance to reply, she added more loudly, "You're very kind. I think I have everything now." She looked at Calista directly, an unspoken warning in her eyes and a polite, distant smile on her lips, then rose to her feet, glanced quickly around, and immediately slipped past a cluster of cleaning women and disappeared in the crowd.

Calista scarcely had time to regain her feet when Rhys was at her side with Sullinian right behind him. "I've been looking for you," Rhys said. "Our host is kind enough to escort us to our rooms, so come along."

It cost an effort to appear appropriately docile under the arrogant command, but Calista managed somehow and fell into step behind him. Unfortunately, the boor who had suggested the after-dinner tour of the red-light district fell into step with *her*, and for the entire walk Calista had to silently endure the man's rude comments and even ruder stares.

By the time they reached their quarters, she was ready to burst with repressed outrage. Once the door was closed behind them and they were left alone, she would happily have vented her feelings if Rhys hadn't clamped a hard hand over her mouth and hissed in her ear, "Shhhh. Be quiet. At least until I'm sure we're not being watched."

Calista stiffened, then nodded to indicate she understood. He was right, damn it.

Satisfied, Rhys let her go, then reached into an inside pocket of his gaudy jacket and pulled out a small, slightly flattened sphere that Calista immediately recognized as a spy seeker.

He punched a button at one end to activate the seeker, then set it free. It hung suspended in the air in front of them for a minute while it oriented itself, then silently sailed off to do its job of probing every corner of the room for spying devices. The seeker was virtually silent and so small even the best hidden viewers had a hard time picking it up.

While they were waiting for the seeker's report,

Rhys strolled about the room with every appearance of a casual, curious visitor. Calista surreptitiously watched him, her irritation slowly fading in a rising fascination. Even the ridiculous clothes he wore couldn't disguise the grace and latent power of his body. Without the clothes . . .

Calista drew her thoughts up short on that one. As distraction, she grabbed Rhys's overstuffed bag and dutifully started unpacking. She was doing it for the sole benefit of any watchers, she assured herself firmly. The minute she was sure they weren't being spied upon, she'd dump the bag and let Rhys unpack his own junk.

Calista watched him step through the open glass doors at the far side of the room, onto the balcony beyond, then turned her attention to the bag's contents.

The extra clothes, so far as she could tell from a cursory inspection, were even more tasteless than the ones Rhys was wearing now. With a dismissive shrug, Calista tossed the garments out of the bag and onto the bed. One immediately slid off on the floor, but Calista, heedless of possible hidden observers, didn't bother to pick it up. Let *him* pick it up. After all, he hadn't done anything all afternoon except stroll around, smile, and stuff his face. *Her* feet were killing her.

A justifiable feeling of indignation rose in Calista. She'd had to adopt unpleasant customs for the sake of trade negotiations before, but never had she been forced to such demeaning subservience. She'd just about had it with pretending she liked waiting on a male hand and foot. And as long as she was thinking about it, what had he meant by ogling that one serving girl with the curly black hair? Fitting into the role he'd assumed was one thing, but Rhys could carry it too far!

101

With a muttered imprecation against all males, Calista turned the bag upside down and shook the remaining contents out onto the bed. It was a much more efficient way to unpack.

An old-fashioned kit for personal items tumbled out, but Calista scarcely gave it a thought. Rhys Fairdane had a passion for antiquated gadgets and customs that she'd never understood. It was crazy, but that was his business. But why in the world would he bring two huge towels? Even Tarkis II had dry booths.

The sight of the towels brought back the unexpected memory of how he'd looked on her view screen just after she'd arrived at Karta, clad, or so he'd said, in a towel and nothing more.

Sudden heat rose in Calista at the vivid images the memory roused. Cautiously, she picked up one of the towels. It was heavy, slightly coarse, and larger than she'd expected. The cloth had a sweet, fresh scent, but there was no trace of Rhys in the smell. Unreasonable disappointment bit at her. She tossed the towel on the untidy pile of items on the bed. She wasn't interested in the silly thing, anyway.

At that moment, the sound of Rhys's footsteps on the polished stone flooring drew her attention. She turned to find him leisurely crossing the room toward her.

Rhys stopped two feet away, but he wasn't looking at her. His gaze was fixed on the mound of his possessions in the middle of the big bed. After a minute's careful inspection of his ill-treated property, he brought his dark gaze around to meet hers. One eyebrow arched.

"How thoughtful," Rhys murmured.

In response, Calista casually flipped the bag, which she was still holding, on top of the pile. It landed bottom up and knocked his small bag of toiletries off the pile. They both watched as the bag tumbled off the bed, then rolled to Rhys's feet as if seeking protection from its rightful owner.

"I take it your seeker didn't find any bugs."

"No." Rhys reached down to pick up his maltreated property, then looked around for somewhere to put it. There wasn't anywhere, so with a shrug he tossed it back on the pile, then added his absurd jacket to the heap, as well.

He'd shed his cape long ago. Calista supposed some properly trained Tarkisian female had already hung it up, ready for the next time he needed it. If he was lucky, he might get the same woman back to take care of the rest of his things, as well.

Sans cape and jacket, Rhys looked a lot less silly and a lot more intimidatingly male. The full-sleeved white shirt and tight leather breeches outlined his form in breath-catching detail. If it weren't for the painted boots and that absurd object—what did he call it? a fish something or other—at his crotch, he'd look very impressive.

If she'd wanted to be impressed, that is. Which she didn't. It had absolutely nothing to do with Rhys if the muscles of her lower belly suddenly contracted under the influence of a rising heat or her nipples hardened and pushed revealingly against the fabric of her gown.

Calista sat on the edge of the bed with an inelegant plop. Rhys sat on the opposite end of the bed, which caused the bed itself to dip a tad. Calista pretended not to notice.

"My feet are killing me," he muttered. "I don't understand how anyone could be crazy enough to wear boots like these."

With a great deal of grunting, he pulled off first one boot, then the other. Then he leaned back on his elbows, stretched his legs out in front of him, and wiggled his toes.

"Ah, bliss."

Calista eyed him with disfavor, but Rhys appeared totally oblivious. He threw back his head, arched his spine, scrunched the muscles of his shoulders together, and extended his legs in a luxurious stretch that brought a moan of satisfaction from him.

It brought something else entirely from Calista. She brought her knees up and wrapped her arms tightly about her legs, trying to suppress the surge of hungry fire that suddenly threatened to consume her.

With his back arched, Rhys's chest thrust up and out until it looked like a mountain of hard rock. The front of his shirt had come open, providing Calista a glimpse of dark skin and curly black hair that roused unwelcome memories of how easily her fingers had once slid through that soft, silky mass.

She forced her eyes down, away from his chest, but that view wasn't any better. Even under the leather of his breeches she could see the way the muscles of his thighs and hips bunched with his stretching.

Worse, his position made the jeweled pouch at his groin thrust out even more arrogantly. Light caught in the fake gems, flashing with every slight shift of his body.

Calista forced her gaze away, struggling for breath. Was he deliberately tormenting her, or was he completely oblivious to the effect his actions were having on her?

"What did . . . um . . . uh." She gulped. "What did you think of this afternoon?"

"This afternoon?" Rhys gave one last stretch, then sat up and eyed her thoughtfully. "Am I wrong, or is there trouble brewing?"

Calista wasn't sure if it was his change in position, or his having the same doubts she had about Tarkis II that made her sigh in relief. "No, you're not wrong.

From some of the comments I caught when you men weren't close, I'd say a few of the women here, at least, aren't going to take these overfed males ruling their lives much longer."

Rhys studied her for a moment, his brows furrowed, then shook his head. "It's not going to be easy. The guards are heavily armed."

He started to lie back, but found the pile of clothes in the middle of the bed in his way. With an irritated grunt, he swung around and swept everything onto the floor, then leaned back against the pillows heaped at the head of the bed and stretched his long legs out beside Calista.

"You know what's crazy?" he asked, propping his hands behind his head. "I didn't get any hint that the Tarkisians I dealt with realize there's anything going on. They seem to think everything's sunshine and light in this comfortable little world they've built themselves."

Irritated by her intense awareness of him, of his body lying so close to hers, Calista wrapped her arms even more tightly around her legs and scowled at the floor.

"Tyrants don't have to think about the poor slobs that serve them."

"I take it you don't like the Tarkisians?"

"That's right. We're committed to sell them the silk this time, but I don't plan on coming back." Calista glared at Rhys, ready to squash any objections.

He startled her by nodding. "It shouldn't be any problem to find another buyer."

"You agree?" Calista wasn't sure she'd heard right. She scooted up the edge of the bed toward him. "The Tarkisians pay good money for the silk. You're willing to cut them off, just like that?"

Rhys frowned, then dropped his arms from behind

his head and pushed back in the pillows until he couldn't go any farther.

"Sure. Why not?"

Insistent, Calista slid closer. "What if we don't find another buyer?"

Rhys pulled himself up into a sitting position, back flat against the wall. "I'm sure we will. It shouldn't be that hard."

Calista couldn't believe what she was hearing. Rhys Fairdane agreeing to cut off a profitable customer, just like that? Just because she said so? She scooted forward until there were only a few inches between them and stared directly into his eyes.

"Are you feeling well, Fairdane?" she demanded.

Rhys blinked, then rolled off the far side of the bed. "Sure, but I *am* feeling a little hungry. How about if we order some food brought up?"

It was long past midnight when Rhys was awakened by the sound of stealthy footsteps and the soft whoosh of the door to the balcony being pushed open. He sighed. When he'd spotted Calista and that Tarkisian servant with their heads together at the end of the dinner, he'd suspected something was brewing. He'd hoped he was wrong, but it seemed he wasn't.

Rhys rolled out of bed and reached for the clothes he'd dumped on the floor earlier. The breeches and the absurd jacket he'd worn earlier, turned inside out, were as close as he could come to a black suit that wouldn't be spotted easily.

He crossed to the balcony, then cautiously peered over the railing. Though the guest quarters in which they'd been lodged were dark, there was just enough light from some of the other buildings in the vast government compound for him to spot Calista, silently gliding through the shadows in the garden one floor below him.

Swallowing a curse, Rhys swung over the railing with effortless grace, then used the ornamental stonework to climb down. After a quick glance up to identify their rooms, he set off in pursuit of his troublesome partner.

The night air was heavy with impending rain and the lichen that passed for grass on this planet was slick beneath Rhys's feet. Thank the stars he'd thought to bring along a decent pair of shoes. He would have risked permanent crippling if he'd been forced to wear those abominations the Tarkisians called boots.

Despite the heavy mud in the garden, Calista was moving silently and quickly through the shadows, taking advantage of every scrap of cover available.

Not that it mattered all that much. Her light-colored gown made her surprisingly easy to follow once his eyes adapted fully to the dark.

But then, when had being an easy target ever slowed Calista down? Rhys thought in disgust. Judging by the risks she took, the woman must consider herself immune to the dangers that afflicted mere mortals like himself. The best he could hope for was that she'd managed to bring a weapon—plasteel, perhaps—just as he had. The Tarkisians' security system hadn't been as efficient as the Kartanese against such easily concealed weapons.

Calista had almost reached the better lighted—and therefore more dangerous—main buildings of the compound when a sharp scream from the shadows at the far edge of the garden stopped her.

Rhys froze, too. An instant later, two armed guards emerged from the shadows dragging a struggling woman between them. They almost had her subdued when a second woman attacked by jumping on one guard, forcing him to abandon his grip on his captive.

Rhys didn't see Calista leave her hiding place behind a bush until she was half out of the shadows. She was moving fast, but he was faster. He tackled her, throwing her face down on the lichen matting the ground.

"Wha—?"

It wasn't easy with her writhing beneath him, but Rhys managed to clap his hand over her mouth before she could say anything more. "It's me, you idiot," he whispered urgently. "Be quiet or you'll bring more guards down on us."

At the sound of his voice, Calista relaxed slightly. Relieved, Rhys started to remove his hand.

She bit him.

"Why you—!" He clamped down harder.

Calista began to squirm, trying to break free. It wasn't easy keeping hold of her, but he might have subdued her if he hadn't been distracted by the angry cries of three more women who suddenly attacked the guards.

Even unarmed, the women managed to keep the guards sufficiently occupied that neither was able to use his weapon. A well-placed blow to the head knocked one man unconscious. The second guard threw off one of the women clinging to him, but instead of firing on his attackers, he turned to help his unconscious partner. The women grabbed his weapon and the fallen guard's, then fled.

"Let's get out of here," Rhys hissed, releasing his grip on Calista. "This place is going to be swarming with guards in a minute or two." He pushed away from her and rose to a crouch, careful not to lose his balance in the slick mat of lichen.

Assured of the women's escape, Calista nodded

curtly, then pulled herself up into a similar crouch a good three feet away. Even in the dark shadows near the building, Rhys could see the angry tension quivering in every line of her body—no mean feat when she was covered with mud and crushed lichen.

To make matters worse, the clinging humidity had turned to a slow, heavy drizzle that managed to chill but did little to remove the grime covering them. The only comfort it provided, Rhys groused silently, was that it would quickly obscure any tracks they'd left.

With every sense alert for the sound of pursuit, Rhys followed Calista back to their rooms. Behind them, sharp, angry cries and the sounds of booted men running across pavement announced that help was arriving for the two guards.

Despite the commotion behind them, they reached the spot beneath their balcony quickly and without incident. Calista shimmied up the rough stone wall with surprising ease. Rhys followed, though not so gracefully. The slime from the lichen, his sodden garments, and the increasingly heavy rain, which turned everything he touched slick and hard to grasp, made it difficult to move.

His hand slipped, scraping the skin painfully. Rhys cursed under his breath. If it hadn't been for Calista, he wouldn't have gotten into the mess in the first place. He could have been comfortably asleep in his comfortable bed instead of getting soaked, chilled, and covered with filth—and all because she couldn't keep out of trouble for more than five minutes.

Calista was going to pay for this. He didn't know how, yet, but she was going to pay. He'd make sure of it.

His irritation back full force, Rhys closed the balcony door and drew the heavy drapes shut before he asked for any lights. Then he turned to confront

Calista—and burst out laughing.

"Just what's so funny, Fairdane?" Calista's pugnacious stance might have been more intimidating if her hair weren't hanging in bedraggled clumps around her face and she hadn't been plastered with green goo so thick the rain had only managed to carve a few tracks through it.

But even the slime couldn't disguise the way her once tidy garment clung damply to breast and waist and hip, revealing every line and curve of her body. As Rhys let his gaze roam over her, his laughter died, replaced by a sudden, hot flare of desire that made his throat clamp shut and the muscles of his belly and thighs contract.

He swallowed, gulping for air and struggling to regain the anger that would have made him master of the situation, regardless of the . . . distractions. "Just what did you think you were doing, sneaking out like that? You could have gotten us both killed! You ought to know better and—"

"Don't start telling *me* what to do, Fairdane." Calista propped her fists on her hips and scowled. The effect was marred by a sodden hank of hair that flopped down across her eyes and stuck to the bridge of her nose. She shoved the errant lock away from her face, but her hand plowed a path through the green muck, leaving a streak of white across her forehead.

Without thinking, Calista ran her hand down the side of her skirt, trying to wipe off the slime. Rhys's eyes followed the path of her hand as she dragged it over her hip and halfway down her thigh.

"Just who do you think you are, Fairdane?" she demanded. "And who appointed you my guardian, anyway?"

Rhys brought his attention back to her face with a snap. "Nobody appointed me your guardian, but if you keep pulling dumb stunts like this one tonight, someone should!"

Calista drew herself up as tall as she could. Her chest swelled with indignation. "Well of all the arrogant, self-righteous—"

If his life had depended on it, Rhys couldn't have kept his eyes on her face. His gaze dropped to the tempting arch of her breasts. Even under the coating of crushed lichens he could see the sharp, hard points of her nipples thrusting against the wet fabric. An urge swept through him to brush away the goo and touch the soft skin beneath. He thought of how quickly her damp skin would warm to his touch, and he groaned.

It was an involuntary sound, torn from him before he was aware of it, and it brought him to his senses with a rush of anger and resentment that she could still drive him to distraction without even trying. He ought to take charge of the situation, ought to give her a rousing lecture on the foolish risks she'd run, ought to lay down the law against any further such escapades.

Instead, Rhys retreated.

"I'm taking a shower," he said. Even to his ears the declaration sounded more like the resentful challenge of a child than it did a statement of fact by a rational adult.

Without glancing at Calista, Rhys grabbed one of the towels from the heap of his possessions on the floor, then stalked past her to the luxurious bath and shower facility attached to the suite.

Calista had her own shower. She could darn well use it.

Once safely behind closed doors, Rhys stripped off his clothes and left them in a damp, dirty pile on the floor. The leather breeches, especially, were hard to remove. The wet leather clung to his skin, chafing unpleasantly and irritating his sensitive, swollen male flesh.

Disgusted at his uncontrollable and unwanted reaction to Calista, Rhys chose a hard, stinging shower setting in the hopes it would ease the fire in his veins. It didn't help. He turned the hot water off, leaving only the cold. The icy spray did no good.

All he could think of was Calista, writhing beneath him. Though his eyes stared at the shower wall opposite him, all his mind could see was Calista with her clothes plastered to her body and every luscious curve, every angle and swell of flesh revealed to his hungry gaze.

Even an energetic rubdown with one of his specially made towels didn't help. It wasn't his body he wanted to touch, it was hers.

At the thought, Rhys trembled with the wanting that coursed through him. It had been so long, yet he remembered how she felt and tasted. How easily she responded to even his slightest touch. How hungrily she had once reached for him, demanding more, then yet more.

With an impatient tug, Rhys wrapped the towel around his waist. Despite its generous size, the heavy expanse of cloth was insufficient to disguise his arousal. In disgust, Rhys ripped it off.

He threw open the door and stomped out with the towel still in his hand, only to draw up short at the sight of Calista, dripping wet and clutching a thin, skimpy rag to her chest, stooping over the untidy heap of his possessions that still lay on the floor by his bed.

Chapter Seven

At the sound of the shower door opening, Calista jerked upright and whirled around.

The sight of Rhys, magnificently, gloriously naked—and intimidatingly aroused—made her gasp, then clutch the sorry excuse for a towel the Tarkisians had provided even more tightly to her.

"Just *what* do you think you're doing?" he raged.

"There's no dry booth for my room!"

"That gives you the right to rummage in my possessions?" Glowering, Rhys came a step closer.

Calista backed up two. "I needed something to dry off with. All these jerks provided was this crummy rag." Indignant at the insult, Calista started to wave the scrap of cloth she held in Rhys' face. She immediately thought better of that foolhardy gesture, but it was too late.

Eyes glittering dangerously, Rhys advanced on her.

"So you decided to grab my towel, hmm? Without asking permission?"

He tossed the damp towel he held to the side, then bent to drag the second towel out of his jumbled heap of clothes. He stood, the towel in his hand. With spurious innocence, he asked, "Is this what you were looking for?"

Calista tried to back up even farther, but stumbled instead on a boot that had rolled behind her. Instantly, Rhys caught her, pulling her to him.

His body was hard and hot and overpoweringly male, his skin still damp. The thick, black hair of his chest and thighs brushed against her, showering the tiny drops of water that still clung to the individual strands across her skin. To Calista's whirling senses, it was impossible to tell if the drops burned or if it was her own heated flesh that made her so intensely aware of those tiny beads of wetness.

"I don't mind sharing, you know," Rhys said, very softly. His breath was warm on her face. He plucked the scrap of cloth from her fingers and flung it to the side. "I don't mind sharing at all."

Rhys brought his own heavy towel up to brush off the moisture still clinging to the edge of her jaw and throat. With tormenting attention to detail, he dried the line of her collarbone and shoulder, then swept down her back, carefully following the curve of her spine before stooping to drag the towel over her buttocks and down her thighs.

The towel was rough and warm against her skin, but it wasn't that which stoked the fire rising within her. It was the feel of his fingertips moving beneath the heavy cloth, the pressure of his hand against her body, the heat and strength of him that were all-male and all-consuming.

Rhys straightened. The slight motion generated a

distracting friction at Calista's breasts and belly and the front of her thighs. Unable to resist her need for him any longer, Calista wrapped her arms around his neck and drew his head down to hers, tangling her fingers in the long, wet strands of his hair.

He bent to her demand. His mouth crushed down on hers. Vaguely, Calista felt his towel slide down her legs as Rhys dropped it to enfold her in his arms. With the towel went the last, faint trace of her self-control.

Her knees buckled and Rhys pulled her down onto the bed.

It's been so long—" His voice was rough-edged with desire.

Calista gave him no chance to say more for she rolled on top of him, covering his mouth with hers, his body with her own.

Pure sensation flooded through her, triggered by a thousand memories as well as by the intoxicating feel of their bodies pressed so tightly together. She knew him. Every inch of him. In five years she hadn't forgotten, and yet she was driven by a hunger to explore that memory could not assuage.

Abandoning his mouth, Calista brushed her tongue and lips across the rough shadow of beard that was just beginning to darken Rhys's cheek. She pressed a hot kiss against the pulse that beat just below the angle of his jaw and was rewarded by his swift intake of breath and the scrape of his fingers and nails across her back as his hands involuntarily clenched in response.

Her own breathing was none too steady. Calista pushed herself up on one elbow and gazed down at Rhys, wanting to see as well as feel the effect her touch was having on him.

His black hair streamed across the pillow, framing his dark features. His eyes glittered, half-hidden by heavy lids, and his mouth worked, his lips opening to gulp at the air that, to Calista, suddenly seemed in such scarce supply. Rhys's chest rose and fell with his quick, uneven breathing.

Exultation rose in Calista. That she hadn't forgotten; that she still had such power over him.

The exultation was short-lived. Rhys slid his hands around to cup her breasts, letting his callused palms rub against her skin and slowly brushing his thumbs against the sensitized tips until Calista had to dig her fingers into his shoulder to keep from collapsing.

"I remember," he said softly. His breathing was too uneven to allow more. "So much—" With a groan, he released her breasts and wrapped his arms around her.

Calista braced herself against his chest. "I remember, too. I remember this—" She brushed a kiss along the line of his throat, scarcely touching him. Rhys stopped breathing for an instant.

"—and this—" With her tongue, Calista traced the pale line of a scar, half-hidden in the silken hair of his chest, that slashed downwards across hard muscle to end just below his left nipple.

"—and this." She bent to take that pale circle of flesh in her mouth. Rhys arched against her with an involuntary cry, then pulled her down and under him.

As Rhys moved to reclaim her mouth, Calista raised her hands to the sides of his face, forcing him to meet her gaze.

"This is crazy," she said. Her voice was ragged, the words uneven with her labored breathing.

His eyes were black, shaded under his heavy lashes. "I know," he groaned. "And I'm a madman, but it doesn't matter, Calista." He turned his head to brush a soft kiss against her palm. "It doesn't matter."

The last words were no more than a whisper, faint,

almost unintelligible. But they were enough.

Calista slid her hands behind his head, drawing him down to her. As their lips met and their breath mingled, she silently acknowledged the truth. However dangerous their need for each other, however great the risk, they were one—had always been one. No rational arguments or carefully considered plans could stand against that truth, or the hungry fires of desire that came with it.

Rhys claimed her, then, swiftly and without hesitation. At the moment of joining, he cried out her name and Calista willingly answered. She arched to meet him, meeting thrust with eager thrust as their bodies melded in the age-old rhythm that made them one.

"So long. It's been so long." Calista wasn't sure if the words were his . . . or hers. It didn't matter.

He called her name again, more urgently, and Calista was lost, all care for past or future burned away in the flaring heat of the here and now. With him she climbed, then soared, until even the present disappeared and she was cast with him into the realm of joyous, overwhelming sensation that was all she'd ever known of forever.

Dawn was not long past when Rhys finally awoke.

He came to full consciousness slowly, too caught up in the sweet remnants of his dreams to want to abandon them. He shifted slightly, stretching under the sheet, and his eyes flew open.

The warm, soft form pressed close against him was no dream, but a woman. Calista!

Hesitantly, and very gently, he ran a hand over her hip and the top of her thigh, reveling in the feel of firm muscle beneath the silken skin, the human heat of her cradled in the angle of his body.

Like her, he'd had his moments of doubt during the

night. He would have them again. They were both too strong-willed, too used to having their own way for any relationship to be easy.

But they would find a way to deal with that. Five years without her had been too long and empty and cold for him ever to let her go again.

Slowly, savoring each inch, Rhys slid his hand up and around to cup her breast. At the touch, she sighed, then stirred slightly in her sleep, cuddling into the warmth of his body. The slight motion and his body's instant response made Rhys draw in a sharp breath, but he forced himself to keep his touch light.

He brought his hand up to brush aside the curls that obscured her face, then bent to kiss the curve of her shoulder, the base of her throat, the warm, secret flesh just behind the lobe of her ear. The scent of her, sweet and tormenting, was like a drug to his senses.

When he ran the tip of his tongue back down the line of her throat, she sighed and her eyes fluttered open. Rhys remained still, watching her, drinking in every subtle nuance of her waking. He knew the moment she became fully aware of his body touching hers, knew the moment her body responded to that knowledge with an answering heat of its own.

She turned towards him, shifting in his arms so she was open to him, eager. If he'd had any last doubts, they faded in the radiance of the smile that lit her face.

The first kiss was gentle, almost shy. The ones that followed were hotter and more demanding but no less sweet.

Their lovemaking was gentler, too, as if their joining in the light of early morning were some token offering, an acknowledgment that the fires that had consumed them the night before had not burned away the deeper emotions that lay beneath.

Afterwards, they lay quiet, tangled in each other's arms, content to let the day wash over them without their moving or speaking.

It was the faint sound of voices in the gardens below their balcony that finally roused Rhys to action. He propped himself up on one elbow but his gaze never left Calista's face. Her hair spread out across the pillow in a tangled, golden mass. Several strands clung to his forearm. Without thinking, Rhys gathered them up, then slowly wrapped them around his finger. With each circling motion, his hand drew closer and closer to her. She watched him, unmoving, a slight smile upon her lips. Just as slowly, he unwound the silken strands, drawing them across her cheek and mouth, letting his finger brush against her skin.

As he traced the line of her mouth, she pressed her lips against the back of his finger, his hand. It was a slight gesture, yet he felt his groin tighten in response. His hand clenched in a fist.

Still holding the lock of hair, he traced the curve of her mouth with a knuckle of his second finger. Even the faint warmth of her breath against his skin, the almost imperceptible brush of her lips against the dark hairs on the back of his finger stirred him.

"We can't stay here, you know," he said. There was a rough, slightly breathless edge to his voice.

Calista smiled. "I know."

"We have work to do."

"That's right."

"So, what are you going to do about it, woman?" he growled.

Calista's smile became a grin. "I'm going to take a shower—using *your* dry booth—and then I'm going to get dressed and come along to make sure you get every *penny* you can out of these jerks."

Rhys grinned. "Heartless wench."

She laughed. "You got *that* right!" She rolled out of bed abruptly, only to be stopped by Rhys tugging on the heavy lock of hair he still held.

"Not so fast." He dragged her back.

Calista came willingly, drawn by the wicked gleam in his eyes as much as by his hold on her. She even more willingly submitted to the kiss he bestowed upon her, despite the hungry heat it instantly roused in her.

He drew back at last, slightly breathless. "Go take your shower. And *don't* come looking for *my* towel!"

Calista fled, laughing. Yet as she stood, poised to get in the shower once the water warmed, she hesitated. His scent and the musky smell of their lovemaking still lingered on her skin.

She didn't regret the night behind them. For the first time since she'd left Rhys, she felt free of the aching loneliness and need that had become so much a part of her.

She didn't want to think about what lay ahead. At least, not right now. They were partners. They'd been lovers and now they were again. The tensions that had crackled between them ever since their first contact in orbit above Karta were gone, vaporized in the heat of last night's passions.

Calista couldn't help wondering how long it would last. They had always been good in bed. Always. But she couldn't let the euphoria of what she'd shared with Rhys over the past hours color her judgment. Being good in bed hadn't been enough five years ago. What made her think it was enough now?

There was no answer except the sound of water drumming against the shower walls. With a shake of her head, Calista plunged into the stinging spray.

The future would have to take care of itself. For now, they had some serious trading to do.

*   *   *

They had three more stops before they were able to head back to Karta. After the satisfaction of obtaining a highly profitable agreement with the Tarkisians, the last three negotiations seemed sadly flat.

Calista didn't mind. The growing closeness between her and Rhys was enough to occupy her mind. When they were together, when he was touching her, making love to her, there was no room for anything but the incredible ecstasy he brought her, and that she knew she brought him.

When they were apart, she had enough work with the ship and preparations for each negotiation that she didn't have much time to think about what might—or might not—lie ahead.

Whenever she got to worrying, she comforted herself with the thought of the commissions she'd earned on this one, relatively short trade run. The thought warmed her. Every credit earned brought her that much closer to buying her freedom. If all the trade runs as the Dorinor's rep were this profitable, it wouldn't take long to reach her goal. That thought alone was enough to quell any doubts.

A warning bell sounded, informing her they were close to the Kartanese system. Calista dropped her equipment check and headed toward the bridge of the *Independence*.

To her surprise, Rhys was there ahead of her, comfortably ensconced in the navigator's chair and staring at the image of a blue-green planet that slowly spun on the view screen in front of him.

"What's that?" Calista asked, glancing over his shoulder.

"The third planet of the Kartanese system." Rhys didn't even look up.

Calista shrugged, then took the pilot's chair beside

him, her interest already focused on the command console and its flashing displays. "That planet's uninhabited."

"I know."

At the slight, almost wistful catch in Rhys's voice, Calista glanced up, surprised. Rhys's attention was still concentrated on the screen before him.

"No people, no trade, Fairdane," she said practically.

This time his gaze swung around to meet hers. "So you're not interested."

"That's right." She quirked an eyebrow. "Should I be?"

He scratched his chin, studying her, then shrugged and shut off the screen. "No, I don't suppose there's any good reason you should be interested."

"But tell me," he hesitantly added a moment later, "what *does* interest you, Calista? Do you have a dream? Something you're working toward? Something you want more than anything else you can possibly imagine?"

My freedom, she thought. *I want my freedom.* She almost said it out loud. Instead, she said, "Money. I want lots of money."

"That's it?"

"That's not enough?"

A long pause, then, "For some, maybe. I don't think it's enough for you, no matter what you say."

Rhys's eyes were dark and unreadable, and they were fixed on her with an intensity that Calista found distinctly uncomfortable. "What is it you think I want, then?"

Another pause. He shook his head slowly. "I don't know, but I know it's not money."

Calista snorted. "How perceptive of you. When you figure it out, would you let me know? I'd hate to think I've been wasting my time trying to make a fortune if what I really want is to, say, raise flat-nosed geckels."

Under the flippancy was a sudden, dangerous urge to tell Rhys—about her childhood as a slave on Andrus, her escape, her dream of freedom. All the things she'd kept hidden for so long.

All the things she still had to keep hidden.

"Why all this curiosity about my motives, Fairdane?"

He pursed his lips, then frowned. "No reason, really." He turned his attention to the console in front of him. "We'll drop out of hyperspace in three minutes."

He wasn't going to get off that easily. "What about yours?"

"My what?"

"Motives. What are *your* motives? What's driving you?" Suddenly, Calista found herself wanting to know. In all the years they'd been together, she'd never really thought about it before, but now she was curious. "Why did you become a trader?"

"Same reasons as you, it seems—money. I want lots of it, too." His attention was focused on the console's display. He keyed in a command, then adjusted a control.

"You're lying, Fairdane. And you're avoiding the question."

"What makes you say that?"

"You're just fiddling. The autopilot is perfectly on track. I can see the same information on my console, remember?"

Rhys scowled at her. "I thought I'd follow your frank and open lead. You want to tell me what really's driving you? I'll share if you will."

Stalemate. There was no way she was going to tell him her secrets, and no way she could force him to tell her his.

Did knowing really matter anyway? It wasn't their

123

past that had ever caused problems between them, it was their own strong-willed natures.

And his pigheadedness. Calista reminded herself not to forget that. If he hadn't tried to run her life five years ago, they'd probably still be together.

Or maybe not. She wasn't sure she'd ever find the right moment to tell him about her past. Confession brought too many risks—risks she'd probably never be willing to take.

The thought brought a vague sense of sadness.

A buzzer sounded the drop out of hyperspace. A minute later, while monitors flashed green to signal a successful drop, a picture of Karta automatically appeared on the view screens.

Unlike the third planet, which had glowed with the brilliant colors of water and lush vegetation, Karta was painted in shades of gray, red and ocher.

It wasn't a dead planet, by any means, Calista knew. Yet it would never be a welcoming environment for humans. If it weren't for the silk, most races would have passed Karta by, seeking more comfortable conditions.

Strange how so simple a thing as that rather drab-looking cloth could so radically change one's perspective. If there was a trader in the universe who wouldn't have given his eyeteeth for the position of rep, Calista knew she'd never met him.

A chime informed them a message was coming in. Rhys cued the system to respond. "Larr, it seems, has been waiting for us."

An instant later, the handsome representative to the Dorinor of Karta beamed at them from their view screens. "I take it you had a pleasant—and profitable—trip."

"You've seen our reports." Calista wasn't sure why Larr irritated her so much.

"Indeed." Larr coughed discreetly. "I was . . . intrigued by the rather astounding increase in the revenues from your sales to Rudgo Beyloraff."

"Your last rep was cheating you, Larr."

Larr greeted Rhys's flat statement with a slight smile. He seemed more pleased than surprised by the news. "If I had been fully . . . satisfied . . . with your predecessor, you wouldn't be in his place now."

"Do you have the next shipment ready?" Calista asked. One of these days she was going to get a better explanation of exactly what *had* happened to their predecessor. She'd tried to trace him more than once, but the man seemed to have disappeared. Not that it really mattered, since his departure was to their distinct benefit.

"Such enthusiasm. It's impressive, but not really all that necessary." Larr beamed.

His expression made Calista think of a feral pig, smug—and highly dangerous.

"However, do come down as soon as you're ready," Larr added. "The Dorinor is anxious to see you. We can celebrate your achievements and plan your future successes. You may use the same coordinates as before."

Without further comment, Larr cut the connection. The view screens went blank.

Rhys leaned back in his seat, staring at the empty screen thoughtfully. "So Larr found out about that little arrangement on Sindrakis with Beyloraff." He glanced over at Calista. "Have you ever wondered what happened to the man we replaced? What was his name?"

"Tull. Porganis Tull. And yeah, I've wondered. Do you know what happened to him?"

"No, and I never much cared to find out. It would seem Larr fired him."

"Wouldn't you?"

"About five seconds after I found out he'd been cheating me." Rhys shrugged, then rose from his seat. "It doesn't matter. But keeping the Dorinor happy does. Shall we go?"

Larr was waiting for them. Unlike Rhys and Calista, who were wearing simple robes over their protective skin suits, the Dorinor's representative had chosen an elaborately embroidered and embellished floor-length coat over a brilliantly colored robe. Larr's choice of clothing lent an exotic elegance to his tall, slender figure.

The man was impressive, Calista thought. Handsome enough and more than intelligent enough to have made a success of just about anything he might have tried. So what, besides the money, kept him here on a desert world like Karta where his only human contacts were with the small staff under him?

Thinking of her earlier conversation with Rhys, Calista couldn't help wondering what secrets Larr kept hidden behind his smooth, unflappable facade. Not that it mattered, really, but it might explain her antipathy toward the man.

Calista dismissed the thought with a shrug as Larr led the way out of the room. They took a side passage that led directly into one of the main Kartanese tunnels. Even though the labyrinthine passages ran deep within the rock, they were notably drier and hotter than the conditioned air maintained in the human quarters.

This time, Calista carried no weapons. Neither did Rhys, evidently. They were halfway past a Kartanese guard, carefully tucked into his niche in the passage wall, before she realized it. If it hadn't been for the flash of color as her glow-light reflected off the creature's dark fur, she might have passed him completely unaware.

A sobering thought, given her unarmed state.

The Dorinor was in the same chamber where they'd met him the first time. Another Kartanese sat on the lower platform at the side. Calista couldn't tell if it was the same one who'd been there on their first visit or not. This time, both Kartanese were studying a 3-D chess game set up on a table between them. The Dorinor had his head cocked awkwardly to one side so he could focus an eye on the board.

While the three humans stood respectfully silent, he picked up a piece in one clawed forefoot and moved it to another level. His companion sucked in a breath, then responded by moving one of his pieces. The Dorinor gave what sounded like the Kartanese equivalent of an exasperated cluck and stared somberly at the board.

"It's mate in three moves, Excellency," the second Kartanese said.

"I should have realized when you risked your knight that you were aiming for this."

Even though the translator behind her ear rendered speech in an uninflected monotone, Calista thought she could detect the note of disgust in the Dorinor's harsh, hissing speech.

The Dorinor spent another two minutes studying the board, then dejectedly reached out and tipped over his king with the flick of a claw. "I concede, Karnor. That's three of the past four games you've won."

With evident relief, he turned his attention to the three humans standing before him. He bent his head to focus on Rhys. "Larr tells me you have had a successful trading run."

"Very successful, Excellency. We think you'll be pleased when you study the report."

The Dorinor waved away the suggestion. "Larr

127

handles those details." He bent lower. "Do you play chess?"

"No, I don't. But I—"

"Do you?" The Dorinor swung his head around to focus on Calista.

"A little, but—"

"Good. We will play a game."

"Uh—"

"You may go with Larr," the Dorinor said dismissively to Rhys. "The female will stay with me."

"Calista?" Rhys cocked an eyebrow, clearly caught between irritation at the creature's dismissal and concern for her.

"No problem. I'd be pleased to take on his Excellency." It was a lie. She'd never been more than an adequate player and she hadn't played for a long time. She ought to remember enough to be able to give the Dorinor a run for his money, however.

Her optimism was totally unfounded, Calista discovered. The Dorinor trounced her thoroughly in sixteen moves in the first game.

Larr and Rhys had left her, at her insistence. Since there were no chairs, she'd simply sat, cross-legged, on the stone floor. If the two Kartanese were intimidatingly big when she was standing, they were almost overwhelming from that perspective.

Once, when the Dorinor had curled his upper lip in scorn at a particularly inept move, she'd been treated to a glimpse of numerous very large and very pointed teeth. It was a disconcerting reminder that the Kartanese were carnivores and she, if they were so inclined, was free meat.

They didn't appear to be so inclined. In fact, their attention was totally focused on the chess board and the game. When she tipped her king over in acknowledgment of defeat, the two Kartanese drew back, shaking their heads slowly in evident disappointment.

"You should have won in only thirteen moves," Karnor said.

"How was I to know she was so weak?" the Dorinor protested. "At her third move, I thought she might be trying the Weidensham gambit, so I countered. If it hadn't been for that—" His voice trailed off in a series of disgusted clicks and grunts. Things were clearly not going well for the Dorinor.

He brought his head down to Calista's level. The golden eye he fixed on her almost glowed in the dim light of the chamber. "You said you knew how to play chess," he hissed accusingly.

"Well, it's been a long time, Excellency," Calista snapped, indignant at both the accusation and her ignominious defeat. "I'm just getting warmed up. You won't have such an easy time of it the next game."

She was right. The Dorinor needed seventeen moves to trounce her the second go-round.

"All right, so I'm *not* the world's greatest chess player." Calista squirmed uncomfortably on the stone floor. Her rear end was beginning to protest the hard seating.

She didn't like being beaten. She especially didn't like being beaten by an overgrown beast whose race hadn't even invented the game, for star's sake!

"How are you at bakal?" The question was really a challenge, but Calista doubted the Dorinor's translator was up to such subtleties.

"Bakal?" The Dorinor scratched his belly. If it weren't for the fact that the bony ridges over his eyes couldn't move, Calista would have sworn he was frowning. "Is that another form of chess?"

"It's a card game. You bet on the cards in your hand.

Whoever gets the most money, wins."

"Bet?"

"Wager. Gamble. Bakal's a game of chance, as well as skill." An idea was beginning to form.

The two Kartanese looked at each other, then looked at Calista. Karnor said, "What are cards?"

Calista smiled.

Like lambs to the slaughter. "I'll teach you," she said.

Chapter Eight

Air filtering and treatment equipment. Chemical converters. Security and alarm systems. Rhys reviewed the extensive list of equipment Larr had provided.

According to Larr, their next trip would involve only a couple of major trading stops; then they were expected to pick up the machinery on the list and bring it back to Karta.

The whole setup puzzled Rhys. First, even if Larr didn't trust anyone else to deliver such large shipments of the silk, he could easily have scheduled those deliveries when he and Calista were out negotiating new trade agreements and opening new markets for the silk. Why waste their time by sending them on what was essentially a glorified delivery run?

Second, why have them pick up the equipment Larr had ordered? They'd have to modify the cargo bays of the *Fair Trade* in order to accommodate the massive machinery. It wouldn't even fit on the *Independence*. A large cargo ship, on the other hand, could easily have loaded everything, with room to spare. Granted, the ships were slower than his, but with the time lost in refitting the *Fair Trade* and making their trade stops, the cargo carriers could have delivered everything.

It didn't add up, and that made Rhys distinctly suspicious.

On top of all that was his sharp, if illogical irritation at Calista being singled out by the Dorinor for a game of chess. That sort of personal contact was just what *he* needed in order to win the creature's confidence and eventually, he hoped, convince the Kartanese to grant him settlement rights to the third planet in the system.

The trouble was, he'd never learned to play chess. That particular lack had never bothered him before, but it irritated the hell out of him now.

Calista would make the most of her chance, but it wouldn't be on his behalf. He could count on that.

Or could he?

Was he being unfair? Sure, she'd sabotaged some of his negotiations over the past few years, but that had been from a desire to provoke him. He'd always managed to return the favor in equal or greater measure. And she didn't know just how much he needed to get on the Dorinor's good side. Never once, in all the time they'd known each other, had he even hinted at his search for a world where his people could settle.

What was it Calista wanted? What secret had she protected with such zeal for so long?

He'd always known, somehow, that it wasn't the money that drove her. Yet not once had she ever revealed what *was* behind her relentless striving for wealth.

Rhys glared at the comp screen and Larr's inexplicable list of equipment. Everyone had secrets. Calista.

Larr. Himself. With those secrets went doubt, distrust, and a lot of energy spent trying to protect them.

For the first time, Rhys wondered if he'd been wise not to tell Calista of his quest. Over the past few weeks, he'd come to realize just how much had been missing in his life.

Without her, he'd been only half alive, too wrapped up in the pursuit of his goal to notice that there was more to life than just struggling, more to living than just working from day to day for a dream that might never be realized in his lifetime.

Watching Calista, he'd realized that it wasn't just their lovemaking he'd missed, it was her. Her laughter and passions, her volatile emotions. He'd missed her pride and cleverness and quick mind, her sometimes cynical, sometimes idealistic reactions to the people they met, the worlds they visited. He'd missed *her*.

Rhys was damned if he had any idea what that meant for the future. He wasn't even sure he wanted it to be that way. All he knew was that Calista had slipped back into his life and thoughts as easily as if she'd never left.

And that made him wonder what she was up to now.

The ship's computer found her in the reception chamber with the Dorinor and his companion.

For a moment, Rhys wondered if he ought to ask Larr's permission to transport down. He wasn't sure exactly what role the man played on Karta, but it was clear he would prefer to control their contact with the Dorinor. The expression on his face when the Dorinor had invited Calista to stay and play a game of chess had made that clear.

With a shrug, Rhys gave the transport computer the command to beam him down to where Calista was. He'd worry about Larr's reactions later.

It took a moment for his eyes to adjust to the dimmer light in the Dorinor's cavern. When they did, Rhys blinked.

Instead of being somberly bent over a chess set, the Dorinor, Calista, and Karnor were seated in a circle around a mound of what, from this distance, looked very much like betting tiles for bakal. Worse, the two Kartanese had pitifully small stacks of tiles in front of them while Calista had an enormous heap on the floor in front of her.

Rhys groaned. The sound failed to catch anyone's attention. They were far too intensely involved in the game in progress.

"I will venture another million to match yours, trader," the Dorinor rasped after a careful study of the jumbled cards he clutched so awkwardly in his front feet. As he reached to transfer some of the tiles from his stack to the pot, he dropped three cards. In trying to pick those three up, he dropped two more.

With only a wrist claw, instead of a fully opposable thumb, he lacked the physical capacity to easily handle anything as small and slippery as the cards. Worse, with his big body, long neck, and eyes mounted on the sides of his head, rather than directly in front, it was almost impossible for him to spot anything as small as the cards once he'd lost them.

Calista finally had to pick up the fallen cards and return them to him. He cast an anxious eye at the cards he held, as though unsure he still had them all, then awkwardly shoved a small stack of tiles forward to add it to the betting pile.

That task accomplished, he sat back on his tail with a grating, grumbling whistle that sounded like the Kartanese equivalent of a sigh and looked at Karnor expectantly.

Karnor rustled his wings uncertainly, studying the

cards he held. Twice he started to speak, then seemed to think better of it. Eventually he settled for carefully placing his cards face down on the floor. "I withdraw."

"You have four hundred thousand credits in the pot," Calista said. "Are you really sure you want to back out now?"

Karnor scratched his belly, obviously perplexed. His head swung from Calista to the Dorinor, then back again. "Is it a terrible disgrace if I withdraw?"

"No, not at all," Calista reassured him. "It will just be very, very expensive."

"Oh. That's all right, then." Karnor leaned back and crossed his forelegs across his stomach. Rhys could swear he looked relieved at being able to back out. "You may continue."

Calista shrugged. "All right. But don't say I didn't warn you." She fanned her cards out in front of her, studying them. When the Dorinor extended his long neck over her shoulder and cocked his head in a blatant attempt to see her hand, Calista hid the cards against her chest and rocked back so she could peer disapprovingly up at the Kartanese leader.

"That's cheating, your Excellency," she admonished him sternly, apparently unintimidated by the huge head and sharp teeth hovering so close above her.

"Oh." The Dorinor retreated posthaste. "That would be very dishonorable."

"Quite right." Calista brought her cards out to look at them again, then folded them into a stack and counted out a quantity of tiles to add to the existing bet. "I'm going to stand on this. What cards do you hold, your Excellency?"

"You stand. That means I have to match your bet and show you my cards, right?"

"You got it."

"I do? What do I have?" The Dorinor held his cards as far away from his body as he could, trying to get a clearer view.

"I mean, you're absolutely right."

"Oh." With a last, uncertain review of his cards, the Dorinor laid them on the floor, then pushed the remainder of his tiles forward.

Calista glanced at the Dorinor's cards, then placed her cards down with the neat efficiency of someone who knew her bakal—and had the full advantage of an opposable thumb. "Ten shooting stars, three fifth-class rockets, and a planet. Two stars better than your hand. I take the pot." She bent forward, swept up the center pile, then added it to her heap.

"But how can that be?" Karnor's wings rustled in his confusion. He flipped over his cards, then used one claw to spread them out. After a careful study of his discarded hand, he craned to see Calista's cards in their neat array on the floor in front of her. "Do not my cards exceed yours by five planets and two first-class rockets?"

"That's right, but you withdrew."

"Yet even with an inferior hand, you stayed in the game?"

"Right." Calista grinned up at the Kartanese. "It's called bluffing, Karnor."

"Is that like lying? Lying is very dishonorable, you know." The prospect of any possible dishonor clearly troubled Karnor.

"No, it's not lying. It's just not letting the other guy know exactly what you have."

Rhys decided it was time he intervened. "From the size of that stack of tiles in front of you, Calista, everybody must already know what you have."

Three heads swung around in surprise. Which only

showed how engrossed in the game they'd been. He'd made no effort to be quiet.

The Dorinor was the first to speak. "Twenty-seven million, nine hundred forty-five thousand, six hundred fifty."

"Seven hundred," Karnor added.

"I beg your pardon?" Rhys frowned, confused.

"Six hundred fifty," the Dorinor insisted.

"Seven hundred." Karnor wasn't budging. "You forget the fifty that I dropped and didn't notice during the first hand."

The Dorinor scratched his belly, considering. "You're right. Twenty-seven million, nine hundred forty-five thousand, seven hundred."

"They're talking about the credits I won," Calista explained, rising gracefully to her feet.

"What?" Rhys choked.

"This bakal is a very confusing game," the Dorinor added. "It is not at all logical."

Even through the translator's flat tones, Rhys could hear the Dorinor's disapprobation.

"Still, it is . . . interesting." The Dorinor swung his head down to Calista's level. "We thank you for introducing us to this new human game."

"You're welcome, Excellency. Maybe we could play it again some time."

Rhys grabbed Calista's arm. He was looking at the huge Kartanese, but he didn't let go of Calista. "We wouldn't dream of disturbing you, Excellency."

"I'd be glad to give you a chance to win your money back." Calista graciously smiled up at the Dorinor. At the same time, she gave Rhys a swift, hard kick on the shins that brought a grunt of pain. He dropped his hold on her arm.

"Win my money back?" the Dorinor asked.

"She means she had no intention of claiming the

credits she just won from you, Excellency," Rhys said between clenched teeth. He was fighting the urge to rub his injured ankle. Good thing he'd chosen to wear boots.

"I don't understand." The Dorinor glanced at Karnor, obviously seeking enlightenment.

"He means I'd be delighted to play some more games of bakal, Excellency." It was Calista's turn to grab Rhys's arm. "In the meantime, I thought we'd just wander around, get to know your place a little better." She waved her hand vaguely at the huge cavern around them as she backed up, drawing Rhys with her.

"Of course."

From the expression on the Dorinor's face, there was no "of course" about it, Rhys decided. The creature hadn't the faintest idea what Calista was talking about.

As he followed Calista toward a passage leading from the cavern deeper into the mountain, Rhys heard the Dorinor say, "Why would we want to win our money back, Karnor?" He didn't catch Karnor's reply before Calista had dragged him around the first turn in the passage.

Rhys planted his feet and tugged his sleeve out of Calista's grasp, forcing her to halt. "Just what's going on? And why were you skinning the Dorinor at bakal?"

"We were playing bakal because I didn't last more than ten minutes in a game of chess." Calista pulled a glow-light off the utility belt hidden under her robes, then a small tracker that would allow her to retrace their route if they became lost. "Come on."

"Where are we going?"

"I haven't the faintest idea. We'll find out when we get there." She set off down the passage without bothering to see if he was following her.

Rhys gave an exasperated snort of disgust, but he did move to catch up with her. "Calista, those two creatures hadn't the slightest idea what they'd gotten into. They had no more notion what twenty-seven million credits represented than—"

"That's the point." Calista stopped so abruptly, Rhys almost ran into her. "Twenty-seven or twenty-seven billion. It didn't make any difference to them."

"Then why—?"

"Don't you see? They're brilliant with numbers, Fairdane. Incredible at chess. They're probably good at anything that depends on logical thought and analysis. But they have no conception of what it means to bluff and absolutely no clue to what credits represent. They'll get the numbers right down to the hundredth decimal point, but it means nothing to them because the money means nothing."

Rhys started to protest, but shut his mouth before a sound came out. He'd been so intent on her trouncing the Kartanese in a card game, he'd missed the obvious.

"You mean—"

"That's right. The Kartanese didn't get into trading the silk because they wanted money or thought they had something to gain. Someone talked them into it. Someone who *did* know what he had to gain."

"Larr."

"That's my guess. If he wasn't the first, he's sure top dog now. He's in a perfect position to manipulate the setup."

"But that doesn't automatically mean he's cheating."

"No. But you know him as well as I do. What do *you* think he'd do under the circumstances?"

"Mmm." Rhys stared at the rock wall across from

him, considering. "Even if Larr *is* cheating the Kartanese, I don't see there's anything we can do about it."

"Not right now, no. But that doesn't mean things won't change."

Rhys grinned at the sudden thought that struck him. "If you're so opposed to cheating, Red, how do you explain that little trick you pulled on me in those negotiations with the Corellians?"

Calista scowled, but Rhys wasn't sure if it was at the question or his calling her Red. "That was different. It's not cheating when the other side knows how to play the game as well as you do. Besides, you got that contract, remember?"

"I almost didn't, remember? And all thanks to your meddling."

The scowl turned into a smug grin. "I should have had that one, Fairdane."

Even in the dim light of the passage, the grin illuminated her face. Rhys's heart skipped a couple of beats. "You almost did. If I could have gotten my hands on you—" His words trailed off and he leaned closer, all thought of where they were or what they were doing fading from his mind.

"You'd have wrung my neck. I believe you said that at the time." Calista's smile faded. Her lips parted and her eyelids lowered until Rhys could barely see the bright blue of her irises through the heavy fringe of lashes. She swayed toward him.

"I believe I did." It was barely a whisper. Then he was incapable of saying more, for his mouth had claimed hers.

The kiss didn't last long. A sharp hiss, almost in his ear, made Rhys jump back. He automatically tried to thrust Calista behind him as he turned to confront the intruder, but she wouldn't budge.

"You have permission to be here?" The Kartanese whose massive body blocked the passage and whose head was only a couple of feet away eyed them suspiciously.

"We've just come from the Dorinor," Calista said. She waved the glow-light. "We're trying to learn our way around this place."

"The Dorinor permits?" Calista's bold assumption of confidence didn't seem to impress the Kartanese.

"Of course he does." Rhys moved a step closer to the creature, partially shielding Calista. "Unfortunately, however, we have to get back to our ship. Business, you know."

"But—" Calista let her protest die unspoken. "That's right. Business. But it's been nice talking to you."

Rhys waited to be sure Calista gave the command to beam up before he did, too. Just before he disappeared, he waved at the immobile Kartanese. "Have a nice day."

Rhys wasn't going to like it. Calista drummed her fingers on the command console, considering.

Five days had passed since she and Rhys had been forced to abandon their explorations of the tunnels, and she hadn't had even one opportunity to try again. They'd both been extremely busy with the rebuilding of the *Fair Trade's* cargo bays. When they weren't on the *Fair Trade*, Larr had kept them occupied with discussions of future trade runs and exhaustive analyses of existing accounts.

The rest of the time she'd spent in trouncing the Dorinor in more rounds of bakal than she cared to count. Even Karnor had given up trying to keep track of all the "credits" she'd won.

Although she was heartily sick of the game, Calista was grateful for the chance to learn more about the

Kartanese and to gain their trust. The trouble was, the information she'd gained only confused her more.

Despite their carnivorous nature and their intimidatingly sharp claws and teeth, the Kartanese were essentially gentle creatures. The only thing that seemed to rouse their ire was any threat to the safety of their caves, their females, and their young, which Calista never saw.

They were passionately addicted to long, involved discussions on issues of honor or questions of logic or the theology behind their small pantheon of gods. They were also addicted to chess, which humans had introduced to them about fifty years earlier, when the planet was first discovered.

Without a written language, they relied on their phenomenal memories to track their race's history, although, so far as Calista could tell, their only real interest in such matters lay in tracing the convoluted genealogies of their leaders. Perhaps because of their extremely limited ability to hold or manipulate a physical object, they'd never developed any of the technical, scientific, or artistic endeavors that occupied human minds. They had absolutely no interest in trade, even though every Kartanese social group maintained close ties with every other group.

Despite numerous attempts, Calista had learned nothing that could explain how the Kartanese, with their clumsy, clawed feet and lack of interest in commerce, had managed to produce something as delicate and highly marketable as the saitha silk. Which suggested the silk was completely natural. That possibility brought a host of questions that were even harder to answer.

The more she'd thought about it, the more puzzled she became. And puzzles, as far as Calista was concerned, absolutely required solutions.

Right now, Rhys and Larr were running a final inspection of the redesigned cargo bays. That meant for the next two or three hours she didn't have anything to do.

Anything, that is, except try to satisfy her curiosity.

With sudden determination, Calista pushed back from the command console. She couldn't go far—there wasn't enough time for that—but she was going to see whatever there was to see of the passages she *could* get to.

As she attached a couple of glow-lights and a tracker to a utility belt, Calista considered the problem of where to start. She could beam directly into the Dorinor's cavern, but she'd just as soon not risk being drawn into another game of bakal. She could also beam into the passages leading to the cavern that she'd used before, but there were guards posted in every one of them.

Which left the passage she and Rhys had started to follow after that first card game with the Dorinor. It wasn't safe to try getting into other passages if the computer didn't have the exact coordinates—the prospect of materializing inside solid rock really didn't hold much appeal.

The passageway, when she arrived, was empty. Calista breathed a sigh of relief. Setting the tracker, she headed away from the main cavern and toward whatever it was that might lie ahead.

Fifteen minutes later, Calista was beginning to wonder if she should bother going farther. There was absolutely nothing of interest. Both the main passage she followed and the five or six intersecting passages she'd crossed were formed of the same dull gray rock she'd seen everywhere else. Walls, floors, and ceilings were all worn smooth with the creatures' passing. At no point were there any lights. Presumably the Kartanese found their way by sense of smell.

This deep in the mountain, she'd almost be able to manage that trick herself. Without cross ventilation, the heavy, musky scent of the Kartanese hung on the air. It wasn't an unpleasant smell, but it was impossible to miss.

Calista hesitated, irritated by the waste of her time so far. She hadn't known what to expect from her unauthorized explorations, but she certainly hadn't expected to be this bored. She could always backtrack and try one of the branch passages. Or she could go forward.

With a mental shrug, Calista decided to keep to the passage she'd been following. She'd give it another ten minutes. If this route didn't pan out, she'd try a side passage. If that didn't work, she'd give up and head back to the ship. The one thing she did want to be sure of was not to go so deep the ship's transporter couldn't reach her.

The allotted ten minutes were almost up and Calista was nearing the transporter's maximum range when she heard the faint sounds of activity ahead. She switched off the glow-light and was startled to find a light showing at the far end of the passage.

Her irritation at the so far fruitless exploration evaporated immediately. The lights were the first indication she'd seen that the Kartanese used any artificial aids or tools of any kind.

If, that is, it was the Kartanese at the end of the passage. It was always possible that Larr and his people were there, instead.

And that might prove just as interesting.

Guided only by the dim glow and her hand on the passage wall, Calista moved cautiously forward. The dark was no protection against the Kartanese, but it would shield her against human eyes. There was no sense in giving away her presence if she didn't have to.

Calista was almost three-quarters of the way to the passage's end before she was able to identify the vague sounds emanating from beyond the light. They were Kartanese voices, lower pitched and softer than those she was accustomed to, but Kartanese nonetheless. The sibilants and gutturals of the creatures' language were unmistakable.

This close, the air was hotter and more humid. The smell of the beasts was stronger, too.

The passage opened onto a broad platform, then a winding stone ramp that appeared to lead down to the chamber

Calista cautiously peered around the end of the passage wall. The voices came from below her on the far side of the cavern, but that didn't mean there were no Kartanese guards posted nearby. Though she still couldn't spot the source of the chamber's illumination, the light was strong enough to make it almost impossible for her to see anything clearly in the darkness at either side of her.

Dropping on all fours, Calista quietly wormed her way toward the platform's edge. Just before she was close enough to look over, she paused, every sense alert, and tried to decipher the muffled sounds from below her. She could hear an odd rustling sound and the low grunts and hisses and grumblings that seemed to constitute their language, but she was still too far away for her translator to make any sense of the conversation.

No sound came from anywhere close that indicated she'd been spotted. Reassured, Calista eased forward and peered down into the chamber below.

Chapter Nine

The cavern was big, perhaps half again the size of the Dorinor's chamber. From her vantage point, Calista could see five other ramps leading down to the cavern floor. At the top of each ramp gaped the dark holes of passages similar to the one behind her. None were set at the same level. Fortunately, the platform she lay on was the highest, which meant no one would be able to spy on her from above.

All six ramps wrapped around the cavern walls in an erratic spiral, their descent broken at intervals where they crossed broad shelves cut into the solid rock. The shelves were wide enough for three humans to walk abreast, but each shelf was so tightly packed with bulky, cocoonlike cylinders that no one would be able to move more than a foot off the ramp without tripping.

The vast space was illuminated by what looked like luminous plants hung at regular intervals along the walls. Heavy mists rising from a circular pool of steaming, blue-green mineral waters set in the middle of the floor softened and diffused the light, obscuring Calista's vision of the activity at the pool's edge.

At this distance, she could vaguely discern the shapes of two or possibly three Kartanese. She thought she also spotted several heavy-bodied, two-legged creatures in the mist, but she couldn't be sure. Whatever they were, they were so pale-skinned they blended into the enveloping vapors.

For an instant, Calista hesitated. She was too deep in the mountain to be able to transport back up if she ran into trouble. On the other hand, she might never again have an opportunity like this to learn the Kartaneses' secrets.

Curiosity inevitably won out over prudence.

With one more quick look to be sure she hadn't been spotted, Calista rose to a crouch and cautiously started down the ramp.

At the first intersecting shelf she reached, Calista paused, then crossed to the cylinders neatly laid in a row stretching away from the ramp.

The first cylinder appeared identical to all the rest, bulky and irregularly shaped, rounded at both ends. At a guess, Calista judged it would be half again as tall as she was and weigh at least two or three times more. The ivory-colored shell appeared to be formed of layer upon layer of what might be long strips of paper or cloth pasted together with some substance that created a hard, protective covering for whatever was inside.

Calista lightly touched the shell. Instantly, energy flowed from it into her fingertips and up her arm. Stifling her exclamation of surprise, she pressed both hands to the shell. Energy surged through her, followed by the same sense of well-being the saitha silk had brought her once she'd conquered that first, overwhelming pain.

Wonderingly, Calista ran her fingers over the rough surface of the shell. Had she discovered the source of the silk? Or was this something different?

The answer, Calista was certain, lay below with the Kartanese and the shadowy figures working around the pool.

Abandoning the shell, Calista set off down the ramp, moving more quickly now. Briefly she stopped at each of the next three shelves to study the ivory-colored cylinders arranged there. Two of the three she checked were like the first, alive with energy. The third was a darker, duller color. When she touched it, there was only a faint flicker, as if whatever lay within was weak or dying.

Calista stopped on the last platform. All the way down she'd kept close to the wall and away from the edge, minimizing the risk of being spotted from below. Now she needed to get closer to the edge, so she could see what was happening. At the same time, she needed some sort of cover to prevent being spotted by anyone entering the chamber from the passages above her. The only cover available was the rows of cylinders that stretched out along the shelf beside her.

Calista quietly worked her way along the back of the shelf until she'd put what she hoped was sufficient distance between her and the ramp, then crawled forward so she could peek over the edge of the shelf.

Though she was still too far away for the translator to function, Calista was relieved to find she could clearly see what was going on below.

To one side, three Kartanese sat propped on their tails, intently watching the efforts of eight of the strange creatures Calista had glimpsed through the mist earlier.

The eight were covered in gray-white fur that made them blend in with the mists, obscuring their outlines. With their relatively short, pudgy bodies awkwardly balanced on two stumpy legs, the creatures provided an odd contrast to the dark bulk of the Kartanese. Unlike the Kartanese, however, the grays possessed the advantage of eyes located squarely in the center of their flat faces and what looked like three-fingered hands with opposable thumbs. Each wore a sort of work apron tied around its waist whose pockets appeared to be stuffed with a variety of small hand tools.

Right now, all eight were intently engaged in working on two of the ivory-colored cylinders which lay on the stone floor by the pool. Both were lying in puddles of water, as though they'd been dumped in the pool first. One of the two jumped and twisted with the struggles of whatever new life lay within. The other twitched occasionally, then lay still.

The dunking in the pool seemed to have dissolved whatever substance had stiffened the shells, loosening the individual layers of material that had formed them. The grays were slowly and rather awkwardly unwinding the ivory-colored lengths of fiber of the shell, then cutting them into odd lengths, depending on convenience, and dumping the lengths into untidy heaps on the floor.

As the grays worked, the three Kartanese kept up a running commentary that seemed to consist of irritated advice and sharp criticism in about equal measure. Instead of rebelling against the verbal attacks, however, the grays scuttled to respond as quickly as they could. More than one tripped or got in the way of another by rushing about in blind response to one of the Kartaneses' dictates. The end result at times seemed more chaos than productive accomplishment.

Although Calista had never seen any creature that even vaguely resembled the eight around the pool, their cringing subservience and anxious haste to respond to the frequent, harsh scoldings from the Kartanese was all too painfully familiar to Calista. There was no mistaking it. She'd seen more than enough of it on Andrus. Whatever else the creatures were, they were bound to the exacting, intolerant Kartanese as slaves, or something very like it.

Bile rose in Calista's throat and she sank, trembling, to lie flat on the hard stone shelf beneath her.

The Kartanese kept slaves.

The knowledge was like a knife in her heart, twisting viciously. In serving them, she helped maintain others in the bondage she'd fought so hard to escape. Only a well-honed instinct for self-preservation kept her from screaming out the anger pouring through her. She pounded her fist on the stone beneath her, but that hurt and accomplished exactly nothing.

She forced her hand to unclench and her breathing to still. She could do nothing to help the grays—at least, not right now—but there was always the chance that she could learn something that would be of value in the future. But she'd have to be paying attention first. Reluctantly, Calista turned her attention back to what was happening by the pool.

The grays were still working on the two cylinders, slowly unwrapping what Calista was now convinced was raw saitha silk. Just a few short hours ago she'd been thinking of her plans for the profits she'd make in selling the silk. And now . . . !

As she watched the silk slowly being unwound from the living creatures it protected, Calista knew she was watching her dream of freedom being unwound, as well. Angry tears burned her eyes.

Freedom or no, she refused to profit from anything gained with the labor of slaves. The Dorinor could take his contract and . . . She wasn't sure just what he could do with it, but she hoped it hurt. And to think she'd actually grown to like the big lunk!

By now the first and most active cylinder was almost completely unwrapped and five of the grays were struggling to keep hold of it. Suddenly a leg burst out of the remaining shell, shredding the protective sheath.

The action brought the three Kartanese to their feet, scolding, clucking, and milling about and further hampering the harassed grays. The three even managed to get in each other's way. When two bumped heads in their eagerness to get a better look, it looked like a fight would erupt until the third reared back, wings flapping angrily, and gave both of them a sound cuffing.

In the confusion, the actual appearance of the newborn Kartanese almost went unnoticed. The baby, its fur still wet and its tiny wings dragging on the ground, awkwardly flopped out of the remaining wrappings and directly into the path of the still squabbling adults. If it hadn't been for the quick intervention of two grays, who pulled the squawking creature out of harm's way, it might have been trampled.

Not that matters improved much, because the baby almost immediately ended up being dumped in the hot mineral pool. Calista held her breath, tensely waiting for the dark head to reappear. She hadn't been able to tell if the action was deliberate, but it certainly managed to get everyone's attention. The three Kartanese and eight grays immediately gathered at the pool's edge, their eyes fixed on the softly bubbling waters.

Calista heard the baby first. It was half out of the pool on the far side, scrabbling for a grip on the slick stone and complaining lustily at the rough treatment. By the time its two- and four-legged attendants rushed around the pool, it was shaking itself vigorously, clearly none the worse for the dunking.

Assured of the newborn's health, the Kartanese began berating the hapless grays, who stood silently, clearly unsure what to do next. The combination of some hungry squawks from the baby and a couple of feeble thumps from the remaining cylinder settled the matter. One of the Kartanese and three of the grays promptly led the newborn out of the cavern, leaving the rest to tend to the second baby.

Even though her translator wouldn't work at this distance, Calista had no difficulty understanding the gist of the consultation between the remaining Kartanese and grays as they contemplated the second unborn baby in its protective wrappings. They were worried.

Compared to the vigorous struggles of the first, this baby's efforts to free itself were pitifully weak and ineffectual. When it became clear it wasn't going to be able to fight free, one of the grays hastily slit open the remaining layers of the sheath.

Unlike its sibling, this small Kartanese flopped into the world with a whimper. Its withered limbs scraped uselessly at the rock beneath it. After a couple of shivering, halfhearted attempts to move toward the pool, it gave up and lay still.

The two Kartanese scarcely moved. Only their wings quivered across their backs as they watched, necks outstretched, eyes glowing, while the small life before them faded, then died.

One of the grays broke the leaden stillness. It stepped forward and gently tried to wrap the baby in the discarded sheath. Its actions roused the smallest Kartanese, who immediately began a painful, keening wail of grief that echoed off the walls of the chamber, filling the empty space.

Suddenly, without warning, the other Kartanese let out a roar of angry denial. In its grief, it lashed its tail and thrashed about blindly, sending the smaller, defenseless workers scurrying for safety.

Horror-struck and helpless, Calista watched as the grief-maddened Kartanese struck one of the grays with its tail and tossed it against a wall, then barely missed a second, which had tripped over some of the discarded sheath in its efforts to flee.

Before the Kartanese could wreak further havoc, its companion roused enough to divert its attention so the remaining grays could get safely out of reach. Three prudently chose to disappear down a nearby passage. The one who had tripped paused long enough to gather up the gray that lay slumped against the far wall before it, too, sought safety in a side passage.

The first Kartanese paid no heed to their departure, but stormed about the chamber, wailing its grief until exhaustion calmed it sufficiently so the second could lead it away down the passage where the first, much happier group had gone only a short while earlier.

In the quiet that followed, Calista could neither move nor think. She stared at the still, small form lying beside the pool, remembering another time, another world.

She'd been nine, almost ten. A family, friends of her master's, had come to visit and her mistress had given a huge garden party in their honor. The family's eldest son, acting on an unwise dare from the neighboring boys, had tried to climb the steep roof of the main house and fallen to his death.

Calista could still see him there, lying on the ground

just as dead as the baby Kartanese on the floor below her. In his grief, the boy's father had lashed out at the frightened slaves who'd run to help, but there'd been no one to stop his violence. He'd struck one of the slave boys in the head with his weighted overseer's whip. He hadn't meant to hurt the boy, but there'd been two bodies to bury that day, not one, and Calista had never forgotten.

Slowly the memories receded, to be replaced by a leaden weight in the pit of her stomach and a cold, biting anger. On Andrus she'd been powerless to act, just as she was here. But at least this time around she had an alternative.

She wasn't going to work for slaveholders. It was as simple as that. And if she had anything to say about it, neither would Rhys Fairdane.

Calista cast one last glance at the sad, silent form below her. To her surprise, four of the grays had returned and were tenderly wrapping the dead baby in the discarded wrappings. None spoke, but two of the four snuffled and sniffed. If they'd been human, she would have said they were crying.

That kind of emotional reaction wasn't unusual either, Calista thought grimly. She'd cried when her master's boy had died, too. But her tears then had held a note of fear, as well as of pity and pain. She imagined the grays' crying did, too.

As quietly as she could, Calista eased back into the shadows behind her, then stood and began to retrace her steps. She was far too deep for the transporter to pick her up, but as soon as she was back on the *Fair Trade*, Rhys was going to get an earful about the creatures they were working for.

"I don't believe you." Rhys had his arms crossed his chest and was scowling at her, obviously shaken but unwilling to accept the truth of her unwelcome news.

Calista had found him on the bridge of the *Fair Trade* when she'd beamed back up to the ship. She was growing increasingly frustrated with his unexpected opposition. "Look, I know a slave when I see one, and those creatures were slaves."

"Where did they come from, then? The Kartanese had no contact with other worlds until humans discovered them. No other intelligent species has ever been found on this planet. Certainly none that resemble the creatures you described."

"How should I know where they came from?" Calista threw up her hands in disgust. "Maybe their ancestors were space travelers who crash-landed on Karta generations ago. Maybe they're native to Karta, but they've been slaves so long that now they only exist in the Kartanese caves. The how and why of it doesn't matter. What matters is that we can't work for slavers."

Rhys's lips tightened in frustrated anger. He started to speak, but a chime from the command console interrupted. With a quick warning glance at Calista, he sat down in the pilot's chair and scanned the bank of instruments before him. His fingers drummed on the arm of his chair in a rapid tattoo that made Calista want to scream. When several lights flashed all together, he punched a series of controls as if he were stabbing them. Satisfied, he turned back to face Calista.

"You have a contract—"

"Contracts be damned!" Calista snapped. "I'll not work for slavers. Period."

"You're not thinking. Remember the penalty clause for breaking the agreement? You'll forfeit just about everything you own—and so will I."

The hot reply she'd been about to make froze on Calista's tongue. She *had* forgotten the penalty clause.

"There are ways to get out of contracts," she muttered at last. At the moment, however, she hadn't the slightest idea how she was going to manage that little trick. Larr had made the pertinent clause extremely tight. At the time, she hadn't protested because she hadn't been able to think of any reason why she'd want to get out of the most lucrative agreement of her entire career.

"Besides," Rhys continued in a level voice, "You can't even prove the creatures you saw really are slaves. Regardless of the way the Kartanese treated them, there might be any number of reasonable explanations for their presence."

"Name one."

"Well—" Rhys's mouth twitched in irritation. "I can't think of anything off the top of my head, but I'm sure—"

"So am I. And I don't want to work for anyone that keeps slaves."

"Neither do I, but I don't want to go off half-cocked, either." Rhys was beginning to lose his temper. "If you can prove those creatures are slaves—"

"They are."

"—and if you can find a way to get out of our contract that won't bankrupt us both, then I'm willing to listen." Rhys paused, clearly fighting for control. Calista could think of nothing to say in rebuttal. When she didn't speak, he added, "In the meantime, we have a trade run we're obligated to complete."

Frustrated, Calista snapped, "Count me out. I'm not about to lift a finger to help anyone who keeps slaves. It's that simple."

"It's not that simple." Rhys's efforts to control his

temper weren't working. "If you'd only—"

"I'll just wait on the *Independence* until you get back." Calista was halfway to the door when Rhys's response stopped her cold.

"Whether you like it or not, you're going on this trip, Calista. The *Fair Trade* has already moved of orbit around Karta and we'll be slipping into hyperspace in a few seconds."

"What?" Calista whirled back to face Rhys. One look at his face told her he wasn't lying, but she couldn't help pushing past him to study the command console. Even as she checked the instruments, she felt the slight, disorienting tug at her senses as the ship crossed the invisible barrier between normal space and the dark, amorphous nothing of hyperspace. There would be no turning back now.

The knowledge didn't stop the protest that rose to her lips. "You can't get away with this, Fairdane. I'll—"

Rhys held up his hands in a placating gesture that did nothing to soothe her irritation. "I programmed the ship before you came on board. The minute you were back, it automatically moved out of orbit."

"You could have stopped it! When you checked the board a couple of minutes ago, I thought—"

"I just confirmed my instructions. We were already out of transporter range by then."

A dozen possible responses occurred to Calista, none of them socially acceptable. Instead of speaking, she turned on her heel and stalked out of the room.

It was a shame the doors were automatic. She wouldn't have minded slamming one. She wouldn't have minded in the least.

Rhys watched Calista storm out, then sank into the pilot's chair.

Was she right? Did the Kartanese really keep slaves? If they didn't, what were the gray-furred creatures Calista had seen, and what was their relationship to the Kartanese?

The thought of working for slavers twisted in his gut like a hot knife. He no more wanted to make his living off the work of slaves than Calista did. The difference between them was he wouldn't jump into any decision without knowing the whole story or considering the consequences.

You jumped fast enough when Larr offered you the position of rep, his conscience chided him.

And look where it had gotten him.

Maybe.

Calista might be wrong. She'd only seen the creatures from a distance, too far even to decipher what was being said. And though he had to admit the Kartanese treatment of the grays was suspicious, that didn't automatically make them slaveholders.

Which left him nowhere and sinking fast.

Between the penalties for breaking his contract and the loss of the chance to obtain the third planet, there was far too much at stake for him to act precipitately. Until he knew for sure, there was nothing he could do except hope that Calista was wrong.

Or was there?

His brow furrowed with thought, Rhys turned to the command console and began keying in a series of questions for the main computer.

Nine days later, he conceded defeat. An exhaustive search of the ship's files had failed to yield even a hint as to the grays' origin. So far as the computer was concerned, the creatures didn't exist. Period.

There were other sources, to be sure. The xenobiology library at Moralla Core, the best of its kind in the known universe. The exploration records at Empire. If the grays had ever had contact with any space-faring species, the information would be there.

But he had neither the time nor the patience for such an extensive search. He had a commitment and he couldn't break that agreement on the basis of Calista's unsubstantiated interpretation of what she'd seen and heard in that cavern on Karta.

Wearily, Rhys rubbed his face. He was tired. Tired and frustrated and lonely. Calista had refused even to speak to him since they'd left Karta. She'd also refused to have anything to do with the two deliveries of silk they'd had to make.

Not that she hadn't pulled her fair share of work. Rhys knew she'd put in long, hard hours in the maintenance section, making sure every ship system was functioning properly. She'd even gotten a couple of the less efficient housekeeping robots to work, something he'd given up on long ago. If they'd been human, he'd have said she'd put the fear of god into them. He couldn't think of any other way she could have managed to get the pesky machines in line.

She'd also spent as many hours poring over the computer files as he had, though her focus had been on contract and trade laws. Rhys didn't have any trouble figuring out her purpose there. Judging from the almost constant frown on her face, she wasn't having any more luck than he had, either.

The worst part of it all was the emotional gulf that had opened between them. After those too-short days when they'd come together again as lovers, he was finding it harder than ever—damn near impossible, in fact—to cope with the need for her that held him in its grip and wouldn't let go.

He felt like a drunk who'd fallen off the wagon and couldn't get back on. He dreamed of her. Waking and sleeping, she was with him, tormenting him, driving him mad with the aching hunger he could not assuage. And the longer she maintained her cold distance from him, the worse his need for her became.

The emotional distance he'd spent five long years trying to put between them had evaporated in the space of one night's loving. Rhys wasn't sure he could ever regain it. He was sure he wouldn't if he spent any more time alone with Calista on the ship—despite her obvious efforts to keep out of his way, he couldn't forget she was there.

More than once he'd walked down a hallway and stopped short, sure, somehow, that she'd passed that way just a short time before. Perhaps it was some trick of his senses. Perhaps it was her scent lingering on the air, faint but just enough so his unconscious mind, at least, could identify it even if his conscious mind could not. He was constantly encountering some small reminder of her presence. A piece of equipment that wasn't put back exactly the way he would have put it back. A chair left out of place. A view screen adjusted to suit her, not him. Trivial details. Details he'd scarcely have noticed if it had been anyone but her.

But it *was* her and he *did* notice and it was driving him mad. Certifiably, irrevocably mad.

And all because of creatures she'd seen once and knew virtually nothing about.

It couldn't go on this way. With sudden decision, Rhys did what he'd fought against doing for the past nine days. He went looking for her.

She was at a workbench in the weapons room. A disassembled stun gun lay before her and she was bent over some small part, intent on whatever adjustment she was making.

She glanced up at his entrance, obviously startled. For an instant, Rhys could have sworn he saw relief in her eyes. But only for an instant, then her eyes dropped back to her work. "You need something in here? I'll be glad to—"

"Let's stop these games, OK, Calista?" Rhys grabbed a stool and sat down beside her. "This is driving us both crazy. You as much as me."

She stiffened, but she didn't take her eyes off her work. "I'm not playing games."

"All right. No games. Stars know there's nothing funny about it. But whatever you want to call it, it has to stop. We're both too old for this, and it's too damn much work to keep out of each other's way for this to go on any longer."

She looked up at that. "Then you believe me? About the Kartanese?"

Rhys drew a deep breath, praying for reason. "I neither believe nor disbelieve. I'm waiting for proof, one way or the other."

"And meanwhile?"

"Meanwhile, I'll do the work I've agreed to, in the best way I know how."

"I won't work for slavers."

"You've said that before. But you can't be sure that what you saw was what you think it is. What ever happened to being innocent until proven guilty? You've condemned the Kartanese for something they may not even be guilty of, something that's legal on a hundred worlds in the Empire."

Calista's fingers tightened around the part she held until the knuckles turned white. "Being legal doesn't make it right."

Rhys sighed. It was hard arguing for his side of the matter when she had so much right on hers. "I'll grant you that. But that's not the issue here. The issue is, are we both going to blindly assume the Kartanese *do* hold slaves? Are we going to risk everything we've spent our lives trying to build, all on an unfounded supposition?"

With a choked exclamation of mingled frustration and disgust, Calista threw the part on the worktable, then leaned toward him, as if eliminating the distance between them would eliminate the differences, as well.

"All right, Fairdane," she said. "Let's assume I play it your way for now, that I do my best to sell that damned silk, that I help you load the equipment we're supposed to pick up. What then? How do we prove those creatures are slaves? How do we disprove it?"

Her body was stiff and awkward with the tension that held her; her eyes sparked with the intensity of her emotions. "What are you going to do if the answer's not what you want? What then?"

"I—" Rhys thought of the people waiting on half a dozen worlds for him to find a home for them, a future. He thought of Glynna and his mother, who had sacrificed and saved for a future they could only dream of. Did he dash their hopes, give up the best chance he'd ever had of obtaining the world he sought, all for the sake of a principle that didn't amount to a hill of durmquats in light of the reality they lived in?

"I don't know, Calista," he admitted at last. "I just don't know."

"You're in it for the money and to hell with anything else? Is that it?"

"Is that what you think?"

"If not, how can you justify—"

"Can't you just trust me?" The question burst out with explosive force, driven by the frustration, uncertainty, and doubt that had hounded him ever since Calista had told him about the gray-furred creatures.

Calista hunched her shoulders, drawing her head down in a protective gesture that spoke more clearly of her distress—and determination—than any words could. "No, I can't."

Rhys could only stare, wide-eyed. She couldn't trust him. Or wouldn't. It amounted to the same thing.

Despite everything that lay between them, despite every feeling they'd had—still had—for each other, she wasn't going to budge an inch for him. Her opinions, her wants, were all that mattered to her. They were probably all that ever would matter.

Rhys rose to his feet slowly. Suddenly he felt very, very tired. Calista refused to look at him. She'd picked up the part she'd been working on and was bent over it, ignoring his presence.

Without speaking, Rhys turned and left the room.

Chapter Ten

"Just what're you guys up to, there on Karta?" the loading master asked. He looked Rhys up, then he looked Rhys down. He didn't seem too impressed with what he saw.

After three days on Empire checking out the shipment of heavy equipment that Larr had told him to pick up, Rhys was glad to have the question out in the open. More than one person had clearly wanted to ask him. The loading master was the first who had.

Which didn't mean he had any intention of answering the question. "What do you mean?"

"Equipment like this, it's not usually used by humans." Sharp intelligence shone behind the master's pale, washed-out gray eyes. He cocked a thumb in the direction of the machinery on the grav hoist. "In fact, there aren't many races that can handle this equipment, period. Controls aren't in the right places. Everything's designed to be used by someone who's a heck of a lot bigger'n you or me. I know you can't use it. Neither can those Karta dragons, from what I've learned about 'em. So that makes me want to ask questions."

"Does it, now?" Rhys hedged. He wished he didn't have quite such a good idea of who *was* going to use it.

"It does." The master wasn't backing down. "Though I will give you credit for not trying to cheat on the billing, as that Tull fellow did. Shameless, that man was."

"So I understand. But there'll be no cheating while I'm handling this."

"And no talking, either, eh?" The master cocked an eyebrow at Rhys.

"That's right."

The master considered that for a moment. "Fair enough. But don't think we're not curious. That's unusual equipment you're hauling, make no mistake. And that Larr fellow has bought enough of it over the past few years to make one wonder."

"There's no charge for wondering." Rhys snapped his hand comp to his belt. Everything was properly accounted and paid for. This load would be the last, for this run, at least.

Maybe the last ever. Rhys frowned. Ever since Calista had returned from Karta with her accusations of slavery, he'd been trying to concentrate on the task at hand. He couldn't afford to waste time and energy worrying about something like that. At least, not yet.

That thought made him frown even more. Some of Calista's passionate, almost irrational, antipathy for slavery was beginning to sink in. He didn't need that kind of distraction.

The arrival of the cargo hauler forestalled both the

need for further thought on the issue, or conversation with the master.

Rhys watched as the handlers loaded the last of Larr's equipment in the hauler and stowed it properly. He'd ride up on the cargo hauler instead of transporting, he decided. Calista would no doubt be in the cargo bay stowing the equipment that had already been delivered and preparing to receive this last load.

The thought made Rhys scowl. He would have to make a decision soon. Calista had already made it clear what she expected him to do. He knew her too well to think she'd back down on the issue now.

That left him exactly nowhere. He'd considered the situation from a hundred angles over the past few days, and still no answer had presented itself. Even if he were certain the Kartanese kept slaves, he wasn't sure that he could, or should, break his agreement with them. The line between his own feelings and the needs of his people had never been less clear. Or more difficult to deal with.

The ride back to the *Fair Trade* was all too short. Calista was at the controls of the airlock, but not by the slightest quiver of a muscle did she acknowledge his presence. Her attention was fixed on overseeing the transfer of the equipment from the hauler to the *Fair Trade's* cargo bays, a job the computers could easily have handled. Human supervision provided no more than a small additional margin of safety.

Safety, however, wasn't her main concern. It didn't take her pointed avoidance of him as she stepped around him on her way to the bays to tell Rhys that.

Something snapped in Rhys. With a growl, he grabbed her arm and pulled her around to face him. He would have welcomed a physical attack.

She came close to obliging. Her right hand balled

into a fist and an angry fire leaped into her eyes. With a muffled curse, she started to swing at him, but something she must have seen in his eyes or his expression stopped her.

"I wouldn't give you the satisfaction, Fairdane." She wrenched free of his grip.

"What kind of 'satisfaction' were you thinking of, York?" Rhys decided he'd'd settle for a verbal sparring match if he couldn't provoke a physical one.

He came close to getting that. Although it clearly cost her an effort not to respond in kind, Calista settled for glaring at him, then pointedly turning her back and stalking away.

Rhys watched her go, his body quivering with the effort required not to run after her. Damn her!

She wasn't giving him a chance, either to fight or to find a solution to their dilemma.

Did you ever give her a chance? a small voice in his head asked. *Did you ever try to explain your situation, ever try to tell her about your search?*

That was different, another angrier voice said. *There were reasons . . .*

Yeah, sure, the first voice responded. *What reasons?*

Rhys shook his head, trying to rid his conscience of the annoying arguments. No matter what he ought to have told her in the past, he sure as blazes wasn't going to start trying to explain anything to that hardheaded female now.

Three days more. That's all she had. Just three days until they reached Karta and she had to make a decision.

Calista slowly ran her hands over the command console. It was just a console, but it was Rhys's console and there was some small comfort to be had in touching the same controls he'd so often touched.

Since leaving Empire with their load of equipment, she'd spent a lot of time on the empty bridge of the *Fair Trade*. She couldn't bear to see Rhys or talk with him, but here, at least, he didn't seem so far away.

If only he would believe her. If only she hadn't seen what she'd seen. If she'd never gone exploring, if she hadn't found that cavern . . .

A lot of ifs—and not one of them mattered. Not any more.

The chime indicating an incoming communication provided a welcome interruption to her thoughts. Calista cued the communicator to respond, then put the transmission on the view screen.

The woman who appeared would have been beautiful if she hadn't been so thin or so obviously under stress. There were circles under her dark eyes and lines of strain around her generous mouth. Her long, black hair was pulled back in a simple queue, accentuating the high cheekbones and firm jawline.

Calista sat up straighter, startled. Rhys had never spoken of his past nor ever mentioned a family, but there was no mistaking the resemblance. The woman on the screen was either a sister or a close relative.

"You must be Calista." The woman's expression lit with interest, despite her obvious weariness.

"That's right. And you're . . . ?"

"Glynna. Is Rhys there?" Static blurred her voice and disrupted her image on the screen.

"Your transmission's breaking up." Calista tried to strengthen the communication link, without success. "Can you fix it on your end?"

"—equipment problems. Don't know . . . Rhys?" Glynna's image winked out, came back on, then lost focus in another burst of static.

"Rhys isn't here. If you'll wait a minute, I'll have the

computer track him down and transfer your—"

"No." Glynna shook her head. "—no time . . . lose connection . . . Mother's dying—" The screen roared with the hiss and crackle of interference. "—should come. If he can." Glynna paused, as if the words she wanted to say wouldn't come. At last she added, "Tell him we understand if he can't. If—"

There was another surge of interference, then the screen went blank. Calista tried to reestablish the connection, but to no avail—the communication had been too brief for the computer to identify the source. Her hands went still on the control panel.

Rhys's mother was dying. Beyond the pain of the message itself was a host of questions Calista had never asked. Questions about his home and family.

The message from Glynna—whoever she might be— was a reminder of how many secrets lay between them, of how much they'd never shared with each other. The reminder hurt.

The computer located Rhys in the exercise rooms, but he didn't cue the view screen right away. When he finally appeared, sweat beaded his brow and lay in a slick sheen across his bare chest and arms. He was breathing heavily.

"Yes?" The single word was sharp with impatience.

Calista hesitated. There was no easy way to say what she had to say. "I just spoke with Glynna. Your mother is dying."

"My mo—" Rhys's face paled under the tan, but that was all. An instant later, all trace of emotion was gone. "Why didn't you transfer the communication to me?"

"The link was very weak. I lost her before I could do anything. She said—" Calista hesitated. "She said they'd understand if you couldn't come."

Rhys didn't respond to that, but the muscles of

his jaw jumped as he clamped down on whatever he'd been about to utter. "I'll be on the bridge in a minute."

"Rhys, I—"

The screen went blank before she could say more.

It took four minutes for Rhys to reach the bridge. They were some of the longest minutes Calista had ever known. What was she supposed to say? What *should* she say? What could she do to help?

The answer, of course, was absolutely nothing. She'd never felt more useless.

Rhys came onto the bridge, cold, hard, implacable, seemingly unmoved. Ignoring Calista, he bent over the control panel, rapidly keying in a series of commands, checking the information the computer gave, then confirming his acceptance.

This close, Calista could feel the heat radiating from him, smell the mingled scent of clean, male sweat that clung to his skin. The intense awareness disturbed her. It wasn't right. Not now.

"Here's your chair." Calista tried to slip out without touching him. He was too close, yet when she brushed against his arm and hip, there was no response. He took the vacated chair without even glancing at her, his attention focused on the screens and monitors before him.

"If there's anything—" Calista faltered. "I'd like to help, so—"

"We're a day and a half away at maximum speed," Rhys said, ignoring her offer. He glanced up at her, very briefly, his face as still as if it had been carved in stone.

Calista wasn't even sure he saw her. His eyes were bottomless pits of black that contained nothing, not even anger.

Involuntarily, she clutched the edge of the control

panel, suddenly feeling as helplessly adrift as she had the first time she'd stepped into the weightlessness of space, as though she'd been cast away without an anchor to tie her to anything she knew or cared about.

He turned back to the controls. "I can't say how long we'll have to stay—"

"Rhys, it doesn't matter. I'll stay—"

"—but however long, you'll just have to wait."

"I can wait."

If Rhys heard, he gave no indication. His attention was totally focused on the controls. Satisfied, he stood abruptly and pushed past Calista as if she weren't there.

Suddenly desperate for some sign that he'd heard her, that he understood she was concerned for him, she grabbed his sleeve. He stopped, then turned to her. The stone carving was still fixed on his face.

"Whatever I can do . . . I want to help. I just wanted you to know —" She'd been ready to walk out of his life, yet Calista found herself frightened by his lack of interest in including her in his life now, when it really mattered. He didn't need her. That fact suddenly frightened her.

"Do you realize," he said, his voice distant, his gaze unfocused, "that we don't have a scrap of silk on board? The rich and powerful of the universe line up for the chance to buy it from us. They pay whatever we ask, and then they order more. We control it. We sell it. And we haven't even a small scrap that might give my mother the strength—" He choked.

His voice dropped to little more than a whisper. Calista had to strain to hear him.

"Not even a scrap."

Without another word, he turned and left the bridge.

*   *   *

Their destination proved to be a small farming community in the middle of some of the bleakest, ugliest territory on one of the poorest worlds Calista had never seen.

Rhys hadn't asked for her company, but when she'd appeared in the transport chamber he hadn't said no, either. Calista wasn't sure there was anything she could do to help, but she wouldn't let him go through what lay ahead alone. She couldn't.

They materialized on a dusty, brick-paved square set in the center of the small village. Glynna and two men who looked to be in their sixties or seventies awaited them.

The instant they materialized, Glynna abandoned her companions to wrap her arms around Rhys's neck. She didn't speak, but tears stained her cheeks and she looked grateful for Rhys's strength and bulk, as though she'd held on for as long as she could and now needed someone else to support her, someone to cling to.

Rhys's face softened. He clung to the slender woman as though he were afraid she, too, were slipping from him.

He released her at last and, his arm still protectively wrapped around her shoulders, turned to face the two men who'd stood silent throughout. None of them paid any attention to Calista.

"Tell me," Rhys said. His voice was steady, his eyes haunted.

The oldest man, a scrawny, gray little fellow who looked as if he'd passed too many nights without sleep, shrugged helplessly.

"What can we say? Your mother's dying. She never fully recovered from that bout of fever two years ago. Now her heart is failing. General systemic collapse." He met Rhys's gaze directly. "After so many years, your mother's tired of fighting, Rhys. She's giving up. That's the best way I can put it."

Rhys didn't say anything, but Calista saw his hand on Glynna's shoulder tighten its grip until his sister—she had to be his sister—looked up in worried inquiry.

"You'll want to see your mother, Rhys," the second man said. "I know it's not a good time, but we need to talk to you as soon as you're free. We've had some bad news from Salaca Minor about the settlement there. Tellus communicated with us a week ago. His negotiations for the continent on Tettrel III that we had such hopes for fell through. And that's not all."

Rhys sighed, then nodded. "All right, Marlott. I'll come as soon as I can. But first, I want to see my mother."

"Of course, of course." The man Rhys addressed as Marlott stepped back, obviously relieved his part of the greeting was over. "I'll come to you later, when you've had a chance—"

"You can stay with me while you're here, if you like," the first man added, leading the small contingent down a dusty side street while Marlott headed toward a cluster of two-story buildings on the far side of the square. "You and your partner . . . ah—" He glanced at Calista, embarrassed. "I'm sorry, I don't remember your name."

"Calista," Rhys said shortly, not even bothering to glance at her.

"York. Calista York," Calista added, uncertain if she should extend her hand or not. It would have been awkward, since Rhys didn't stop for introductions and they had to watch for loose stones and potholes in the narrow, crudely paved roadway.

She was saved from having to decide by Rhys halting abruptly in front of a squat, reddish-brown, mud-walled house indistinguishable from its neighbors.

"Wait here," Rhys said with a brief, warning glance at her. It was the first time he'd recognized her presence directly.

Calista would have responded, but he'd already turned back to open the door to the little house. His broad-shouldered body filled the opening; then he was gone, swallowed up in the shadows on the other side. Glynna was next, followed by the older man whom no one had bothered to introduce. He closed the heavy wood door behind them, shutting Calista out on the street.

Calista stared at the door, uncertain what to do next. Rhys had told her to wait. Under most circumstances, a command like that would have been all the excuse she needed not to. But what if Rhys needed her?

Restless, she started to pace. Perhaps she shouldn't have come. What, after all, could she possibly do to help? If Rhys had really needed her, wouldn't he have asked?

Silly question. Of course he wouldn't. Neither would she. If there was one thing both of them had learned, it was to rely on themselves, not others. Judging by the list of problems of that man Marlott, not everyone had learned that lesson, however.

Sweat trickled between Calista's breasts and shoulder blades and down her sides. Irritated, she rubbed the front of her jumpsuit against her chest, trying to blot up the wet. She should have worn a protective skin suit instead of this standard cloth suit. She could beam back up to the ship . . .

Running away, York? a small voice in her head asked. *Can't stand being on the outside looking in, knowing you're not wanted? It's one thing to refuse*

*an invitation, quite another not to be invited in the
first place, isn't it?*

Shut up! Calista commanded that mocking voice.
That's not it at all.

She stopped her pacing abruptly and came close
to twisting her ankle as a loose paving stone shifted
under her foot.

Or maybe it was. Maybe she *couldn't* accept being
excluded. Shutting Rhys out of her life was one thing.
Having him shut her out of his was another entirely.

Shaken, Calista abandoned her pacing and sought
refuge in a small strip of shade clinging to the front
of the houses opposite. It wasn't much, but at least it
offered some slight respite from the merciless sun. She
settled on the ground with her back propped against
the wall behind her. From here, she could watch the
door through which Rhys had gone without being in
the way of any passersby or other householders.

Who was she trying to fool? Rhys didn't need her.
If she'd had any sense, she'd have stayed on the *Fair
Trade*. And if Rhys's mother hadn't chosen such an
inconvenient time to die . . .

Calista tensed and looked around guiltily, half
expecting to find someone staring at her, shocked
by the thoughts going around in her head.

Life had been so simple, once. It wasn't at all
simple now. Now she was confused, angry, resentful,
worried, and uncertain. She was also very, very
lonely.

That scared her. She'd never been lonely before.

Calista drew her legs up close, propped her chin on
her knees, and frowned down at the paving stones
without really seeing them.

What was she going to do? Slowly she ran her hands
up and down her legs, knee to ankle and back again.
The protective cloth of her jumpsuit was rough and

real under her hands, the steady, monotonous motion oddly comforting.

What *should* she do?

Forget it all, probably.

Go back to the ship. That was, after all, a better idea. A very much safer idea. If she was on the ship, she couldn't get dragged into the emotional maelstrom that had already threatened her confidence and self-composure.

Calista half rose to her feet. The sight of that heavy wood door, firmly shut against her, made her sink back down.

Rhys's mother was dying. Calista's stomach twisted painfully inside her at the thought of how easily, how callously, she could ignore that fact. Had she become so distanced from others, from the basic facts of life like being born, and loving, and dying, that she was incapable of caring? Had she fought so hard for her freedom that she had cut herself off from everything else that mattered?

Or was it that she couldn't bear the thought of Rhys with a family when she had none? She'd never known her mother and father. She had no idea if somewhere on Andrus she had brothers and sisters she'd never met. Blood relationships didn't matter if you were a slave. There, the fact of your bondage was all that counted. Here, those same relationships were an important part of who and what each person was, of where they fit in the broader society.

So what? Calista picked up a pebble near her boot and flung it at the wall opposite.

What difference did it make that Rhys had a family, connections to a society of which he was obviously a valued member? Why should she care that he'd never spoken of Glynna or his mother? What did it have to do with her, anyway?

Her gaze dropped to the pavement beneath her feet. Without thinking, Calista gathered up a handful of pebbles and sand, but instead of flinging them away, she closed her fist and squeezed until the sharp granules dug into the palm of her hand.

The heavy door of the house opposite swung open. Calista tossed the pebbles aside and jumped to her feet, struggling to show none of the feelings that had shaken her so badly. She relaxed slightly, oddly grateful, when the only one to appear was the old man.

"How . . . Is everything all right? Is Rhys—" Calista faltered.

"Dorana Fairdane will live a day or two yet," the old man said. With the awkwardness of someone hampered by age and stiff joints, he carefully settled on the ground beside her.

Calista sat, as well, uncertain what to do.

"I am called Powdran," he said, extending his hand.

"Calista York," Calista replied, ignoring the fact that she, at least, had already been introduced. She took his proffered hand, grateful for that slight human contact.

"You have known Rhys a long time," he said. It wasn't a question.

"A while. We've worked together before."

Powdran nodded. "So I understand. We have followed his work closely, you know. As our lead seeker, what Rhys does is always of interest."

"Seeker?"

"That's what we call the men and women who are looking for a new home for us." The old man let his gaze roam over the narrow, dusty street, the small houses crowded so close together. "We miss the green of our world, you know. The trees and flowers. Water that runs free instead of being hoarded in covered cisterns and buried in irrigation channels."

Calista watched him, waiting. Obviously, Powdran thought she knew about his people's history. Perhaps she would have, if she and Rhys had ever learned to trust each other enough to share their secrets. It hurt to think they never had.

Powdran looked back at Calista. Sadness cut deep grooves in his wrinkled old face. "We have to find a world soon. There are almost three million of us, scattered across a dozen planets. It's close to twenty years since we were forced off Ziana and we're slowly but inevitably drifting apart. Our children learn about our history, but for them it's just another story their parents tell. It's not real, and it never will be if we can't bring them back together, can't rebuild what we lost."

The old man slumped wearily against the wall behind him and let his head fall back, so that his face was turned toward a sky the same bleached blue as his faded eyes.

"Dorana came as a stranger to Ziana long ago, but she has become a part of us, a part of who we are. When she dies, she will take so much with her," he said. His voice faded to a whisper. "So much."

Calista was saved from having to answer by the door opening once again. This time Rhys emerged, closely followed by his sister. Rhys's expression revealed nothing.

"She is asleep," he said.

His words were directed to Powdran, not to her. Calista felt the chill of exclusion even as she rose to her feet. Hurt, she turned to offer her hand to Powdran, but the old man was already up.

"It is best so," Powdran said. "She will wake refreshed and with more energy to share what time remains with you."

Calista saw pain flare in Rhys's eyes, but even as she instinctively reached to touch him, to offer him comfort, his brief flash of emotion was gone, hidden behind the invisible barrier he had erected between them. He turned from her, pointedly ignoring her outstretched hand.

"I'll go see Marlott. I doubt there is anything I can do, but—" Rhys's words trailed off. He shrugged, his expression grim, then turned and strode toward the square where they'd arrived.

Calista stood silently, watching him walk away and fighting to ignore the hurt trembling inside her. So much for good intentions and human compassion. A gentle touch on her arm roused her.

"I'm sorry you were left out here, alone in the heat," Glynna said. Her features, so like Rhys's despite their more feminine cast, were softened by an expression of worried apology. "I wasn't thinking, I guess. It's been so difficult and—"

"That's quite all right. I didn't mind waiting."

Unlike her brother's, Glynna's smile was sweet, without any trace of his frequent mockery. "You're kind, but not a very good liar."

Calista couldn't stop the brittle laugh that rose to her lips. "No one's ever accused me of that before."

"Then come. Powdran will watch Mother while she sleeps and I will take you to the eating hall. It's cool there. We can get something to drink, then we can talk."

Glynna obviously didn't stop to consider that Calista or Powdran might have other plans. She gave the old man a quick kiss on the cheek, then started up the street in the direction Rhys had gone. Despite her obvious physical and emotional weariness, she walked quickly, with the firm stride of someone who knows exactly what they're going to do next.

Calista had to hurry to catch up with her. A sudden eagerness to be with Glynna, to get to know her, caught Calista by surprise. She found herself wondering what the younger woman thought of her and her working with Rhys.

At the same time, she felt strangely shy, as though she were forcing her way in where she was neither wanted nor needed. "You don't have to put yourself out. I'm quite all right. Really. I can—"

"It won't matter. For a little bit, anyway." Glynna glanced at her, then just as quickly looked away. "These past few days, with Mother weakening so rapidly—" She shook her head sharply. Her straight, shoulder-length black hair swung back and forth with the motion, rustling on the slick fabric of her jumpsuit. "An iced fruit drink would be good, I think."

Glynna said nothing more and Calista made no effort to ask any questions, contenting herself with quick glances out of the corner of her eye as she tried to trace the points of resemblance between this woman she'd just met and the man who, only a few days earlier, she'd thought she knew so well.

Once, Glynna caught her surreptitious glance and threw her a brief, understanding smile. Calista couldn't help smiling in response, touched by the unexpected hint of acceptance.

The eating hall proved to be a massive, brick-walled building without windows set at the far edge of the square. As they pushed through the second set of protective doors, a rush of cool air greeted them, flowing past into the warmer air beyond and bringing with it the smell of damp, fertile earth and the murmur of voices in conversation.

Calista stopped short just inside the entrance, stunned by the verdant jungle before her. Masses of trees and shrubs of all kinds filled the space, transforming it into a haven of green. Two stories overhead, skylights filtered the harsh sunlight, illuminating the area. Quarried stone served both as floor and as path through the lush verdure, leading the visitor into sheltered nooks holding small stone tables and wooden chairs. With the luxuriant foliage blocking her view, Calista couldn't tell how many of the tables were occupied.

Calista breathed deep, savoring the sweet, flower-scented air and the sound of water lazily dripping over stone somewhere in the background.

"We can get a drink over here," Glynna said, leading Calista toward a service area half-hidden by plants at the far side of the room.

Following Glynna's lead, Calista chose a tall glass from a rack, then filled it to the brim with ice and a pinkish-colored liquid from a pitcher. When she refused the offer of something to eat, Glynna led her to a small table with four chairs nestled among towering masses of flowers, bushes, and low-growing trees. The few people they passed glanced up curiously, but made no effort to speak or to detain them.

"We won't be disturbed here," Glynna said, settling into her chair. She glanced about them, as if to assure herself of the truth of her words, then met Calista's questioning gaze with an even more direct one of her own.

Oddly, Calista felt no resentment at the assessment. With anyone else, she would have bristled immediately under the force of such a steady, questioning gaze. Something about this woman deflected anger, as if she had a natural right to judge that could not be disputed. Or perhaps it was the real and very human . . . understanding . . . that seemed to emanate from her.

Whatever it was, Calista found herself liking Glynna

and irrationally hoping that she measured up to whatever standards Glynna was judging her by.

At last Glynna's gaze dropped to the drink she held. As if deep in thought, she dragged the tip of one finger along the condensation on the side of the glass, marking a strip of dark against the moisture. She rubbed the tip of her finger with the pad of her thumb, seemingly concentrating on the icy dampness. Then her head came up and her dark eyes, so like Rhys's, met Calista's.

"Tell me," Glynna said, "are you in love with my brother?"

Chapter Eleven

"What?" The single word was more a squawk than articulate speech. Calista could only be grateful she hadn't been trying to drink. She would have choked.

"I said, are you in love with my brother?"

Calista took a quick breath to counteract the sudden shortage of oxygen. "That's what I thought you said."

"Are you?" Glynna wasn't backing off.

Hedge, Calista thought. That's what she'd do if she were negotiating a trade deal. Or lie if she had to. But she wasn't negotiating, and neither was Glynna. A direct question hung in the air between them; it demanded a direct answer.

Calista hedged. "Why do you ask that?"

"I want to know." Glynna, it appeared, didn't believe in hedging.

"We've worked together pretty well. Rhys is very good at his work."

"I didn't ask that."

Calista's grip tightened on the glass she held. The question—and Glynna's insistence on an answer—made her distinctly uncomfortable. "We're partners, that's all. And we're not going to be that for much longer."

Glynna's mouth dropped. "Not going to be partners? What happened? I thought—"

"Differences of opinion," Calista muttered. How much did Glynna know? What had Rhys told her about their working relationship? And why did it matter anyway? Calista asked herself, retreating into anger rather than face the pain the truth brought with it.

After all, she thought wildly, no one had offered to explain anything to her. Not about this Hall, not about the village, not about anything. Rhys had never even mentioned Glynna's existence. What made Glynna think she had the right to ask such questions now? Anger rose in Calista, a welcome alternative to the dangerous emotions Glynna's original question had roused.

"I'm sorry." Glynna grimaced. "Friends tell me I'm often rude, but I don't mean to be." The words carried a sincere note of apology. "It's just that . . . well, I worry about Rhys," Glynna added. "With all his responsibilities, the demands he puts on himself . . . Oh, I know how he can be. Sarcastic. Smiling, but in a way that makes you want to hit him. Laughing as if nothing mattered." Glynna met Calista's gaze directly, pleading for understanding. "That's not the way he is, you know. Not really."

No, she didn't, Calista wanted to say, but right now she wasn't sure who it was she *had* known. She was familiar with the mocking devil Glynna described. She knew the passionate lover, the shrewd trader, the arrogant, hardheaded male who had to have things his way, always. Never once had she glimpsed the serious, dedicated man these people seemed to know.

So where was the real Rhys Fairdane in all of this?

Calista felt cast adrift on a sea of confusing emotions, battered first by one tide, then another. Because she wasn't sure what to say, Calista chose to say nothing. Instead, she took a sip of the tangy juice Glynna had poured for her—and waited. Her hand trembled, ever so slightly, and the muscles of her shoulders ached with tension.

The silence stretched until Glynna gave up expecting a response and changed the topic.

"I imagine this Hall was a surprise for you," she said, indicating the artificial forest that surrounded them.

Calista nodded, grateful for the diversion. She struggled to keep her voice level and unemotional. "You might say that. I don't think anyone expects to find a jungle in the middle of a brick building."

"It's our way of keeping the memory of home alive," Glynna said, tugging on one huge, dark green leaf, making the intertwined branches, leaves, and vines rustle softly. "Many of these plants are native to Ziana, our home world. A number of us chose to bring seeds and roots and cuttings from our gardens rather than more practical items."

"Why did you leave? And why would you choose a desert world like this to settle on?" Calista gratefully grabbed at the opportunity to drag the conversation away from Rhys to less emotionally taxing but no less intriguing questions.

Glynna's face darkened. "We had no choice." She released the leaf. Freed of the tension, its thick, springy stem snapped back into place, sending rustling tremors through the foliage. "When the Imperial

Armed Forces discovered Ziana contained immense deposits of targanite, the metal that makes the hulls of their spaceships virtually impregnable, there was no talk of rights. We were simply deported."

"A whole world?" Calista tried to imagine transporting the population of an entire world. The undertaking must have been enormous.

"Yes. There weren't that many of us. A little over three million," Glynna added hastily. "We were an agricultural colony. Three or four generations isn't much, but it was enough for us to consider ourselves as one people, not just settlers. That's why we decided to find another world where we could rebuild our society, as well as our farms."

"You didn't get resettlement rights?" Calista asked, surprised.

"Sure we did. A village here, a town there. Whatever anyone else had abandoned, we got." Bitterness gave Glynna's words a harsh sting. She pointed to the skylight and the planet's fierce, bright sun beyond. "We got this. An agricultural outpost the first settlers abandoned thirty years before we arrived. And this was one of the more desirable spots."

Calista studied the younger woman's angry face, then the artificial jungle surrounding them. She'd always known it wasn't necessary to be a slave to be at someone else's mercy—all it took was power on one side and an inability to fight back on the other. "What will you do if you can't find a suitable world, Glynna? What will your people do?"

Glynna's eyes glittered with the same dark, angry fires Calista had seen in her brother's. "We have to find a world. We *have* to."

She roughly shoved back from the table and stood up. "I'd better get back."

*　　*　　*

By the time they reached the Fairdane house, Glynna's flare of anger had abated. When Calista paused uncertainly on the doorstep, she said, "Come. It's cooler in here and far more comfortable, even if we can't offer the amenities of the Hall."

The outer door opened directly into a central room that served as living area, work space, and garden, all in one. As in the Hall, plants of every description divided the areas and partially hid the four doors that led to what Calista assumed must be sleeping chambers and bath.

Without speaking, Glynna slipped through the left-hand door and quietly closed it behind her, leaving Calista alone.

Restless, uncertain what to do next, Calista stood where Glynna had left her. Though she didn't like admitting it, the younger woman's revelations had touched her deeply, reminding her of the vague dreams of belonging somewhere, of being a part of something bigger than herself, that had so tempted and tormented her as a child.

Calista had forgotten those dreams. Until now, they'd been buried under the more compelling dream of freedom that had driven her for so long. Strange that Glynna's few, simple words could have brought those earlier, deeper longings back so easily.

It would have been better if she hadn't remembered. There was no sense wanting something you could never, ever have. Calista forced her awareness back to the present. Concentrate on the now, on what's real, she told herself firmly. It was always safer that way.

Careful to keep her distance from the door through which Glynna had gone, she began to explore the room around her. As in the Hall, chairs and tables were clustered in whatever space wasn't taken up by greenery. What looked like handwoven fabrics in shades of blue and green covered the chairs, as if the multitude of plants and the tiny fountain half-hidden in the shrubbery weren't enough to maintain the illusion of the lush, green world they'd lost.

There was no sign of a central computer and no luxury. Just simple comfort and an obvious effort to make this place of exile as much as possible like the home they'd once known. Thoughtfully, Calista trailed her fingers along the stone of one planter, then brushed against the densely packed leaves. Her action stirred a faint, sweet scent from the delicate blue flowers clustered on one heavy limb and showered petals on the floor around her.

Hastily, Calista gathered the fallen petals, unwilling to mar the orderliness of the room through her careless gesture. The petals were soft and silken, temptingly sensual. Piled in her hand like this, they emitted an even headier fragrance.

Calista brought the petals to her nose and inhaled, reveling in the rich, sweet scent, then brushed them across her cheek before letting them filter through her fingers onto the damp soil.

"Aasanith. Dorana's favorite flower."

The softly spoken words startled Calista. Hastily, almost guiltily, she brushed off the few petals that still clung to her skin. "Rhys. I . . . I didn't hear you come in."

He stood just inside the door to the street, oddly tense despite the weariness dragging at him. His eyes fixed on her warily, as if he were uncertain of her reaction to his presence.

How long, Calista wondered, had he been watching her?

"Mother—?"

"Still sleeping, I think. Glynna went in a few minutes ago."

Rhys glanced at the door to his mother's room, then looked away and fixed his attention on the flowers he'd called aasanith.

"You're tired," she said, struggling to keep her voice neutral. "Come sit down." Calista gestured to a chair beside her, uncertain whether he would accept her invitation or not.

He hesitated, but only for a moment. She pulled a stool forward for herself, close enough to indicate her willingness to accept a truce, but not too close. Once seated, however, Calista had no idea what to say next. Rhys didn't help. He just slumped in the chair and stared at the floor, a vague, abstracted expression on his face.

An unaccustomed protectiveness rose within her. He looked so tired. What could she offer, Calista wondered, that would comfort him? She wanted to take him in her arms, to pillow his head upon her breast and let him rest. She wanted to find the right words to say, wanted to do the right things, but she'd spent far too many years alone. She didn't know what to do or say.

Uncomfortable with the silence, she began to run her finger along the edge of the planter, tracing the uneven surface of the stone and the scarcely visible veins of lighter colored minerals trapped within the darker mass of rock.

"She brought it with her when we were driven from Ziana," Rhys said unexpectedly, very low.

Calista looked up, startled, to find his gaze fixed on the blossoms of aasanith.

"At first, she would save part of her own water ration in order to keep it alive." He tentatively touched a cluster of flowers, generating another shower of petals

189

that cascaded across the leaves below and onto his hand and Calista's.

Rhys froze, as if transfixed by the sight of the fallen petals. When Calista didn't shake off them off, he reached over and, with the tip of his finger, gently brushed a petal from her thumb.

Calista couldn't prevent her sudden intake of breath or the electric awareness that thrilled through her hand and up her arm at the contact, but she made no move to pull away as he flicked at another petal, then another.

Slowly, he moved up her thumb to her wrist, then back down across her hand and along the length of her first finger, brushing off each petal, one at a time.

Calista trembled. Her hand quivered and she could feel the heat of his skin against hers, yet still Rhys continued, his brows knit in concentration on the task he had set himself.

Flick, flick, until only one petal remained, caught in the vee of skin between her third and fourth fingers. Rhys paused. His gaze never wavered from that last small scrap of blue. Slowly, ever so slowly, he ran his finger along the inside of her third finger, up the narrowing gap between the third and fourth until he brushed against both. He scarcely touched her, yet as he reached the last petal, then brushed it away, Calista gasped.

Rhys stared at his hand as though seeing it for the first time. His fingers curled into his palm, forming a fist. He took a deep breath, held it a moment, then released it and brought his eyes up to meet hers.

Though he was looking directly at her, Calista couldn't read the emotions hidden within those black depths. Deliberately she drew her still-trembling hand into her lap, too shaken and uncertain to speak.

"You should return to the *Fair Trade*," Rhys said.

His voice was rough, slightly ragged around the edges. "Take it to Karta, deliver the equipment. You can send it back here on automatic pilot when you're done."

Before Calista could think of a word to say, the door to Dorana Fairdane's room opened and Glynna emerged.

"Mother's sleeping again. She was restless and Powdran gave her a draft of something that helped her relax." Glynna was halfway across the room before she noticed Rhys. A tired smile lit her face. "I didn't hear you come in."

Rhys straightened. He inhaled deeply, then let the breath out in an unsteady sigh. His hand uncurled slowly, as if forced. He pulled a chair forward for his sister. "I didn't want to disturb you. Are you all right?"

"Yes. Just tired." Glynna stretched, easing the muscles of her back, then dropped into the chair. "How did the meeting with Marlott go? I hope he didn't dump all his problems on you at one go."

Rhys shrugged, but the lines around his mouth deepened. "He told me about the fire in the settlement on Salaca Minor. He said the place is a total ruin, that they've nowhere else to move everyone."

"That's right." Glynna frowned. "We heard about it a week ago. From all accounts, there's not much we can do but provide temporary shelter and food until we know more."

"And Tellus failed to win the right of colonization on Tettrel III."

"Rhys—"

"Marlott also said the condensers are failing here. That you need major replacements before the plantations are affected. And he said the subspace communication system is almost useless now."

Glynna's frown deepened with obvious displeasure. "He didn't need to tell you—"

Rhys angrily waved aside the objection. "Who else was he going to tell? There's no one here that can help. They're all tied up with just getting by from day to day."

"There's no one anywhere that can solve all those problems! We'll cope, just as we always have. The people on Salaca Minor will cope. Tellus will cope, and he'll keep on coping."

Glynna's voice rose on a note of protective fierceness that took Calista by surprise. She'd never thought of Rhys as anyone needing protection, but obviously his sister did.

"Why do you always have to take on the burdens for the whole world, Rhys? Why can't you set aside everyone's problems, just for a while, and worry about your own for a change?"

Rhys flushed and a muscle at the corner of his mouth twitched. His eyes dropped from his sister's sparking gaze. "You're right. I should have been here sooner. I came as quickly as I could but—"

"That's not what I'm talking about." Glynna leaned forward to wrap her hand around his wrist. "I'm talking about *you*."

Rhys's head came up. Calista could see the confusion in his face. Clearly, he hadn't the slightest idea what his sister was talking about. For that matter, neither did she.

Glynna's gaze swung to her. A question shone in those dark eyes but Calista lacked even a faint clue that would allow her to decipher it. Uncertain, she glanced at Rhys, looking for an explanation. There was none. He simply sat and stared at his sister, too taken aback by her attack to respond.

"You don't even know what I'm talking about, do

you?" Glynna demanded, her attention once more fixed on her brother. She studied the strained, puzzled expression on his face, then sighed and leaned back in her chair. "You haven't the slightest idea. You never have."

"If there's something I should have done, something—" Self-blame sounded clearly in his voice. Rhys's frown deepened. "You should have let me know sooner. I'd have come. You know I would have come."

"I know. You always have." Glynna's features, so delicate, yet so like her brother's, softened as she met Rhys's worried glance. "I imagine you always will, whatever the cost."

Glynna bent forward once more and gathered Rhys's right hand in both her own. "Don't blame yourself for Mother, Rhys. You've done your best, but no one, not even you, could have brought back Father or the world we lost. No one."

"We can get help somewhere else. Give me time to return to Karta, get some of the silk . . . The settlement needs her, Glynna. Our *people* need her." Rhys's voice vibrated with the intensity of his emotions.

Glynna shook her head sadly. "You've always looked ahead, Rhys, given all your energies to the future. I don't think you ever understood how little Dorana cared about that future. No matter how hard she worked to make this settlement home for us, she never really looked forward. She only looked back." Glynna paused, biting her lips to control the quaver that had begun to creep into her voice.

"Glynna—"

"She's tired, Rhys. Can you understand that? As much as it grieves me to lose her, I won't begrudge her dying. She's earned her peace. Blaming yourself for not being here, for not doing this or that or whatever—that won't keep her here. Nothing will. Not now."

Before Rhys could respond, Glynna turned her attention to Calista. "You'll stay, won't you? Here on the planet, with us, not on the ship. For a few days, just until—"

Calista found herself nodding before she could even question the wisdom of her acquiescence. She'd intended nothing of the sort, but she would stay. She couldn't refuse, not with Glynna watching her so intently.

But what did Rhys think of his sister's invitation? Did *he* want her to stay? Calista studied him, looking for some hint of his reaction. She wasn't sure what she hoped to see, what she wanted him to say. She wasn't sure what she'd do if he told her to leave.

His expression gave nothing away.

Glynna hadn't missed Calista's silent query or Rhys's lack of response, but she didn't say anything, just pursed her lips thoughtfully, then rose to her feet.

"I'm tired. I'm going to lie down for a little bit. Powdran needs to rest, as well. He's been helping me care for Mother ever since she fell ill—and he's older than she is."

A wry smile softened her expression and she gently brushed a hand over Rhys's long, dark hair. "I'd tell you to rest, too, big brother. But you never listen to me, do you?"

The stars shone brilliantly silver in the night sky, a radiant carpet for the heavens above him. Rhys had often thought those distant pricks of light the most beautiful thing about this stark, harsh planet to which his people had been brought.

Despite the weariness dragging at him, he'd been unable to sleep and so had walked out to this barren ridge at the far edge of the village. The ridge, and especially this rough outcropping of rock on which he sat, had come to be his favorite refuge whenever he was on the planet and needed to escape the myriad demands that inevitably threatened to swamp him. With the village asleep below and nothing to break the vast sweep and silence of night except the stars and the mournful wind, he could find peace, at least for a little while.

Tonight that peace, like sleep, eluded him.

It wasn't Dorana's dying that troubled him so much. Glynna had been right—there was nothing he could do to change the past, and nothing that would give his mother back the will to live that she had lost so long ago. He would mourn her, and he would go on, regardless.

What bothered him was the deep, aching uncertainty that assailed him whenever he thought of Calista.

Why had she come with him? What did she think, now that she knew he'd kept so much from her for so long? Did she understand why he'd done what he had, or did she resent the secrets more?

Would she take the *Fair Trade* back to Karta as he'd suggested, or would she stay? He didn't want her here, not when even knowing she was close could distract him from the almost overwhelming problems he'd have to deal with in the days ahead. He didn't want her, but he needed her. Badly.

Her fire, passion and invincible spirit gave him courage. She was the only one besides Glynna and his mother who didn't depend on him, who didn't look to him for advice and guidance and the solution to their problems.

Whatever it was in her past that had made Calista so fiercely independent, she was the only person he'd ever met who had always known exactly what she wanted and how she was going to get it. She was the only one who never faltered, never doubted, and never looked back.

With all that lay ahead of him, he could use some of her courage now.

Yet though he needed her, Calista might now be the single greatest obstacle between him and his goal. Whatever it was that drove her to react so violently, almost irrationally, to what she'd found on Karta, it threatened everything he'd worked for, everything he'd dreamed of for so long.

A dull, hot, heavy anger coursed through him at the thought. The anger burned, but it didn't stop him from wanting her . . . and that angered him most of all.

Calista hated having nothing to do.

She'd swept the floor, dusted the shutters, straightened the chairs and tables, watered the plants. The floor gleamed; the shutters let in more light; the chairs and tables looked uncomfortably stiff and formal. Whether the plants would survive being drowned was up to them.

She hated housekeeping. That's what robots were for, and there wasn't a robot in the entire house.

She'd spent the night on a small cot set up in the main room. She hadn't slept well, caught between her own confused thoughts and the half-dozen interruptions when Glynna had gotten up to check on Dorana and Rhys, who had chosen to sleep on a pallet thrown on the floor in his mother's room.

They'd all risen early. Calista hadn't needed more than one quick glance to know that neither Rhys nor Glynna had slept any better than she had.

While Rhys sat with his mother, she'd joined Glynna

for a simple breakfast of fruit and bread in the Hall. Neither had said much.

Rhys left shortly after they'd returned, headed for another meeting with the village leaders. With Glynna tending to her mother, there'd been nothing for Calista to do except the simple housekeeping chores that had obviously been neglected for the past few days. She was grateful to have even that much to keep her occupied. Any physical activity was preferable to being free to think about all the tangled emotions, doubts, and insecurities that tugged her first one way, then another.

Now the house was done, however, Calista was growing restless. She tried pacing and soon grew tired of the limited space. She tried studying the files on the antiquated computer she'd found half-buried under plants in a corner of the room, but she wasn't in the mood for agricultural analyses or economic reports when there was no benefit to be had from the information. Not that she'd ever enjoyed reading those sorts of things, anyway.

That left her with absolutely nothing to do but escape and hope she found something—anything— outside that might occupy her time for the next few hours. At least she would be free for a short time of the emotions that pressed so hard around her in the Fairdane house.

As before, the street outside lay empty, deserted even by its inhabitants. Heat and light enveloped her, drawing the air from her lungs and making her squint against the brightness.

Calista stopped where the lane opened onto the square, trying to decide where she should go, what she could do next. She could always try the Hall, but she wasn't hungry and exploring an artificial garden wasn't exactly her idea of a fun time. Maybe she should have taken more of an interest in botany when she'd had the chance.

Four or five buildings had enough traffic in and out their doors, relatively speaking, to promise something of interest. Calista decided to try the building on her right, for the arguably justifiable reason that it was the closest.

No luck. It only required one quick glance in the door at the banks of comp stations to realize she'd found the local data bank. Useful only if she'd wanted to research anything, which she didn't.

Calista couldn't figure out what the next building was, but it didn't matter. It didn't look any more interesting than the first.

The ancient saying of third time to charm seemed to hold true, however. She was five feet inside the door when she spotted one of the few faces she could recognize: Marlott.

He seemed as pleased to see her as she was surprised to find him. Abandoning the two women with whom he'd been talking, he crossed to her, a smile of welcome on his face.

"You are Calista York, are you not?" he asked, staring up at her curiously.

"That's right." Not knowing his title, Calista decided to avoid the risk of offending by not using any name at all. "I had some time free and thought I'd come exploring."

"Good. Good." The old man nodded in approval, but the smile quickly disappeared from his face. "It is well that you come to know us. Perhaps, with your skills and Rhys Fairdane's experience—" He shook his head abruptly, back and forth in short little swings as if shaking off a bad idea. "No, no, I go too fast," he apologized.

Before Calista had time to think of any rational

response to that, he added, "I am headed out to the plantations. Would you care to accompany me?"

Calista's mind boggled trying to imagine what a plantation on this dry world would look like. "Thank you. I'd like that."

"Good. I have a buggy at the back, if you'd care to follow me—" Marlott didn't wait for a response, just led the way to a back door and a two-passenger, six-wheeled vehicle unlike anything Calista had ever seen.

Following Marlott's lead, she climbed in and strapped a safety belt around her hips, then helped fasten down the protective cloth and plastiglass covering.

"Why don't you use hoverers?" she asked. "Wouldn't they be more efficient?" And more comfortable, she added silently as they started off with a neck-snapping jerk and a bounce.

"Too expensive. These were left by the first settlers, just like the houses and the communication system and the plantations." Marlott had to shout over the grinding of the vehicle's gears and the whine of its fat tires on the baked dirt road. "Hoverers would have to be shipped in, then we'd have to buy replacement parts, fuel cells. Not practical."

"Surely a generator could produce what you need."

"That's not practical, either."

Calista couldn't help staring in surprise. No generator to produce the routine articles of clothing, spare parts, and whatnot that were needed by the villagers? Everyone with the level of technology these people surely possessed used generators, even if they were the less efficient models that relied on solar energy for their operation. "You don't use solar power?" She ducked her head so she could peer out the filtered plastiglass at the huge golden ball that hung in the sky, baking both color and life out of everything around them.

"Dust storms," Marlott shouted in explanation. "Sometimes they go on for days. We can't afford to waste the energy we need for our operations on running a generator, no matter how much we'd like to."

Marlott swerved the vehicle around a couple of gaping potholes. "Everything's falling apart here," he added apologetically. "With a substantial investment in equipment and improvements, this could be a reasonably profitable settlement. But we don't belong here, any more than the first settlers did. We don't *want* to be here. Never have. The Imperial Army put us here and we'll stay here until we find a decent home, but we won't stay a minute longer than we have to. In the meantime, we save every credit we can and invest as little as possible in our operations here."

Before Calista could think of a response, they dropped over a low ridge and her attention was captured by what looked like a vast array of huge, plasti-glass houses spread across several square kilometers of desert before them. The only trouble was, the houses were no more than a meter or two high, far too short for any human habitation.

Marlott took an abrupt turn to the right onto a wide ramp that led down between two mud-plastered walls to a set of double doors the same baked dust color as the earth around them.

Chapter Twelve

At their approach, a smaller door set in the main bay on the right side swung up to let them pass. As they jounced through the narrow opening, Calista realized Marlott and his people hadn't been quite as crazy for keeping these clumsy vehicles as she'd thought. The door was the exact size needed to let the vehicle through, and not a meter bigger. A hoverer would either have had to be parked outside, at risk of the dust storms Marlott had mentioned, or they would have had to rebuild the doors. Bigger doors would have meant more loss of the humidity inside.

And humid it was. Calista couldn't help gaping at the immense rows of green, growing plants that stretched before her. The plantation was nothing more than a huge greenhouse!

Marlott chuckled at her obvious amazement. "Not what you'd expect in the middle of this dry country, is it?" he asked, slowly driving up a narrow lane that ran through the middle of the rows of plants. "The first settlers here, almost sixty years ago, planned to establish a vast system of protected farms that could provide real food to a dozen nearby worlds."

"Cassala fruit," he said, gesturing to a section of waist-high plants covered with clusters of a pinkish-gray pods. "That's kahnish, a vegetable favored by the people on Theok II, not far from here. I don't much care for it, myself, but it brings us excellent profits. Kahnish is very hard to grow and the conditions here are ideal."

"I can't believe it. A farm? Here?"

Marlott grinned, clearly pleased that he'd managed to confound her. "The soil here is high in the minerals needed for good crops. The original settlers had the right idea. Go into farming in a big way, produce everything that's relatively scarce and highly prized on the neighboring worlds and produce it better and cheaper than they can. They got a good market established, started seeing a real demand for their product. The trouble was, they just weren't farmers. They hadn't realized what hard work it is and they grew discouraged, then gave up and abandoned the settlement to the Imperial government."

Marlott pulled into a small, clear space at the side and shut off the buggy. He gestured to the rows of carefully tended plants, his expression suddenly grim. "The government no doubt thought they were doing us a favor by dropping this great opportunity in our laps. They didn't know how much work it was, either. Or maybe they didn't care."

He sighed. "Anyway, this is where they brought us— some of us, at least—when they forcibly removed us from Ziana. Unfortunately, the settlement was pretty badly run down. We refurbished the village and houses, such as they are, replanted the plantations with the root and seed stock the Army so 'generously' gave us, and then we set up our trade markets. It isn't much, but it is a place to live."

Marlott drooped in his seat. "I'm getting old," he said, his voice pitched very low. "I'm not sure anymore that I'll ever see our people on a world of their own. It's what I dream of, what I pray for, but I don't think I'll ever see it." His voice trailed off.

"Why don't you turn your efforts to making this one work?" Calista asked. She let her gaze sweep over the rows and rows of vegetables and fruit that stretched around them. "You've done well here so far. The worlds near you are all wealthy enough to afford the cost of fresh food, rather than settling for generator-produced food. You wouldn't become wealthy, but you'd earn enough to be able to invest in something else, maybe even to begin reforming the climate of the planet itself."

The old man sighed. "We don't own the planet. All we have are settlement rights on this continent. That means we could be kicked out tomorrow if the Imperial government chose, just as we were kicked off Ziana." He shook his head gloomily. "Besides, what we do have rights to can't support all three million of us. It doesn't have enough water. Too many of our resources would have to be funneled into making food for us to eat, instead of for selling."

"Then one of your other settlements—"

"Different situations, same basic problems. No, we need our own world, one we can't be kicked off of whenever someone has the whim."

Calista thought of the years she'd spent as a slave, never knowing what to expect from one day to the next because so much depended on the whims of others. She remembered the anger that fact had so often generated in her, and the sense of utter helplessness. "I can understand that," she remarked, her voice strangely tight.

"Our seekers are trying. Rhys has helped arrange for settlement rights on two new planets, but no one has found a suitable world that we can claim." Marlott glanced over at her, a wry, sad smile on his face. "Good, green, rich worlds are almost always claimed by those who find them, and we haven't found any."

"What happens if you never do?" Calista asked softly. She knew what it was to long for something that was always just out of reach. Even if she could not understand their passion for the land, she could understand the dream that drove Rhys's people as her dream drove her.

"I don't know," Marlott said softly, his eyes fixed, unseeing, on the green fields in front of him. "I don't know."

Shaking off the somber mood, he put the buggy back in gear and carefully pulled back into the center path. Calista joined Marlott in his consultations with two managers and an inspection of the work of a four-person crew engaged in extending the buried irrigation system, but she kept silent, not asking questions and content to observe.

It was only as they were leaving that Marlott returned to their previous conversation. Waving his hand at the flat, dry landscape around them, he said, "Dorana always claimed we should look for a world that was like this. Not so desirable, but workable. One we could build and change to suit our needs. We never even found one of those."

Calista looked out at the hot, barren land, wondering what it would be like to face it, year after year. Such a life would, she thought, be frighteningly close to a kind of slavery.

"I took her place on the Council, you know," Marlott

said abruptly. "Dorana's place, I mean."

"It's an elected position among all our settlements," he added when Calista said nothing. "I'm honored, of course, but it will be very difficult to fill her shoes. The people trusted her because she always put their interests first. She could get opposing factions to work together better than anyone else ever could." He fell silent for a moment. "She served for so long— over forty years—it's hard to imagine her not being there."

"Forty years *is* a long time," Calista murmured politely.

"She came to Ziana as Jovane's bride. It was an arranged marriage, but that didn't matter. For them, it was a case of love at first sight. I'd never believed in that old superstition, but it was true for them." Marlott sighed reminiscently. "Eventually she served on the Council in her own right. She was almost forty when she had Rhys and Glynna. Wanted both of them to serve on the Council, too. Glynna may, someday. Rhys never will. He was always too independent, even as a boy. What he does now is more important, anyway."

The old man glanced at Calista. "You probably think we expect too much of him, that I was unfair to share all our problems so soon after he came back, but I had to," Marlott said defensively. "With his contacts, his freedom of movement, he can do things we can't."

Calista suddenly thought of all the hours Rhys spent on the bridge when they were onboard ship, all the coded communications he sent flying in every direction. And she'd suspected he was trying to work up private deals on the side!

"What happened to Rhys's father, Jovane?" she asked.

"He died in the fighting on Ziana. It was foolish, but we tried to resist the Army when they first attempted to move in." Marlott's round face sagged with remembered pain. "It took less than a week for them to slaughter our fighters, round us up, and force those who survived into transport ships."

The old man's hands tightened on the buggy's steering handles. "They took our past from us," he said grimly. "They can't take the future."

Calista was still thinking about those words long after Marlott dropped her off at the entrance to Dorana Fairdane's house.

Glynna was waiting for her. "I'm glad you're back," she said. "Mother has been asking to see you."

Before Calista could object, Glynna thrust her into Dorana Fairdane's room, then quietly closed the door behind her.

The only illumination in the room came from sunlight seeping through the slatted shutters and casting bars of pale gold across the stone floor. A high, narrow bed stood in the far corner, pushed close against the wall. It took a moment before Calista could discern the frail, gray figure under the light coverlet. Even the long, white strands of Dorana Fairdane's hair strewn across the pillow disappeared against the white of the bedclothes.

When the silence became unbearable, Calista spoke. "Glynna said you wanted to see me."

The pale face shifted on the pillow. "Come closer. It's so dim in here, but the light hurts my eyes—" The words were scarcely a whisper.

Calista took the chair indicated, conscious of an intense scrutiny from the woman in the bed.

"You are Calista York, my son's trading partner." Though the voice was still weak, there was steel in the words and an uncompromising glitter in the faded brown eyes that watched her so steadily in the dim light.

"I am."

"You resent me, resent my dying and distracting Rhys." ·

"I—" The denial died before Calista could say it. Dorana was right. She'd never realized it before, but some small part of her soul *did* resent the claims these people so rightfully held on Rhys's time and emotions.

"You did not know of me, or Glynna."

"No."

"Do we seem a threat to you?"

The question hit with illuminating intensity. That was part of the problem, Calista realized, startled. She'd been on her own so long, she'd come to see others only in terms of how they fit in her life. She'd even expected her relationship with Rhys to fit in the comfortable little niche she'd made for it. Not once had she considered that he would have other plans, other loyalties that claimed his attention first.

Dorana shifted on the pillow so she could look directly at Calista. Even that slight movement cost her an effort, but the small smile she gave Calista was filled with understanding.

"I felt that way when I first arrived on Ziana as Jovane's bride," she said softly. "It's not easy sharing when you've never had to."

Calista stared at the dying woman, too shaken by the unexpected insights into her own feelings to know how to respond.

Dorana sighed. "You don't want do be here now, do you?"

The woman was a witch, a mind reader, Calista thought wildly. She'd expected an inquiry into her relationship with Rhys, perhaps a plea that she take care of him or love him or keep him happy. She wasn't prepared for these harsh, unsentimental questions spoken in the wavery voice of a dying woman.

The answer was hard to get out. "No, I don't want to be here," Calista said.

"Ah." Dorana's head shifted ever so slightly on the pillow, then her eyelids slid shut.

Calista wasn't sure, but she thought Dorana had nodded—in understanding, perhaps, or agreement. She sat still, waiting.

After a few moments, Dorana, without opening her eyes, said very faintly, "I have never liked this world we have been forced to live on. I will not be sorry to leave it."

She paused, then opened her eyes and stared directly at Calista. "Do you have a home?"

"A home?" Another question Calista hadn't expected.

"A world where you belong. People. A family."

Calista thought of the slave quarters on Andrus, of the dirty streets and the squalid inns on a dozen worlds where she'd slept until she'd won her first small ship. She thought of the *Independence*. "No. No home."

"Do you want one?"

Calista's eyebrows rose. A home? She considered the question. "No." Her freedom would be enough. She'd decided that long ago.

Dorana nodded slightly, the movement scarcely perceptible. "You are wise."

Something, perhaps the presumption of the questions, irritated Calista, but she shoved down her annoyance. The woman was dying, after all.

"My questions make you angry," Dorana said. "You resent them, but since I am dying you think you will not protest. Am I right?"

She'd had years of practice in dealing with unexpected questions, but this one made Calista stare.

Dorana's gaze didn't waver. Calista couldn't help grinning. "You're right."

Dorana chuckled, a dry, wheezing cackle that left her gasping for air, but when Calista moved to help her, she waved her away. "No," she said, then, when she'd recovered her breath, she added, "Laughter is worth any price."

"Even now?"

"Especially now." Dorana sank back in the pillows and closed her eyes, gathering her dwindling strength. "Especially now," she whispered, as if to herself.

While she waited for the old woman to recover, Calista studied the face on the pillow curiously, trying to trace the features the mother had bequeathed to her son and daughter. There, obscured by age and pain, were the same straight brows, the same high cheekbones and finely shaped chin. But Dorana's nose was less aquiline, her jaw less strongly sculpted, and though her eyes must once have gleamed with the same dark intensity as her children's, they were now half-hidden by the heavy, drooping lids.

Strange how a man and a woman could create a child of their own bodies who was a part of them and yet so different. Calista found herself wondering what her mother and father had looked like, what kind of people they'd been. She had no memory of anyone who had cared for her more than they'd cared for any other child in the crowded slave quarters, no one to whom she'd mattered more than any one else.

For the first time, the thought brought neither pain nor anger. Dorana Fairdane, Calista decided, would probably disapprove of such sentiments.

As if to confirm that thought, Dorana stirred, then opened her eyes. With her pale, skeletal hands—hands that must once have been very beautiful—she twitched feebly at her covers.

"Rhys will not rest until he has found a world for us," she said, as though Calista had tried to argue with her. "He will let nothing stop him. Glynna is the same. They both remember the invasion of Ziana. They remember the fear and the anger and the threats." Dorana sighed. "We made a lot of threats. None of them made any difference."

"And now?"

"Now?" The old woman seemed to consider the thought. "Now I am dying because I am tired of living on this world of dry sand and hot sun. I was a stranger to Ziana, but I learned to love it." She sighed again. "I buried my husband there, and now I'm tired of waiting for a future that is for the young, not for the old and tired like me."

Calista watched as the heavy eyelids sagged even more, until only a dark rim of iris showed beneath the folds of wrinkled skin. Dorana Fairdane was weakening visibly with the effort of talking, but Calista made no move to stop her. The woman had the right to spend her last energies as she wanted. Dorana had a purpose in this conversation, though Calista couldn't guess what that purpose might be.

"Rhys will bring that future," Dorana continued, her voice now so weak Calista had to lean forward to catch what she was saying. "Whatever the cost."

The weighted lids flew up and Calista suddenly found herself looking directly into the faded brown depths of Dorana's eyes.

"He is a fool," the old woman said clearly, staring back at Calista, daring her to challenge her assertion. "He will sacrifice everything for it—for the sake of others, not for him."

Drained, Dorana fell silent. Her eyes once more slid slowly shut and she sank into the bed as though the very weight of the air about her had grown too heavy to bear.

"Everything," she said, her voice not even strong enough for a whisper.

Several minutes passed and Dorana did not stir. Only the almost imperceptible rise and fall of her chest revealed that she still lived. Calista rose, taking care that the chair didn't grate against the stone floor. She was backing away from the bed when Dorana spoke again.

"I loved Rhys's father," she said firmly. Once again the old eyes were open. They glittered in the dim light. "It was worth any pain since."

Calista waited, but there was nothing else. Silently, she turned and left the room.

Dorana Fairdane died in her sleep that night, quietly and without fuss.

The three of them, Calista, Glynna, and Rhys, kept a vigil in her room, not speaking but taking comfort from each other's presence until the last faint, soft exhalation that said Dorana was gone from them forever.

Glynna cried, then dried her tears and helped Powdran and one of the village women prepare her mother for burial. Rhys, his eyes like cold, hard stones set in his stiff, white face, set about organizing the final details of the funeral.

The funeral itself was short and simple. Judging by the mass of people clustered around the new grave dug in the rocky soil of the community cemetery, Calista decided most of the village must have come to pay their last respects to Dorana Fairdane.

It wasn't the first grave on the low hill. Long rows of engraved stone markers indicated the end to other settlers' dreams. Beyond them, even more worn, rounded markers betrayed the cost of the first settlement.

Wood was too scarce and plastiglass too precious to be used for a coffin. Dorana's body was placed directly in the grave, wrapped in a winding shroud the same reddish-brown color as the dry earth. Remembering the sternly honest and unsentimental woman she had talked with for such a short time, Calista thought Dorana must have appreciated the symbolism.

The memorial service afterwards filled the eating hall. Since the few people she knew were fully occupied, Calista wandered through the crowd sipping a fruit drink she'd been handed and trying to look inconspicuous. She'd never felt more alone and disconnected, not even in the hundreds of traders' inns she'd visited over the years.

In those places, she hadn't known anyone and had never expected to see any of them again. It hadn't mattered because no one belonged there any more than she had.

Here, everyone belonged but her. Everyone had a position, a role within their society. She had none and the fact that she didn't want one did nothing to lessen the emptiness of not belonging.

It didn't matter, she reminded herself sternly. She'd be free of this place soon. In the meantime, the main doors to the Hall and temporary freedom lay just ahead. She dodged a woman carrying four glasses filled with a pinkish-gold liquid, pushed past a cluster of farmers debating the relative merits of various planting methods . . . and pulled up short.

Ahead of her, a group of a dozen or so people clustered in front of the main doors, blocking her escape. It only took a second to spot Rhys at its center; his black hair and broad shoulders would have made him stand out, even if the attention of everyone else in the group hadn't been focused on him.

From this distance, he appeared calm, attentive, and

concerned, but Calista could sense the strain in the way he held his shoulders, in his stiff, formal stance, so at odds with his usual grace and air of leashed power.

Anger, not mere irritation, rose within her. His mother was scarcely buried and already they clamored for his attention, dumping their petty concerns on his shoulders as if his grief were of no consideration.

Calista's hands balled into fists at her sides. If she thought it would do any good, she'd shove into the group and pull Rhys out, then beam him back to the *Fair Trade* where he could have some peace and a chance to rest.

He wouldn't have come. If she'd learned nothing else in the last two days, she had discovered that behind the facade of careless, tormenting mockery he showed to the rest of the world, Rhys was a man driven, totally committed to the goal he'd set himself of finding a home for his scattered people. Nothing would stop him or turn him aside. Certainly not any plea from her.

Not that it mattered, she reminded herself. Why should it bother her that his people put such heavy demands on Rhys? What difference could it possible make to her? Wasn't she leaving, after all? Hadn't she made that perfectly clear, to herself as well as Rhys? So why did she feel so . . . hollow?

"—settlement on Davinal is threatening to leave the Council if they don't get more support."

The rough, low voice broke in on Calista's thoughts. She peered through the foliage, trying to discern who had spoken.

"Maybe Rhys can think of something. I hear Salaca Minor was saying they'd leave, too, if they didn't get more help after the fire. This plan of his to trade for mining rights has already stopped that talk."

The first speaker, a woman, sighed loudly. "I don't know how long we can keep patching the Council together. With each settlement's leaders pulling in different directions, we'll break apart if we don't have a world to settle, and soon. I don't—" The words faded as the two speakers moved away.

Calista remained where she was, staring at the rough, green-black surface of the leaf in front of her. What was it Marlott had said?

"We all, every one of us, watch Rhys and pray that he'll find what he's searching for." Then he'd added, "For all our sakes."

For the first time, Calista began to understand what he'd meant.

They spent five more days on the planet while Rhys dealt with the myriad problems Marlott and others had so willingly heaped on him.

Once Glynna protested indignantly that he was letting himself be used. He'd scowled at her, too tired to argue, then returned to the problem he was working on.

"The trouble is," Glynna had admitted to Calista afterwards, "even though he's outside the Council, people still listen to him because of Jovane and Dorana, and because he *has* managed to resolve issues that everyone else had just about given up on. With all the settlements vying for resources and influence, Rhys is one of the few who's seen as representing *all* of us, and not just one faction."

Thwarted by her brother's unwillingness to heed her concerns, Glynna adopted a number of under-handed methods to protect him from the importunate demands of others. She feigned a lack of knowledge about his schedule, managed to forget messages others asked her to pass him, and refused to let most visitors inside the door of their little house. When all else failed, she lied, shamelessly and fluently.

To her surprise, Calista found herself adopting the same protective ploys. She even found herself handling a number of the problems herself.

When Marlott insisted, and rightly so, that the community's long-range communication system had to be repaired, Calista used the *Fair Trade's* generators to produce the necessary replacement parts, then worked with the local technicians to install and test the new equipment. The heavy drain on the ship's power reserves required to produce the parts was justified, she decided, by the elimination of one of the more pressing problems weighing on Rhys.

Even though she knew absolutely nothing about selling agricultural produce, when two of the settlement's traders approached her for advice on negotiations with a neighboring planet, Calista found herself drawn into the deal before she knew it. After a couple of hectic hours spent reviewing everything she could find on previous contracts and the other side's situation, she managed, by dint of hard bargaining and some nerve-racking bluffs, to finagle a far more advantageous—and profitable—agreement than anyone had thought possible.

It was only as she was crawling into bed late that night that Calista realized she hadn't earned even one credit on the deal. For an instant she froze, shocked. Then she remembered the delight of the traders and administrators as they'd calculated what the additional profits would mean to the settlement, and she smiled and slid beneath the covers.

Calista couldn't help wondering what Rhys would have thought of the deal. He'd be proud of her, she decided sleepily. She was pretty pleased herself. She hadn't realized how satisfying it could be to know she'd made a difference in the lives of others. Almost as satisfying as seeing her own credit balances mount up. Almost.

As she drifted into sleep, the smile remained in place.

Her success brought demands for more assistance. Two days later she was deep into planning the strategy for another, potentially far more profitable deal, when Rhys walked into the room. Ignoring the plantation manager, the trader, and the administrator who were bent over their hand comps and the mass of papers spread on the table before them, he crossed to her.

"I heard about your help with some of the trade negotiations," he said without preamble. His eyes bored into hers like lasers, hot and piercing.

Calista stiffened, unsure of his intent.

Slowly, a smile lit his tired face. He stretched out his hand and brushed away a stray lock of her hair. The back of his finger grazed her cheek in a fleeting caress and heat flared instantly within her.

"Thanks, Red," he said softly. A moment later, he was gone.

Ignoring the fascinated interest of the others around the table, Calista remained frozen, staring at the door through which he'd disappeared. Her cheek burned where he'd touched her.

Only much later, as she gathered her few belongings in preparation for their departure, did it dawn on her why he'd seemed so different.

He hadn't changed. Lines of strain and exhaustion still etched the corners of his eyes without dimming the glittering awareness of those dark orbs. His body, so intimidatingly male and powerful, still radiated the energy and tension that had driven him for so long.

What had changed wasn't Rhys, but her perception

of him. Only here, on this planet, had she felt the pride, the driving commitment, and the passionate love for his people that had always been there, hidden beneath the surface where only those who knew his secrets could see them.

It wasn't that he'd let her get any closer to him emotionally, Calista had to admit, shaken by the unexpected insight.

No, she'd felt the presence of the real Rhys only because, for the first time in her life she, too, had learned what it was like to be needed by others. For the first time she'd tasted the pride and the humbling awareness of how much still remained to be done to ensure a future, not just for herself, but for all the others who had come to depend on her.

It was a revelation, Calista decided, she might have been better off never knowing.

Chapter Thirteen

Calista returned to the *Fair Trade* first. By the time Rhys beamed aboard over an hour later, she had the journey back to Karta programmed into the main computer and had completed a detailed systems check.

Rhys came to the bridge directly from the transport chamber. Calista hadn't seen him since that strange, brief moment two days before, when he'd thanked her and called her Red. His appearance now brought a shocked exclamation of protest to her lips.

A day's growth of beard roughened his chin. Dark circles made his eyes sink back in their sockets and deepened the lines of strain at the corners. Stray locks of his long, black hair had worked their way free of his usual neat queue and now hung loose about his face, giving him the appearance of a madman.

He glared at her, clearly warning her against

any unwonted displays of concern or any meddling interference.

Calista ignored the warning. "When's the last time you got any sleep, Fairdane?" she demanded.

He shook his head, irritated. "It doesn't matter."

"That's what *you* say. I make it a point of never trusting a man who looks like he's about to collapse. Sit," she commanded, pointing to a chair.

He shook his head again, stubbornly insistent on remaining on his feet, and studied the command console. "Why such a slow trip? If you set—"

"The power core needs time to rebuild its energy levels," Calista interrupted. She pointed to a reading on one of the console's instruments. "See? Using the generators to produce the communications equipment your people needed drained the reserves. At the speed I've set, the core will be fully recharged by the time we reach Karta."

"Oh." Rhys frowned at the instrument reading, then wearily rubbed his face.

Calista could hear the rasp of his hand dragging across the stubble on his chin. She squeezed between him and the console, placed her hands on his chest, and pushed him backward. "Sit, Fairdane. Before you fall over."

Too tired and too surprised to do anything else, Rhys stumbled back two steps to collapse in the chair Calista had indicated.

Calista followed him all the way, still pushing. Once he was seated, she slid her hands up to his shoulders, ready to shove him down if he tried to rise, and looked him straight in his red-rimmed eyes. "When was the last time you had any sleep?"

"Mmm, yesterday. I think."

"You think." Calista snorted in disgust. "How long did you sleep?"

219

"What is this? The Inquisition? I've got work to do, things that won't wait."

Rhys started to get to his feet, but Calista was ready for him. "Not so fast, Fairdane. How long? An hour? Two hours? If you had any more than two or three, I'll eat my boots."

"A couple of hours," Rhys mumbled, clearly irritated.

"That's what I thought. I'd be surprised if you had any more the day before or the day before *that*." She released him and stepped back. "Wait here. I'll be back in a couple of minutes."

"And don't touch the controls in the meantime!" she added from the doorway as Rhys started to get to his feet.

It was closer to five minutes later when she walked back onto the bridge and found Rhys blearily staring at a computer screen and swearing. He keyed in some commands, his tired fingers stumbling over the console, then swore some more. He hadn't even noticed her return.

Calista crossed to him and shoved a mug filled with a dark, steaming hot liquid in front of him. "Here. Drink this."

"What is it?" Rhys demanded, eyeing the mug doubtfully.

"Earth-grown coffee. With lots of sugar."

After a quick glance at her to make sure she was telling the truth, Rhys took the mug from her hand and cautiously sipped the strong brew. The first sip was followed by a second, then a third, more generous gulp that slid down his throat slowly.

Rhys sighed and leaned back in his chair. "Thanks. That helps."

"Ten or twelve hours of sleep would help even more."

He shook his head. "In a while, but not now. There are still a couple of things I left dangling that need to be taken care of first."

Calista eyed him thoughtfully while he took another swallow of coffee. Assured that he wasn't going anywhere, at least not for the next few minutes, she turned her attention to the control panel. A quick check showed everything functioning normally and ready to go so she gave the final command to take the *Fair Trade* out of orbit and into hyperdrive.

With the ship operating smoothly, Calista abandoned the console and dropped into the seat beside Rhys, feet over the armrest, elbow on the seat back, and her head propped on her hand.

Rhys appeared not to notice. He was slowly rocking the mug he held cradled in one hand, his gaze fixed on the dimly reflective surface of the coffee as it swirled up one side of the cup and down the other.

Before she could speak he asked, very softly, "What happens once we get back, Calista?" His eyes never wavered from the dark, swirling liquid.

Calista stilled, her breath halfway to her lungs. She dropped her hand until it lay along the back of the seat and dug her fingers into the soft, heavily padded leather.

Rhys looked up then, directly into her eyes.

This is how mind stealers do it, Calista thought, trapped by the unwavering gaze. *They look at you and look at you and you can't look away. And when you can't look away, they take your soul.*

She didn't want to answer. Not now. Please, not now.

"What happens, Calista?" Rhys insisted.

Calista straightened as far as she could in her cramped and awkward position. "I understand your goal, Rhys. I understand how important this contract

221

is for you. But if the Kartanese really do keep slaves—" She hesitated, then said, "You tell me, Rhys. Do the ends ever justify the means?"

She held his gaze for a minute, unblinking. It seemed an eternity. He was the first to look away.

Once again his gaze dropped to the mug he held. Not even a slight tremor of his fingers betrayed him; he stared back into the dark coffee as if, somehow, he expected to find an answer more to his liking beneath the surface.

With an abrupt motion, he brought the mug to his lips and drained the contents. Calista could see the muscles in his throat contract as he swallowed. For an instant more he stared at the now-empty mug, then pushed out of his seat and set the mug on the edge of the console.

"Thanks for the coffee," he said. Without another word, he strode across the bridge and out the door.

Four hours later, after tending to tasks elsewhere on the ship, Calista found Rhys back on the bridge, slumped over a console and sound asleep. The communications screen in front of him still showed the recognition code for the last transmission.

He'd showered and changed his clothes since she'd last seen him. Calista had no doubt it had been a *very* cold shower. He would have tried anything to keep himself awake.

But even though he might not be willing to admit it, Rhys Fairdane was human, with human needs for rest. He'd pushed himself too hard for too long and his body had finally insisted on claiming the sleep he'd denied it. He'd sleep better, however, if he were in his own bed.

Calista reached to grab his shoulder and shake him awake. She stopped her hand only inches from him, uncertain why she did so but knowing she didn't want to wake him. Not yet, anyway.

He lay with his head pillowed on his left forearm, his right arm stretched out in front of him. His face was slightly turned toward her. Calista could see the heavy sweep of his thick, black lashes, the aquiline arch of his nose. From this angle, his mouth looked softer, perhaps because the curve of his shoulder partially hid the hard, strong line of his jaw.

He hadn't shaved. Calista repressed an urge to run a finger across the rough stubble, to follow the hollow of his cheek until she reached his lips. If she traced the swell of his lower lip, she would be able to feel the soft flow of his breath, in and out, warm against her skin.

She longed to touch him but her hand still hovered just above his head. What if he wakened and, angry at her presence, drove her away? Worse, what if he ignored her outstretched hand and merely stared at her, as cold and hard and distant as the stars that shone like pinpricks on the monitors?

In her unwillingness to agree to continue working with the Kartanese, she'd drawn a clean, sharp line between them, and she was the one who would have to erase it, for Rhys would never cross it.

Carefully, her fingers trembling, Calista traced the curve of his head and shoulders in the air above him. Her hand was so close she could feel the coolness against her palm of his still-damp hair, feel the heat of his body under the crisp fabric of his shirt. Yet she never touched him.

In the long years they'd been apàrt, Calista remembered her dreams had been like that. She'd reach out to him. She'd see his face, hear his voice. The heat of him had caressed her palm, just as it did now. The smell of him had tantalized her. Like now.

And like now, she'd never touched him. Her hands had always stretched toward him, but they'd never, never touched him.

The memory hit her with the devastating force of a sun gone nova. Trembling, Calista sank to her knees beside Rhys.

Is that what she wanted for the rest of her life? To reach for Rhys in her dreams only to wake and find he wasn't there? To stretch out her hand and know that all it would find was empty air and memories?

She let her eyes roam over him, let her mind remember each small detail. The way his chest rose and fell with each breath. The hard muscles of his arms and the surprisingly soft, dark hairs on his forearms that were so temptingly springy beneath her hand. And she shouldn't forget how sensitive the inside of the crook in his arm was. If he were awake and she ran the tip of her finger, just so, across that spot . . .

She was like a wild creature gathering its store of food for the long, cold winter that lay ahead, only her food would be the images, the small memories her mind could tuck away, then give back when there was nothing else left her.

Calista sank back on her heels, aching to touch him, afraid of what would happen if she did.

He looked so . . . vulnerable.

Unbidden, a fierce protectiveness rose in her.

His people had no right to demand so much of him. They knew he would give until there was nothing more to give, drive himself until he dropped, yet still they demanded more.

But isn't that what you've *always done?* The thought flashed, hot and bright, across her conscience.

Surely not! Calista protested, shocked.

Ah, but you have! her conscience replied. *How much*

have you demanded of him, how many changes have you required he make in his life to suit you? Can you count them? And how much have you changed to suit him? Not at all! How many times has he put himself at risk to protect you? Remember how he placed himself between you and the Kartanese guard? Remember how on Tarkis II he stopped you from plunging into a dangerous fight where you had no business sticking your nose?

But that was different!

Remember?

She remembered. Calista drooped, suddenly ashamed.

But she would change, she vowed silently. For Rhys. He needed her, even if he didn't know it. She would protect him, be the buffer between him and the pain that life had brought him, be the rational voice that kept him from driving harder and harder until he dropped. She could do it.

Slowly Calista rose to her feet. She would change, she'd learn.

She had to, because she loved him.

She loved him . . . Calista hung suspended, caught on the words as her mind spun madly.

She loved him. She always had.

That was impossible. Love belonged to the tales old women told. It wasn't supposed to happen to her.

It had, and now she wasn't sure what she ought to do next.

Put him to bed.

Calista almost burst out laughing at the thought. She felt breathless, dazed, disoriented, and confused. She felt like singing and she wanted to burst into tears, and all she could think to do was put Rhys to bed.

It was a beginning, at any rate.

Stooping over him, she gently brushed back a lock

of hair that had pulled free of his queue. The strands were heavy, yet smooth to the touch, still damp. Calista tucked the errant lock behind his ear, then bent to kiss his cheek.

"Rhys," she whispered in his ear. "Wake up and come to bed."

He stirred, mumbled drowsily, "Calista?"

"Come to bed, Rhys."

He blinked, then raised his head and shook it, still groggy. "Whad'ya say?"

"Come on." Calista grabbed his arm and tugged until he came heavily to his feet. "This way."

When he just stood there, weaving slightly and frowning in confusion, she wrapped his arm around her shoulders. "Move it, Fairdane."

Some vague notion of what she wanted seemed to work its way through the mists that fogged his exhausted mind. Leaning heavily on her, Rhys obeyed her command to move it.

He almost moved it right into the door frame. Calista barely managed to steer him away from the frame and through the door, then down the passage.

Even the walk to his private quarters wasn't enough to rouse him completely. The long days of stress, grief, overwork, and little sleep had taken their toll. Once Rhys had given in to his need for rest, his mind and body had collapsed. They weren't about to start working properly again until they'd had a chance to recover from the abuse he'd heaped on them.

Calista guided Rhys to the big bed that dominated his quarters and dropped his arm. "Sit down, Rhys," she commanded, panting slightly. Rhys was a big man, but she'd swear he'd added another stone or two of weight.

Rhys still stood, staring around him vaguely and frowning. "Can't stay here," he said. "Work t'do."

"Later. First, you have to get some sleep." Calista edged around him to pull down the covers on the bed, then turned back to find him watching her. This time, however, there was a gleam in his eyes that said some, at least, of his drowsiness had dissipated.

Calista caught her breath at the unexpected surge of heat within her. "Why don't you—"

Rhys kissed her. Very gently. When she tried to object, he pulled her down on the bed with him.

His arms felt good around her. Strong, comforting, and so very right. He kissed her again, his beard rasping against her cheek, then shifted so she was cradled in his arms, her back to him. An instant later, he was asleep.

Calista turned out the lights from the control panel at the head of the bed. Even after Rhys's breathing indicated he'd fallen into a deep sleep, Calista remained where she was, grateful for his warmth and the weight of his arm about her.

She loved him. A little while ago, that knowledge had made her laugh. Now it frightened her.

It ought to be so simple, but it wasn't simple at all. Nothing in the outside world had changed. The responsibilities Rhys had borne for so long and the commitments he'd made wouldn't go away just because she willed it so. Ahead of them lay Karta. What was she going to do about that? Calista wondered. Where did love fit in there?

Rhys awoke to an insistent tugging on his foot. He peered groggily toward the end of the bed where a black mass, scarcely distinguishable against the darkened room, bent over his feet.

His conscious mind wasn't working clearly yet, but his instincts for self-preservation hadn't stopped functioning. Without thinking, he kicked out at the unknown shape, then rolled off the far side of the bed.

Tried to, anyway.

The bedclothes tangled around him and instead of rolling free, he landed in an untidy heap on the floor.

Rhys swore. It took a second before he realized his unknown assailant was doing the same, and far more fluently.

"Calista?"

"You couldn't have asked that *before* you tried to break my ribs?"

It took a minute's fumbling before Rhys found the room controls set in the head of the bed. As hidden lights cast a soft, golden glow along the walls, he gave up trying to fight free of the bedclothes wrapped around his legs and settled for propping his arms on the edge of the bed.

At the far side, Calista was trying to get her feet under her, push her wildly tousled hair back from her face, and scowl at him, all at the same time. The only thing she was managing with any success was the scowling.

"Did you have to kick me?" she demanded.

"Just what did you think you were doing?" He could scowl as well as she could. Landing on the floor like that hadn't felt too great, either. "And why are you in my room?"

"I was trying to take your boots off. Or do you always sleep in them?"

"My boots?" Rhys glanced down at his feet, ingloriously stuck out of the twisted covers. He was still in possession of his left boot, at least.

"That's right. Last time I do you any favors, Fairdane." Calista was on her feet by this time. She stomped around the end of the bed and extended the missing boot. "Here. Since you seem so attached to this."

Rhys didn't grab the boot. He grabbed Calista's wrist instead and with one, strong tug, pulled her down into his arms. Instead of resisting as he'd expected, she readily molded herself to his embrace and just as readily welcomed the kiss he immediately claimed.

She tasted like honey. Honey and sweet dreams and fire. Rhys groaned, dipped deeper, and felt the fire burn deeper still.

"That's better," he said at last, his voice grown dark and husky. He rolled her onto her back. "Now, what was this about trying to undress me?"

"Do you have a problem with that, Fairdane?" she asked.

Her voice, too, was deeper, rougher. It made him tighten with a hot, rising urgency that threatened his control.

"Not if I'm awake to enjoy it." He kissed her again. "Just how were you planning to manage this little task?" he asked, his lips only inches from hers.

"I thought I'd start with the boots."

"Consider them done."

"I only got one, you know."

"We'll get to the other one later." He ran the tip of his tongue along the inside of her lower lip, then caught that tempting swell of flesh between his teeth, briefly, before releasing her. "What comes next?"

"Hmmmm." Calista tilted her head back across his arm. Her eyes were half closed, as though she were deep in thought.

Through the dark brown lashes Rhys could see the blue of her irises, blue as the oceans of his homeworld and just as deep and secret. Her tongue flicked out to wet her lips, to taste the traces of himself that he'd left, and the heat within him rose another notch.

"The seal on your suit's next, don't you think?" Without waiting for him to reply, Calista placed a finger at the top of the front seam and slowly, with a steady, tormenting pressure that made it increasingly hard for him to breathe, traced the line down his chest and belly. The seam sprang open in the wake of her finger, revealing his body to her.

Rhys groaned and arched against her. She ignored his response and slipped her hand inside the suit. Her fingers barely grazed him. Then, just as slowly as she'd descended, she followed the opening upward, her touch so light he could barely feel it, so searing he wasn't sure he could endure it.

"The sleeves are next, I think," she murmured, even though her breathing had become as quick and shallow as his. She shoved her hands inside his suit and dragged it over his shoulders and down his back.

Rhys pulled his arms free, but other than showering kisses along her face and throat and shoulder, he made no effort to interfere as she deliberately and very carefully tugged the suit farther, below his waist, then over his hips and down his thighs as far as she could reach.

He wanted her—now. He wanted to take her as quickly as he could, to fill her until she ached as he did. He wanted to share her warmth and passion and vibrant sense of being *alive*. He *needed* it—his body, his very soul, trembled with the needing.

Instead, Rhys pulled away from her, stilling her protest with a kiss, and removed his suit and remaining boot. Tossing aside the unwanted clothing, he knelt and took her right foot in his hands.

Fighting to suppress the husky note of desire in his voice, he said, "Now that you've shown me how, I thought I'd practice a little. Like this."

Unlike his boots, the simple shoes Calista wore were

easy to remove, but Rhys didn't hurry. He eased the first one off with infinite care, then gently kneaded her foot. She came up on her elbows, watching him, her eyes heavy and dark with the hunger he could see rising within her.

Rhys forced down the urge to allay that hunger and instead gently laid her foot in his lap and turned his attention to the other shoe.

The second shoe proved far more difficult. Not because of the shoe, but because Calista chose to distract him by pressing her unshod foot against his lower belly and kneading the taut muscles with her toes. Rhys struggled to concentrate, fought to keep control, but when she moved lower he could no longer resist the tension building within him.

With a low, hoarse cry that was part plea, part exultation, Rhys abandoned all restraint. There was nothing smooth or calculated about the way he removed her suit. It was just one more barrier that divided him from her and in that moment, in his need, he would not allow anything to keep them apart.

All the loneliness and longing and heartache of the past few days, all the desperate, aching emptiness were gone, burned to ashes in the fire that now raged between them, threatening to consume them both.

At the moment of joining, Rhys cried out, a sound of exultation and release that was instantly stilled as Calista pulled his head down and claimed his mouth in a kiss that promised everything his heart desired, and more. Then her hands slid down, over his shoulders and along his back, pulling her even more closely against him as the rhythm of her body matched the rhythm of his, bending with him, arching to meet his thrusts, sharing the joy that was both of theirs for the taking until the stars rushed down to engulf them.

* * *

The vague light from the small, concealed fixtures near the floor illuminated the room when Rhys awoke.

He was alone. The sheets where Calista had lain were cold. Only the indentation on the pillow and the fading, musky scent of their lovemaking remained as proof that she'd been there at all.

Rhys lay still, staring at the traces of her presence, trying to recapture the sense of wonder, of the rightness of it all, that had so overwhelmed him before. Nothing came to him except a sense of loss that carried a nagging uncertainty with it.

He pushed himself up on one elbow, his gaze fixed on the rumpled pillow. Without knowing why he did so, he stretched out his hand and, after a moment's hesitation, ran his open palm over its surface, tracing the indentation where her head had lain.

The pillow was like his soul. When she was gone, a portion of him was left hollowed out, with only memories of her to fill it. Rhys's fingers tightened around the edge of the pillow, crushing it and obliterating the indentation.

Was that what he wanted, to be a malleable, crushable pillow for her, someone with whom she could find comfort when she needed it, then discard when it suited her?

Rhys flung the pillow away with disgust. That was unfair. Whatever it was that drove her, whatever it was she wanted, she'd never used him. Not in that way.

Which didn't mean she wasn't capable of hurting him. Rhys took a deep breath, fighting to separate emotion from reason. How much easier it would have been if she'd never walked back into his life.

No, walked wasn't the right description. Elbowed, bullied, stormed, and stomped her way back in.

Calista would never do anything so mundane as merely walk.

Maybe that was the attraction. He'd spent years hiding his emotions behind a protective facade of slightly cynical amusement while she carried hers so openly, never hesitating to let him know what she thought or felt.

Or did she?

Rhys frowned. She'd stuck with him, even through the difficult days just past, but did he really know why? And what would she do once they reached Karta? Did what lay between them matter enough for her to stay, or was her passionate hatred for slavery so much greater than his people's needs and the ties that bound them to each other?

Those questions ran around in Rhys's head while he showered, shaved, and dressed, driving out the last remnants of the peace he'd found in their lovemaking. By the time he located her on the bridge, only one thought, one driving question remained in his mind.

"What happens when we get to Karta?" he asked. "And this time, Calista, I want a straight answer."

Chapter Fourteen

Calista slowly twisted round in her seat. She'd had hours to think about her response to his inevitable question. She still wasn't sure she was making the right decision.

Rhys stood in the doorway, just as he'd stood in the doorway once before and challenged her for an answer she couldn't give. Gone was the passionate, tormenting, teasing lover of a few hours before. In his place, Calista saw a man who'd had time to think and to remember all the unanswered questions that lay between them, a man who didn't like unanswered questions and never would.

"What happens when we get to Karta?" he asked again.

"I thought maybe . . . maybe sometimes the ends *do* justify the means," Calista said, very carefully. "Like you said, there might be some explanation, some reason—" Her voice trailed off. Another question

234

lay beyond her answer, a question she didn't want to face.

Rhys asked it. "And what if the Kartanese really do keep slaves? What then?" He was very still, very quiet, as though he held every emotion in check so no hint of what he was feeling would betray him, make him vulnerable to the hurt that would inevitably follow.

Calista took a deep breath, then slowly expelled the air, fighting for a calm she didn't feel, for a strength that wasn't there. She'd asked herself the question a hundred times since she'd left his bed, asked herself if the knowledge that she loved him—truly, deeply loved him—was enough.

"I . . . I don't know, Rhys."

There. She'd said it. The back of her throat burned. She squeezed her eyes shut, fighting back tears.

The seconds ticked by and Rhys just stood there, watching her, his eyes dark hollows as empty as the depths of space.

After an eternity, he took a deep, deep breath. Calista could hear the sighing intake of air even halfway across the room. His chest swelled and the cords of his neck strained with his effort to control his reactions. Then, just as slowly, he let out the breath he held, straightened, and looked away from her.

His gaze didn't move far. Just to the view screen in front of Calista and the image of a brilliant blue and green planet that floated there. Rhys's brow furrowed in sudden recognition. Without taking his eyes from the screen, he crossed the room to stand by her chair. "That's the third planet of the Kartanese system."

Calista stared at the screen she'd been watching for hours. With what she'd learned over the past few days, it hadn't been hard to figure out why the third planet fascinated Rhys so much. "Yes."

"I was hoping to convince the Dorinor to grant me

rights to the planet." Rhys silently studied the world slowly spinning on the screen before them.

Calista could feel the tension in him, and the fear. Not for himself, but for his people.

Although there was no guarantee the Dorinor would grant him the rights to the planet if she stayed, the failure of his plans was virtually assured if she left. On her decision rested the future of millions who'd spent the last twenty years in exile, without a home and with little more than a vague hope of ever gaining one.

Rhys had spent his entire adult life working toward the goal of finding his people a world they could call their own. Now the fulfillment of that dream might almost be within his grasp, yet it could all crumble to nothing in the space of a few seconds, depending on what choice she made.

A surge of anger rose within Calista. It wasn't fair! She hadn't asked for this kind of responsibility, this kind of power.

If she followed her heart and remained with Rhys, if she put the needs of his people first, she would compromise everything she'd stood for, everything she'd fought against all her life. How could she, an escaped slave still at risk of being discovered and sent back into slavery, condone, or even tolerate the enslavement of others?

The answer was, she couldn't.

But if she didn't, how could she live with the knowledge of what Rhys's people would lose because of her? Now that she'd met Glynna and Marlott and Powdran, how could she refuse to do what she could to help them?

She didn't know the answers to those questions. Even thinking about them was far too frightening.

"So we wait, is that it, Calista?" Rhys's voice quivered with the anger rising within him. "Wait until you decide if you can accept a culture that has existed for thousands of years, a culture that isn't ours and that we have no right to judge. Is that right?"

"I . . . That's right." Her words sounded to Calista as if they came from a great distance, from someone who wasn't her, someone who didn't ache inside with a pain that threatened to last a lifetime.

"I see."

He didn't say any more. Just turned on his heel and stalked off the bridge.

Larr contacted them when they were only an hour out from Karta. Calista monitored the call from a comm panel in one of the workrooms instead of joining Rhys on the bridge. She'd managed to keep out of his way for most of the past week—she might as well keep trying for a little while longer.

She even overrode the panel's automatic instructions to show both Rhys and Larr on the screen. It would hurt too much to see the cold, distant expression that told, more clearly than words, how far Rhys had withdrawn from her.

"Welcome, traders," Larr said. As before, the smile on his face was beautiful. Perfect and balanced and so very, very appropriate to his handsome face.

It chilled Calista to her soul.

Rhys didn't bother to reply.

One of Larr's perfect, golden brows quirked upward. His voice lost even the faint trace of human warmth it had held a moment before. "I'd expected you over a week ago."

"I sent you word we'd be delayed."

Calista could hear the restraint behind Rhys's words.

"That's right, you did. But you didn't explain why you were delayed."

237

The silence before Rhys answered couldn't have lasted more than a couple of seconds. To Calista, it seemed to stretch forever.

"No. The delay had nothing to do with you, Larr. We're here now, however, and we have all the equipment you ordered. It's too massive to transport. I assume you have a hauler or a shuttle that can pick it up."

"We do. A fairly substantial hauler, as it happens. It came in very handy when we were trying to build our accommodations here."

While Larr and Rhys worked out the details of the equipment transfer, Calista studied the blond man's face. The more she saw of the man, the less she liked and trusted him. The trouble was, she could never quite put her finger on the reason for her reaction.

Her instincts had served her well in the past, however, and she saw no reason to lose faith in them now. Whether she stayed as trade rep or not, she'd be careful to keep an eye on the man.

Did Rhys hold the same opinion? she wondered. She couldn't tell anything from his voice. If he did, he'd never mentioned it, even toward the end of the first trip when everything had gone so well and they'd felt comfortable in sharing their opinions about the deals they were working on.

Calista listened to Rhys's voice, mentally blotting out Larr's image on the screen and substituting Rhys's instead. It wasn't hard. That dark visage was in her dreams each night and with her during the day, no matter how far apart they were.

Was this what she would be doing in the years to come? Conjuring up mental images of his features because that was all that would be left her? What perversity kept her from letting her fierce hatred of slavery go and committing herself to Rhys and his struggle? She'd gain nothing and help the grays not at all, no matter what she did, while she had the world—and Rhys—waiting for her if she stayed.

Calista scarcely noticed when Larr and Rhys finally ended their discussion. Even after Larr broke the connection, a light glowed on Calista's comm panel to indicate Rhys was still there.

"Calista?"

She didn't answer.

"I know you're there, that you can hear me. Turn on your screen so I can see you." Barely repressed anger rang in the words.

Reluctantly, not knowing why she did so but unable to refuse, Calista activated the visual link.

Rhys instantly appeared on her screen. Unlike Larr, who had kept his mask of perfect politeness in place throughout, Rhys made no effort to hide his feelings. His dark eyes sparked and his lips thinned to a narrow line.

"You can't hide from me forever, Calista. Not once we're on the planet."

Goaded, Calista snapped, "I'm not hiding, Fairdane." The lie was acid on her tongue.

"All right. Let's not call it hiding. Let's say you're doing a pretty good job of avoiding me. Does that sound better?"

When she didn't answer, Rhys snorted in disgust. "Make your choice, Calista. I can respect your reasons for not wanting to work for the Kartanese—if, that is, they really do keep slaves."

He paused, as if waiting for her to deny she'd ever thought of leaving. When she still remained silent, he continued, "I don't have to agree with your choice and I don't have to like it, but at least I won't be slinking down hallways and dodging around corners to avoid you."

"You don't understand!"

"Have you tried to help me understand? Someday, Calista, someday you're going to have to start thinking of someone besides yourself. And when that day comes, pray there isn't anyone there who can take everything you're fighting for and destroy it without a moment's thought."

Rhys broke the connection then. Calista didn't move. She just kept staring at the blank screen as two words kept chasing round and round in her mind. *Tell him.*

Simple words. Not so simple a deed.

Tell him. Tell him. Tell him.

She drew her feet up on the chair and wrapped her arms around her legs, huddling into a tight ball. How could she explain? After all these years of keeping silent, how could she find the words to describe the fears that were always with her, the memories that still had the power to make her tremble and look over her shoulder, wondering if the slave hunters were right behind her?

If she told him of her past, of Andrus and her escape, of all the years spent desperately trying to hide her tracks and disappear, he'd understand her refusal to work for the Kartanese. Of that she was certain.

He'd understand, but he wouldn't change his course, either. Not for her.

Calista's arms tightened around her legs. She knew he cared for her—at least a little. He cared, but he didn't love her. A tear, one of the many she'd been struggling for days to suppress, seeped beneath her lid and trickled down her cheek.

Life had been so much simpler when she could divide it into columns of profit and loss, and see the careful calculations that translated into her freedom slowly take on reality.

If she could forget her love for Rhys she gladly would, but how did she do that when she didn't understand how it had come to her in the first place? Calista stared at the view screen where his image had been brief minutes ago, but the only answer she got in return was a blank screen and a silent room.

Slowly, reluctantly, she uncurled and stood up. At least there was work to do. Overseeing the transfer of their cargo from the *Fair Trade* to Larr's hauler wasn't much, but it would keep her mind off questions that had no answer.

By the time Rhys brought the *Fair Trade* into orbit around Karta, Calista had checked and rechecked the cargo manifest a dozen times. The first crates were already loaded on the grav hoist, ready for transfer.

Rhys entered the cargo area a few minutes later. He didn't speak, just brushed past to inspect her work, verifying load arrangements, security, and identification marks as if she were a novice trying her first transfer.

Calista glared at his broad back, indignant at the mistrust. "Find anything, Fairdane?"

His dark eyes narrowed. "The *Fair Trade* is my ship. Nothing comes on or goes off it unless I check it first."

Calista was saved from having to answer by the sound of the alarm that warned of an approaching ship. She started to respond when Rhys pushed her aside and began the security procedure that would allow the hauler to connect with the *Fair Trade's* cargo bay.

Once the two ships were joined, Rhys strode across the connecting bridge and into the hauler's bay. After a last check of the arrangements, Calista followed.

The only occupant of the hauler was a dour, muscular brute whom Calista had never seen before. He nodded curtly to Rhys, ignored Calista, and turned his attention to the robots that were already beginning to transfer the equipment.

Since it didn't require many of the big crates to fill up the hauler's cargo area, the transfer of the first load didn't take long. The hauler's pilot ran a final check, then stepped to the side without a word, obviously expecting Calista and Rhys to return to the *Fair Trade*.

Her help wouldn't be required once the hauler reached Karta, so Calista started to cross back. She stopped when she realized that Rhys, at least, had no intention of returning to the ship.

"I'm going down with you," he said to the pilot. He didn't even bother to see what Calista's reaction was.

"With me?" The flat statement obviously caught the pilot by surprise. "You can't. I don't need you and Larr won't like it."

Rhys shrugged, unimpressed. "I brought the cargo in. I'm going down with it to be sure it's delivered safely." Without another glance at the startled pilot, he strode toward the door that divided the cargo area from the bridge.

With a quick "Me, too" tossed over her shoulder to the pilot, Calista hurried after him. She wasn't sure what Rhys was up to—if anything—but she wasn't going to be left behind.

Though the pilot eyed them narrowly when he finally joined them on the hauler's bridge, he didn't say anything. With a rude grunt to warn her out of his way, he shoved past Calista and settled into his seat.

As Calista took her own seat, she couldn't help thinking that good manners seemed to be in seriously short supply lately.

Calista was still trying to decide how to behave if Larr met them at the unloading area when the pilot landed and opened the cargo bay. She was up on her feet, off the bridge, and striding toward the open doors before Rhys could stop her.

She did stop, however, before she was halfway down the loading ramp. Her mouth dropped open in surprise. She didn't even bother to snap at Rhys when he ran into her.

All she could do was stare at the massive gray creatures standing at the bottom of the ramp, apparently waiting for permission to come up and retrieve the cargo.

"What in the stars are those things?" Rhys demanded, obviously stunned by their size.

"It's the sla...the grays. The ones I told you about." Calista could feel her own eyes grow round with surprise.

Four of the creatures crowded up the ramp, oblivious to their stares. They were so big, Calista had to step back out of their way. Unfortunately, back meant right into Rhys.

His hands automatically clamped down on her shoulders, steadying her. Calista would never have admitted it, but she was suddenly profoundly grateful for his massive presence.

The creatures were big. Huge, in fact. She'd only seen them—or at least their relatives—once and from a distance. There in the cavern, the grays hadn't looked quite so enormous. Especially not when compared to the Kartanese who'd been present.

Right now, only a few feet away from her, they were intimidating. Moving ponderously on their stump-like legs, they entered the cargo bay and immediately headed for four different crates. In an instant, a shrill discussion broke out in the Kartanese language.

Calista's translator strained to sort out the jumble of voices, but one thing was clear: each of the grays wanted to unload what it had immediately decided was its own crate.

It needed the shouting, cursing pilot to straighten out the confusion. "That one!" he roared, indicating the crate nearest the ramp. "Then that one. One at a time, you stupid lumps!"

Cowed, the four rushed to cluster around the crate indicated. Matters progressed slowly, however, while they tried to work out exactly which side of the crate belonged to whom, and who would get to lead. No matter what they were doing, each of the four dropped everything to bow, scrape and cringe every time the pilot came anywhere close to it.

Eventually, Calista wasn't quite sure how, the details were sorted out to the satisfaction of each and the first crate was carried down the ramp and carefully set at the side of the unloading area.

As the grays passed them, headed for the second crate the pilot indicated, Rhys muttered, "So these are your slaves?"

"You don't see any of the Kartanese lending a hand, do you?" Calista demanded.

"No, but that would be pretty hard to manage since they don't really have any."

"Any what?" Calista's attention was drawn by the confusion around the second crate while the grays squabbled over the same issues they'd resolved only minutes earlier.

"Hands. They don't have any hands."

"Oh. So? Isn't it clear these creatures are used for the work the Kartanese don't want to do?"

Rhys started to reply, but his attention was drawn to the circus in the cargo bay, instead. The four grays, each with a firm grip on one side of the crate, were dancing around in a circle trying to work out the issue of who got to go first down the ramp this time. All under the screaming, red-faced supervision of the apoplectic pilot.

The issue resolved, the grays emerged with the crate and Rhys returned to the argument.

"Somehow, I can't imagine anyone wanting to keep such incompetent slaves. Can you, Calista?"

Calista's forehead wrinkled in angry puzzlement. "I can't imagine them paying for this kind of service, either."

No answer came over the next quarter hour while the grays, under the supervision of the increasingly frustrated pilot, unloaded the hauler.

By the fourth crate, Calista had had all she could take of the pilot's shouting and cursing. She stomped up the ramp and over to the man.

"For stars' sake, quit screaming at the poor creatures," she snapped. "Can't you see you're confusing them?"

"You think *you* can do better, go ahead and try!" the pilot snarled, his patience clearly at an end. He gave a mocking bow and, with a sweep of his right hand, indicated Calista should take over.

Calista pretended to ignore the smirk of anticipation on the pilot's face while she tried to get the grays' attention. Ten minutes later, her voice growing hoarse from shouting, Calista gave up. The grays not only ignored polite requests and helpful suggestions, they didn't pay any attention when she yelled at them, either. Instead of running more smoothly, the unloading efforts had come to a complete halt while the huge creatures once again argued about which crate belonged to whom.

Chastened and thoroughly irritated by the grays' stupidity, Calista slunk back down the ramp, pointedly ignoring Rhys's silent, and obviously amused, stare.

It took another half hour of the pilot's shouting to get the rest of the crates unloaded. As the grays hauled down the last one, the pilot, sweating and swearing, stomped down the ramp to stand by Rhys and glare at the hapless creatures.

"Stupid, clunk-headed, low-brained . . . Arrgh." He wiped his brow on his sleeve, then turned and spat in disgust. "It's like this every time we bring a load in. They want to treat every piece as if it were one of their precious eggs and each of 'em had one to take care of."

Calista didn't miss the sudden gleam of interest in Rhys's eyes as he murmured sympathetically. "Frustrating."

"Frustrating don't half describe it." The pilot broke off to shout at the grays, who were avidly inspecting the crates now standing at the side of the hauler. "They're trying to figure out who gets what. As if it mattered."

"But surely since the equipment is designed for their use—" Rhys let the question dangle, inviting more information.

"That's only 'cause Larr still hasn't convinced the Dorinor to let us manage the stuff. Don't imagine he ever will, either," the man huffed. "That pigheaded, winged monster might have agreed to us installin' it, but he won't let us near it once it's in."

Calista opened her mouth, ready to jump in, when a warning glance from Rhys stopped her. Irritated, she subsided. Rhys was right. The pilot, who had ignored her ever since she'd boarded the hauler, was opening up to him, not her.

"That's odd," Rhys said to the pilot. "The creatures . . . mmm . . . well—"

"You got that right," the pilot agreed heartily. "Only

a few of 'em have any sense of how all the equipment works together. Most of 'em just want their own little baby to care for and to hell with all the rest. They're muckin' it up, too. You saw. They won't let us use robots for handling the cargo and they don't want us around the hatchin' caves. If Larr can't convince the Dorinor to let us run it—" He shook his head and spat again.

Despite the grim implications of the pilot's words, Calista had to struggle to repress the grin that threatened. However mad Rhys could make her, she had to admit he was very, very good at worming information out of people. He hadn't said anything, but he'd managed to get the pilot to reveal information, no matter how vague, that she was sure Larr wouldn't want them to know.

At least, not yet. At some point, he'd have to share his plans, if only to keep them from making a mistake in their dealings with others. Until then, she didn't think he'd be pleased.

She was right.

Five minutes later, as she and Rhys were helping the pilot stow everything in preparation for their return to the *Fair Trade*, Larr strode into the loading area.

The expression on his face when he spotted them clearly indicated the man was not happy. Not happy at all.

Chapter Fifteen

"What are you doing here?" Larr demanded. The question sparked with distrust.

Calista's hackles rose. Fortunately, Rhys responded before she had a chance to.

"I always make sure any cargo I carry is delivered safely," he said calmly, meeting Larr's glare with a steady gaze that dismissed, rather than confronted, the other man's anger.

"That wasn't necessary!"

"No? From what I've seen so far, I think I'll make sure anything I carry in the future is packed a little more securely."

"The *drenn* haven't dropped or broken anything yet."

"Miracles happen, but I wouldn't count on them."

Larr scowled, then subsided. Rhys didn't look as if he'd been even slightly interested in the interchange, but Calista suspected he was as irritated by Larr's belligerence as she was, and just as intrigued by his use of the word *drenn*.

Her translator had hesitated for a fraction of a second on the word, which meant the substitute was close, but not exact. The substitute, however, was enough to give her hope. Larr had called the grays "servants," not slaves.

Calista glanced toward where the crates were standing. The grays had had time to sort out which crates belonged to whom and now hovered over the inert boxes with all the anxious attention of mothers over their newborn babes.

How could anybody be dumb enough to keep servants as inept as these clumsy creatures? What possible use could the Kartanese have for servants who didn't even recognize a packing crate when they saw one?

She shook her head, puzzled. It still didn't make any sense. Even slaves had a purpose, but Calista couldn't figure out what the grays' purpose would be. What, after all, did the Kartanese need? They were hunters, not farmers. They had few possessions, none of which required any great effort to maintain. The grays had clearly served a role there in the cave, with the hatching of the two babies, but beyond that, what did they do?

And what was the equipment for, anyway?

Before she could think of any more questions for which she had no answers, Rhys called her name, snapping Calista out of her thoughts.

"Did you hear anything we said?" he demanded. "The Dorinor wants to talk to us. Now."

"I was going to have you come down as soon as all the crates were unloaded, but as you're already here—" Larr's disapproving frown deepened. Without waiting for a reply, he strode toward one of the passages on the far side of the loading area.

Calista glanced at Rhys, wondering what his reaction to this peremptory summons was. Instead of looking at her, he glanced over at the grays, his eyes narrowed in speculation. Knowing Rhys, he was asking himself the same questions she had. But what kind of answers was he getting? And what would it mean to them? To her?

She didn't have a chance to find out. From the far side of the cavern, Larr called out in irritation, "Are you coming? The Dorinor probably knows you're here by now and he won't appreciate waiting."

The Dorinor, it turned out, hadn't minded the wait at all. He was deep in a game of bakal with Karnor. The two Kartanese scarcely accorded their entrance a glance before their attention was back on the cards they held in their claws.

"I'll match that and raise you ten thousand," the Dorinor said after a careful scrutiny of his cards and the pile of coins heaped on the floor between them.

"Ten thousand! Why would you want to do that?" Karnor demanded, clearly nonplussed.

"It seems to me a very reasonable bet," the Dorinor replied calmly. He clumsily fanned his cards and cocked his head to stare admiringly at them.

"But given the cards that have already appeared and what I now hold, the chances of you having anything worth betting on are ridiculously small!" Karnor had clearly opted for a mathematical approach to bakal.

The Dorinor appeared to consider that possibility, then he glanced at his cards once more and grinned.

Calista had seen him grin before. All those long, sharp teeth would have made any other player who wasn't Kartanese flinch.

"You must match my bet or I win," he said to Karnor, obviously pleased with himself.

Karnor muttered to himself, too low for Calista's translator to catch the words, and scratched his belly uncertainly. Still muttering, he studied his hand, the Dorinor, and his hand again, then reluctantly placed the cards he held facedown on the ground.

"The game is yours," he conceded, his gaze fixed on the cards the Dorinor held.

The Dorinor's wings rustled as he laid his cards down, face up, then sat back and crossed his front feet over his belly in satisfaction.

"Two stars, a red sun, four planets, all unmatched, and a fifth-class rocket," Karnor said, clearly not believing his eyes. "You don't have *anything* worth betting on!"

Calista grinned. So the Dorinor had finally figured out what bluffing was all about, had he?

Her grin disappeared when the Dorinor turned his attention to them. His claws scraped on the stone floor as he rose to his feet and crossed to them. Calista had to tilt her head back to meet his unblinking gaze.

From a distance, watching him fumble his cards with claws that were ill-suited to holding anything, he'd looked—amusing. It had been easy to feel slightly patronizing.

This close, with his black body looming huge in the cavern's shadowed interior and his golden eyes gleaming bright, he didn't look amusing at all. He looked, Calista thought, downright intimidating. She found, suddenly, that she didn't have the slightest urge to patronize him.

Calista backed up three steps. Just to relieve the strain on her neck, she silently reassured herself.

"You were expected back over a week ago," the Dorinor rumbled, studying both her and Rhys with disapproval.

"I am the one responsible for the delay," Rhys said,

chin up. In the low light, with his black eyes, black hair, and black skin suit, he seemed as intimidatingly powerful a force as the massive creature he faced so unflinchingly.

"Indeed?" The Dorinor swung his head around and down, until his eyes were on a level with Rhys's. His lips pulled back and his sharp teeth gleamed white only inches from Rhys's throat.

Rhys didn't move. "That's right. I have commitments to others as well as to you."

He didn't say any more. He didn't seem to need to. The Dorinor, after several long seconds when he continued to stare silently at Rhys, nodded slowly. Then he turned away and crossed to the platform at the far side of the cavern and sat on his haunches.

After a quick, questioning glance at her, Rhys advanced to stand in front of the platform. Calista was right beside him. Larr took a position a discreet five or six steps back.

"You have brought the equipment Larr sent you for?" the Dorinor asked.

"Yes." Rhys obviously intended to take charge of the conversation.

"You know what its purpose is?"

"No."

Calista held her breath, wondering what the answer would be.

There was no answer. Instead, the Dorinor posed another question, his golden gaze fixed on Rhys. "Can you work on heavy machinery such as the equipment you brought?

Rhys hesitated for only a fraction of a second. "Yes."

"Can you?" The Dorinor swung his head around to stare directly at Calista.

"I'm as good a mechanic as he is." Calista frowned.

What was the point of all these questions?

The Dorinor swung his head up and back so his chin almost touched the curve of his long neck. Calista counted the seconds as he stared down at them, unspeaking. A minute passed, then two.

Calista was beginning to fidget under the silence when he spoke again.

"I want you both to oversee the installation of the new equipment," the Dorinor said, as flatly as possible for any creature who spoke in rasps, whistles, and grating grunts.

Calista looked at Rhys. Rhys looked at her. She couldn't think of anything to say in response. From his expression, he couldn't either.

Larr jumped into the breach. "But, Excellency, my people—"

"Call in Pa'a, Karnor," the Dorinor instructed, ignoring Larr's protest.

Without moving from his spot, Karnor gave a loud, grating shout. A few minutes later, one of the gray-furred creatures trotted into the cavern and up to the foot of the Dorinor's platform. Ignoring the three humans, it threw itself on the floor.

"I have come as you bid me, O Great One. My life is the life of Karta, my soul your servant—"

"Never mind that now," the Dorinor rasped. "I have work for you."

"Of course, Master. As you say, Master." The gray clumsily scrambled to its feet, then thrust its three-fingered hands into the pouch which hung from a belt around its thick waist.

Before it could open its mouth to renew the protestations of respect, the Dorinor said, "These two humans have brought new equipment." He gestured toward Rhys and Calista with one clawed forefoot, but he didn't take his eyes off the nervous gray. "They

253

will work with you to install it."

"But, Excellency—"

"Our contract didn't say anything—"

"Now, just a minute—"

Larr's, Rhys's, and Calista's simultaneous protests were cut short by an outraged roar from the Dorinor.

"These are my orders! You *will* obey them!" The Dorinor half rose on his massive hind feet while his forefeet came up for battle, sharp claws clearly displayed.

Calista crouched, muscles tensed. She had no weapons. After those first couple of encounters with the Kartanese guards, she'd given up trying to carry them. But she wasn't going to agree to something before she knew anything about it.

When a hand wrapped around her arm, she whirled, ready to defend herself, only to find it was Rhys who had taken her in such a tight grip.

"We'd be delighted to do what we can to help, Excellency," he said calmly. Without taking his eyes off the still angry Dorinor, he tugged on Calista's arms, pulling her around behind him.

Out of the side of his mouth he hissed, "Shut up, you fool. We're unarmed."

If they'd been anyplace else, Calista would gladly have socked him. As it was, she settled for wrenching her arm free of his grip. "We'll consider it, anyway," she said, loudly enough for both Larr and the Dorinor to hear.

The concession was grudging, in the very least, but it evidently was enough to pacify the Dorinor. He sank back on his haunches and tucked his forefeet closer to his body.

"Very well."

Calista would have responded to that, but Rhys was tugging on her arm again. He was distractingly insistent. As he pulled her away from the platform, Larr pushed past, clearly intent on protesting the Dorinor's decision.

"Let's get out of here and drag this Pa'a creature with us," Rhys said, low enough so only she could hear. "Do you want to lose this chance to finally find some answers?"

He didn't wait to hear her response. Without letting go of her arm, he gestured to the big gray creature the Dorinor had called Pa'a. "Let's go."

Pa'a hesitated, clearly wavering between following the strange humans he'd been assigned to work with and the urge to abase himself before the Dorinor once more. It wasn't duty so much as the Dorinor's irritated grunt of dismissal that decided the issue. Head drooping, hands twisting nervously, Pa'a followed them out of the cavern.

Once they were well into the passage from which Pa'a had emerged earlier, Rhys dropped Calista's arm and turned to face the lumbering gray creature.

"All right, Pa'a. What's this all about?" Rhys demanded, hands on hips.

"About, master?" Clearly puzzled, Pa'a scratched his belly and stared down at them.

"What is it we're supposed to work on with you? What's this equipment we brought being used for? What are Larr's people doing here?" Calista had had enough of keeping quiet and she had a *lot* of questions that needed answers.

At least a small part of what she'd said got through. Pa'a straightened and nodded eagerly. "I will work with you. The master has said so."

"But what is it we're going to work *on*?" Calista's level of frustration was rising rapidly.

"The equipment. We will work on the equipment

with you. The master has said so." Pa'a tucked his hands back in his pouch then just stood there, waiting for them to make the next move.

"Great. This is just great," Calista muttered in disgust. She looked at Rhys for help.

He looked back at her and shrugged. "Your guess is as good as mine. But at least we know where to start." He turned to the gray. "All right, big guy. Lead us to the hauler. Once we've got the equipment, you can show us what we're supposed to do with it."

The hauler was still sitting where they'd left it, but the equipment was gone. Calista drew up short. She wouldn't have thought they'd been away long enough for the grays to have moved all of the crates this quickly.

Pa'a paid no attention to her reaction. He just kept walking and didn't stop until he'd reached the base of the hauler's ramp.

"Here it is," he said simply.

"Here what is?" Rhys demanded, irritation sharpening his voice.

"The hauler," Pa'a said. "You told me to lead you to it. I have done as you required."

"What?" Calista wasn't sure Pa'a's explanation made any more sense than the disappearance of the crates.

The hauler's pilot suddenly appeared at the top of the ramp, an amused expression on his round, red face. "You gotta be careful what you tell the stupid brutes," he said. "They'll do exactly what you tell 'em and that's about it. Sometimes they can't even manage that."

Rhys grimaced in disgust. He studied Pa'a, who stood there watching him with an air of patient expectancy, then looked at the pilot. "Where'd the new equipment go?"

The pilot shrugged. "The *drenn* took it to that cavern they're working on. You ready to pick up the next load? If we don't finish today, it might be a week before I can come back."

Rhys hesitated. "Calista?"

Calista considered her options. She should go back to the *Fair Trade* on the hauler. Rhys didn't like strangers on his ship and things would go much faster with both of them working to get the crates loaded. On the other hand, she could stay on Karta and try to find some answers to the myriad questions nagging at her. The Dorinor *had* been pretty insistent.

"I'll go with Pa'a," she said.

A few minutes later as the hauler, its engines whining, lifted off the ground to hover for a moment, then swing around and fly out the now-open doors of the cavern, Calista wondered if she'd made a mistake in remaining behind.

She hadn't promised to stay and help Rhys—at least, not really—but by not trying to get out of this ridiculous assignment the Dorinor had given them, she might have committed herself to something she couldn't follow through on.

And what would that mean for her relationship with Rhys?

In just a couple of minutes the hauler was a mere speck against the pale blue sky; then it was gone and the massive doors slowly swung shut, blocking out the harsh sunlight and the world beyond.

As the last clanging echoes of the closing doors died away within the cavern, Calista shook herself, then forced her shoulders back.

"Come on, Pa'a," she said. "You lead the way to where your friends have taken that equipment. I'll follow."

* * *

By the time Rhys finally showed up several hours later, Calista was tired, hot, grumpy, and thoroughly frustrated.

As instructed, Pa'a had taken her to the equipment. He'd even shown her some of the machinery already in place in a series of interconnected chambers deep within the mountain.

But though he'd tried his best to answer her questions, all Calista had gotten out of the conversation was a confused impression that the complex mechanical systems Larr's people and the grays had installed was somehow connected to the well-being of the cocoons, or "eggs," as the translator interpreted Pa'a's words.

Calista was down on her knees trying to peer through a foot-wide tunnel cut out of the solid rock when Rhys's appearance caused a flurry of excitement among the six grays at work around her. She sat back on her heels with a sigh and watched him stride across the chamber to her.

He was still dressed in the black skin suit he'd worn earlier, but this time he'd slung a belt around his slim hips to carry tools, hand comps, and anything else he'd figured might be needed. A small bag dangled from his right hand.

He looked cool, self-possessed, and completely comfortable, despite the crazy situation into which the Dorinor had thrust them. He also looked far more desirable than any man Calista had ever known or ever hoped to know.

She tried, and failed, to blow a stray lock of hair out of her eyes, then swiped her sleeve across her forehead to wipe off the beads of sweat. If she'd had any sense, she would have asked him to bring a packet of food and a skin suit for her. But she hadn't thought to ask and now here she was, looking like a grubby waif while he looked good enough to dazzle a dozen beauties from the Imperial court.

Calista scowled, then wiped at the tip of her nose with a dirty fist to catch the drop of sweat that had trickled down.

"What'd you do, Fairdane? Take a nap?" she demanded, in spite of her best intentions to hold her tongue.

Rhys's right eyebrow rose a fraction of an inch. He stopped four feet in front of her and slowly—and very insultingly, to Calista's way of thinking—let his gaze roam over her.

"Were you studying the machinery here," he asked, "or trying to clean it?"

"At least I was doing something constructive, instead of lounging around on a nice, clean, air-conditioned spaceship," she snapped. The instant the words were out, she regretted them. The comment wasn't fair. It had been her choice to stay on Karta.

"No doubt." His lips twitched.

Calista sighed, then shifted to sit on the stone floor. It was a strain to crane her head back to look up at him, but she didn't feel like wasting the energy needed to get to her feet. "Sorry. I didn't mean to be so—" She shrugged, embarrassed. "I don't suppose you brought anything to drink down with you."

Rhys's mouth curved upward in sympathetic amusement. "As a matter of fact, I did." He tossed the small bag he held at her feet. "There's a jug of cold water, some food, and a skin suit in there for you. Also one of my small washrags that you find so amusing. The rag's damp, so you can cool off a little. I figured if you'd been down here this long working on the equipment, you'd need it."

Calista took the bag, but before she could say

thanks, Rhys added dryly, "You might want to wash your face. It needs it."

Calista didn't give him the satisfaction of responding. Instead, she grabbed the bag and began rooting around inside. A drink of cold water came first. Then the rag. She couldn't help wrinkling her nose in distaste when she saw how dirty it came away after one pass around her face. She shifted to a clean spot on the rag and rubbed again.

While she indulged in the makeshift cleanup, Rhys scanned the grays and the machinery around them, then settled into a cross-legged position on the floor beside her.

"Found anything interesting?" he asked, watching one of the grays caress a piece of equipment it was attending.

Calista took another swig of water, then twisted to see what he was watching. "They do that all the time," she said. "Every one of them. They've got everything divided up among themselves, just like the grays with those crates." She frowned, searching for the right words to describe what she'd seen and learned over the past few hours. "It's crazy, but the way they treat that equipment, you'd think they were taking care of their very own babies."

She reached into the bag again, searching for the qaali fruit she'd seen. After hours spent with only the grays for company, it was comforting to have another human being to talk to.

No, that wasn't right. It was comforting to have *Rhys* to talk to.

Calista froze.

Don't, she told herself silently, fiercely. Not now.

She was the one who'd chosen to put up a barrier between them by not promising to remain on Karta. From his perspective, Rhys had every right keep his distance. She'd be a fool to let her emotions rule her head now.

With an effort of will, Calista forced herself to pick up the fruit and take a bite. She couldn't force herself to meet his eyes when he turned back to her.

"Have they said anything that would explain what they do, who they are?" Rhys asked.

Was it only her imagination, or did she detect a note of strain in his voice? And if she did, was it because of what the answers might mean to them, or to Rhys's plans for the third planet? Calista's fingers tightened around the fruit until her nails dug into the firm flesh.

"No, not a word," she said, biting off the words sharply. "They don't talk much among themselves, and as long as I keep out of their way, they ignore me completely. They're not stupid, but they seem incapable of thinking for themselves. They don't have any pride, but they cling to those damn machines as if the fate of the universe rested on them."

She glanced at the grays guiltily, wondering if they'd heard her and taken offense. The creatures didn't once look their way, oblivious to the presence of the humans in their midst.

"Do you still think they're slaves?" Not by so much as the flick of an eyelash did Rhys suggest her answer mattered.

"I . . . I don't know," Calista admitted reluctantly.

Rhys opened his mouth to respond, but Calista never found out what he was going to say because a Kartanese burst into the chamber at that moment.

The huge, black creature was as silent in its movements as every other Kartanese Calista had ever met, but it didn't remain silent long.

"The waters are not flowing," it roared. In the relatively narrow confines of the chamber, the sound reverberated painfully. "What have you fools done to the waters?"

The seemingly simple question generated pandemonium among the grays.

One, the largest and seemingly the leader, threw itself on the ground before the angry Kartanese. "The waters, Master?"

"The waters, fool! Why must I explain myself twice?"

"Yes, Master, but—"

"Tend to it!" the Kartanese roared.

The grays who were still upright scrambled to be the first out of the cavern. Their haste only added to the confusion since both the Kartanese and the prostrate gray blocked their path. When they couldn't slip past, they settled for milling about in nervous, gibbering confusion.

The first gray, still cringing on the floor, offered the solution. "Perhaps if you would lead, Master?"

It took a moment for the value of the suggestion to sink in. When it did, the Kartanese, muttering fiercely, twisted round and headed back the way it had come. Calista barely avoided being struck by its angrily lashing tail as it left.

One of the smaller, more fragile pieces of equipment nearer the entrance wasn't so lucky. The heavy tail shattered the bank of monitoring instruments and severely dented the heavy metallic shell, but the Kartanese didn't even stop.

The gray who had attended the machine so carefully stopped, however. A rough, grating wail broke from its mouth as it futilely patted and caressed the damaged equipment.

It wasn't given much chance to grieve. The first gray was on its feet by now. Grabbing the distraught creature by the long hair across its back, it dragged it, whimpering and wailing, from the chamber.

The quiet that remained seemed to echo even more loudly than had the shouting a moment earlier. Calista stood, back to the stone wall, too shaken to move. Rhys seemed in little better shape. Only the sound of a vehement, and very human, curse was enough to rouse them.

"Stupid beasts," the woman who stood near the entrance said with repressed passion, staring after the departed assemblage. "You'd think they'd learn to control themselves, but every little problem gets turned into a major production. It's as if they *enjoy* their idiotic theatrics."

Calista stared at her, too startled to speak. She'd seen a few women in Larr's complex, but what was this woman doing here now, and why had she been with the Kartanese? Before Calista could ask, her attention was caught by something else. "Your cheek!" she exclaimed, pointing. "You're bleeding!"

The woman frowned, then wiped her cheek with the back of her hand. The action smeared blood along the side of her face. She stared at her hand in distaste. "Stupid beasts," she said again, even more vehemently.

Rhys crossed to her, then placed his finger under her chin and tilted her head so he could see her cheek more clearly. "It's just a scratch, even if it is bleeding rather heavily. What happened?"

The woman jerked free of his touch. "It was her flapping around like that. I tried to dodge but she caught me with the edge of her wing." She swore again. "You'd think by now I'd know better than to tell those stupid beasts anything. They haven't got the brains of a Seuterian louse."

Something about the sneering words and the blood stirred a long-forgotten memory in Calista. She shook her head, trying to drive it away.

The woman pushed past Rhys and strode over to the broken machinery. "Stupid beasts," she muttered again as she ran her hands across the broken controls.

Her actions were strangely like those of the grief-stricken gray, Calista thought, watching her. "Are you an engineer here?"

The woman thumped the side of the shattered case in disgust, then turned to face them. "Not for long. I've had it with trying to work with these overgrown, pebble-brained—" She stopped in mid-breath to stare at first Calista, then Rhys. "You're the new traders." It wasn't a question and it was definitely hostile.

"That's right." Hostility didn't faze Rhys.

His calm response didn't soothe the angry engineer. "Well, enjoy your profits while you can. Sooner or later, the beasts will either drive you crazy or they'll kill you. If it weren't for the silk—" She shrugged and would have moved past Rhys to the entrance if he hadn't stopped her.

"What do you mean by that?" he demanded.

She smiled up at him, but it wasn't a pleasant smile. "Haven't you ever wondered what happened to your predecessor?" she asked.

Calista could see Rhys's grip on the woman's arm tighten. "What happened?" The two words were as much a command as a query.

The woman pulled free. "Ask Larr." Her feral grin widened. "Better yet, ask the Dorinor's buddy, Karnor."

With that, she turned and stomped out. Calista just caught her parting words.

"Stupid beasts. Stupid, useless beasts," the woman said.

With those words, the memory that had been biting

at the edges of her consciousness came flooding back. Calista gasped at the force of the emotions it brought with it.

She'd been thirteen when the overseer had come storming into the women's slave quarters late one night. He'd been angry, furious. Calista couldn't remember why.

She could remember the confusion and the fear, the way the older slaves had rushed to pacify him, cringing and abasing themselves, trying to appease his anger before the brunt of it fell on them directly.

It hadn't worked. In his rage, the man had flung one of the women against a chest as if she'd been a filthy rag lying in his path. The woman had cried out, once, then slumped in a heap at the foot of the chest.

Calista hadn't known the woman well. She couldn't even remember her name. But she could remember the blood mixed with clear liquid that had trickled from her ear, could remember her dying, ever so slowly, as she lay in a broken, pathetic heap on the floor. The smell of fear had been sharp and acrid in the air, the night sounds from outside painfully loud.

As though engraved in her memory, Calista could see the overseer, his rage only partially appeased, standing in the doorway and glaring at the slaves who were too frightened even to aid their dying companion. "Stupid beasts," he'd said. "Stupid, useless beasts."

Calista's heart pounded. Her stomach churned and cold sweat broke out on her skin.

Stupid beasts. They were words of scorn and disgust—the words of a man speaking to slaves he didn't even count as human. *Stupid beasts.*

"Calista? Calista, are you all right?"

The words seemed to come from far away.

Calista shook her head, fighting to break free of

265

the memory. A hand pressed on her shoulder. With a startled cry, she threw it off and jerked away out of reach.

"What the hell?"

The expletive brought the present rushing back. Calista blinked, gulped in air, and stared at Rhys.

"Are you all right?" he demanded, his brow furrowed in puzzled concern.

"Yes. Yes, of course I'm all right." It cost Calista an effort to force the words past her suddenly constricted throat.

Rhys clearly didn't believe her.

"Why don't you go back to the *Fair Trade*?" he said. "Take a shower, get a decent meal—" He let the suggestion hang in the air between them.

Calista nodded. "Sure. I could do that." She swallowed and tried to ignore her shaking limbs and the icy sweat pooling between her breasts. "Not a bad idea."

Rhys moved as if to touch her. "I'll go with you—"

"No!"

He dropped his hand to his side. His fingers curved into a fist.

"No," she said, this time more calmly. "I'm sorry. It's nothing. Really. I'm suddenly just a little tired, I guess."

Calista wanted him to hold her, to drive out the memories. But he knew nothing of those memories and she still lacked the courage to tell him.

Would she ever find that courage? she wondered, staring at Rhys. Would she ever be able to lay the memories to rest?

Rhys stepped back, uncertain. His eyes seemed lost in their shadowed sockets. "If you're sure you're all right—?"

"I'm sure. Why don't you go after the grays, find out what all the ruckus was about?"

"That's not a bad idea." He hesitated, giving her a chance to retract her refusal of help. When she didn't say anything, he left. He didn't even look back.

Calista watched him go. Once he was out of sight, she sagged back against the wall behind her, grateful for its hard, unyielding support.

She wanted to run after him, but she had no right to because she knew, now, what it was she must do. She should have known it all along.

One wrong did not justify another. It never would. She could not help Rhys right the wrong done to his people if it meant she would perpetuate the wrong done to the innocent grays.

No matter how dull-witted or incompetent the grays were, they were sentient beings. No one had the right to hold them against their will or treat them as the Kartanese did.

If she stayed, she would be guilty of the same cowardly acceptance of injustice that had kept her from going to the side of the dying slave all those years ago. There was nothing she could do to change the system here, but she couldn't—wouldn't—support it by using her skills as a trader to fatten the Dorinor's coffers, not even to help Rhys and his people.

Pain knifed deep in Calista. In leaving, she was not only abandoning Rhys, she was also abandoning any chance of happiness she might have had with him. She couldn't help that, but she could do her best not to trample on his dreams in the process.

Calista pushed away from the wall, her next steps clear in her mind. She did what she could to arrange her hair a little more neatly and to brush the dust and dirt she'd accumulated from her clothes; then, shoulders pushed back as straight as she could make them, she set off to find Larr.

After a number of false turns, she finally found

an entrance to the area he and his people occupied. With the exception of a clerk bent over his computer, she saw no one. The clerk scarcely glanced up from his work when she asked for directions to Larr's quarters.

She found Larr in the spacious room where the three of them had toasted the signing of their contracts—ages ago, it now seemed to her. His blond head showed over the back of a heavy chair that was pulled around to face the window set in the far wall.

Calista hesitated in the doorway, struggling to assume just the right air of anger and determination she would need to convince Larr of her resolve. Once she was convinced her mask was firmly in place, she crossed the room to stand beside Larr's chair.

"I want to talk to you, Larr," she said without preamble.

The Dorinor's representative shifted slightly in his chair, as though suddenly aware of her presence. "Do you?"

"I want out of my contract, Larr. Now."

"Indeed." Larr smiled, clearly amused by her belligerence. He gestured to a chair set at an angle to his. "Why don't you sit down?"

"I prefer to stand." Calista moved to place herself squarely between Larr and the window. "I can't work with Fairdane. I told you that at the start. I've tried, but it's not working, so I want out."

Larr slowly, thoughtfully, ran his finger over his lips, back and forth. His smile widened. "I thought it might come to this."

"Then why—?"

"I had my reasons."

Calista brushed the suggestion aside, irritated. "I'm quitting, Larr."

The smile widened even further, until it lighted his

perfect features with its radiance. "Oh, I don't think so," he said, very softly.

"You can't stop me."

"Perhaps not. But I have a great deal of confidence that the slave hunters from Andrus could. What do you think?"

Chapter Sixteen

The air stuck in Calista's throat. Her heart missed a beat while her mind tried to grapple with the frightening significance of Larr's words.

"What do you mean?" Even as she spoke, Calista knew the bluff wouldn't work.

Larr's thin lips quivered in amusement. "I think you know perfectly well what I mean, Trader York. Of course, that isn't your real name, is it?"

When Calista didn't answer, Larr gestured to the chair he'd indicated earlier. "I really do wish you'd sit down. It's so uncomfortable having to carry on a conversation with you standing over me like that."

Calista took the chair, her movements stiff and awkward. Her eyes never wavered from Larr's face.

For years she'd dreaded this moment. In her worst nightmares she'd imagined what it would be like when she was revealed as an escaped slave. She'd thought of a hundred scenarios for what she would do, how she would react. The only thing she hadn't expected was to be so stunned that no emotions seeped past the shock.

"You're taking this very well, I must say," Larr said pleasantly. "I admit, I rather expected a little more . . . violence."

"How did—" Calista swallowed, then licked her lips. "How did you find out?" She wrapped her hands around the edge of her seat, grateful for something to cling to.

"Chance." Larr smiled reminiscently. "I'd been looking around for new trade reps even before your esteemed predecessor's demise. People sometimes forget that information is a marketable commodity, too," he added, as if anxious to explain a point she might not have caught. "I'd picked up interesting bits and pieces, a little here, a little there. Eventually I had enough little bits to make an intriguing—and useful—whole."

"Why did you bother?" Calista rasped. Anger pushed at the edge of her awareness. The fear, she thought vaguely, would come later.

Larr beamed as though she'd identified a particularly subtle and elusive question. "I've always found it helpful to know the . . . vulnerabilities . . . of those around me. One can never tell when such knowledge will be advantageous. Like now."

"Why didn't you just turn me in for the reward, then find another trader?"

Larr dismissed the question with a wave of his hand. "You underrate yourself, my dear. I would never be so foolish as to waste your remarkable abilities as a trader for the relatively trivial reward your masters would pay. Besides, with the exception of your status as a runaway slave, you have an impeccable record for honest dealings. Such integrity is commendable and, may I say, highly unusual."

"Is that why you chose me? My honesty?" Anger was coming to her defense at last, breaking through the appalling numbness that had held her trapped for the past few minutes.

The corner of Larr's mouth twitched. "It helped that you also happen to be a very shrewd negotiator. You and Trader Fairdane complement one another very well, I think—and you're both admirably suited for certain . . . mmm . . . plans of mine for the future. I look forward to some quite extraordinary successes from you two."

"I told you, Larr: I can't work with Fairdane." The sick feeling in the pit of Calista's stomach returned. Did Larr know about Rhys's search? That kind of information would be extremely easy to get for someone who'd managed to ferret out the truth about her background.

"You'll learn." Larr dropped his pretense of detached amusement. His voice was suddenly hard and menacing. "You'll work with Fairdane and you'll like it, or the slave hunters will be reminded of a certain fourteen-year-old girl who left Andrus illegally. Do you understand?"

Calista stiffened. She didn't like threats, but she hadn't the slightest idea how to deal with this one.

"Do you understand me, trader?" Larr asked again, very softly.

"I understand." Calista had to force the words out.

Larr smiled, his mask of pleasant amusement back in place. "That's good, trader. You're very wise."

Calista rose to her feet. She needed to get away, put some distance between her and Larr. She needed to think, but right now her whirling thoughts refused to focus on anything but the appalling fact that her past had finally caught up with her.

She was halfway to the door when she stopped abruptly, her attention caught by a fleeting memory. Something Larr had said ... A word he'd used ... Calista shook her head, frustrated that the thought slipped out of reach. She swung around to find that Larr was on his feet as well, standing by his chair and watching her with an expression of cruel triumph on his face.

Demise! That was it. Larr had said something about her predecessor's demise.

"What happened to him?" she demanded.

"What happened to whom?" One of Larr's eyebrows arched in polite inquiry.

"Tull. The trade rep before us. What happened to him?"

"I never told you?" Larr looked shocked at the oversight. "How thoughtless of me." He smiled. "Karnor ate him."

Calista could have sworn the floor shifted under her feet. "Ate him?"

"That's right. The Kartanese do that when they feel someone's become a danger to their society. It's a habit I've found rather ... useful now and then."

At that moment, one of the Kartanese flew in front of the window behind Larr. Calista watched, appalled and fascinated, as the huge, beautiful creature twisted in mid-flight, then abruptly dove toward the plain far below.

Larr turned to see what had caught her attention. "It's hunting, you know." He glanced back at her over his shoulder, judging her reaction. His smile made Calista think of a predator stalking its prey. A hungry predator.

"They're such stupidly naive, good-natured brutes, we tend to forget they're carnivores. Rather vicious carnivores," he added, clearly pleased at the thought.

"Especially when they're angry."

Calista couldn't take any more. She turned and fled.

Once out of the room, Calista transported directly to the *Fair Trade*. She had to tell Rhys.

More than that, she had to see him, touch him. She didn't stop to analyze why, she just knew she needed his strength right now. His strength and his calm, clear-headed, rational approach to solving problems. She needed *him*.

She found him on the bridge, bent over one of the communication monitors. His first reaction was obvious irritation at the interruption. His second, an instant after he got a clear look at her face, was sharp concern.

"What the—?" He was out of his chair and across the room to her in three strides. "What happened? Are you all right? For stars' sake, sit down before you fall over."

His hand on her arm felt comfortingly warm and strong. If she'd dared, Calista would have thrown herself into his arms. She didn't dare, but she gratefully accepted his support as he led her to the chair by the one he'd just vacated.

"Sit, Calista, before you fall down," he commanded sternly. He didn't let go of her until she was firmly ensconced in the chair, then he resumed his own. "Now, what happened? You look like—" He shook his head, clearly worried.

"He knows, Rhys." Calista forced the words out, one at a time, very carefully. "Larr knows."

"Knows what?"

"About your people, about your search for an inhabitable world you can claim." Calista gulped, still too confused and shocked to make the words come out right. "At least, I think he knows."

Rhys's brow knit in a thoughtful frown. "That's possible. He would have run a background check on me. It wouldn't be hard to figure out if he really wanted to know." His dark eyes studied her. "But that's not what shook you, Calista."

"No." Calista, eyes downcast, drew the word out slowly, uncertain what to say next. She'd spent most of her life hiding her past. Even now, after Larr's revelation, it wasn't easy to let down the guard she'd maintained around her secret for so many years.

"Larr found out," she faltered at last, "that . . . that I—"

Calista gripped the armrests of her chair, fighting to hold on to something fixed and firm in a world suddenly grown frighteningly unstable. With an effort, she brought her gaze up to meet Rhys's steady, questioning look.

Something in those dark eyes gave her the courage to go on. "I'm an escaped slave. Everything I have, everything I've worked for will be forfeit if I'm ever discovered."

Surprise, shock, and finally understanding showed in Rhys's gaze. He made no move to touch her, offered no words of comfort, but Calista felt the tension inexplicably ease within her. After so many years of keeping her past a secret and repressing even the slightest reference to where she'd come from and what she'd been, it would be good to speak the truth at last.

"I was born into slavery. I don't know who my father and mother were; I don't know where they came from, or if they were born slaves like me. My owners were—are—estate holders on the planet Andrus."

"Andrus!" The word burst from Rhys. Hot anger flamed in his eyes. "That's the worst hell in the

Empire! They treat humans like . . . like . . . My god! Andrus!"

Calista forced her shoulders back and her head up. "I won't go back. I was fourteen when I escaped and I *won't* go back. Ever."

Put up a bold front, never let the other side know if you're uncertain or confused or just plain scared. She'd learned that long ago. Calista faced Rhys squarely.

She'd never done anything harder in her life. Inside, she shook with the fear she'd managed to repress or ignore for so long. She wanted to let go, wanted to cry and for once, just once, she wanted not to be strong.

If only Rhys would hold her. If only he'd stretch out his arms and gather her close. She'd be safe, then. Nothing could touch her if Rhys was there to protect her.

He wouldn't do it. She was sure of that.

Once, perhaps, he might have come to her aid. Once, not so long ago, he would have stood between her and the fears she'd fought against for so long. But not now. She'd shut him out of her life, put her needs first and refused to acknowledge his, and now she had no claim on him, no right to ask for the comfort and assurance she needed so badly.

There was nothing she could say, no plea she could honestly make, and so Calista sat, staring at Rhys and fighting to keep up that bold false front that was all she had left.

Rhys slid from his chair to kneel at her feet. Gently, he cupped her face in his hands, forcing her to look at him.

"We'll find a way out of this, Calista," he said softly. "We can do it, the two of us. Together."

Together. Something inside Calista snapped, some

protective restraint she'd tied around her emotions long ago.

The hot tears she'd never, ever, allowed herself filled her eyes, blurring her vision and spilling over to flood down her cheeks. With a small, anguished moan, Calista slid out of her chair and into his welcoming arms. "I'm so scared, Rhys. I'm so scared."

"I know, Calista," he murmured in her ear as he crushed her against him. "I know."

Worn out by the emotional upheaval of the past few hours and by her faltering, cathartic recounting of her past, Calista had fallen asleep easily.

Rhys, however, was wide awake.

He sat in a chair pulled up to the foot of his bed and watched Calista as she slept.

He'd never been more frightened in his life.

He'd promised her they'd not only find a way to prevent Larr from carrying out his threats, but that they'd obtain her freedom and the world he sought, as well. Bold words to comfort a distraught woman. Right now, those promises looked like nothing but so much hot air.

What had they gotten themselves into, Rhys wondered, and how were they going to get out?

Even if he were prepared to walk away before he'd had a good try at obtaining the rights to the third planet, Larr held him bound in a contract that was as rigidly confining as it was lucrative.

What was more worrisome, the fragile net of trade his people had built to finance their existing settlements was all too vulnerable to outside meddling. Larr could easily destroy what had taken years to build and after his threats toward Calista, Rhys had no doubt that Larr would use the threat of interference if it suited his purpose.

Calista's situation was even worse. She faced what would amount to a death sentence if the slave hunters found her and took her back to Andrus. Her proud and fiercely independent spirit would never survive a return to the horror of the life she'd once known and escaped at such cost.

Rhys had to grind his teeth together in order to keep from cursing. Andrus! Even the name of that hellhole made him sick to his stomach.

He no longer wondered that Calista had always been so insistent on running things her way, or that she'd so strongly resisted the efforts he'd made to intervene whenever her impetuous nature led her astray. To an escaped slave, any sort of restraint or control imposed by others must seem like a kind of slavery, a forced subjugation to the will of others.

He certainly understood why she'd been so vehement in her refusal to work with the Kartanese after her first discovery of the grays. As far as he was concerned, the only wonder was that she'd been willing even to consider staying and working for the Kartanese when every instinct, every fiber of her being must have raged against it.

And he'd accused her of being selfish and self-centered, of thinking only of her own goals! The memory shamed him now.

Rhys studied the pale face on the pillow. How little he'd understood.

True, she'd never spoken of her past or tried to explain her actions, but neither had he—and she'd had far more reason to keep quiet. Silence, for him, had become a trader's ploy to protect whatever advantage he might have in a negotiation. Silence for her had been a matter of survival.

As though responding to his thoughts, Calista stirred in her sleep, murmuring unintelligibly into her pillow and twisting under the light cover as if trying to get away from whatever it was that pursued her through her dreams. She kicked out with her foot, throwing the cover back, but before Rhys could lean forward to soothe her, she quieted and drifted back into sleep.

Rhys waited for a moment, wondering if she would rouse again. When she remained quiet, he reached for the edge of the light blanket to tuck it back in. His hand froze midway as a small, white scar around her ankle caught his eye.

He'd seen it before. In the right light, like now, it was readily noticeable for it cut across the narrowest part of her leg, just above the anklebone. He'd never bothered to ask how she'd gotten it.

Now he was afraid he knew—steel shackles, the kind used to chain recalcitrant slaves, had caused that scar. His hand balled into a tight fist, crushing the soft fabric of the blanket.

She hadn't told him so, but he knew.

On the bridge, her admission of fear had opened the floodgates of memory. In an unstoppable rush, all the hurtful, haunting memories she'd kept dammed up inside her for so long had come pouring out, swamping him with the horror, anguish and pity of it all. But even as he'd cradled her in his arms and listened to her disjointed, sometimes incoherent recital of what it had meant to be young and a slave on Andrus, he'd known she wasn't telling him everything.

Rhys suspected she never would. She was too proud and the memories too painful for that.

She'd told him enough, however. If it cost him his life, he'd ensure she'd never return to Andrus.

Taking care not to wake her, Rhys tucked the edge of the blanket in around her feet, then rose and silently left the room. He needed a plan, a course of action that would free them from Larr's power.

Rhys had no illusions about Larr's ruthlessness. The Dorinor's representative wouldn't hesitate to destroy them both if it served his purpose, but for right now he obviously wanted them alive and working for him. Rhys still hadn't figured out why.

That didn't matter right now. What mattered was getting free of Larr's control. Somehow, someway, Rhys vowed, he'd find a way to break Larr's little game and still gain what both he and Calista sought.

He just wasn't sure how he was going to do it.

"The first thing is to be sure you keep up the pretense of not being able to get along with me," Rhys said the next morning.

They'd been arguing and discussing alternative actions for over an hour, and they were no further along than when they'd started.

"In fact," he added, "it might be better if you transported over to the *Independence* and beamed down from there. What would Larr think if he found that his two traders who didn't get along too well, nonetheless spent the night together?"

Calista started to protest, then immediately thought better of it.

Ever since she'd awakened to a new day and the realization that her past was no longer a secret to be protected from Rhys at all costs, she'd felt strangely light-headed.

She couldn't explain it. She didn't want to. But for the first time in her life she felt . . . human. Fully and completely human. As if her tears had finally washed away the appalling taint of being a slave.

Calista knew such confidence was unwarranted. Larr's threats still hung over her, as did the danger of discovery by the slave hunters she'd feared for so long.

Neither Larr nor the hunters mattered as they had yesterday, however, for between the "then" and the "now" lay a new reality in which she no longer stood alone and vulnerable. There in Rhys's arms, she had washed away the past's bitter legacy of pain with the stinging salt tears that had coursed so freely down her cheeks.

No, not washed it away. Cleansed it, so that it would never again have the same power to hurt her.

Calista sat silent, staring across the table at Rhys, drinking in every detail of his strong, dark features, every nuance of his voice. Nothing seemed changed, yet everything was transformed in ways she could not define. She felt as if she could sit here forever and never grow tired of watching him, listening to him.

"Calista!"

The harsh sound jerked her from her reverie with startling force.

"Have you heard a word I've said?" Rhys demanded, glaring at her across the table.

"Uh, sure." Calista mentally groped for some proof—any proof—that she'd been listening. "I should transport over to the *Independence* and—"

"I said that five minutes ago!" He shook his head, disgusted. "We've signed virtually unbreakable contracts we can't get out of; we're involved in something we haven't even begun to figure out; Larr's threatened you with exposure and a return to slavery—and all you can do is sit and stare at me as if I've sprouted green antennas from my ears."

He sounded angry, yet for the first time Calista heard the fear behind his words. Not for himself, but for her.

No one had ever been afraid for her before. Not ever.

The knowledge that Rhys cared that much brought tears to Calista's eyes.

For someone who had taken such pride in never crying, Calista thought, she was spending an awful lot of time doing just that lately. The fact that she *could* cry was yet another wonder to add to her growing list of wonders.

She ignored the tears and reached to take Rhys's right hand in both her own. "I'm sorry," she said. "I'm still just a little . . . I don't know . . . dazed, I guess."

"Forgive me." Rhys wrapped his left hand around hers. "I didn't mean to yell at you."

Calista couldn't help laughing. "Liar! But that's all right," she added hastily, when Rhys tried to interrupt. "I know nothing's resolved, but—" She shook her head, frustrated that the words escaped her. "I can't explain it, Rhys, but it doesn't seem to matter. Not like it would have yesterday. It's as if . . . as if I've been set free, somehow."

She pulled her hands from his, then stood up and leaned across the table to kiss Rhys on the lips. Slowly. Savoring every subtle detail.

When his mouth opened to her, she pulled back.

"I don't know that I'll ever find the words to thank you for . . . last night, for listening," she said softly. "I only know that I'm grateful and—"

She wanted to say, *and I love you.* She didn't have the courage. Not yet.

"—and that it will all work out. Somehow." She stepped back from the table, loath to leave Rhys but knowing that if she didn't now, she never would. There was still too much to do, too many obstacles ahead.

You're just too scared to find out if he feels the same

way about you, a voice within her whispered. The voice was absolutely right.

"I'll meet you on Karta in an hour," she said. "We might as well get to work installing all that new equipment we brought."

Three hours later, Rhys was bent over the controls on one of the recently installed machines when Larr silently strode into the chamber. Only the sudden nervousness of the two grays he'd been working with alerted him to the man's presence.

Careful to keep all expression from his face, Rhys straightened. "I didn't know you ever came this far into the caves, Larr."

"There are a lot of things you don't know, trader." Larr's gaze flicked over the grays, who had retreated to the far corner of the chamber, and the untidy jumble of equipment and tools scattered about. "The installation is going well, I hope?"

"It'd go a lot better if I had any idea what the hell we're doing."

"If you didn't know what you were doing, why did you agree to oversee the work?"

"I don't recall that Calista and I had any choice. Or did I misunderstand the Dorinor?" Rhys demanded sarcastically.

"No." Larr's thin mouth pursed in a disapproving frown. "You'd do well, trader, not to get too involved with the Dorinor."

"Why's that, Larr? Afraid I'll corrupt him?"

"Hardly. I worry for your safety, you know." Larr's expression gave no hint of the thoughts behind those cold eyes.

"I'm touched." Rhys knew he ought to keep his temper under control, but after Larr's threats to Calista, hiding his dislike of the Dorinor's representative was just short of impossible. "What, exactly, is so unsafe about dealing with the Dorinor? Do I run a risk of him sitting on me, or what?"

Anger sparked in Larr's eyes. "Don't mock me, Fairdane. I'm not in the mood for your silly jests."

"Just what are you in the mood for, Larr?" Rhys's eyes narrowed. "You obviously don't want me working on this equipment—whatever the hell it is—but it doesn't look to me as if you have much say in the matter."

"The Dorinor—"

"The Dorinor didn't *ask* me to take over your people's job, Larr. He *told* me to. Are you suggesting I should go against his orders?"

"No. I'm telling you to watch your step. There's more involved here than you realize."

Larr's suddenly assumed air of concern grated on Rhys far more than the threats had.

"Why don't you tell me just what *is* involved, Larr? How do you know I can't be of use?" Rhys let a hint of suggestive threat into his voice. But no more than a hint. He wanted Larr to open up, not shut him out.

Now it was Larr's turn to narrow his eyes. He didn't answer for a moment, then said, "I will, Fairdane. Soon." He smiled. His teeth shone white in the dim light. "I think you'll find my little proposition . . . interesting."

Rhys let the silence stretch while his thoughts raced. What was it Larr had planned? And why wouldn't he speak of it now?

If he antagonized Larr now, Rhys reminded himself, he might never find out. Forcing himself to relax, he returned Larr's white-toothed smile. "I'm always intrigued by . . . propositions." He paused, letting the subtle promise sink in, then asked, "I'm wondering if Calista will be intrigued, as well."

"She might be." A speculative gleam lit Larr's pale eyes. "Then again, she might not. What do you think, trader?"

Was it safer to count Calista in, or out? Rhys wondered. He already knew which course she'd choose, regardless. "She might. Especially if there are profits to be had."

"Oh, there are profits, trader. Nice, big, fat profits. But whether there were or not, I think Trader York would stay in the game."

He wasn't supposed to know about Calista's past or Larr's threats, Rhys reminded himself, forcing down his anger at Larr's presumption that he could so easily control Calista.

Rhys nodded curtly, suddenly anxious to be as far away from Larr as he could get. "That's all right, then."

"I take it you're still not getting along." Larr seemed pleased by the thought.

"We get along just fine . . . when there's money involved." He started to turn away, but Larr's hand on his arm stopped him.

"There's money involved, trader, but there's power as well. More power than you ever dreamed of. But if you two make one mistake, even one small mistake, on this equipment, you'll lose it all. Do you understand me?"

Rhys didn't understand any of it, but he wasn't about to admit it to this arrogant, manipulative cheat. "Don't threaten me, Larr."

"I'm not threatening you, trader. That was a promise."

This time it was Calista's turn to bring food, water and a damp washrag. Rhys was especially grateful for the rag. Working in the tunnels, even with the protection of a skin suit, was hot, hard, dirty labor.

They'd already spent the better part of a week working and, so far as Rhys could see, they still hadn't accomplished much worth mentioning.

"I don't know about you, but I don't seem to remember signing on as an engineer," he groused as he settled with his back against the cavern wall.

"Section eight, subsection four, paragraph twelve. Something about 'all duties, as required.' I checked," Calista added apologetically when he scowled.

"Since when have you become a space lawyer?"

Calista's right eyebrow rose a fraction of an inch at his bad humor. "I used to think I was pretty good at contracts, until I got involved in this." She slid down into a cross-legged position beside him. "Have you figured out what, by all the devils of Dormat, we're doing here, Rhys?"

"Environmental control. That's all I know. I've tried, but I can't figure out why the Kartanese and Larr think they need to install this kind of equipment. Chemical monitors, water circulation systems, humidity controls." He shook his head in disgust. "It doesn't make any sense."

Calista took a cautious bite of the bread and cheese she'd brought. Rhys watched as she chewed the food carefully, intrigued by her distant, thoughtful air of preoccupation. "Okay. Out with it. What have you found out?" he demanded.

She swallowed, then frowned. "Nothing. At least, nothing I'm sure of. But I've got an idea—"

Rhys waited as patiently as he could. Even a wild guess was better than no guesses at all.

"Remember I told you about that cavern with all the cocoons?" she said at last.

Rhys nodded without speaking. It wasn't something he was likely to forget, but so far he hadn't seen anything like what she'd described.

"It struck me at the time, but I was so engrossed in watching what was going on, I didn't pay that much attention. But now—" She hesitated. "The climate in that cavern was entirely different from the climate in any of the others we've seen. It was humid, for one thing. Everyplace else is dry enough to wilt a rock. And the pool had an odd color, as though it carried a lot of minerals in it." Calista frowned at the memory, then continued. "Remember that Kartanese who burst in the other day, shouting that the waters weren't flowing? He came *here*, not someplace else, which makes me wonder if—"

"You mean—?" Rhys let the question trail off as he considered the implications.

It was Calista's turn to nod. "I think we're supposed to be creating another nursery or hatching ground or incubator or whatever you want to call it," she said. "It's the only explanation I can find that makes sense."

"More baby Kartanese, more silk; more silk, more money. Or maybe it's just more babies, if the Kartanese are behind it and not Larr. You're right. It does make sense."

"So what do we do about it? Assuming I'm right, of course."

"What makes you think we need to do anything about it?"

Calista opened her mouth to reply, then shut it without saying a word.

"If you're right—and I think you are—what I'd like to know is, whose idea was this, anyway? The answer to that question would also answer a lot of others."

"And where do the grays fit in with all of this?" Calista wasn't looking at him when she said it; she was staring at the two creatures who continued to fuss over the machinery they'd each been assigned.

Rhys watched her, trying to gauge the emotions behind her thoughtful expression. In the days since her soul-wrenching revelations about her past, Calista had changed in subtle ways that he couldn't quite describe but that tantalized him with their fleeting insights into the woman who had lived for so long behind every protective emotional barrier she could erect against a hostile and dangerous world.

She seemed quieter, for one thing. More at peace with herself and the past, despite the threat of exposure that still loomed over her. Some of that hard, brittle edge that had made her so ready to quarrel and take offense had softened, too, so that she no longer was as quick to object to whatever he might say or do.

Rhys couldn't help smiling at that thought. He hoped she didn't lose all her combativeness. Their disagreements added a little spice to life and he'd be loath to give them up entirely.

Not that he really thought he'd have to. Calista was too fiercely independent and naturally high-spirited to give in readily to anyone else's ideas, no matter how much she mellowed.

Despite their agreement that the best strategy for right now was to maintain an appearance of mutual antipathy and distrust, Rhys had found it increasingly difficult to keep up the pretense. Just as Calista had changed, so had he.

He wasn't sure he could describe those changes if he had to, but he sensed within himself the same lowering of barriers that he sensed in Calista.

It wasn't anything he was consciously doing, nothing he'd deliberately decided upon. He was still bound by his obligations and commitments to his people. He hadn't given up his search for a new world and he doubted he ever would. Yet even with all that, he felt as though the weight of responsibility he'd carried for so long had somehow been lessened.

Rhys had no rational explanation for it. Perhaps it was because, after so many years of hiding what mattered most from each other, they'd finally found the courage to put an end to the secrets between them. Perhaps by sharing her fears, Calista had made it possible for him to let go of some of his.

He didn't know. Rhys only knew that, whatever lay ahead, he was deeply grateful for what he and Calista had shared in these past few days.

"Rhys? Rhys!"

The sharp note in Calista's voice cut through his thoughts. Rhys looked up to find Calista staring at him, forehead creased in puzzled exasperation.

"I said, can you think of any place the grays could have come from originally? They're not quite like any other creature I've ever seen."

"Maybe Larr brought them." Rhys stopped short, then grinned wryly. "After five days of working with them, I can't believe anyone would go to the effort of bringing them all the way to Karta, then keeping them as slaves. Can you?"

"Nooo." Calista drew the single syllable out slowly. "They're not stupid, but that passion of theirs for adopting one or two machines and ignoring everything else may drive me crazy before we're through. You're right. I can't picture anyone keeping them as slaves. But what are they, then? And why are they here?"

"That," Rhys said, rising to his feet, "is only one of many questions that seem to be so common around here." He extended a hand to help Calista to her feet, but instead of releasing her, he pulled her into his arms. "Are you in any rush to find the answers?"

Chapter Seventeen

Calista didn't have a chance to reply. A gray she'd never seen before appeared at the chamber's entrance. When its eyes lit on them, it shuffled forward apologetically.

"The Dorinor wishes to see you," it said, bowing.

"Me?" Calista and Rhys said as one.

Coming as it did from two people at the same time, the question clearly confused the creature. The gray wrung its hands, its gaze shifting back and forth between them uncertainly. "Both of you?" it said at last on a rising note of inquiry.

Rhys sighed and released her. "I suppose that's a command and I suppose we should be grateful it wasn't one of Larr's men who walked in." He dropped a quick kiss on the tip of her nose and grinned. "But let's not forget where we left off."

They found the Dorinor in the great chamber, morosely flipping bakal betting tiles into a small heap in front of him. He didn't appear to be in a very good mood, but he brightened considerably at their entrance.

Karnor was nowhere in sight, which didn't bother Calista. Ever since Larr had explained his role in Porganis Tull's death, she hadn't felt quite the same about being in the same cavern with the huge creature.

"You have finished?" the Dorinor asked, abandoning the tiles.

"No, Excellency." Rhys shrugged, then added boldly, "It would take less time and be a lot more efficient if we knew the purpose of all this equipment."

The Dorinor scratched his belly in the gesture Calista had come to recognize indicated perplexity. This time there was a hint of irritation in the gesture, as well. "But you brought this machinery. How can you not know its purpose?"

Rhys looked at Calista, his eyebrows raised. Calista could only stare back at him.

"We figure its purpose is to adjust the climate in the caves where you keep your eggs," Rhys finally ventured. "What we don't understand is why you need it in the first place. Perhaps if you'd explain—"

It was the wrong thing to say.

The Dorinor reared back on his haunches, head high and eyes flashing. His claws, extended to their lethal full length, gleamed dully in the dim light. "I am the Dorinor," he bellowed. "I do not need to explain anything."

Rhys jumped, startled by the creature's irate response. Before he could say anything more, Calista moved in front of him.

"Of course you don't have to explain anything, your Excellency," she said soothingly. She'd seen enough of the toadying, cringing behavior of the *drenn* when they were in the Dorinor's presence to know what was expected, especially since Rhys had evidently trespassed on forbidden territory by suggesting the Kartanese leader explain anything.

"If you, in your great wisdom, Excellency," Calista continued in her most ingratiating tones, "could share your knowledge with us and guide us, then we would be able to do a better job for you and for Karta."

The Dorinor huffed indignantly and rustled his wings, but after a moment he sheathed his claws and gradually sank back on his haunches. Calista held her breath until he'd settled himself more comfortably, then let it out in one long sigh of relief.

She glanced over at Rhys and found him watching her, dark eyes alight with laughter. Her new role as conciliator appeared to be a bigger hit with him than it was with the Dorinor.

Her own lips twitched in response, then stretched into a quick but unmistakable grin.

The automatic response came as a surprise, even to her. If anyone had ever told her she'd not only stoop to using blatant flattery, but be willing to laugh about it, as well, she'd have threatened them with a disrupter.

Forcing her features into a more respectfully serious expression, Calista turned back to the Dorinor. She could tell by the way he watched her that he still wasn't quite recovered from the indignity of Rhys's proposal. She'd have to proceed carefully or something might set him off again.

"We have come seeking understanding, Excellency," she said carefully. "The majesty of the Kartanese is evident, but your history is unknown to us. Trader Fairdane and I seek only to comprehend the reasons for the installation of this new equipment in order that we might serve you and your people to the best of our ability."

For a moment, Calista wondered if she hadn't laid the flattery on just a little too thick that time. But from the self-satisfied smirk on the Dorinor's face, she could tell she hadn't.

"Trader York speaks the truth, Excellency," Rhys added, bowing slightly. "I chose my words poorly, but my intentions were good. We would be greatly honored if you would tell us why the equipment came to be installed in the first place."

Mollified, the Dorinor nodded. "Very well." He curled his tail around his feet, crossed his forelegs over his belly. After a moment's thought, he said, "You understand, of course, that for the eggs to grow and produce healthy young, the conditions in the sacred caves must be exactly right. When the gods grow angry, waters cease to flow as they should and the caves change.

"Over forty-seven solar cycles ago—forty-seven cycles and one hundred and sixteen days, to be precise—the gods caused great changes in the sacred caves. The eggs began to die and we feared for our future." He paused. His eyes dimmed and he fixed his gaze on the far wall of the chamber as if he were seeing that tragedy once again.

Calista thought of the Kartanese baby she'd seen lying on the floor of the cave, feebly struggling for the pitiful few breaths it would ever take. She thought of the adults' grief and tried to imagine what it must have been like all those years before.

"We almost gave up hope," the Dorinor continued at last, "and then Larr arrived."

Calista sat up straighter at that bit of information. She'd thought Larr was in his mid-thirties, at the oldest. If the Dorinor's timekeeping was right—and she was willing to bet the *Independence* it was—Larr was probably somewhere between seventy and eighty years old! It must have needed a lot of saitha silk over the years to keep him that young-looking.

Judging from the expression on Rhys's face, he'd come to the same conclusion.

"Larr was selling goods we could not use, but when he heard of our troubles, he said he could help." The Dorinor sighed, remembering. "It is forbidden to let any but the chosen into the sacred caves, but I ignored my councillors and showed Larr what the gods had done. He went away, then brought back the first of this strange equipment. Once his things were installed, the waters began flowing again and the eggs stopped dying."

The Dorinor fell silent. Calista waited, wondering if he would continue, but when the silence stretched, she asked, "What did Larr ask in return for his services?"

"Nothing."

"Nothing?" The word burst out before she could stop it, but the Dorinor didn't seem to take offense.

"He simply chose to stay here and serve us. Perhaps that was what the gods intended all along."

"But what about the fibers, Excellency?" Rhys asked.

From the tone of his voice, Calista suspected he was having as hard a time keeping his surprise under control as she was.

"Oh, Larr and his people gather that. He said it would bring in the money he needed to buy the machines for the sacred caves." The Dorinor didn't appear to be much interested in the fibers or Larr's business dealings.

"I'll just bet he did," Calista muttered under her breath. When the Dorinor swung his head around in inquiry, she said, more loudly, "If Larr installed the first machines, Excellency, why did you choose us to install the new pieces we brought?"

The Dorinor shifted his position, then scratched his belly. Calista suspected the question made him uncomfortable.

"The machines are not working as they were in the past," he said at last. "Perhaps the gods have grown tired of our interference. Perhaps they do not approve that I have tried to open new caves, so that we may have an alternative place for our eggs. I thought perhaps the machines would respond better to a new hand."

Rhys beat her to the next obvious question. "Was it Larr who suggested you start new caves, Excellency?"

"Yes, of course. It seemed a reasonable suggestion."

It must have seemed that way to Larr, anyway, Calista thought in disgust. Not only had he managed to gain control of the most costly commodity in the galaxy, he planned on increasing "production" through the simple method of adding another couple of caves and some more machines capable of creating the environment essential for the eggs' well-being.

Larr's little arrangement had to be one of the most lucrative business deals in the history of the Empire. She couldn't prove it yet, but Calista suspected he hadn't stopped there.

The trick was going to be figuring out what he planned next.

"Stupid piece of junk," Rhys muttered, disgusted, as the connector he'd been trying to force into place slipped out of his fingers again. He squirmed farther into the massive piece of machinery he was working on.

Installing the connector was one of the last things

remaining to be finished before they could turn this particular piece of machinery on. He probably shouldn't have beamed down alone, since the connector really required two people to handle it, but he'd been restless and unable to sleep and this had seemed as good a way as any to pass the time.

He reached to fit the connector again and knocked down the work light he'd mounted so precariously on some of the cabling. The light went out, leaving him with nothing more than the faint glow of the chamber's lights, which were far too weak to be of any use to him.

Rhys cursed silently and fumbled for the light when the sound of footsteps and human voices in the outer passage made him freeze. Some of Larr's people, he told himself, wanting to check on progress. Maybe they preferred to visit when he and Calista weren't supposed to be around.

It made sense. He couldn't explain the instinct that drove him to remain silent and not move.

The footsteps came closer, then entered the chamber and came to a halt. Three people, Rhys decided, judging from the sound of it.

"The two of 'em quit about three, four hours ago, then went back to their ships." It was a man's voice, only slightly familiar. Undoubtedly one of the dozen or so of Larr's employees whom he'd met so far, Rhys decided.

"They don't seem to have made any more progress than the last time I was down here," Larr responded.

Rhys tensed. Somehow, he hadn't expected Larr to be inspecting their work.

"They're taking about five times longer than two of my engineers would have, but they're getting it done."

It took a moment for Rhys to connect the voice with

his vague memory of the woman engineer who'd hated the grays and seemed so passionately attached to the machinery.

"How much longer, do you think?" Larr again.

"Maybe a day or so, at the rate they're going." The woman paused, then added with more passion than Rhys expected, "I want them out of here, Larr. I want those traders and the damn *drenn* out of here. You hired me to get these environmental control systems operating. I can do it, but not if I have to work around amateurs and those stupid, lumbering, thickheaded beasts."

"I can't do anything about the *drenn*," Larr snapped, clearly irritated at what must be a familiar complaint from the woman. "I warned you about them before you came."

"And the traders?"

"The Dorinor dumped them here, not me. And he did it because you and your engineers still haven't straightened out the problems in the old hatching cave, let alone these new ones. If you'd done your job—"

"Me! Listen, Larr, and listen good. Environmental control in these caves is just about as impossible a job as you can get." The woman clearly wasn't taking anything from Larr, not even threats. "If you'd gotten some expert advice at the start, you wouldn't have tried this in the first place. It was your inept bungling and those idiots you hired the first time round that damaged the balance in the original cavern."

"I told you the change in the climate—"

"—was temporary. It would have returned to normal if you'd left it alone. Now it won't be so easy because you've meddled too much. The two new caves are different, since we're trying to change their environment artificially. It can be done, but only if you leave it

297

to professionals." The woman's voice rose with her rising anger. "You get those traders and the *drenn* out of here, Larr. You hear me? If you want the caves to work, if you want to stop the eggs from dying, then you'll get them out of here."

"Don't threaten me. I'll—"

"Don't threaten *me*. You want the caves and more eggs, you do as I say. Period." The woman left the chamber, her footsteps quick, hard, and echoing.

"Got a temper, don't she?" Larr's remaining employee said admiringly.

"So do I, Shaduck." Larr sounded as if he was having a hard time controlling his.

"What're you going to do about her, then?"

"I don't know. She's one of the best anywhere. I don't want her leaving."

"So you're booting out the traders? Going to get rid of them the same way you got rid of Tull?"

"I wasn't the one who got rid of Tull!"

"Well, you weren't the one who ate 'im, that's for sure, but—"

"Forget Tull!"

"Sure, boss, whatever you say." Shaduck didn't sound overly impressed by his employer's threats.

"Besides, in a few days we'll only have one trader to keep an eye on." Larr's voice trailed off as he began pacing.

Rhys held his breath, listening to Larr's footsteps and straining to catch whatever the man might say next.

"I made a mistake in thinking that with their mutual antagonism and competitiveness, having the two of them would make it easier to keep them in line," Larr added in a disgusted tone, coming to a halt beside his subordinate. "That damned, inquisitive female is getting out of line."

"What'd she do, boss?"

"Do! Yesterday she had the nerve to tell the Dorinor he ought to stop work on the new systems. Then she started questioning the *drenn* about the operations in the old cave. She's even had the nerve to ask for a list of all sales for the past thirty years. Said she was going to forecast future demand! Hah!"

"Is that why you called those slavers on Andrus, boss?"

Shaduck's words, so alive with avid curiosity, hit Rhys like a physical blow. He clenched his hands into tight fists, digging his nails into his palms in an effort to keep from betraying his presence.

"Where'd you hear that?" Larr demanded.

"People talk. Sort of hard to decide which is worse, getting eaten by those damn dragons or being sold into slavery on Andrus." Shaduck's voice betrayed nothing more than intellectual curiosity regarding the relative undesirability of the two options.

Larr laughed. The sound made Rhys's blood burn with the urge to wrap his fingers around the blond man's throat and squeeze until the smile disappeared off his face forever.

"I'm not selling her into slavery, Shaduck," Larr said, his good humor restored. "I'm . . . restoring lost property, shall we say?"

"Yeah?" The subtlety of the distinction didn't impress Shaduck. "You don't think that Fairdane fellow's going to object?"

"Not for long. He has other interests . . . and other vulnerabilities."

Even though he couldn't see Larr, Rhys could easily imagine the sly, satisfied smile on his face right now. Maybe, Rhys thought wildly, he could smash that smile off before he choked Larr to death.

"Enough," Larr said suddenly, impatiently. "There's

nothing more to see here. I'll be rid of York and have Fairdane dancing to my tune in no time. Then we can worry about how to straighten out this mess with the damn caves."

Rhys remained still and silent long after the sound of the two men's footsteps died away. His muscles ached with the effort needed to keep himself from smashing something.

Larr had turned Calista in to the slavers. The horror of that fact drowned even the rising anger over Larr's intentions toward him.

He had to get Calista away. Now, while she still had time to cover her tracks, to disappear before the slavers could begin tracing her.

Yet even amidst the anger, the cold, hard, rational part of Rhys knew that wasn't going to be easy. When she'd disappeared the first time, she'd been a starving adolescent, of little value to anyone. Now she was a successful trader with business connections and a ship that would be relatively easy to trace if the slavers wanted to.

Given the reward they'd receive for bringing in a lucrative prize like Calista, Rhys had no doubt they'd want to.

"You *have* to go, Calista. *Now.*"

It was all Rhys could do not to grab Calista and shake some sense into her. After he'd found her on the *Independence*, her first reaction to his revelation of Larr's betrayal of her had been to stay and fight. Her second reaction had been exactly the same. Some part of him wondered dimly why that should have surprised him. The rest of him just got angry, because anger was a far safer emotion than the debilitating fear for her that threatened to swamp him.

"Do you have any suggestions as to where?" Calista

faced him dry-eyed. Only her stiff, straight spine and the slightly awkward angle of her shoulders betrayed just how hard his announcement had hit her.

Where? There was a whole galaxy out there, tens of thousands of inhabited planets where she could hide. Maybe it wouldn't be hard for an escaped slave who knew the backways of a hundred different worlds to vanish, after all. Once safely hidden, Calista could start a new life for herself. And that was the problem. If she was to have any chance at staying free, she couldn't risk contacting anyone she'd ever known before. Not ever. She couldn't risk contacting *him*.

He thought of the future without her in it that stretched before him, unbearably bleak and empty. "Graustauk VII, maybe, to start. No slave hunter in his right mind would go within a hundred parsecs of the place. Or maybe Empire."

"Empire? Are you out of your mind? With the Imperial government there?"

"Exactly. If you were a slave hunter, would you expect a runaway to head right for the central planet? It's the last place they'd look for you."

Calista just stared at him, wide-eyed and silent.

"Do you have money someplace, money or resources that can't be traced to you?" Be practical, Rhys commanded himself. Think of what has to be done to protect her. Think of everything she's too stunned to think of right now. For her sake.

It was better than thinking about how terribly frightened he was—for himself, when she wasn't there anymore—as well as for her.

Rhys paced, forcing himself to concentrate on the issues at hand. He couldn't bear to look at her, to see her eyes grow round with the shock that still held her. "You'll need new identification records. And you'll have to get rid of the *Independence*. You'll take a loss

301

on that, but it can't be helped. Converting it illegally would take too long and leave too many tracks for the hunters to follow. We'll have to think of a diversion, some way of throwing them off track. Maybe I—"

"Rhys!"

Rhys stopped short, his back to her. He couldn't bear to turn and see the anguished query in her eyes that he could hear so clearly in her voice. "Yes?"

"Look at me."

Rhys stiffened. The muscles in his neck and jaw ached with tension. He wouldn't turn. Not now. He didn't have the courage.

"Look at me."

Slowly Rhys turned. He had to bite down, hard, to keep from grinding his teeth together.

Calista stood tall and straight and proud—the way he imagined she always faced whatever frightened her.

"I want to know," she said, her voice taut with strain, "what you're planning to do."

"Do?"

"After I leave. What are you going to do?"

Rhys hesitated, uncertain. There was another question hidden behind the spoken words, but he wasn't sure what it was or how he ought to respond.

"I . . . I hadn't thought that far," he said at last. "Do what I can to confuse them, of course. Pretend to be angry, then glad you're gone and I have the trade to myself. See if I can mislead them. I don't know! I'll just have to see what happens!" The last words burst from him.

"And then?"

"Then? Dammit, Calista! I don't know! Keep working here, I guess. See if I can outwit Larr, get the third planet . . . How am I supposed to know what I'll do then, for stars' sake? I don't know what I'm going to do an hour from now!"

That much was true, at least. Rhys stood still, staring at her and fighting against the words he didn't dare to say—for her sake.

I'll find you, he wanted to say. *Somehow. Once it's safe. We can start over together, build a life for the two of us on a world that's never heard of Andrus or saitha silk. I'll come to you as soon as I can, and then I'll never, ever let you go.*

He wanted to say that, but instead kept silent. He couldn't risk her safety by giving in to his selfish need for her. If the slave hunters even suspected he might contact her, they'd watch him, monitor his communications and study his contacts, looking for the chance to get her through him. He couldn't risk that. For Calista's sake, he had to cut all ties with her, no matter how empty the future would be without her.

"I understand. Of course there's no way you can know what you'll do," she said at last, enunciating every word with careful precision. She drooped suddenly. "I'd best get going."

"Yes." Rhys forced down the urge to go to her, to draw her into his arms and comfort her. He had no comfort to offer, no soothing words that weren't all lies.

She keyed her comm link. An instant before she disappeared in the transport beam, she said, "Good-bye, Rhys. Good luck."

The words seemed to echo in the room long after she was gone.

Graustauk VII. A den of thieves, mercenaries, outlaws, and the outcasts of a hundred worlds. Just the place for a runaway slave to disappear. Especially a runaway who had the money to pay for the false documents and new ship she'd need for whatever came after.

Calista kept her hands flat on the console, unable to give the commands that would start her flight into . . . what?

After she sold the *Independence* and destroyed all traces of the past few years, what came next? She had enough credits secreted in accounts on a dozen worlds to keep her for the rest of her life if she was careful.

If she was careful. The word had a dull, flat sound that rang hollowly within her. Careful to keep low, not attract attention, not do anything out of the ordinary. Careful not to be noticed, because she might not be able to run from the slave hunters and she'd certainly never again earn enough credits to buy her freedom.

Maybe she could get a regular job on some backwater planet that didn't look at a person's past too closely. She could be a mechanic, perhaps, or a laborer. The thought generated a dull pain, somewhere deep inside her.

Or she could buy a new identity, maybe even a new face, then go back to trading once the initial fury of the hunt for her died down.

Slowly Calista ran the palms of her hands across the console before her. She'd been twenty-two when she'd commissioned the construction of the *Independence*. Twenty-two and passionately certain that true independence lay just ahead. A few more deals, a few more credits hoarded and she'd been convinced she'd have all she needed to buy her way to freedom.

Strange, how that elusive dream had always been just a little bit further away than she could reach.

Never had it looked further away than it did right now, and yet somehow that thought didn't hurt half as much as the thought of losing Rhys.

Calista squeezed her eyes shut against the hot tears

that threatened, but the tears escaped and trickled down her cheeks anyway.

If only he'd said he cared, suggested they arrange to meet again at some time in the future. But he hadn't said he cared and he hadn't even hinted at a meeting. She'd been too proud to suggest it herself, but now she wished she had. Perhaps if she'd offered . . .

Calista angrily shook her head at that, shaking off the tears that had slid all the way to her chin. Roughly, she wiped away the last trace of moisture with the back of her hand.

What kind of fool was she? Did falling in love destroy pride as well as common sense? Nothing would have changed if she'd proposed they arrange to meet when it was safe. She would still be a fugitive and he would have far too much to lose to want to get entangled in her problems.

And what difference did it make, anyway? She loved him, but he didn't love her. Of that she was certain. He cared for her, but it would never go beyond that. She was too demanding, too difficult, and far too dangerous to have in his life for long, and he had too many other, more pressing obligations to worry about her. It wasn't callousness, it was practicality, and Rhys was an eminently practical man at heart.

She ought to start applying a little practicality herself.

The longer she stayed here, the less time she'd have to cover her tracks from the slave hunters. She'd need every advantage she could get, no matter how small, because once they realized how rich a prize they pursued, they wouldn't stop until they caught her or there was no more hope of tracing her.

So where should she go?

Calista stared at the navigation screen before her. She'd called up the coordinates for Graustauk VII immediately after she'd come on board because that was what Rhys had suggested. They still showed there, unchanged.

The planet was little more than a galactic cesspool, filled with the dregs of a hundred races who congregated there. Even the Imperial Security forces left the place alone. The slave hunters might reason she'd go there first, but they'd have a hard time finding her.

If Rhys ever chose to follow her, he'd never find her. Calista couldn't help wondering if running was even worth it.

The universe suddenly seemed immensely cold, dark and lonely. Calista felt as if she'd been cast into space without a lifeline, as if she would go spinning and tumbling through the void forever, lost and alone.

Then the instinct for survival that had carried her through so much for so long came back. It couldn't drive out the hurt or the aching emptiness—it never would—but it could get her through whatever lay ahead.

Calista's jaw set. Back straight and eyes dry, she gave the commands that would take the *Independence* out of orbit and set it on course for Graustauk VII.

Even after all visible trace of the *Independence* was gone, Rhys watched the monitors that showed the residual heat of its passing until even that faint indicator disappeared.

Where had she decided to go? he wondered. What was she going to do? Would he ever know?

Not knowing seemed almost as terrifying as her absence. At least the last time they'd split up, he'd been able to keep track of her, know what she was doing and that she was safe. What if she ran into danger? He'd never know and never be able to help.

She'd be all right, he told himself fiercely, shutting

off the monitors. She'd gotten along just fine before he met her, and those first years after her escape from Andrus would have been a lot more dangerous for a young, inexperienced runaway with no credits and no means of earning a living.

So why was he so damn scared?

Rhys shoved to his feet, angry with himself, Calista and life in general. Most especially angry with Larr, whose devious machinations were behind Calista's flight.

He'd have to watch his step in the weeks ahead. Especially he'd have to watch for any hint of further danger to Calista. There might be something he could do, or maybe he'd have an opportunity to warn her . . .

Rhys cursed. Was he deliberately tormenting himself? He couldn't warn her. He'd never see her again.

The thought burned like a brand, searing through him with a hot white pain.

He twisted around, desperately looking for something to distract him, to stop the pain. The bridge was empty except for him. The whole, damn ship was empty.

Rhys drew in a shuddering breath, fighting for calm. He had to be sensible, rational. He still had commitments to his people that should be—*had* to be—the focus of his energy from now on. He couldn't afford to let his emotions get in the way, couldn't afford to waste time wanting something he could never have.

So why did all of it seem so flat and unimportant?

He forced himself to move, out the door and down the passage. He didn't know where he was headed, he just knew he needed movement, action, some purpose to get him through the hours ahead.

Certainly there was enough to do. In the days he and Calista had spent working in the caves, he'd neglected work on his own ship. Equipment needed repairing, the cargo bays still had to be returned to their usual configuration after the modifications they'd made earlier, and he'd planned an overhaul on the guidance system for months now. And that was just for starters.

Rhys chose to start in the maintenance area, simply because that was closest. Several small pieces of equipment lay on one of the workbenches, ready to be worked on. Rhys flinched. He hadn't put them there; Calista had.

Pushing down the thought, he pulled a tall stool up to one of the benches, dragged over the first piece of equipment with his left hand, and automatically reached for a tool with the right. His left hand found the equipment with no problems. His right fumbled, groped, and found nothing.

Irritated, Rhys swung around. He always kept the thing right there and . . . The anger died. The tool was neatly placed in a rack about six inches away from where he usually kept it. It wasn't the only piece not in its right place, either. Calista had moved just about everything to suit her needs, regardless of the fact it was his workspace.

Rhys rearranged the space, returning everything to its proper spot. It didn't help. Even the knowledge that Calista had been here, that she'd sat in exactly this spot, was too much. He couldn't concentrate and he couldn't shake the conviction that some part of her was still here, that some . . . essence . . . that was uniquely hers permeated the walls, the table and the air around him.

He left the piece of equipment he'd picked up on the table, its cover off and its insides half disassembled. He left the work space in cluttered disarray and the stool out of place and the lights on. He didn't care, just so long as he got out of there and away from the intangible and inescapable reminders that Calista had been here.

Rhys tried working in the cargo bay next, with no greater success. The bay's monitors were turned at angles to accommodate Calista, not him. Tools and equipment weren't in their right place and controls were set for her convenience, not his.

It was the same in the study area, the exercise rooms and in the passages themselves. Everywhere he went, with everything he did, he encountered some reminder of Calista until it seemed the memories had transformed into dangerous darts that threatened him at every turn, piercing his defenses until he could bear it no longer.

Driven, Rhys retreated to his quarters, but there was no respite from the memories even then. One glance at the big bed made his body ache and burn with wanting what was already gone from him forever.

With a curse, Rhys retreated into the shower. Stripping off his clothes, he turned the water on as hard and cold as he could make it, then stepped into the icy spray. The shock of the frigid dousing made him gasp, but he forced himself to remain until his teeth chattered and every muscle of his body trembled uncontrollably with cold.

Any good effects of the shower were destroyed, however, the minute he dragged a towel off the rack and started to dry himself.

Unbidden, the memory of Calista, stark naked and dripping wet, rose in his mind. She might have been there before him, so vividly did his memories recreate her. He would have sworn he could see her vivid blue eyes flashing, touch her soft, damp skin, smell the sweet scent of her soap.

Rhys groaned and staggered back, still clutching the towel, until brought up short by the wall behind him. He shut his eyes, willing the bright image to disappear, but when he looked again, something of her still remained, mocking him, tormenting him. Back pressed against the hard wall, Rhys slid slowly down until he huddled on the floor.

The floor was hard and cold against his naked buttocks and icy water pooled under him, unpleasantly chilling. The damp skin of his back rubbed painfully against the hard wall behind him. His hair, freed of its queue, lay plastered against his head and neck like so much cold, wet rope, dripping more icy water down his body.

Rhys scarcely noticed. His awareness was focused inward, caught by a truth that had lain within him for years unnoticed, but that now shone more brilliantly than any sun.

He loved Calista. He always had.

She was part of him. She filled the emptiness in his soul—an emptiness he'd never realized existed until now, when it was too late.

No matter that she irritated him, angered him, drove him to distraction with her opinionated, arrogant, overbearing ways. No matter that her intemperate passions and mercurial moods had so often roused his own hasty temper. She'd harassed him, argued with him, ignored his counsel, flouted his rules, and defied his efforts to control her. She'd driven him mad without even trying, and she'd drive him mad again if she ever returned.

None of that mattered, because he loved her.

It was as simple as that.

Rhys groaned and let his head fall back, shutting his eyes against the agony of so simple and so devastating a truth.

He loved her and he would never, ever see her again.

"Is there something going on I don't know about, Larr? Did you send her off on a sales trip without consulting me? Is that it? Are you giving her a cut that you're not giving me?" Rhys shouted. He stomped. He stormed.

He'd decided the best defense was a good offense and was doing his damnedest to convince Larr that he not only knew nothing about Calista's departure, but that he suspected the two of them of underhanded dealings. At the least, the tactic would keep Larr from asking too many dangerous questions. At best, Larr might reveal something, some small fact that might be of use.

Larr said nothing, just sat impassively behind the big conference table and watched him pace the room.

Rhys came to a halt in front of him, then slapped both hands down on the table and leaned forward aggressively. "Well, Larr?" he demanded. "I want to know what you two are up to and why Calista slipped out like that while I slept."

"I assure you, trader, I know nothing of the reasons for your colleague's departure. I most certainly am not in collusion with her against your business interests."

"Nice, fancy words, Larr. How come I don't believe you?"

Larr's upper lip twitched in irritation. It wasn't much, but Rhys savored even that small crack in the man's annoyingly bland facade.

"I don't know why you don't believe me," Larr said sharply, "nor do I care. I *am* concerned by Trader York's unannounced departure, however, and I, too, want some answers."

311

Rhys shoved away from the desk, eyeing the blond man speculatively. It appeared Larr really didn't know why Calista had run, which meant he'd be off balance and confused, unsure how to react. And that would give Calista a little more time to hide her tracks. It wasn't much, but it was something.

"If you find out anything, Larr, I want to be the first to know," Rhys said at last. He turned on his heel and stalked out the door without giving Larr a chance to respond.

As he strode down the passage leading to the Kartanese caves, Rhys's mind raced. What should he do next? How long before the slave hunters arrived?

He'd already commanded the *Fair Trade's* computer to alert him to the arrival of any small, fast ship like the ones the hunters traditionally used. At least he'd know the minute they dropped out of hyperspace. He could only hope that by then he'd have a good plan for misleading them that wouldn't give any hint he already knew about Calista's past or her escape.

At times during the past hours he'd been tempted to run, too. If it hadn't been for the need to confuse Calista's pursuers as best he could, he might well have followed her.

Despite all his efforts to convince himself there was still a chance to get rights to the third planet, Rhys knew he was fooling himself. He'd never had much of a chance, even at the start. He had even less now.

Whatever it was Larr wanted so badly, his betrayal of Calista made it clear he'd let nothing and no one get in his way. And that included Rhys.

If he couldn't find a way to get around Larr or get him out of the way, Rhys knew he'd soon be helplessly dangling at the end of Larr's string.

Unlike Calista, he didn't have the option of running. With the fragile economic and political structure his people had built to keep their society functioning, there were too many weak links, too many points where they were vulnerable. Rhys did not doubt that Larr would use that vulnerability against him whenever it served his purpose.

The Dorinor's representative held Rhys's people—all three million of them—hostage, and right now there was absolutely nothing he could do about it.

Chapter Eighteen

The streets of Graustauk were as crowded, filthy, and noisome as Calista remembered. From all sides, a deafening babel of squeaks, grunts, whines, shouts, growls, and hisses assaulted her ears as a hundred different species speaking a dozen different languages bargained, quarreled and plotted in the city's open market.

Every sense alert, Calista pushed her way through the crowd. She'd taken care with her disguise, choosing, after much thought, the uniform commonly worn by Shielukk mercenaries. The costume's tight-fitting, dark-gray hood effectively covered her blond hair and the looser gray tunic and breeches not only permitted freedom of movement, they also provided excellent hiding places for the various weapons she'd brought. Not that she'd neglected to sling a hand-held disrupter from her belt, as well. It paid to be prepared on Graustauk.

Calista blinked, irritated by the colored lenses that gave her eyes a dark gray, almost black cast. She'd even gone so far as to temporarily dye the skin of her face and hands a pale gray-green. The disguise was no guarantee that someone wouldn't still recognize her—disguises were a time-honored form of dress on the planet—but it did give her a few advantages. People tended to keep their distance from Shielukk mercenaries, who were infamous for their quick tempers and willingness to fight any and all comers.

She shoved past three Norgonians engaged in heated debate with a six-legged Ekzz that perched protectively on its pile of wares, shrilly insulting its prospective customers. Beyond the Norgonians, a cluster of two Kurs, a Zeilbadian, a human, a Ba'ar, and three creatures Calista had never seen before blocked the narrow path, forcing her to edge around a potter's stall, crawl over heaped bales of woven Kielush cloth, and walk through the carefully arranged display of a miedule seller, who responded by shaking all four fists and shouting vulgar insults at her in three different languages.

If she'd really wanted to assume the persona of a Shielukk mercenary, Calista knew, she should have shoved the Norgonians out of her way, pushed through the middle of the mixed group, and threatened to knife the miedule seller. But her goal was to get through the market without attracting undue attention and without any more problems than necessary, so she settled for tossing a few insults over her shoulder at the seller and continuing on her way. She wasn't even sure what a couple of the insults meant, but she'd heard them often enough in places like this to know they'd served her purpose quite adequately.

Her destination was a traders' tavern hidden down a side street at the far side of the market. She couldn't remember exactly where it was located—wasn't even sure it still existed—but it was the best place she knew of for obtaining information, which was what she most urgently needed now.

Three days in hyperspace had given her time to overcome the first, panicked reaction to the news that Larr had alerted the slave hunters to her existence. Once rational thought had returned, she'd realized something she should have thought of long ago: two could play at the game of information gathering and blackmail.

When Larr first proposed the position of trade rep to her, she'd made a perfunctory effort to learn what she could about the man and the operations. The trouble was, every trader with any experience at all had heard of the Dorinor's representative and the fortune to be made through the sale of saitha silk. She'd heard plenty, all of it glowing. Only in the last few days had she begun to wonder how much of that information had been nothing more than wishful thinking and exaggeration.

She'd been a blind and greedy fool to so readily believe everything she'd heard. She didn't intend to continue being a fool. There were no guarantees she could stop Larr and it might already be too late to divert the slave hunters from her trail, but until she was absolutely sure she had no options except running, she'd do her damnedest to thwart Larr's plans, whatever they were.

It was the only way she could figure out to get free of this mess she was in—and to see Rhys again.

At the thought of Rhys, Calista stopped short, suddenly overwhelmed by the bitter, aching loneliness that had been her constant companion since she'd left Karta.

Her abrupt halt wasn't well-received by the Gorridian behind her, whose path she was suddenly blocking. He snarled at her, snapping his long, sharp teeth in irritation and flexing his even longer claws. Calista snarled in return, her hand on her disrupter, then added a disparaging remark about his home nest's breeding practices for good measure. She didn't really feel like a fight, but Gorridians interpreted good manners as a sign of weakness.

Apparently, her manners were sufficiently poor to meet the creature's low standards because he grinned nastily, exposing even more teeth, then walked around her.

After a mental shake for her momentary lapse, Calista followed. The last thing she needed was a fight, but if she didn't pay attention, she'd end up with one, anyway.

The tavern she was seeking was a little farther along the narrow street, but just as dirty, crowded, and dark as she remembered. She ordered a Fallarian ale, a drink she particularly disliked but which had the advantage of being something she could nurse for a couple of hours. Without a drink, she wouldn't be allowed to stay. On the other hand, if she was lucky she'd find enough loquacious traders for whom she could buy drinks to keep the management from watching her too closely.

Three hours later she was beginning to wonder if she shouldn't try another place altogether. She'd met no one with either information or contacts she could use and staying too long would attract just the sort of attention she didn't need.

The arrival of a new customer, a human male who had to be well over seven feet tall, attracted her attention first. He stood in the doorway for a moment, casually scanning the inn's occupants, then

317

crossed to the bar to place his order. Calista sank back in her chair, waiting. She'd swear he'd noticed her. Something about his stance, about the way his gaze had slid so smoothly past her, suggested it might be worth her while to see what he did next.

She didn't have to wait long. Drink in hand, the new arrival pushed through the crowd to her table and, without asking permission, took the vacant seat beside her. His eyes met hers once before he turned to study the occupied tables near them. He took a sip of the drink he held, then, still without looking at her, said, "The word is you want to know about the Kartanese and their representative, Larr."

Calista pushed down the sudden eagerness within her. She'd known that rumor spread fast on Graustauk, but she hadn't expected anything like this quite so soon. Too great a show of eagerness now, however, might either drive the stranger away, or raise his asking price beyond her ability to pay.

"That's right," she said. Like him, she kept her eyes on the crowd around them.

"How much?"

Calista shrugged. "That depends. What do you have?"

The man took another swig and appeared to consider her question. "That depends, but it's not me who's interested in talking to you. Do you know an inn called the Nova in the Balbek quarter?"

Neither the inn nor the area of the city were familiar to Calista and she said so.

The man nodded, unsurprised by her lack of knowledge. In a few words he gave her directions on how to reach the Nova, then rose to his feet. "Come tonight after dark. You'll be expected."

Even after he'd disappeared, Calista remained where she was, considering her options. She'd expected to gather information bit by bit, a little here, a little there. This clandestine meeting promised far more—and that made her leery. Very leery indeed.

The Nova proved to be a reasonably decent inn, by standards on Graustauk, at any rate. As instructed, Calista had waited until after dark to come, which made finding the place ten times more difficult, since streetlights weren't much appreciated by the planet's denizens.

The tall human was seated in a dark corner of the inn's entrance, waiting for her. At her appearance, he stood and, with a jerk of his head, indicated she should follow him.

He led Calista up narrow stairs at the back of the inn, then down an equally narrow, dark hallway lined by closed doors. Stopping in front of one of the doors, he knocked softly in what sounded like a simple, prearranged code. The door opened almost immediately, although, behind him, Calista could see no one inside the room.

Still without speaking, the man stepped to the side and gestured to the open door, indicating she should enter. He made no effort to follow her, but by the time Calista realized that fact, the door had already shut behind her.

She was alert, ready to react to any threat. Although she carefully kept her hand away from the disrupter hung so obviously on her belt, Calista's right hand rested on the end of the plasteel hidden in the seam of her tunic. Her left hand was only inches from a second disrupter in a secret pocket.

At sight of the two people awaiting her, her jaw dropped. Calista had thought she was prepared for just about anything, but one thing she *hadn't* expected to see was two elderly humans, a man and a woman, both caught between fear and an emotion Calista could only describe as wild hope.

"Please, come in. Sit down," the old man said. He moved away from the door to sit beside the woman. From the solicitous way he took her hand, patting it comfortingly, Calista assumed she was his wife.

After another quick glance around to verify they were alone, Calista took the seat indicated. Her mind raced trying to figure out how to handle this unexpected turn of events. She couldn't think of anything, because she couldn't think of any reason this old couple should be here on a planet where even the youngest and hardiest didn't always survive.

"We understand you are seeking information about the Kartanese and a man named Larr," the man said. "May we ask why?"

Calista had thought up a dozen different stories that might serve, depending on the situation. None of them seemed appropriate here. "I have a friend who has been . . . approached by Larr to work for the Kartanese," she ventured at last. "He wants to know more about the situation there than he has been told so far."

"That is very wise." The old man nodded his head sadly. "If only our—"

"We have information we are willing to trade," the old woman interrupted. Her free hand balled into a tight little fist in her lap. "We want to know what happened to the last . . . trade representative for the Kartanese. If you can answer our questions, then we will share what we know about the Kartanese."

Calista couldn't help but admire the woman's courage in demanding a trade. A real Shielukk mercenary wouldn't have hesitated to slit their throats if the possibility of profit were involved. "What representative do you mean?"

"Porganis Tull. Do you know anything of him?" the woman asked.

She knew rather a great deal about Tull, Calista thought, but was any of it suitable for sharing with this rather naive couple? "I know something of him," she acknowledged at last, hesitantly.

"Do you know where he is?" The old man leaned toward her, suddenly eager.

Calista flinched. Karnor had eaten Porganis Tull for dinner months ago.

Her hesitation wasn't lost on the two before her. "He's dead, isn't he?" the old woman whispered, her face white with the shock of the answer she must have expected, and dreaded, all along.

"Yes." Calista would have left it at that, but it was clear the other two wouldn't let her, so she added, "The Kartanese . . . killed him. They thought . . . they thought he'd threatened their young. That's all I know," she added miserably, unable to bear the stricken looks on the couple's faces. She wasn't about to tell them anything of Tull's crooked business dealings.

Neither the man nor the woman cried. They simply sat, staring at Calista and holding each other's hands so tightly their knuckles were white.

"I'm sorry," Calista offered softly. "Did you . . . know him well?"

The old man nodded, very slightly. "He was our son."

Before Calista could think of a response to that revelation, the woman added, "We feared something like this. It had been so long since we'd heard from him—" Her voice died away.

Calista didn't say anything. There wasn't anything she *could* say, certainly nothing that would ease the pain of parents who had just had their worst fears confirmed.

All she could do was let the first shock wear off, then pursue the questions that had brought her here in the first place. Not that she thought these two would have much useful information, but she wasn't going to leave until she'd learned everything, no matter how trivial, that might provide the leverage on Larr that she sought.

After several minutes had passed and the two simply continued to sit, staring blankly at her, Calista cleared her throat. "You said you had information to trade—"

The reminder roused the pair. They blinked, glanced at each other, then at Calista. A sharp, hard look suddenly came into the old woman's eyes. Her voice grew sharp and shrewish. "We have information, but we expected more. What would it be worth to you, stranger, to know what Larr's plans are?"

Calista's mouth twisted in distaste. Poor Tull. So soon forgotten when it was a matter of money. It appeared the man had come by his dishonest habits quite legitimately—he'd inherited them.

"It's worth exactly what I've already paid you," Calista snapped, all sympathy at an end. She pulled the disrupter off her belt and pointed it at the startled couple. If she was going to deal with crooks, she might as well take advantage of her disguise. A Shielukk wouldn't tolerate treachery for any longer than it took to press the trigger.

"Of course, of course! I didn't mean—" the old woman gabbled.

"We'll tell you!" the old man said, eyes wide. "My wife didn't want to suggest—"

"Then tell me what you know, or—" Calista waved the disrupter suggestively.

They told her. It wasn't much, but it would be enough, Calista thought. Used properly, it would be more than enough.

When she was sure the two had told her everything they knew, Calista rose. "I'm not going to hurt you," she said, disgusted, when the two shrank back. "Are you from Graustauk?"

The old woman shook her head. "Weavering. We're from Weavering. Porganis first met Larr here and he was here the last time we heard from him so we thought—"

Had they just come in search of their son? Calista wondered. Or had they hoped to use the information he'd given them to their own benefit? Their inept attempts at extortion indicated they possessed neither the skill nor the nerve to wring a profit from the knowledge they held, but perhaps their son's grandiose boasting had misled them. And now they were left with nothing.

"Go back to Weavering," she said harshly, hoping an implied threat would serve where good sense had not.

She found the tall man still in his place in the shadows at the foot of the stairs. What was his role? Calista wondered. Did he work for pay, or for the profits he'd never see?

"They're going back to Weavering," she said, coming to a halt in front of him. "If you're owed any pay, you might want to collect it now, before they leave."

The man grinned, exposing three broken teeth. "Much obliged. For such a sweet old couple, they're surprisingly quick when it comes to protecting their credits."

He was already headed up the stairs by the time

Calista reached the main door. She didn't care. She was trying to work out how long it would take to reach Karta if she traveled at top speed.

"So you have certain eggs you're supposed to watch, and when they're ready, you move them, is that it?" Rhys asked.

The gray, whose name was Na'a, sat awkwardly on the ground in front of him, trying its best to please but clearly uncomfortable with the strange position. "Yes, Master. That's right."

Rhys bit his lip at the answer, which was almost identical to every other answer he'd gotten from the creature. He had to remind himself to be patient.

He wasn't sure why, but this afternoon only one *drenn*, Na'a, had been assigned to help him. He'd decided to take advantage of the opportunity and for the last twenty minutes he'd been trying to question the creature about how things worked in the caves.

It hadn't been easy. Na'a was willing enough, but it never ventured any information on its own, so he had to pull the answers out, a little at a time. Most of the answers were the same, "Yes, Master. That's right," which didn't get him very far.

Rhys was growing exceedingly weary of the whole process and beginning to wonder if even the possibility of gaining information that might help him discredit Larr was worth the frustration of dealing with this gentle yet incredibly simpleminded beast.

"How do you decide who takes care of which eggs?" he asked.

"The eggs are given to us, Master." Na'a bowed its head ingratiatingly and added, "I would be honored to take care of *your* eggs, Master."

Rhys couldn't help blinking at the offer. "Uh, thanks. Thanks very much." He wasn't even going to attempt explaining human reproduction. "So the eggs become like the Dorinor, is that it?"

Na'a's mouth dropped open. It plunged its hands into the crude work apron tied around what passed for its waist and started wringing them nervously.

Over the past few days Rhys had come to identify the action as a sign of agitation and worry. What, he wondered, had he said to upset the creature so?

"They don't become like the Dorinor?" he asked.

Na'a wrung its hands some more. "Oh, no, Master. There is only one Dorinor."

"Only one?"

"Yes, Master."

Rhys waited, hoping for more. When the gray said nothing, he sighed and asked another question. "What *do* they become, then?"

Na'a cocked its head to one side, struggling to grasp the meaning of the question. "The eggs are what they are, Master," it timidly ventured at last.

Rhys threw up his hands, his patience at an end. "So what *are* they?"

That question, at least, seemed to make sense to the gray. It immediately began reciting a litany of words whose meaning even the translator didn't seem to know. There were so many words, Rhys's attention began to wander. He almost missed the one word he did know.

"Wait! Stop!" he commanded, holding up both hands. "Did you say *drenn*?"

"Yes, master."

"The eggs become *drenn*?" Rhys's voice was tight with eager tension.

"Only the *drenn* eggs become *drenn*, master," Na'a replied, clearly puzzled by Rhys's incomprehension.

"Can you show me the eggs?" Rhys asked, expecting

to be rebuffed. Na'a's ready acquiescence caught him by surprise.

The creature awkwardly clambered to its feet, clearly relieved to be able to stand. When Rhys was on his feet, it said, "This way, Master." Without waiting to see if Rhys followed, it set off at a brisk, if lumbering, pace down a passage Rhys hadn't yet ventured into.

Rhys scarcely paid any attention. His thoughts were too eagerly turning over the implications of Na'a's revelation. If the *drenn* hatched from the same kinds of eggs as the Kartanese, then they were Kartanese, too, regardless of the obvious physical differences. And if they were Kartanese, then Calista could stop worrying . . .

The memory of Calista and her passionate objection to what she saw as the *drenn's* evident slavery brought Rhys's thoughts to a confused halt. No matter how hard he tried, he couldn't force her from his mind.

He'd have to, somehow, Rhys reminded himself. She was gone and she wouldn't be coming back, and any effort on his part to find her would only put her at greater risk with the slave hunters.

A hot, hard tightness caught in Rhys's throat, compounded of all the longing and regret and all the tears he'd refused to shed since she'd left. Calista was gone. The words burned painfully, but if he said them often enough, perhaps he'd come to accept them.

It hadn't helped so far.

All he could do was hope that time and his own demanding work would eventually soften the memories so they were at least endurable. He didn't have much confidence even in those traditional remedies for a wounded heart.

It only needed a few turns and intersecting passages for Rhys to lose all sense of direction. He had a glowlight, but he hadn't thought to bring a tracker as part of his regular equipment, which meant he'd be dependent on Na'a to lead him out again.

Just as Calista had described, Rhys's first hint of the hatching cavern was a faint glow at the end of the tunnel. He soon discovered the cavern even looked like Calista's, with lighting from what appeared to be ferns hung on the wall, a mist-shrouded mineral pool in the center of the cavern floor, and a series of unevenly spaced spiral ramps leading down to it. The difference was, this cavern had only a few hundred eggs, all neatly laid out on the shelflike lower levels of the ramps.

Na'a immediately headed down the ramp but Rhys paused a moment, trying to gauge the atmosphere of the big area. It was certainly warmer and far more humid than the passages, but it didn't seem to be quite as hot or humid as Calista had described the cavern she'd seen.

Was this cavern's climate being controlled by the equipment already installed? He tried to estimate where the cavern's location was in relation to the equipment, but he was too disoriented even to make a guess.

The easiest solution, of course, was to ask Na'a. Thinking of the readiness with which the gray had responded to his request to visit the cavern, Rhys wondered if he hadn't made a mistake all along in not asking the *drenn* for more information.

On the other hand, he couldn't help wondering what he was getting himself into by entering the cavern. No one, not even the Dorinor, had specifically made the hatching caves off limits, but the frequently repeated refusals to let him trace any of the conduits and access tunnels connected to the equipment they'd been installing clearly indicated he wasn't welcome outside certain areas. And hadn't the Dorinor said something about only the chosen being allowed in the caves? Though if Larr had been allowed in almost fifty years ago, the Kartanese must surely have eased up on that restriction since then.

The rationalizations sounded good. Now, if they just didn't get him in trouble.

He'd find more answers if he did something besides stand still, however. Na'a was already at the lowest level of the ramp, patiently waiting for him to catch up.

As he came up beside the gray, Rhys asked, "Are you responsible for tending any of these eggs, Na'a?"

The big gray came as close to giving a happy grin as anything Rhys had seen.

"Yes, Master." It gestured toward the neatly aligned eggs lying on the shelf to Rhys's right. "These are my eggs."

Na'a led the way along the ledge, moving with an odd grace Rhys had never before seen in any of the grays, solicitously bending over first one egg, then another, touching each gently in passing as though to reassure itself that all was well.

To Rhys, all the eggs looked pretty much the same, dull, off-white, rough-surfaced ovals like the ones Calista had described. Curious, he asked, "What are these eggs, Na'a?" He couldn't remember any of the words Na'a had used to describe the different types.

Na'a stopped, then touched first the egg in front of it, then the egg to the side. "This is a *shue*, Master, a hunter. And this is a *drenn*. This is *shue*, and this a *dra'a*, a mother." It looked up at Rhys. "I am honored to have a *dra'a*, Master. I have watched it very carefully, ever since it was given to me."

"I'm sure you have," Rhys murmured, touched by the creature's obvious concern for the precious eggs entrusted to its care. Strange that neither he nor Calista had considered the possibility that there might be more than one kind of Kartanese.

Though such division of roles was rare among the more intelligent species, it was fairly common throughout the galaxy among the lesser species. The Dorinor himself had even provided a hint the first time they'd met. Something about him and Calista each having their role. If the grays hadn't been so very different from the Dorinor and his kind, perhaps . . .

An inarticulate cry of concern from Na'a interrupted Rhys's train of thought. The gray was crouched beside one of the eggs, clearly worried about something.

"Na'a?" Rhys moved to the creature's side, even though there wasn't much he could do to help with whatever the problem was.

"The egg, Master. It weakens." Na'a's dark eyes had grown dull with worry. It rose to its feet, towering over Rhys. "I must go for help."

"Of course. I'll wait for you here." He couldn't do much else, Rhys thought grimly. Without a tracker, he'd have trouble finding his way back to the equipment chamber, and he was far too deep to beam back up to the ship from here.

Besides, he wouldn't mind exploring further to see if he could find any outlets that would indicate whether the environment in this cavern was artificially controlled. Na'a's absence would give him a few minutes alone. He might as well make the most of the opportunity.

Na'a didn't wait for his answer, anyway. Moaning softly to itself, it left Rhys without a backward glance and disappeared down one of the nearby passages.

Ten minutes later Rhys was trying to squeeze past some of the eggs so he could get close enough to inspect what looked like an equipment access tunnel when an enraged roar from behind him made him spin around, every sense alert.

A Kartanese—at least, what he still thought of as a Kartanese—stood on its back feet at the entrance to the passageway through which Na'a had disappeared. Its eyes glittered, its teeth were bared, and its front feet, claws out, were raised for battle. Beside it, perhaps half a dozen grays clustered, uncertain what was expected of them.

"He's tampering with the eggs!" the Kartanese roared, pointing at Rhys. "Seize him!"

Chapter Nineteen

For an instant, Rhys couldn't believe he was the target of the Kartanese's wrath. He hadn't touched any of the eggs. He hadn't even moved very far from where Na'a had left him. That meant it had to be someone or something else that had triggered the creature's explosive anger.

The sight of three *drenn* headed directly toward him as fast as their ponderous legs would take them quickly disabused him of that notion.

Whether he was innocent or not, it didn't look as if anybody was going to stop long enough to hear his side of things before they trampled him to death. A brief, vivid flashback to what Larr had told Calista about Porganis Tull's demise served as a potent reminder that there were worse ways of dying than being squashed.

Rhys scanned the area around him, desperately searching for an escape route. He was too deep

331

for the *Fair Trade's* transporter to reach him. The conduit he'd been inspecting was too narrow for him to squeeze through, even if he'd been sure where it led, and he couldn't climb to the next higher level because the stone wall behind him was too smooth to provide even minuscule handholds. The *drenn* were already thundering along the ledge he was on and getting closer by the second.

That left one option—jump down to the main floor of the cavern and run for the nearest clear passage, praying like hell it would take him up to within transport range and not deeper into the mountain.

Rhys jumped.

Even though he tried to flex, then roll, the shock of landing on the stone floor made his teeth rattle. He didn't take time to see if anything was broken. If he got back to the ship, he'd have plenty of time to check things out. If he didn't, it wouldn't matter a lot, anyway.

Fortunately, the hard landing hadn't affected his glowlight. He switched it on the minute he was in the passage, heedless of whether it made him easier to spot. The Kartanese could find him by sense of smell, anyway, and he'd be able to move a lot faster if he could see where he was going.

Despite the glowlight, Rhys didn't see the black-furred Kartanese ahead of him until he was almost under the creature's nose. He had a horrifying glimpse of two golden eyes, glittering with rage, and huge jaws filled with what looked like hundreds of very white and very sharp teeth closing shut just inches in front of his face. He barely saw the clawed forefoot that hit him and flung him against the passage wall, but he did have an incredibly vivid vision of what those claws would do to him just an instant before everything went black and he lost consciousness.

* * *

Calista dropped out of hyperspace above Karta with all weapons fully armed and sensors set to their maximum to detect any slave hunters who might already have arrived. The *Fair Trade* hung in its accustomed orbit, but she caught no trace of any new arrivals.

Which didn't mean they hadn't already come through. Had Rhys seen them? Would they have left one of their number on the planet, in case she came back?

There wasn't any sure way of finding out unless she asked.

She signaled the *Fair Trade*, but got nothing more than a standard response from the ship's computer. She tried sending a direct message to Rhys. No response at all.

Calista drummed her fingers on the console, considering alternatives and not liking any of them. If Larr's people hadn't fallen asleep at their work, they either already knew she'd returned or they'd find out pretty quickly.

Were they in touch with the hunters? Would they pass the word that the prey was back in the trap, or would they merely wait and see what happened next on the assumption the hunters would catch her, no matter what?

And where was Rhys? Why couldn't she contact him? No trader was out of touch with his ship for long, so why didn't he respond?

She had to talk to him. *Now*. He needed to hear what she'd learned from Tull's parents. With that information, Calista possessed the leverage she needed to stop Larr, or at least hold him at bay. It might not be enough to protect her from the slave hunters, but it would give Rhys a fighting chance of gaining the world that he sought so desperately.

Unable to sit still any longer, Calista jumped up and began pacing, considering her options.

There was, of course, another way she could find him. She could transport to the *Fair Trade* and use the ship's computer to trace him. Unless he'd abandoned his communicator, the computer would maintain a low-level link that would allow her to locate him.

The trouble was, the minute she left the *Independence*, she left behind her means of protection and escape. Once off the ship, she was dangerously vulnerable.

On the other hand, staying here and waiting for Rhys to show up, whenever that might be, wasn't too bright an idea, either. The longer she was here, the more people who would know of her presence—and be able to do something about it.

Yet Rhys had to know what she'd learned. Getting that information to him had been worth the risk when she'd left Graustauk VII. It was worth the risk now.

With sudden decision, Calista left the bridge headed for her quarters. The green skin dye had worn off, but she still had the mercenary's clothes she'd worn on Graustauk. The garments hid an impressive array of weapons and tools that might prove useful.

Ten minutes later she was on the bridge of the *Fair Trade*. The ship's computer traced Rhys immediately.

Calista swore.

He was in the Dorinor's chamber, and from the readings the sensors had picked up, the place was jammed with both Kartanese and humans. Not exactly what she had in mind for a safe, quite reunion.

If she were smart, she'd wait. Rhys was bound to be back in a few hours, at most, and she'd be a lot safer on the *Independence* than she would be traipsing around on the planet below if Larr was anywhere near Rhys.

The trouble was, her curiosity was growing. Just what was going on down there that required all those Kartanese and humans to meet at one time? Was Larr plotting something? Had the Dorinor, perhaps, decided to throw a party?

Or was Rhys in some kind of danger?

That possibility made her grow cold. What could have happened in the few days she'd been gone that could put Rhys in trouble?

She had no doubts that Larr would be perfectly amenable to using threats, blackmail, and physical force to get his way, but he already had leverage over Rhys. With what Larr was plotting, he needed the silk and the profits it brought him to succeed. Now that she was supposedly gone, surely he wouldn't risk losing his remaining trade rep. Or would he?

Calista studied the sensor readings again. Despite the large number of Kartanese and humans congregated in the main chamber, the side passages appeared empty. If she could transport directly into one of the passages, there was a chance she'd be able to see and hear enough to figure out what was going on without being spotted herself. If Rhys wasn't in any danger, she could return to the *Independence* and wait for his return.

If he *was* in danger . . .

Calista pushed down the sick, nervous feeling in the pit of her stomach at the thought. He was a big boy and had been in more than his fair share of trouble over the years. He was perfectly capable of taking care of himself. She hoped . . .

With a last, quick check of her weapons, Calista gave the order for the transporter to beam her down.

Calista heard the uproar coming from the Dorinor's chamber first. As her eyes adapted to the lower light levels, she could pick up the faint glow showing at the end of the passage ahead. She'd deliberately chosen a smaller side passage, one that opened into the chamber at a level that would give her a view of what was going on without running so much risk of being spotted herself.

With a last check of her hidden weapons—she'd taken the disrupter off her belt—and a quick prayer that she was wasting her time, Calista crept toward the Dorinor's chamber and the ruckus within it.

Her caution was so much wasted effort. Nobody was watching any of the passage openings. Their attention was focused on the raised platform where the Dorinor sat on his haunches, angrily surveying the crowd before him.

In front of the platform, a Kartanese harangued the Dorinor in an impassioned speech whose words Calista couldn't catch. The creature was so agitated it kept flapping its wings and lashing its tail, which made things remarkably uncomfortable for the two Kartanese guards and the five grays who stood behind it. The guards, intent on staying close to the speaker, had to duck more than once to avoid getting hit.

The grays weren't so quick. Calista saw two of them take a dive as the tail slashed through the space where their heads had been a moment before. In their haste they bumped into each other, then into a third, and sent it sprawling as well.

On one side of the Kartanese who was speaking, another gray lay prostrate on the floor in front of the platform, wailing and gabbling senselessly. Calista thought she detected someone or something on the other side of the Kartanese, but she couldn't be sure because her view was blocked by the creature's massive body.

Beyond, Larr and two of his henchmen stood

coldly watching the circus in front of them. Near them, seated on his lower platform, Karnor sat with his forefeet protectively placed on his belly, morosely staring at the ground rather than watching the commotion. The big Kartanese looked distinctly unhappy, but about what, Calista couldn't tell.

What worried Calista was Rhys's absence. The *Fair Trade's* computer had indicated he was here in the chamber, but she couldn't spot a trace of him. She scanned the chamber again with the same results. Unless he was standing on the far side of the still-shouting Kartanese, he wasn't there, and yet he *had* to be present.

There was only one way to find out for sure. Calista stood up as straight as she could, thrust back her shoulders, and nonchalantly strolled down the ramp leading to the chamber floor.

At first, no one noticed her. They were all too intent on what was going on in front of the Dorinor's platform.

Larr was the first to spot her. His head snapped up and his eyes narrowed with suspicion and anger. His reaction roused his two lieutenants. Their mouths dropped open in surprise, but at a gesture from Larr, they started toward her, ready for a fight if she was.

They didn't get far. Their movements attracted the Dorinor's attention. At the sight of Calista, he roared for silence.

The Kartanese who had held the floor for so long stopped in mid-sentence, startled by his leader's abrupt command. He turned to see what had interrupted his speech, and that made everyone else turn around as well.

Nothing like making a grand entrance, Calista thought. And where in the hell was Rhys?

Repressing the urge to rush forward, she calmly

pushed past the grays and the Kartanese guard at the back of the crowd.

"Hello, Larr," Calista said pleasantly, meeting the man's venomous gaze. "What are you doing, having a little town meeting?"

Larr couldn't quite master his fury. "I didn't expect you back, trader."

"Why wouldn't I come back? We have a contract, remember?" She stopped a respectful distance from the Dorinor's platform and bowed. "I give you greetings, Excellency."

Still in a deep bow, she craned her head to see around the Kartanese, who was huffing indignantly at being required to shut up just because another human had appeared.

Calista almost lost her balance as shock and sudden panic rocketed through her. Rhys! Battered, bloody, and on his knees with his hands bound behind his back!

At the sight of her, he tensed and his brow creased into a tight, worried frown. He started to speak, but the Kartanese cuffed him soundly before he could get a word out.

Calista reached for her hidden disrupter, but stopped at the last second. She'd gotten the weapons past the guards only because they'd been too engrossed in whatever was going on to pay any attention to her. There wasn't any sense in losing that advantage yet.

"Hello, Fairdane," she said, forcing down her panic. "I hope you don't mind my saying so, but you look like hell."

Rhys scowled, clearly unimpressed by her levity at such a moment, then winced in pain.

From the look of him, just about everything must hurt. A huge and rapidly darkening bruise shaded the right side of his face from temple to jaw. Several cuts and scrapes added a colorful touch to the purplish black of the bruise. Rhys's skin suit hung in tatters. It was shredded from his right shoulder to his left side, exposing long, bloody scratches across his chest that looked like the result of one strong swipe from a Kartanese's claws.

He was lucky he'd been wearing a skin suit, Calista thought. Otherwise, those claws might have cut to the bone.

"He has trespassed in the sacred caves," the Dorinor said. His voice rumbled dismally in the chamber, even over the constant whimpering of the *drenn* who still lay face down on the floor before him.

"Are you sure?" Calista challenged him.

"I found him there! He was tampering with the sacred eggs, endangering their well-being!" Rhys's captor didn't take long to get into full swing with his ranting. "He *must* be punished for such sacrilege! He defiled the sacred cave, disobeyed the rules that only the chosen may enter therein, then—"

"Enough! We've heard your accusations, Tharnok!"

From beside the angry Dorinor came the Kartanese equivalent of an anguished whisper. "Oh dear. Oh dear, oh dear!"

Calista swung around, surprised by the both the plaintive exclamation and its source. Karnor sat on his platform, anxiously watching the proceedings and solicitously rubbing his belly with both forefeet. She'd swear he looked paler than he had a few minutes earlier, though how a huge, black-furred beast like Karnor could manage that feat, she couldn't guess.

"All that fat," he added pitifully, his gaze fixed on Rhys's lean, muscular frame. "Oh, my digestion! My poor digestion."

Larr came closer, a coldly hostile smile on his face.

"It rather appears I'm going to have to look for new representatives, trader."

"Did you set this up, Larr?" Calista demanded angrily.

He raised his hands, palms out, and assumed an expression of innocence. "I had nothing to do with this. Your partner managed to get into this mess all by himself."

"Quiet!"

The Dorinor's angry roar reverberated in the cavern. Even the prostrate *drenn* shut up this time.

"The issue here is the protection of our sacred caves," he continued sternly, though at a slightly lower decibel level. "If this human has trespassed, then he must be punished."

"But I saw him!" the accusing Kartanese protested.

"I said quiet!" The Dorinor eyed the creature for a minute, as though daring him to disobey again, then said, "I have heard from everyone except the human." He looked at Rhys. "Do you have anything to say?"

"I do, your Excellency." Rhys glared at his accuser, then struggled painfully to his feet. "I intended no harm in visiting the cave and did not threaten your eggs." He glanced at the *drenn* who had been making all the noise. "Na'a is not responsible. He took me there at my request because he had been instructed to follow my orders. My only reason for going was to learn what I could do so the equipment that you required I install would function properly."

Rhys stared at the Dorinor in an open challenge that didn't quite go beyond the limits of what was acceptable. When the Dorinor didn't respond, he added, "Besides, you never forbade me to go in the caves. I didn't know it was a crime to do so."

The Dorinor briefly considered that, then shook his head. "That is beside the point. You were found with the sacred eggs. Endangering our young—"

"Your Excellency!" Calista stepped forward.

Now was her chance to use the information she'd gained on Graustauk VII and what she'd pieced together herself. But what should she say? Given the Kartanese's lack of knowledge about anything except mathematics and their precious eggs, what arguments would be the most convincing to them— and damning for Larr?

Ignoring the Dorinor's irritation at her interruption, she said, "If endangering the young is a crime, then it is not Trader Fairdane, but your representative Larr who should be punished!"

"What?" The Dorinor's head came up.

Larr's head jerked up, too. He stared at her, his eyes hard and bright with hostility.

"He is using you for his own ends," Calista insisted, "and he will stop at nothing—including killing some of the eggs in the sacred caves—to get what he wants."

"Excellency!" Larr interjected angrily, stepping forward. "The woman is mad! You know how I have worked for the benefit of Karta and your people. You know I have given years of my life so that the caves are protected and—"

"Lies! Excellency," Calista hotly replied. "All lies! I have information that—"

"The woman is nothing more than an escaped slave, Excellency! Would you believe her over me, who has served you for so long?"

Calista took another step forward, fighting against the urge to drive her fist into Larr's face. "Larr has used you for years! He's never cared about the Kartanese, only about his own profit and his dreams of power! If you will let me explain how—"

"Quiet!" The roar wasn't quite as loud this time, but it was no less effective. The Dorinor stared first at Calista, then Rhys, then at Larr. Then he scratched his belly.

After a moment's consideration, he lowered his head to Calista's level and said, "I will listen to what you have to say. That does not mean I believe you." He turned to Larr. "You will keep quiet while she speaks, then I will listen to what *you* have to say."

Larr clearly didn't like it, but he remained quiet.

"May I untie Trader Fairdane first, your Excellency?" Calista asked. If her ploy didn't work, she and Rhys might well have to fight their way off Karta. They wouldn't have much of a chance if Rhys was still bound.

When the Dorinor looked like he was about to refuse, Calista added, "It's only fair! Larr is not tied!" As an argument, her protest lacked even a speck of logic, but it worked.

The Dorinor nodded reluctantly and said, "All right," then sat back, distancing himself from them as if he wanted to show he wasn't going to be taking sides.

Pleased to have gotten at least that much of a concession, Calista moved to free Rhys's hands. As she bent over the clumsily tied knot, she whispered, low enough so no one else could hear, "There's a disrupter in a hidden pocket on the left side and a plasteel in the outside seam of my sleeve."

"I hope you know what you're doing," Rhys whispered back, rubbing his wrists, careful not to look at her.

So do I, Calista thought. *So do I*.

"Your Excellency," Calista began, "Larr wants much more of the fibers—what we call saitha silk—than would normally be produced, so he's decided to stimulate its production artificially."

She paused, letting her words sink in, then, in the most impressively ringing tones she could muster, added, "He has been dumping chemicals into the waters of the sacred caves. Those chemicals artificially encourage your mothers to produce more eggs."

Calista glanced over at Larr, but instead of the shock and fear she'd expected to see in his face, she found only irritation and anger. Puzzled, she turned back to find the Dorinor staring at her with a quizzical expression on his face.

"Have I explained myself clearly, Excellency?" she asked. She wanted to ask if he'd understood a word she'd said, but that approach wouldn't get her much of anywhere except in trouble.

The Dorinor gave a snort of disgust. "Larr has told us of these chemicals, which he says are needed to make the air and water of the caves well again," he said sharply. "We have been pleased at the greater number of eggs, for they are our future. But that is not why we are here. Do not waste my time."

Calista sensed Rhys moving closer to her, undoubtedly preparing to grab her hidden disrupter, but she didn't look his way. They might eventually have to fight their way out, but she wasn't ready to give up yet.

"You see, Excellency?" Larr demanded before Calista could continue. "She's trying to trick you. I have served you and your people for too long for you to doubt me and she knows that. Her intentions are to buy time so she and her partner can escape without punishment. She's already tricked you into letting her untie him."

"She has not tricked me!" the Dorinor snapped, swinging around to glare at Larr.

"And *he* has not told you the full truth about those chemicals, Excellency!" Calista added, taking advantage of Larr's tactical mistake in insulting the Dorinor.

343

The Dorinor's attention swung back to Calista. "What *is* the truth?" he demanded.

"That they produce more eggs, but many of those eggs die. You know how many are dying, Excellency! It isn't these new machines that will stop it, but removing the old machines, stopping the chemicals, and letting the caves return to their normal state!" Calista tried to pour every possible ounce of conviction into her voice. It didn't work.

"Larr has explained all that." The Dorinor shook his head sadly. "The gods were angry with us before Larr came. They changed the sacred waters and allowed many of our young to die unborn. If he had not brought his machines and chemicals, we might have lost all our eggs, but even he can not restore the caves to what they were."

Calista glanced at Larr. He simply glared at her, angry but not yet nervous. The man had covered his tracks very cleverly. It wasn't going to be as easy to discredit him as she'd first thought.

She turned back to the Dorinor. "The eggs wouldn't be dying now if it weren't for the artificial control of the caves' environments." That was pushing the truth, Calista guessed, but Tull had been convinced that was so, and everything she'd seen so far led her to believe he'd been right. "Larr doesn't care if the eggs die, because he can still use the silk they produce. It isn't as effective and it doesn't last as long, but it's good enough for some of his customers."

The tip of the Dorinor's tail twitched, just a little, and his wings rustled. Maybe she was making some headway after all. Calista could hear Rhys shifting impatiently behind her, but she made no effort to turn around and look at him. The last thing she needed was to divert any attention from her accusations against Larr back to the charges still pending against Rhys.

Calista pushed on. "None of the new caves you're adding can function without the equipment that's been installed, Excellency. If anything were to happen to that machinery, every single egg in there would die because there would be no natural systems to keep the cave functioning properly. At least when there are changes in any of the real sacred caves, most of the eggs survive because the changes aren't that drastic."

The Dorinor glanced uncertainly from Calista to Larr and back again. "But why—?"

"Money, Excellency, and power." Out of the corner of her eye, Calista watched Larr. What she was going to say next might not make much of an impression on the Kartanese, but it might put the first dent in the man's self-control. Maybe.

"Over the past forty years, Larr has used the sale of the silk to gain influence over rulers on a hundred wealthy or powerful planets around the galaxy." Calista let that thought sink in, then continued, "These people have become so dependent on the silk that they will pay anything—*do* anything—to maintain their supply of it."

From the corner of her eye, Calista watched Larr, hoping for some indication that she'd hit a sensitive nerve. The testimony of Tull's parents had confirmed what she and Rhys had begun to suspect, but Calista was willing to bet Larr thought his secret still safe.

Still watching Larr, she added in ringing tones, "Larr wants to become not only the richest, but also the most powerful man in the galaxy, and he will stop at nothing until he does!"

The charge produced the first real chink in Larr's emotional armor that Calista had seen so far. His face flushed with rising anger, which meant he was losing control. People as coldly unemotional as Larr

345

never learned how to handle strong human feelings, especially rage. The more out of control they became, the more vulnerable they were.

She pushed him a little further by letting him see her gloat.

Calista could sense the growing uncertainty of the Kartanese around her, could see the doubt and worry in the expressions of Larr's two escorts. None of that mattered in comparison with the faint hint of fear that now showed in Larr's eyes.

From here on out, she was going on speculation. If the Dorinor insisted on proof, she was in trouble, but if she could force Larr to make a mistake . . .

"Larr intends to control everything and everyone he can, your Excellency," she continued, choosing her words carefully. "He will turn you and your people into virtual slaves in his greed to possess more power and more wealth. He doesn't care how many of the precious eggs die to achieve that ambition."

"Excellency!" Larr protested, red-faced with anger. "After all the years I have served you, will you now let this conniving, unprincipled woman insult me and lie about me like this?"

The Dorinor, who had watched and listened without moving, now sat up straighter, clearly unsure how to react or whom to believe.

"Good try, Calista," Rhys said in a low, tight voice close behind her, "but your bluff's not working. I'd suggest we beam up to our ships and get the hell out of here while we still can."

Bluff. Calista could scarcely breathe, she was so tense. Rhys was right; she'd bluffed, and it hadn't gotten her much advantage. A little, but not enough.

What would she do in a game of bakal if her bluff wasn't working? The answer was easy. She'd double the ante and go one more round.

There *was* one last card she could play, but she had no proof. Calista wasn't even sure the information was true, for Tull's parents had only mentioned it in passing and they'd had no more information to offer when she'd tried to press them about it.

But true or not, it was her last chance.

Calista took a deep breath, then demanded in clear, ringing tones, "Ask Larr about the eggs he stole, Excellency. Ask him about his plans to establish caves on other planets so he could have more eggs and more fibers if anything went wrong here."

"What? How did you . . . ? You scheming witch!" Larr's last vestige of self-control vanished in that instant. His features twisted in rage as he lunged toward her, hands curved to wrap around her throat.

Chapter Twenty

The Kartanese who had accused Rhys of tampering with the eggs let out a deafening roar and moved to block Larr's attempt to reach Calista. "The missing eggs! So *you* are responsible!"

The two Kartanese guards, eyes glittering fiercely, rose on their back legs, unsheathed their deadly front claws, and advanced on him. With a harsh, angry cry, Karnor plunged off his platform toward Larr, as well.

Larr might have evaded Calista's trap even then, but in his fury he didn't stop to think. Ignoring the enraged Kartanese, he launched himself at her, blindly intent on revenge.

Calista wasn't quick enough to dodge his attack. She pulled out her hidden disrupter, but Larr wrenched it from her before she had a chance to use it. She barely avoided the vicious, backhand blow he aimed at her before he swung around to confront the Kartanese, her disrupter in his hand.

At the sight of the weapon, the guards attacked. Larr fired, hitting one in the shoulder. The creature's cry of pain fueled the other's rage. Teeth bared, the second guard sprang toward Larr. If it hadn't been for the frightened *drenn* that blundered in front of him, he probably would have killed the man right then.

"Down! Calista!" Rhys shouted, grabbing her and pulling her to the far side of the Dorinor's platform. It wasn't much protection, but it was safer than getting in the way of the enraged Kartanese, who would have trampled them without thinking in their fury.

"Do something, you fools!" Larr screeched at his men, dodging out of the guard's reach and firing again.

The two unarmed humans, eyes and mouths open wide with terror, made no effort to help. Instead, they ran right over the fallen *drenn* in their panic-stricken haste to reach the passage leading to the human quarters where the Kartanese couldn't follow them.

They almost made it, but one of the Kartanese guards blocked their way, driving them back toward Larr.

Evidently realizing his men would be of no assistance, Larr glanced toward the Dorinor. There would be no help from that quarter either. The Kartanese leader, forefeet up and claws bared, was already headed toward him, as ready for battle as the two guards.

Larr dashed around the *drenn*, which was struggling to get to its feet, then used its heavy body as a shield while he fired first at the Dorinor, then Calista and Rhys.

The shots missed, but Larr didn't stay long enough to find out. With a choked cry, he abandoned the fight and fled toward the same passage his two guards had tried to reach.

Unlike them, Larr managed to dodge the Kartanese who tried to block his way. Long robes flying, he raced up the ramp, into the smaller tunnel, and out of sight. The two Kartanese guards and Karnor were right behind him, but their greater bulk and the smaller passage slowed their pursuit.

The disappearance of their boss destroyed whatever fighting spirit remained in the two human guards. They crouched back to back, their hands up in a gesture of defeat. Even that wouldn't have saved them from the remaining Kartanese's rage if it hadn't been for the Dorinor's shouted command to leave them alone.

Rhys nudged Calista, then rose to his feet. "We'd better do something before those two end up being someone's dinner," he said, nodding toward the two terrified humans who cowered at the feet of the two angry Kartanese.

"Your Excellency," Rhys called, moving toward the Dorinor with as much of an air of calm confidence as he could muster. "Don't hurt them. They can help us find Larr for you."

Rhys could only hope he sounded convincing. He wasn't at all sure the men would be any use whatsoever. He wasn't even sure they didn't deserve punishment for whatever they might have done at Larr's instigation. But no matter what they'd done in the past, they didn't deserve the appalling punishment the Kartanese would have meted out. Nobody did.

The Dorinor hesitated. "These creatures have helped Larr defile our sacred caves and steal our eggs. By all our laws, they must be punished."

"It is Larr who is responsible, not these men," Rhys said. "If you will release them, they can help us track him down."

After a moment's consideration, the Dorinor grudgingly stepped away. "You may take them," he grumbled.

Dazed and frightened, the two men scarcely understood Rhys at first. Then the fact that they'd been reprieved sank in.

"I'll help," the bigger of the two readily offered, now that there was no enraged Kartanese looming over him.

The second merely nodded, then swore under his breath and nervously glanced at the Dorinor.

A few minutes later, however, they almost backed out of the deal when they caught sight of the three Kartanese blocking the narrow passage ahead of them. Karnor and the two Kartanese guards had chased Larr as far as they could go and were now jammed in the passage, snarling and snapping at each other and futilely trying to cram their way farther in.

Rhys had to shout to get their attention, then convince them to move out of the way and not try to rend Larr's men limb from limb in the process before the Kartanese eventually, and very reluctantly, let them through.

He had expected the heavy door between the Kartanese and human sides of the tunnel to be locked. It wasn't. In his haste, Larr hadn't even stopped to close it. He seemed to have swept through like a whirlwind, sucking everything up in his wake, for they saw no one in the deserted offices. Only a couple of glowing monitors or a chair or two out of place gave any indication that people had recently occupied the rooms they passed.

They paused only once to find disrupters, then continued on as quickly as they could. Rhys called a halt before the passage they were following reached the main work area near Larr's quarters. "Where will Larr go? What will he do next?" he demanded, studying the two men, wondering just how far he could trust them.

Now that they were safely out of the Kartanese's reach, the men's courage had returned with their rising anger and resentment of Larr's abandonment of them. The anger would serve his purpose, Rhys thought, but only so long as it was kept in control. If the men's hunger for revenge took over, they might be as dangerous to Calista and him as they would be to Larr because they might not stop to think about the possible consequences of their actions.

The bigger man, who seemed to be the leader of the two and who was clearly eager to hurry on, scowled at the question. "He'll run, I guess," he said after a moment's thought. "He keeps a four-passenger flitter that can handle hyperspace, but there's no other transport off this damned rock except the hauler."

"You mean he'd leave us here?" the second man squawked, outraged. When the realization sank in that his partner was right, he started cursing again.

"We've no time for that now," Rhys snapped, forcing the men's attention back to the problem at hand. "The question is, what will the rest of your people do? Will they protect Larr, or will they help us?"

The first man mulled that one over briefly. "Some of them might help us, if we can explain what's happened. There's nobody here who didn't come for the money, and that's a fact. If Larr would leave Rogh, here, and me to the beasts, he'd do the same to any of the rest of them."

"Pirock's right. And if I ever get my hands on that—" Rogh's hands twisted in a graphic description of just what he'd do with Larr.

"I want him alive!"

Calista's sharp words startled Rhys with their vehemence.

"He's the only one who can send away the hunters, the only one who's got a chance of convincing them it was all a mistake," Calista continued, her gaze insistently fixed on his, her body strung tight with tension.

Guilt stabbed at Rhys. He'd been so focused on the pain of his bruised and battered body and on his own desire for revenge on Larr for having so readily abandoned him to the Kartanese that he hadn't even thought of why Calista was here or what she risked by having returned. He didn't want to think of what would have happened if she hadn't come back.

He nodded once, then gestured to the two men. "Lead the way, but remember, we want Larr alive."

The command to take Larr alive didn't seem to sit well with Rogh, but both men were too accustomed to following someone else's commands to question Rhys's now. Their faces set in grim determination, they set off at a jog trot in the direction of Larr's quarters.

Their first indication of the presence of other humans was a frantic hum of voices, then the confused sound of hurrying feet. Rhys started to warn the men ahead to wait, but it was too late. They'd already burst into the middle of the open work area outside Larr's quarters.

"Where's Larr?" Pirock demanded, loud enough to catch the attention of everyone there. He brandished the disrupter, drawing a squeal of panic from one of the startled people there and frightened stares from the rest.

"Where's Larr?" Pirock repeated. "Where'd he go?"

One of the women, more calm than the rest, gestured toward Larr's quarters. "He's in there. He came

353

running through here a few minutes ago screaming at everyone. What in the hell's going on, Pirock?"

That released a stream of questions from the rest, who clustered around Pirock and Rogh, faces avid with curiosity.

"What happened? Why is Larr having to leave so suddenly?"

"Who are the strangers who are here to see Larr?"

"Where's Larr going?"

"What—?"

Pirock, feet aggressively wide apart and shoulders hunched as though poised to strike, silenced them with an angry curse. "That bastard is in deep trouble with those damn dragons, and he left Rogh and me to face them alone, just like he's trying to walk out on you now. I want him! Will any of you help me get him?"

Rhys couldn't stop a grimace of distaste at the man's words. For someone who hadn't seemed too concerned when he, Rhys, was on his knees, bound and helpless and about to become the Kartanese main course, Pirock was making a good show of moral outrage now.

Calista brought his attention back to the moment by lightly touching his arm. "Did you catch the reference to strangers visiting?" she asked. "Do you think . . . maybe . . . the hunters?"

He nodded. He'd caught it, but he'd hoped she hadn't. Rhys pointed toward the door set in the far wall that opened into Larr's quarters. "Let's see what's going on," he said, "while they're still distracted out here. Keep behind me, in case those strangers with Larr *are* hunters."

Calista followed him immediately, as he'd known she would. If he had his way, he'd stick her in a locked room, safely out of the way, but Rhys knew she'd never tolerate any attempt to leave her behind.

Not that there was any safe place for her. She couldn't even risk beaming up to the *Independence*, in case the hunters—if it really was them—had boarded her ship.

By coming to his rescue, Calista had put herself in enormous danger, and that fact both infuriated and frightened Rhys.

Larr had a lot to pay for. An awful lot to pay for.

They were almost to the massive door when it burst open and Larr emerged.

"Why has no one brought the trunks of silk I asked for?" he demanded. "Where's—"

He stopped abruptly at sight of Rhys. "You!" He spun around to confront this unexpected threat. "And you!" he added as he caught sight of Calista.

Before Rhys had a chance to respond, Larr pointed at them and cried, "Seize them!"

Not one of Larr's people moved.

Rhys pointed his disrupter straight at Larr. "It seems you've lost some of your powers of persuasion, Larr. Or is it they're not too fond of the idea of becoming somebody else's dinner whenever you can't be bothered with them anymore?"

"What are you waiting for?" Larr shouted, half-turning to his people, who remained frozen in place. He caught sight of Pirock. "You're my guard. Shoot them!"

Pirock stepped forward. "I don't think so. They weren't the ones who left me, Larr. You were." Slowly he raised his arm until his disrupter pointed straight at Larr's heart.

Larr swung around, but that direction was blocked by a grim-faced, disrupter-wielding Rogh. He backed up a step. "I didn't mean . . . They were after me, too!"

"Yeah?" Rogh waved his disrupter dismissively.

Desperate, Larr turned back to the still-silent cluster of employees who watched the exchange, all of them too uncertain or too frightened to act. "Are you all just going to stand there and let them threaten me like this?"

He got no answer.

"You can't do this!" Larr shrieked, his eyes wild.

"I think we can, Larr." Pirock advanced another step. "No problem."

"No! Don't hurt him!" Calista's clear, commanding tones made Pirock hesitate.

Rhys tried to stop her, but she pushed past him. "He's mine," she said, "and nobody's getting to him except me."

Larr took a step back, then another, his eyes fixed on Calista. "You're nothing more than a runaway slave," he spat, desperately trying to regain control over both himself and the situation. "You can't do anything."

"Are you sure about that?"

"He's sure." A burly man about Rhys's height but much more massive emerged from the room behind Larr. In his hand he held what looked like a small recording device, and it was pointing right at Calista.

"Her voice is a clear match, Frell," he added over his shoulder. "She's the runaway this guy reported."

Shock hit Rhys like a physical blow. For an instant, it seemed as if his heart stopped beating and the air remained trapped in his lungs, hot and tight.

The slave hunters were here and they'd identified Calista before he was even aware of their presence. He started to turn, to shield Calista, but it was too late.

The man addressed as Frell stepped out of the doorway, raised his stun gun, and fired at Calista before Rhys had moved two feet.

With a faint sigh, Calista collapsed in a heap, slowly folding in on herself in the limp, helpless motion of someone who'd been hit by a strong stun charge.

Rhys whirled back, disrupter raised and ready to fight the slavers, only to find the stun gun pointed directly at his chest.

"I wouldn't advise it," Frell said in a flat, unemotional voice.

"Good work!" The first slaver cautiously edged around Rhys to bend over Calista. He pulled her hands behind her back, then strapped on the unbreakable electronic bonds and gag that would hold her immobile and silent for as long as they liked.

Anger and fear churned in Rhys, matching the anger, fear and utter helplessness he briefly glimpsed in Calista's eyes before the slaver rolled her onto her stomach against the wall.

Slowly and very deliberately, Rhys lowered his disrupter. In that position, Calista would have little chance to move, even once the effects of the stun gun wore off. If she were ever to get free, he would have to do it, and he'd have to do it soon, before the slavers hauled her away.

"Well done!" Larr crowed, some of his haughty bravado coming back now that one of his opponents was effectively vanquished. "You see, trader?" he said, gloatingly. "You should have stayed with me."

Before Rhys could reply, he turned on Pirock. "As for you! I'll sell your contract to the slavers here. Yours and your friend's. Don't think I can?" he added in response to the horrified expression on Pirock's face. "You didn't read the fine print! I—"

Whatever Larr had been about to add ended in a choked cry of pain, then a small, faint gasp as he collapsed under the deadly beam of a disrupter set to kill.

Rogh stepped forward, disrupter in hand, to stare down at the lifeless body of the man who'd been his employer. He swore, spat on the floor, then glanced at the motionless slave hunters. "You want to follow up on what this bag of slime was saying?" he asked, waving the disrupter suggestively.

The hunter named Frell remained expressionless, unmoved by Larr's death. The first hunter shrugged. "Don't know that we can, now he's dead." His lips curled back in an ugly mockery of a grin. "Besides, with him dead, Frell and me don't have to pay the finder's fee for leading us to the runaway."

Rhys stepped forward. "About the slave . . . We need to talk. Now that Larr's dead, I'm in charge here, and there are a few things I need to know. Maybe," he added carefully, "there are a few things you ought to know, too."

The hunter stared at him, clearly assessing this new factor. "Who are you?"

"I'm Rhys Fairdane, the Dorinor's trade representative and now," he glanced at Larr's body, "by default, the Dorinor's personal representative, as well."

"Can't say as I'm impressed."

"You might be."

For a long, long minute, the hunter wavered, uncertain. He glanced first at Larr, then at the impassive Frell, then at Calista, who was beginning to throw off the effects of the stun. He turned back to Rhys. "All right. I'll listen."

"Good." Rhys tried to put every ounce of confidence he could into that one word. He wasn't at all sure his plan was going to work, but he had no intention of letting the hunter see his doubts.

Assuming a strong note of authority, Rhys waved at Larr's body. "Take care of him," he said to Pirock and Rogh. "Get whatever help you need and find a place to bury him decently. You," he added, pointing to the woman who had appeared so calm earlier, "get these people back to work. Larr's dead, but we still have work to do and I imagine it's going to be hell trying to straighten out some of his dealings."

Rhys held his breath, wondering if his bluff was going to work. He hadn't the slightest idea if they would be able to continue collecting and selling the silk, or if they'd be lucky just to get off the planet, but it wouldn't do anyone any good to admit that right now. Least of all Calista.

Fortunately, the woman to whom he'd given the order had the sense to see the wisdom of returning to work, regardless of whether they stayed or not. In a matter of minutes, Pirock and Rogh, with the help of two other men, had carried off Larr's body. Everyone else had returned to their places, wide-eyed and still in shock, but undoubtedly relieved that someone at least appeared to be in charge.

As Larr's former employees dispersed, Rhys turned his attention back to the slave hunters. He couldn't bear to look at Calista.

"We might as well make ourselves comfortable," he said, leading the way into the room with the window looking out on Karta. "I trust Larr offered you something to drink?" he asked, coming to a halt by the table where Larr had kept his crystal goblets and decanters of wine.

"Yeah. We don't need nothing more," the first hunter said impatiently, warily following him across the room. "Cut the chitchat, trader. Are you thinking of buying the slave? If so, what're you willing to offer for her . . . and why should we sell her, anyway?"

Out of the corner of his eye, Rhys could see Frell dragging Calista into the room as if she were a sack of tumwort seeds. His fingers tightened around the goblet he'd picked up. Briefly, he considered throwing it at Frell and had to force himself to relax his grip before he shattered the glass.

At least Calista's fighting spirit was back. Her blue eyes flashed with anger and she was struggling against Frell's grip. Not that her struggles could free her—the bonds that held her were unbreakable—but they did irritate Frell. The hunter, with the first sign of emotion Rhys had seen him display, almost threw Calista into a heap in the middle of the floor.

"Well, trader?" the first hunter demanded. "What are you willing to pay for the slave?"

"Not much," Rhys said in the most offhand tone he could manage. He settled into one of the chairs that gave him a good view of both Calista and the hunters, then took a sip of wine, openly studying Calista as though she were a commodity at auction. "She's useful and not too stupid. The thing is, I wouldn't bother except that I'm going to be a little shorthanded and she already knows the trade." After a moment's apparent consideration, he ventured a figure for the purchase price that was low, but not unreasonably so. He wouldn't gain anything by insulting his adversaries.

The hunter snorted in disgust. "That's not even enough to cover the cost of fuel to get here!"

Calista didn't seem to think much of the offer, either, for she glared up at him from her uncomfortable position on the floor, then squirmed angrily in her bonds.

Whether Calista's anger at him was real or feigned, Rhys was grateful for the diversion. The slavers would be difficult to deal with in direct proportion to their estimation of how badly he wanted her. They must already know the price she'd bring on the open market, which made it that much harder to negotiate.

"All right," Rhys said at last, shrugging. "What do you want for her?"

The hunter's shrewd gaze flicked from Rhys to Calista and back. He offhandedly suggested an extortionate sum.

Rhys forced a convincing imitation of a laugh. "Don't be ridiculous. You know as well as I do she's not worth anywhere near that much."

The dealing was on. They bluffed, argued, cajoled, made offers, and then made counteroffers. They assumed masks of boredom, irritation, friendly willingness to cooperate, regret, and any other emotion they thought would serve their purpose.

They got absolutely nowhere.

And all the while Calista lay on the floor, trussed like a pig in the market while Rhys's anger at her situation grew inside him until it was all he could do to keep from pulling out his disrupter and killing her captors right there. He was prepared to kill the two slavers, but only if no other means of freeing Calista sufficed. So desperate an act would turn both of them into fugitives, for other slavers would make it a point to track down anyone responsible for killing two of their own. What the next hunters would do to Calista didn't bear thinking about.

She had to be free, Rhys reminded himself fiercely again and again, fighting to control his temper. Really free, with no need ever to look back and wonder who was behind her and why.

At the same time, it sickened him to see anyone benefit by so much as a credit from Calista's inhumane bondage. Whatever the cost of her freedom, he would pay it, but he wouldn't give ground easily to scum like the two before him.

Rhys bargained and bluffed as he tried to force the hunter's price down toward some more reasonable, if still extortionate, sum. Despite the slave hunter's growing anger, Rhys was beginning to think he was making real progress when the man abruptly rose from his seat.

"I'm tired of negotiating, trader," he snarled, glaring down at Rhys. "I'll make one last offer, take it or leave it."

Tense silence gripped the room. Rhys waited, scarcely breathing. This was it, his trader's instincts told him. Negotiations stopped here, whether he wanted them to or not. Whatever the hunter's next demand, he would have to meet it—or he would have to resort to violence.

"And what's your offer?" Rhys asked at last, as calmly as he could.

"My last price—plus your ship, the *Fair Trade*."

Chapter Twenty-One

Rhys stared at the man, stunned by the unexpected demand. Give away the *Fair Trade*, the ship he'd designed himself with such love, such careful thought and attention to detail? It was like asking him to give up his firstborn child. Even Frell, who had remained silent throughout the negotiations, sat up at the demand.

The hunter's eyes gleamed with avaricious challenge. "That's right. The *Fair Trade* and my last price in credits, or we leave with the slave."

Rhys's hand inched closer to his disrupter while his gaze turned toward Calista. He couldn't risk her safety—or her freedom—he reminded himself. He still had more than enough financial resources to buy another ship, but that wasn't the point. His trader's soul rebelled at a price that was nothing short of piracy.

That thought brought Rhys up short. Piracy. Of

course! He barely repressed the silly grin that threatened to force its way onto his face.

"My ship?" he croaked instead with a note of dismay worthy of the most renowned Imperial actors. "You want the *Fair Trade*?"

The hunter nodded, too eager for the profits to sense the possible pitfalls. "And the credits. After all, we'll have the slave's ship if we don't sell her."

"But my ship!" Rhys protested pitifully. "I know it's got some crazy quirks, but—"

"Take it or leave it." The hunter waited for a second, oblivious to the subtle warning and clearly delighted by what he took to be Rhys's vulnerability. Then he spun around on his heel and headed toward the door. "Come on, Frell," he snapped. "Grab the girl and let's go."

"No! Wait!" Rhys hoped he'd gotten just the right note of desperation in his voice. "Don't take her. Don't take Calista! I'll trade if you'll only promise me right of first refusal when you decide to sell the *Fair Trade*. If you give me some time, I can get some more credits, maybe take a partner . . . I've got a few deals with the silk coming up and—"

The hunter stopped dead. "The credits *and* the ship, trader. Right now, with the transfer confirmed by Imperial code."

"Of course! The credits and the ship! Whatever you say. Just don't take the girl." For a minute, Rhys was afraid he'd overdone the act, but the two slavers were too excited by the thought of their unexpectedly rich haul to notice.

Under the watchful eye of the eager hunter, Rhys used Larr's hand comp to key in the transfer of rights to both Calista and his ship, then transmit the agreement via the *Fair Trade's* main communications system to Imperial records half a universe away. With the mass of details involved in the transfers, he hoped the hunter wouldn't notice the extra line of data that wasn't part of the agreements and that would never go beyond the *Fair Trade's* central computer.

When the essential data line slid on to the screen, then off without the hunter ever noticing, Rhys relaxed. His ploy might not work, but just thinking about the problems that now lay ahead for the two hunters was going to bring him a lot of satisfaction.

The thought of Calista, free at last, was dizzying.

"Done," Rhys said when the official confirmation of the transfer appeared on the hand comp's screen. "The *Fair Trade's* yours and the credits are deposited into the account you specified. The girl is mine." When the hunter moved to grab the printed confirmation, Rhys stretched out his hand, palm up. "I'll take the key to her shackles first."

The transporter image of the hunters hadn't even disappeared when he was down on his knees beside Calista releasing her from her bonds.

"You're free, Calista!" Rhys exulted, helping her to her feet. He wanted to dance with her across the room, wanted to kiss her until her head spun, then make love to her right on the floor if they couldn't find anything more comfortable close at hand.

He reached to take her in his arms, but instead of joyfully falling into his embrace as he'd expected, Calista stiffly pushed away.

Her gaze was fixed on her wrists, wrists that only a moment before had been bound by the slave hunter's shackles. "Am I, Rhys?" she asked, her voice tight with strain.

Rhys froze, uncertain of her meaning. "Of course you are. I have the documents to prove it."

Calista brought her gaze up to meet his. Her lips trembled slightly as she shook her head. "You have the documents that prove you *bought* me, Rhys. I'm still a slave, it's just that now I'm *your* slave."

"That's ridiculous!"

"No, it's not. It's fact."

"But—" The words trailed away. She was right, although that was easily remedied. All he had to do was sign her release to set her free forever. He would have done that without thinking, but her expressed doubts of his intentions stung. Did she really think he would be capable of freeing her from her former master only to hold her as his slave? Did she know him so little—or distrust him so much?

"Well, Rhys?" Calista's chin came up an inch higher. "Am I *really* free?"

Angrily Rhys grabbed up the hand comp and gave the commands that would legally set Calista free, from him or anyone else. When confirmation that the release had been recorded in Imperial records flashed on the screen, he thrust the comp at Calista. "Will this satisfy you?" he asked, his voice cold.

Head still proudly high, her eyes unwaveringly fixed on his, Calista took the offered comp. She glanced at the screen, then her hand tightened around the comp until the knuckles grew white. She drew in a deep, trembling breath and stared at the information glowing on the tiny screen.

"Well, Calista? Are you satisfied?" Rhys demanded again. He, too, kept his head high, his back stiff.

"I'm free." Calista's words were scarcely a whisper, but they vibrated with mingled wonder and disbelief.

"I said you were."

"Free." The word was so faint, it might have been no more than a breath passing across her lips. Calista raised her head, bringing her gaze back to his.

In the depths of those blue eyes Rhys read her confusion, uncertainty and dawning hope. His resentment evaporated in the sudden realization that it wasn't his intentions she'd doubted, but the possibility that what she'd dreamed of for so long might really be true.

Fool! He cursed silently, ashamed of himself and his doubts. Calista had thrown away her chance to escape the hunters, even risked her life to return to Karta with the information that had saved him, and he'd repaid her courage with his own unwillingness to trust.

They both, Rhys thought, his heart twisting within him, had a lot to learn about believing.

Gently, he touched her cheek in a gesture of reassurance. "You're free, Calista," he said softly. "Free to go where you want, do what you want, when you want. No one can ever take that away from you. Not ever again."

She trapped his hand in hers, but made no effort to push him away. Rhys slid his hand down to the side of her neck, then slowly ran his thumb along the edge of her jaw. Her skin was warm beneath his palm and he could feel her pulse pounding just beneath the surface. The feel of her, the heat of her made him ache with wanting.

"You have nothing left, Rhys," Calista said at last, hesitantly. "You don't even have the *Fair Trade*."

He chuckled. "I'm not quite destitute. At least, not yet." He paused, then added softly, "It wouldn't matter if I were, so long as you're free."

"What about your people? What about your dream of obtaining rights to the third planet? What are you going to do now?"

A sharp, burning pain suddenly lodged in Rhys's chest. She spoke as though she watched the future from afar, as though whatever happened to him had nothing to do with her and never would. The possibility that she wouldn't stay with him had never occurred to Rhys. If it had, he might never have set her free.

That thought brought him up short. No, that wasn't right. Calista would either stay with him because she chose to, or she would leave him. The choice was hers—*had* to be hers. No matter how much he wanted her, no matter how bleak the future looked without her in it, he would not hold her against her will. He wouldn't even suggest she stay because she might feel that she owed him too much and was obligated to remain, whether she wanted to or not.

He loved her far too much for that.

Rhys brushed his hand along her cheek, then pulled away from her. He shrugged, as if his answer to her question didn't matter. Without her, not much of anything would matter.

"The Dorinor might want some help in cleaning up the mess here," he said. "Pirock mentioned Larr had a small flitter. Maybe I can use that until I get some good deals going and find another ship."

"That sounds like a reasonable plan," Calista said hesitantly, as though expecting him to say more.

"I'll just have to see what happens here."

"Of course."

Rhys took a deep breath. He didn't want to ask the question, but he had to know. "What are *you* going to do?"

Calista shook her head. "I . . . I'm not sure." She gave a shaky laugh. "It's all so . . . unexpected. I hadn't really thought—"

She bit her lower lip, then moved a fraction of an inch closer, her eyes fixed on his with such intensity that Rhys suddenly found it hard to breathe.

"You don't need a partner, do you?" Calista asked.

"A . . . what?"

"A partner."

Hope flared in Rhys, making it difficult to think, to grasp her next words.

"I figured, maybe . . . well, you might need help here. There's the equipment in the caves that has to be removed, for one thing. It's not going to be easy to convince the Dorinor to grant you rights to the third planet. And there are all those customers, Larr's mess, I—" The words tumbled faster and faster, until Calista tripped over them in her hurry.

She stopped, then took a deep breath. Rhys's heart seemed to stop beating while he waited for what came next.

"I don't want to leave, Rhys," Calista said at last, very softly, very simply. "I want to stay here with you, work with you. I—" She swayed forward, raising her hands and pressing them against his chest as if she wanted to reassure herself of the reality of his nearness.

"I belong to you, Rhys," she insisted passionately, "no matter what the law says. I love you and I—"

She didn't have a chance to say anything more, for Rhys did what he'd been wanting to do ever since he'd released Calista from her bonds—he swept her into his arms and brought his mouth down on hers in a kiss that threatened to set the world afire with its hungry heat.

Calista could have sworn she was floating. Despite her weariness, despite the evidence of the floor beneath her feet and the hard rock walls around her, she felt as if she were soaring over Karta, climbing on an updraft until she could touch the sky and everything beyond.

She felt . . . free.

Over and over she'd repeated the word to herself, savoring the taste of it, still not quite believing that what she'd worked for and dreamed of for so long was now hers. Freedom. Complete and limitless freedom.

How strange that at the very moment she'd known she was truly free, she'd found herself irrevocably bound to another human being. Not by chains or the law's restrictive tenets, but by the unbreakable bonds that tied her heart to his.

She watched Rhys now, wondering at her certainty that she'd made the right decision, treasuring even his slightest gesture, his most fleeting expression.

They'd emerged from Larr's quarters to find people once more milling aimlessly about, too upset by events to focus on their accustomed work. Still too disoriented herself to concentrate on more mundane matters, no matter how pressing, Calista had retreated to the far side of the reception area and left Rhys to handle the endless details and answer the myriad questions with which Larr's staff had bombarded him.

He seemed born to command, she thought, watching him deal with a disagreement between two of the workers. Without raising his voice or forcing his opinions on anyone, Rhys had managed to assume control and restore order as easily as he ran his ship.

That thought brought Calista's mind into focus with a snap. Rhys didn't have a ship any longer. He'd traded it for her freedom, leaving himself without the essential transportation every trader needed to make a living.

Or had he?

Calista tried to remember exactly what Rhys had said to the hunters, how he'd acted. The details eluded her—she'd been too emotionally wrapped up in what was happening to remember clearly now—but she had the distinct impression that Rhys hadn't been quite as disturbed by the transaction as she might have expected. It wasn't a matter of him taking the trade calmly, she thought, but rather an impression that beneath his protestations of dismay lay an almost gleeful satisfaction in the trade. Which didn't make any sense at all, even if she considered that it was her freedom he'd been trading for.

So why—?

"You're awfully quiet for a woman who's just gotten what she wanted most in life."

Calista jumped, startled by Rhys's sudden appearance at her side. She'd been so lost in thought she hadn't noticed his approach.

"You didn't give away the *Fair Trade*, did you, Rhys?" she demanded.

He grinned. "I traded it for you, remember? I seem to remember that not twenty minutes ago you were telling me you belonged to—"

"That's not what I mean and you know it. You had something up your sleeve when you agreed to trade your ship for my freedom." Calista eyed his innocent expression, convinced now beyond a doubt that somehow Rhys had managed to get the better of the deal.

His grin widened. "Not up my sleeve, exactly. More like buried in the *Fair Trade's* main computer."

"Buried . . . What do you mean?"

"Beginning about a hour after their first jump into hyperspace, those two gentlemen are going to find their new ship has a few odd quirks in the way it responds to commands. And the longer they hold it, the worse those quirks are going to become."

"You mean—?" Comprehension was beginning to dawn.

Rhys nodded, his eyes dancing. "When I transmitted the authorization to transfer ownership, I sent a code that triggered a protective program I buried in the main computer years ago in case the ship was ever boarded. Every system on that ship is slowly going to go haywire—not enough to endanger the *Fair Trade* itself, but enough to drive anyone on it crazy trying to find the problems."

Calista couldn't repress an answering grin. "What if they try to sell the ship elsewhere?"

A shrug was eloquent answer. "Who's going to buy a ship with a fault in its basic programming? Eventually the *Fair Trade* will be abandoned. Even if whoever has it can put up with things like the food generators producing garbage or the waste disposers dumping raw crud back into the ship, they won't risk transporters that are just as likely to put them in the middle of a mountain as at their original destination."

Rhys paused and for a moment his face assumed an expression of rapt satisfaction. "If it's abandoned, the *Fair Trade* will return to the spot where I triggered the original protective program. That means it will come right back here."

Calista couldn't help laughing at that. "And what if it's not abandoned? What if those slavers show up demanding satisfaction?"

"Oh, I think Larr's coffers will provide enough resources for us to resolve that little problem. After I've replenished my own accounts, of course."

Calista grinned. She quite liked the idea of Larr paying for her freedom, even after he was dead. There was a certain justice to it, since he'd been the one to betray her to the slave hunters in the first place.

The problem of regaining the *Fair Trade* could wait for the future, however. Right now they had more pressing matters to attend to.

"Are you through here?" she asked, glancing back at the now empty reception area.

"It would seem so." Rhys followed the direction of her glance, then turned to look down the passageway behind her that led to the Dorinor's cavern. "Are you thinking what I'm thinking?"

"That we have to tell the Dorinor what's happened?"

"And discuss a little matter of the third planet." Rhys's dark eyes met hers with a steady, questioning gaze. "Are you sure this is what you want, Calista? They're my people, not yours, but—"

"But?"

"I love you." He spoke the words softly, but with all the force of passionate conviction. "I love you, Calista, but I can't walk away from my responsibilities. Not yet. Not until I know I've done everything I can to help my people."

Calista didn't respond for a minute. She wasn't even sure she could find the words to express her jumbled feelings. It was all so new—her freedom; this strange, sweet love that seemed to sweep away every other thought, every opposing consideration.

"I love *you*, Rhys," she said at last. "I didn't understand that until I realized I couldn't separate you from your past any more than I could separate myself from mine. Maybe that's part of what loving is." She hesitated, then continued more slowly, "I won't make promises I can't keep. I'm not sure how well I can adapt to the responsibilities that you and Glynna have assumed. I only know I'm willing to try."

She stretched upward to brush a gentle kiss across his lips, then slipped out of his reach before he could take her in his arms. "I'm free, Rhys, free to choose whatever path I want." Her chin came up. "I choose to go with you, no matter what."

He let out his breath then—a deep, sighing exhalation that spoke more powerfully than words of just how uncertain he'd still been of her answer—and how much it had mattered to him. "Then we'd best get on

373

with it. The Dorinor's going to start wondering what we're up to if we don't report in soon."

They passed three Kartanese guards posted at various points along the passage from the human quarters, but found the Dorinor and Karnor alone in the main chamber. Calista thought she sensed the presence of more guards in the other passages leading out of the chamber, but she couldn't be sure.

"Well?" the Dorinor demanded the instant they came to a halt at the foot of his platform. "Where is that lying, vermin-ridden, nest-fouling thief? Where is Larr?"

"He's dead, Excellency," Rhys said, tilting his head back so he could meet the Dorinor's gaze.

"Dead!" The great creature half-rose to his feet, indignant. "How can he be dead?"

"Someone else ate him?" There was no mistaking the relief in Karnor's query.

"One of his men killed him, Excellency," Calista added. "He betrayed the humans he brought here just as he betrayed you. They didn't know what was going on, either."

Actually, she wasn't convinced that statement was true, but there was no sense in making the situation worse by digging too deeply into past events. "We've already got Larr's people trying to sort out some of the mess he left behind."

"If those other humans aren't involved, then I won't have to eat anyone else, right?" Karnor asked, eager for reassurance.

"Right." Rhys nodded at Karnor, then turned his attention back to the Dorinor. "You're going to need help removing the equipment Larr installed in the sacred caves. We can provide that help. We can also try to find the missing eggs."

"Indeed?" The Dorinor didn't appear impressed, but he did at least sit back down.

"We can't give you any guarantees, of course," Calista said. "We don't know where the stolen eggs are or what condition they're in, and we don't know how long it will take the sacred caves to return to their normal state."

"What *can* you promise me? And what do you expect in return?"

The Dorinor's questions caught Calista by surprise. Up until now, the great creature had seemed so confused by business details that she hadn't expected him to be quite so . . . direct in negotiations.

"We can promise to do our best to help you and your people," Rhys said. "I don't think you'll want to count on the grays . . . er, the *drenn*, to get everything back the way it was."

"Rrmmph."

Calista recognized a noncommittal grunt when she heard one, even though the sound the Dorinor made more nearly resembled the grating scrape of rough stone against stone.

"The *drenn* mean well," the Dorinor reluctantly conceded at last, "but they never have mastered all that complicated human machinery."

Though it had nothing to do with the present discussion, Calista couldn't help asking, "Just what *are* the *drenn*, Excellency? I never have figured out where they come from."

"Come from?" The question clearly caught the Dorinor by surprise. "They come from here, of course."

"But where do they live?"

"They live in the caves, just like any other Kartanese."

"But—" Calista stopped short as understanding suddenly dawned. "They're *Kartanese?* They're like *you?*"

"Of course not," the Dorinor snapped, irritated. "They are *drenn*, just as I am the Dorinor. They are shaped in the egg to be what they are and I cannot change that."

The *drenn* were Kartanese! Neither servants nor slaves, but another form of the species! Calista could have laughed in relief if it wouldn't have offended the Dorinor. With that knowledge, the last, niggling little doubt about working with the Kartanese disappeared as if it had never been.

"Of course, Excellency," she said hastily. "I didn't mean to offend. I—"

"Calista was just concerned that any work done on the caves be done right, your Excellency," Rhys interjected smoothly, giving her time to recover. "The *drenn* can, of course, do much of the work in removing the equipment that Larr had installed, but they'll still need the guidance of humans who—"

"You still haven't answered my second question," the Dorinor interrupted.

"Your second—?"

"I want to know what you humans expect in return."

Rhys didn't miss a beat. "We want rights to the third planet of Karta, Excellency. The next planet farther away from your sun than this one."

"I know what planet you're talking about." The implication he wouldn't understand clearly irritated the Dorinor.

"And the continued right to represent you in selling the fibers," Calista interjected. Might as well go for the whole pot of stew. "Now that Larr has built a market, you can't just refuse to sell or you're likely to have unscrupulous individuals trying to invade Karta and take the fibers from you."

"That's right. And my people can provide extra protection to Karta from settlements on the third planet." With the smooth assurance of a skilled trader, Rhys built on Calista's points and, at the same time, reinforced his own. "It could be an extremely productive and useful arrangement for both sides, Excellency."

Calista tried to decipher the expression on the Dorinor's features. There was an odd tension about his mouth and a glitter in his eyes she'd never seen before. If he'd been human, she'd almost have thought he was plotting something, but that didn't make sense. Not with a Kartanese, anyway. The creatures had shown themselves too guileless to be capable of plotting anything.

"I was considering posting guards at all the entrances to your human caves," the Dorinor said at last, reflectively. "The minute someone appeared, my guards could eat them."

Karnor groaned. The Dorinor ignored him. "It would take time, but it would be effective in ensuring that you humans never again attempted to harm our eggs." The Dorinor gave the Kartanese equivalent of a frown. "Of course, you humans are ridiculously fat. It *would* be hard on my guards' digestion."

Karnor whimpered, very softly.

"Is there any reason," the Dorinor continued, ignoring his companion's discomfort and fixing his attention on the two humans instead, "that I shouldn't simply order you all killed or starved to death?"

Calista swallowed hard, astounded by the Dorinor's plan. She'd considered a dozen possible reactions to her and Rhys's proposals, but nothing like this.

Rhys recovered his voice first. "Killing us wouldn't

do you much good, Excellency. Humans know about the silk now. There will always be somebody willing to risk the danger of being eaten alive in the hopes of gaining control of the silk. Do you really want your people to waste their time protecting Karta against attack when working with us would prevent that happening in the first place?"

The Dorinor swung his head down so he could stare directly into Rhys's eyes. His lips pulled back in a frightening imitation of a human grin, exposing what seemed like hundreds of long, sharp teeth. "Can you guarantee there will be no more betrayals such as Larr's?"

"Calista and I risked our lives to help you and protect your eggs!" Rhys exclaimed angrily. "Why would we have done that if we weren't honest?"

The Dorinor made an odd, choking sound Calista had never heard before. It bore an odd resemblance to a human laugh, but that comparison was absurd. Wasn't it?

"I will grant your request," he finally said, drawing his head up so he once more towered over Calista and Rhys, "but on somewhat different terms than you had before."

The Dorinor sat back on his tail, crossed his forefeet across his belly, and cocked his head to stare contemplatively at the chamber ceiling. "You may have the planet, but in exchange your people will be required to provide protection to Karta at all times. You will also have to return the sacred caves to the way they were before Larr interfered."

Calista could hear Rhys's sharp, exultant intake of breath but her attention was fixed on the huge Kartanese in front of her. There was something about the Dorinor's behavior . . . "What about the trading rights?" she asked suspiciously.

The Dorinor rolled one eye around so he could see her, then returned to contemplating the ceiling. "You can have the trading rights, too," he said at last, "but the percentages will have to be changed."

Calista frowned, but before she could say anything, Rhys burst out, "How much?"

Once more the bright, golden eye rolled around in the big, black head. "You can have five percent. I'll keep the rest."

"What?" Rhys almost choked on the word.

Calista burst out laughing. He was bluffing. The Dorinor was bluffing!

"Ninety percent," she managed to get out, ignoring Rhys's spluttering objections. "We'll keep ninety percent and you can take ten. That seems fair."

Suddenly the ceiling didn't seem to have quite the attraction of a moment earlier. The Dorinor's head came down until both eyes focused on Calista. There was no mistaking the grin now, even if it *was* the first one she'd ever seen on a Kartanese.

"All right," the Dorinor said, "You can take ten percent and I'll keep the rest."

"We'll concede you twelve percent," Rhys offered, suddenly catching on. "That leaves us eighty-eight percent. Considering how costly it is to run a trading operation like this, that's an eminently reasonable proposal. Just ask anyone."

For a beginner, the Kartanese leader didn't do too badly at negotiating. Unfortunately, the creature didn't stand a chance against two experienced traders like her and Rhys. Calista suspected the percentages didn't really matter, anyway. Just as in bakal, it wasn't the money, but the game itself that was important to the Dorinor. Considering how fast he was learning human ways, however, she wouldn't want to bet on what he'd do in the future.

"So we're agreed," Rhys said at last. "My people will receive title to the third planet in exchange for providing protection to Karta. We will also ensure the caves are returned to their normal state and you will grant us trade rights to the fibers, what we call saitha silk."

"That's right," the Dorinor agreed, clearly pleased with the results of his first trade negotiation. "And with the thirty-five percent of the proceeds *my* people will receive from your trading, we will help pay for the ships and equipment you will need to protect our home."

Everyone has won, Calista thought, watching Rhys teach the Dorinor how to shake hands. She made no effort to repress the grin that stretched across her face. *This is what a fair trade is all about. Rhys has his world. The Dorinor has gained protection for his people and a guarantee that the sacred caves will be returned to normal. I have my freedom and a future.* Calista blinked, her vision suddenly blurred.

The hot, stinging sensation in her eyes couldn't be tears, she told herself fiercely. She never cried. Especially not when she was happy.

Yet when Rhys, his face alight with joy, swept her off her feet and into his arms, the tears whose existence she'd denied spilled over her lashes and streamed unchecked down her cheeks.

"To the future, Calista," he said, his lips only a breath away from hers.

"To the future, Rhys," Calista said, eliminating even that small distance between them.

Epilogue

"It has to go there." The dour-faced man thumped the big map rolled out on the center of the table, clearly challenging the other nine individuals grouped around it to disagree.

"No, it has to go *there*. I can't imagine anyone wanting it anywhere else." The gray-haired woman across the table from him spoke with far less force but no less determination as she indicated her own favored spot.

A tall, thin man at the end of the table piped up, "Well, personally, I think—"

"It's a good thing we all realize this discussion is academic," Glynna Fairdane interrupted smoothly. "Since the Structures Design Committee is the one responsible for determining where the Main Hall will be built, all we have left to worry about is how to relocate a few million people to New Ziana in an orderly fashion. We should get back to our original discussion, which was how to get three different settlements going at the same time. I believe Derrif was saying—"

Calista sat back in her chair and let Glynna's voice fade into a blur. Getting the Dorinor to grant Rhys's people rights to the third planet had been easy compared to the effort required to get the people themselves in agreement on how to go about settling it. After so many months of negotiations and discussions among representatives of the scattered communities, she was heartily sick of the whole process.

Even watching Glynna skillfully maneuver the disparate members of any given committee into arriving at some consensus had begun to pale as entertainment. Calista couldn't deny the younger woman had inherited her mother's flair for political dealings, however, nor could she ignore the growing talk of proposing Glynna for the new Council being formed.

What worried Calista was that Rhys's name had already been proposed for the Council. After these past months on New Ziana, she wasn't sure she could endure a lifetime spent in politics, no matter how much she loved him. And that uncertainty troubled her deeply.

The breaking up of the meeting roused Calista from her thoughts. She knew Glynna wanted to talk to her about the negotiations underway for transport to bring the settlers to their new world, but Calista quietly slipped from the room before she could be stopped. There had been three meetings already and the day was not yet half over. She couldn't bear one more serious discussion. Not right now.

Calista hesitated at the top of the steps leading from the building that presently served as both eating hall and administrative center. Before her stretched a muddy confusion of roads and half-constructed buildings that would eventually form the nucleus for the community they were creating out of the rich, raw world they had claimed.

This particular view had become one of her favorites, for already Calista could envision the way the finished structures would blend in with the lush, carefully protected greenery around them. It was comforting to know that everyone, despite their numerous disagreements, was deeply committed to ensuring the new settlements brought no harm to the world the Dorinor had entrusted to their keeping.

Restless and unwilling to return to yet another meeting, Calista cautiously picked her way across the rough ground that would eventually be transformed into a central park. A number of the settlers called to her as she passed, but she acknowledged their greetings with no more than a wave of her hand. She wasn't in the mood for company, even though these people had become close friends over the past year.

If only Rhys would return! He'd been gone almost three weeks. An urgent mission, he'd said, without giving any further details. If it hadn't been for her numerous commitments here on New Ziana, she would have gone with him.

That was the problem with belonging somewhere, Calista thought in growing frustration. The people around her, people she had honestly come to care for, were always far too ready to claim her time and emotional energy. That it was usually for a worthy cause only made it more difficult to refuse them, and made her all the more resentful.

Troubled by her own discontent, Calista chose the path that would take her away from the settlement and up the hill to the small house she and Rhys had built shortly after their arrival with the first settlers.

It was a simple shelter of glass and native stone situated on a bluff overlooking the forested slopes and open valleys of New Ziana. At night, she could stand on the ridge while the stars slowly wheeled across the black depths of the sky and feel, at least for a while, that she was once more in space with all the universe awaiting her.

Such feelings stirred an unaccustomed guilt within her, guilt which Calista carefully kept hidden from Rhys. Not by so much as a whisper would she add to the pressures his people and the Dorinor had already heaped on him in such abundant measure.

At least they'd recovered all the stolen Kartanese eggs. Calista smiled, remembering the objections a couple of the eggs' caretakers had raised to returning the Dorinor's property. A disrupter waved suggestively under their noses had eliminated most of their complaints, but Rhys had taken a light phaser burn on his left arm before he'd managed to persuade a couple of them to release their purloined prize.

If only the important work of building the settlements on New Ziana could be that much fun! It didn't help to admit that concentrating her efforts here, rather than on expanding the trade in saitha silk, had been her own choice. After living and working alone for so long, the chance to work side by side with others had held an immense appeal.

Unfortunately, even her years spent in the crowded slave quarters on Andrus had not prepared her for the constant pressures, the incessant give and take of communal living. If it weren't for her deep love for Rhys and the knowledge that he had relied heavily on her support over the past few months, Calista had to admit she would have given up long ago.

Calista spotted the blinking light on the comm panel the minute she walked in. For an instant, she considered not answering the waiting message, but her newly acquired sense of responsibility wouldn't let her.

She keyed an order to respond while trying to erase any hint of her present emotional state from her expression. The effort wasn't necessary—the moment Rhys's familiar, dark visage appeared on the screen, all Calista's torments were forgotten in a searing burst of joy.

"You're back! Are you still on the *Independence*? When are you beaming down?" The questions tumbled out before Calista could stop them.

Rhys's eager, answering laugh was all the confirmation she needed that he'd missed her as much as she'd missed him. "I'm back, I'm not on the *Independence*, and I'm not beaming down. You're beaming up."

Before Calista could ask another question, her house and New Ziana disappeared, to be replaced by the soft lights and hard floors of a transport chamber. She had a brief, vague sense that she'd been in that particular chamber before; then she was in Rhys's arms and nothing mattered except his strong arms around her and the hot, hungry kisses he rained down on her mouth, face and throat.

"Three weeks, Rhys!" Calista moaned when he finally gave her a chance to breathe. "How could you stay away three weeks?"

"Two weeks, four days, seven and a half hours. But who's counting?" His dark eyes glittered as he pressed her even more tightly against him. "Did everyone drive you mad with their squabbling and their problems and their needs?"

"Nooo." Calista dragged the denial out, trying to find words that wouldn't reveal the frustrations she'd been struggling with.

"Liar. They'd drive a saint to distraction, and you're

no saint, my love." His lips curved in a dazzling smile. "But I have a solution I think you'll like."

Before Calista could resist, Rhys was sweeping her out the door of the transport chamber and down the passageway beyond. It took a couple of minutes before Calista's memories connected with what she was seeing around her.

"It's the *Fair Trade*!" she gasped, pulling Rhys to a halt. "You've got the *Fair Trade* back!"

Rhys's smile stretched into a delighted grin. "Our friends trashed it, but after a lot of work it's almost as good as new. There are still a few quirks left in its systems, but I figure we can sort those out between here and Beta Andra III."

"Beta An . . . What are you talking about?"

"Our first trading stop, my love. You and I are giving up world-building in favor of a little heavy duty trading."

"We are?" Calista gulped, trying to ignore the tempting visions conjured by Rhys's words. "But what about your people? What about the position on the Council they're going to offer you? What about New Ziana and—"

Rhys pressed a finger to her lips, silencing her. The laughter went out of his eyes, to be replaced by a look of such deep understanding that Calista's breath caught in her throat. "They've already offered me a position on the Council. I turned it down. I figure I've done everything I can to make this new world work, and you've done far more than anyone should ever have asked of you. Now it's our turn to do what we want with our lives."

"But—"

"Do you really think I don't know the price you've paid because of your love for me?" he asked softly. "I had duties I couldn't ignore, people whose needs

I couldn't walk away from, yet if it hadn't been for your strength, your support—"

His voice trailed away as he brushed a soft, exquisitely tender kiss across Calista's lips. "I love you, Calista York," he said. "I couldn't bear to see you chained to such a restricted life because of me."

The corner of his mouth quirked upward in a devilish smile and his eyes once more came alive with that tormenting glint. "Besides," he added, "I couldn't stand spending the rest of my life on a planet, either. Politics drive me crazy."

"What? Why, you—!" Calista wrenched free of his grip, suddenly indignant. "Do you mean I sat through *seventeen* meetings of the Waste Recycling Committee when you—"

Rhys laughed. "Now, Red. You shouldn't let your temper get the best of you that quickly. Why don't you come up on the bridge and I'll show you the trade itinerary I've plotted out? I thought we could hit Garul Lazar next and—"

"You've plotted our itinerary? Without asking me?"

"Just to save time. I thought—"

Calista couldn't help it. After the emotional highs and lows she'd already gone through that morning, having Rhys decide what their first trade route was going to be was just too much. She doubled her fist and took a hefty swing.

Rhys ducked, still laughing, then swept her off her feet and into his arms. "We can always discuss this in private," he said, taking the turn that led toward his personal quarters.

"There isn't anyone on this ship to be private from!" Calista protested.

"But a good trader always negotiates from strength, Red, and I rather fancy my talents in—"

"Rhys! You—!"

Whatever else Calista had to say was cut short as the door to Rhys's bedchamber slid shut behind them.

Only much later—when the soft, almost inaudible sounds of the *Fair Trade* and of Calista's breathing were all he could hear—only then did it occur to Rhys how aptly named his ship was.

At the thought of the *Fair Trade* and what he'd gained in exchange for it, he laughed, rousing Calista from the drowsy half-sleep that had claimed her.

Softly, ever so gently, Rhys ran his hand across Calista's bare breast and side, over the smooth skin of her hip and thigh. He watched her eyes widen and a smile form on her lips, watched her breathing deepen and a soft flush creep across her cheeks and throat in response to his touch.

Even if he'd never recovered his ship, Rhys knew it wouldn't have mattered. It *had* been a fair trade—his heart and soul for a love great enough to fill the universe and more.

An eminently fair trade, he thought, just before thought became impossible. The best deal he'd ever made.

Dear Reader:

Dreams are rare and precious things. Calista and Rhys
had theirs. Dayra Smith of my next book, *Far Star*,
has hers, which centers around building a home and
a future for herself and her orphaned half brother
and sister on the distant world known as Far Star.
Since experience has taught her she can't rely on
any man to help build that dream, Dayra has a
hard time explaining to herself just why she hired
the big, scruffy drifter who offered to exchange some
work for a meal, a bath, and a bed. No woman in
her right mind would count on a man who carries
all his possessions in one well-worn spacer's bag
and whose eyes reveal a loneliness bigger than the
universe itself.

Anne Avery

Coll Larren is a man who knows how easily life grinds dreams into dust. He ought to. He's stood in enough dust for ten men and he has no intention of staying around long enough to see life grind up Dayra Smith's dreams, too. After all, Dayra is the worst kind of dreamer, the decent, caring, building-a-world-for-others kind of dreamer who hasn't the slightest idea of what she's up against and wouldn't admit her plans weren't possible even if she were eyeball to eyeball with failure. So why, he wonders, is he staying? Even worse, why is he suddenly so ready to take up the fight against the overwhelming forces that threaten to destroy the hopeless dreams of a woman he can't possibly love?

Dayra and Coll's story will be told in *Far Star*, available from Love Spell in October, 1994.

I would very much enjoy hearing from readers who love futuristic romances as much as I do. My address is P.O. Box 62533, Colorado Springs, CO 80962-2533. A self-addressed, stamped envelope would be appreciated.

Sincerely,
Anne Avery

TIMESWEPT ROMANCE
TIME REMEMBERED
Elizabeth Crane
Bestselling Author of *Reflections in Time*

A voodoo doll and an ancient spell whisk thoroughly modern Jody Farnell from a decaying antebellum mansion to the Old South and a true Southern gentleman who shows her the magic of love.

_0-505-51904-6 $4.99 US/$5.99 CAN

FUTURISTIC ROMANCE
A DISTANT STAR
Anne Avery

Jerrel is enchanted by the courageous messenger who saves his life. But he cannot permit anyone to turn him from the mission that has brought him to the distant world—not even the proud and passionate woman who offers him a love capable of bridging the stars.

_0-505-51905-4 $4.99 US/$5.99 CAN

TIMESWEPT ROMANCE

TIME OF THE ROSE
By Bonita Clifton

When the silver-haired cowboy brings Madison Calloway to his run-down ranch, she thinks for sure he is senile. Certain he'll bring harm to himself, Madison follows the man into a thunderstorm and back to the wild days of his youth in the Old West.

The dread of all his enemies and the desire of all the ladies, Colton Chase does not stand a chance against the spunky beauty who has tracked him through time. And after one passion-drenched night, Colt is ready to surrender his heart to the most tempting spitfire anywhere in time.

__51922-4 $4.99 US/$5.99 CAN

A FUTURISTIC ROMANCE

AWAKENINGS
By Saranne Dawson

Fearless and bold, Justan rules his domain with an iron hand, but nothing short of the Dammai's magic will bring his warring people peace. He claims he needs Rozlynd—a bewitching beauty and the last of the Dammai—for her sorcery alone, yet inside him stirs an unexpected yearning to savor the temptress's charms, to sample her sweet innocence. And as her silken spell ensnares him, Justan battles to vanquish a power whose like he has never encountered—the power of Rozlynd's love.

__51921-6 $4.99 US/$5.99 CAN

HISTORICAL ROMANCE
HUNTERS OF THE ICE AGE:
YESTERDAY'S DAWN
By Theresa Scott

Named for the massive beast sacred to his people, Mamut has proven his strength and courage time and again. But when it comes to subduing one helpless captive female, he finds himself at a distinct disadvantage. Never has he realized the power of beguiling brown eyes, soft curves and berry-red lips to weaken a man's resolve. He has claimed he will make the stolen woman his slave, but he soon learns he will never enjoy her alluring body unless he can first win her elusive heart.

_51920-8 $4.99 US/$5.99 CAN

A CONTEMPORARY ROMANCE
HIGH VOLTAGE
By Lori Copeland

Laurel Henderson hadn't expected the burden of inheriting her father's farm to fall squarely on her shoulders. And if Sheriff Clay Kerwin can't catch the culprits who are sabotaging her best efforts, her hopes of selling it are dim. Struggling with this new responsibility, Laurel has no time to pursue anything, especially not love. The best she can hope for is an affair with no strings attached. And the virile law officer is the perfect man for the job—until Laurel's scheme backfires. Blind to Clay's feelings and her own, she never dreams their amorous arrangement will lead to the passion she wants to last for a lifetime.

_51923-2 $4.99 US/$5.99 CAN

LOVE SPELL
ATTN: Order Department
Dorchester Publishing Co., Inc.
276 5th Avenue, New York, NY 10001

Please add $1.50 for shipping and handling for the first book and $.35 for each book thereafter. PA., N.Y.S. and N.Y.C. residents, please add appropriate sales tax. No cash, stamps, or C.O.D.s. All orders shipped within 6 weeks via postal service book rate. Canadian orders require $2.00 extra postage and must be paid in U.S. dollars through a U.S. banking facility.

Name _____

Address _____

City _____ State _____ Zip _____

I have enclosed $_____ in payment for the checked book(s).
Payment **must** accompany all orders. ☐ Please send a free catalog.

FROM LOVE SPELL
HISTORICAL ROMANCE
THE PASSIONATE REBEL
Helene Lehr

A beautiful American patriot, Gillian Winthrop is horrified to learn that her grandmother means her to wed a traitor to the American Revolution. Her body yearns for Philip Meredith's masterful touch, but she is determined not to give her hand—or any other part of herself—to the handsome Tory, until he convinces her that he too is a passionate rebel.

_51918-6 $4.99 US/$5.99 CAN

CONTEMPORARY ROMANCE
THE TAWNY GOLD MAN
Amii Lorin

Bestselling Author Of More Than 5 Million Books In Print!

Long ago, in a moment of wild, rioting ecstasy, Jud Cammeron vowed to love her always. Now, as Anne Moore looks at her stepbrother, she sees a total stranger, a man who plans to take control of his father's estate and everyone on it. Anne knows things are different—she is a grown woman with a fiance—but something tells her she still belongs to the tawny gold man.

_51919-4 $4.99 US/$5.99 CAN

TIMESWEPT ROMANCE

A TIME-TRAVEL CHRISTMAS
By Megan Daniel, Vivian Knight-Jenkins, Eugenia Riley, and Flora Speer

In these four passionate time-travel historical romance stories, modern-day heroines journey everywhere from Dickens's London to a medieval castle as they fulfill their deepest desires on Christmases past.

_51912-7 $4.99 US/$5.99 CAN

A FUTURISTIC ROMANCE

MOON OF DESIRE
By Pam Rock

Future leader of his order, Logan has vanquished enemies, so he expects no trouble when a sinister plot brings a mere woman to him. But as the three moons of the planet Thurlow move into alignment, Logan and Calla head for a collision of heavenly bodies that will bring them ecstasy—or utter devastation.

_51913-5 $4.99 US/$5.99 CAN